Sons and Other Flammable Objects

Sons and Other Flammable Objects

Porochista Khakpour

Grove Press
New York

The epigraph from Sadegh Hedayat's *The Blind Owl* is used by permission of
Grove/Atlantic, Inc. The quote was translated by Arta Khakpour.

The epigraph from Forugh Farrokhzad is excerpted from her poem "The Bird Was
Only a Bird" from the book *Remembering the Flight: Twenty Poems by Forugh Farrokjhzad*
[Third Edition—January 2004, ISBN: 1-883819-02-4] selected and translated by
Ahmad Karimi-Hakkak, published by Ketab Corp, 1419 Westwood Blvd., Los
Angeles CA 90024. The author gratefully acknowledges Ketab Corp. and Ahmad
Karimi-Hakkak for permission to reprint it here.

The epigraph from the transcript of Larry King's interview with Barbara Eden on
Larry King Live is courtesy of CNN.

Published simultaneously in Canada
Printed in the United States of America

FIRST EDITION

ISBN-10: 0-8021-1853-4
ISBN-13: 978-0-8021-1853-0

Grove Press
an imprint of Grove/Atlantic, Inc.
841 Broadway
New York, NY 10003

Distributed by Publishers Group West

www.groveatlantic.com

07 08 09 10 11 12   10 9 8 7 6 5 4 3 2 1

To Kingsley,
the son invincible,
who was there from day one
and manages to still be here, forever

I thought to myself: "If it's true that every person has a star in the sky, mine must be distant, dim, and absurd. Perhaps I've never had a star."
—Sadegh Hedayat, *Blind Owl*, 1937

✻

The bird flew through the air
above the red lights
at the height of oblivion
experiencing the blue moments
madly.

The bird, ah, was only a bird.
—Forugh Farrokhzad, "The Bird Was Only a Bird"

✻

KING: If they were doing that show today, would there be sexual implications of Jeannie and. . . .

EDEN: Well, I don't think so. Because the funny part about the show was the fact that she thought she was human and she wasn't. And she wanted to marry him. And he knew she wasn't human. So there's your comedy. She's a fish out of water. You can't have anything really happen between the two of them because she's smoke, but she doesn't think so. You know?

KING: And so, she ain't there?

EDEN: No. Yes.
—Barbara Eden on *Larry King Live*, January 2002

Contents

Sons and Other
Flammable
Objects

Part One

The Birds and the Birds

Another in the long line of misunderstandings in their shared history, what caused Xerxes and Darius Adam to vow never to speak again, really began with a misplaced anecdote, specifically an incident that happened many years before in the summer of Xerxes's twelfth year, known always in the Adam household as "the summer when Darius Adam began terrorizing the neighbors' cats," known privately to Xerxes's future self as "the summer in which I realized something was very wrong with my father, something that would cause us to never have a normal father-son bond—the summer, years later, accidentally triggering the very last straw that would cause us to never communicate again." Ever? "Well, wishful thinking, for starters."

Los Angeles, 1987

Darius Adam began with kindness, kindness and some deception. He began by befriending them: Apartment #14's tabby Tabitha, #3's Pedro, #29's BooBoo (neither Xerxes nor his father knew for sure if this was the cat's *actual* name, hearing it only in the daily coos of Ms. Bialik or Ms. Bialock, whose name they weren't sure of either), and the two nameless identical black kittens who belonged to either #11 or #13 or both, who traveled in pairs and answered to either one door or the other or both. *Gorbeh,* being the Farsi word for cat, was what Darius Adam would resort to when all else failed: "Here, *gorbeh,* here, little pretty *gorbeh,* c'mon, now, damnit, *gorbeh.*" He lured the *gorbehs* with bowls of milk which rarely worked—he blamed it on Xerxes's mother's insistence on only buying skim, something that not only he disapproved of, but apparently the goddamn everyday cats did as well—and so he moved on to cheese singles, which worked for some, especially BooBoo. In the end, he actually began frying slices of liver, taking a few bites himself, playfully offering some to Xerxes—who replied with the children's universal gag face, glad to see the household liver supply dwindle for this cause—and to his wife, to rile her up, for she found the investment a terrible waste, *when for one week all we've had are leftovers, when I could only dream of liver,* she'd claim, every day insisting she was going to make it that night's meal. The cats responded to liver. And when the liver was done for good—because Xerxes's mother eventually retaliated by ceasing to purchase liver altogether—they responded to cookies. It was soon discovered that the *gorbehs* had a thing for her favorite pecan-sandy cookies. It was as if before she could even attempt to draw the line, the very concept of lines had become obsolete. Everything was game.

One by one he lured them into their house. Xerxes's mother was beside herself: *Cats in the house—what's next!* It was almost as if the answer to that question was, *Prostitutes—that's what's next!* Xerxes thought to himself, imagining his father dangling fried meat at these forbidden for-sale women that he'd only just begun seeing in movies —attracting all sorts of crawling, purring, fishnetted, bed-headed women that smelled like a rumored musk he couldn't imagine but assumed was the scent of sex, something furry and sweaty and sweet. But the cats tended to stay close to the door, as nothing about the depths of the Adams' indoors interested any of them. Darius Adam would crouch to their level to negotiate with hands full of cookie crumbs, letting them timidly sniff and lick, and then with an urgency that Xerxes seldom heard in his father, he'd order Xerxes to bring him *the bag*. Xerxes begrudgingly would bring the canvas bag that was draped on his father's armchair, next to the Basic Algebra textbooks and ungraded student papers, the piles Xerxes's mother and Xerxes were never to touch—which Xerxes only once did and discovered a strange postcard with a paradisal sunset scene signed "Miss u—u best teacher man! Hugs&kiss, CeCe," which taught him never ever to go there again. He cringed at the sound the bag made—something like a possessed tambourine girl—a strangely heavy bag overstuffed with an ambitious supply of bell-studded cat collars. Xerxes believed his father when he said, *See, they made these for one reason and one reason only, and that is my reason: to save. These are not* gorbeh *presents*, he reminded them—his mother immediately reaching in the bag for the receipt, moaning about the expense when she didn't even have a winter coat, when her pumps were busted— *this is a necessity*, he'd declare. It was a necessity that he had to invest in, that he had been called on to invest in, he reminded them, because certainly if the neighbors were good cat owners, each and every one would have done this. But because they failed, someone had to. Xerxes knew what he meant although he took some unspoken objection with the *had to;* his mother didn't understand at all and so she bit her tongue and instead did that more powerfully infuriating thing of head shaking all the way through his process. *Madness,* she would think. *Don't say a word, especially in the case of the word not being a nice word,* his father would say, messing up the saying, perhaps purposely; he often botched his usually near-perfect English to make a point, Xerxes suspected, as if to say, *Who cares about this bastard tongue?* In any case, refraining from words-that-are-not-nice-ones—unless you were Darius Adam, that is—had become a family rule in their house of swallowed discontentment, of several future decades' worth of ulcers.

> *I take then you two are happy living in a battlefield?*
> *I take you like dodging daily carnage? Remind you of home?*
> *Death all around you—I take you think that's an acceptable sight?*
> *Tell me, are you Adam or* gorbeh?

Xerxes knew his father believed in a better good, that he was acting out of a certain humanitarian manifest destiny to institute *right* among all mammals of the modern domicile. He *was* trying to save. Save themselves in the end, via saving the spring's batch of blue jays who had suddenly, in their cheery oblivious way, taken residence among the palms and oaks of their conflicted suburban California neighborhood, in particular in their apartment complex, "Eden Gardens," as the sign read (to the embarrassment of Xerxes, who often found himself just shrugging when his teachers or friends or the others of the town's home-owning gentry asked his address and wondered, "Oh, is that The Lanai? Or are you Tropical Terrace? *Oh, Eden Gardens?*") The blue jays had come noticed by no one really, Xerxes was sure, except his father who would rush to their balcony, daily, and call out, *Look! Look! Look! Look . . . blue jays.* The birds would make lackluster eye contact, maybe they would chirp— *Sing!* Xerxes's father insisted, *they really do sing*—and then they would be off with their manic flutter.

Happy-go-lucky idiots, Xerxes thought, *dancing on a death trap like that, the fools.* Because of all the apartment buildings, why theirs? Why at the only pets-welcome complex on the block? Eden Gardens' expansive animal kingdom had no room for easily conquered fragile types—they already had the black potbellied pig on a leash belonging to the lanky Jesus-looking man that Xerxes's mother and father knew only as The Drug Dealer, and who Xerxes, although usually ready to disagree with his folks, had concluded, to his own shock, *was* a drug dealer; the triplet collies belonging to Silent-Arts-and-Crafts-Lady; the ancient pit bull belonging to The Mexicans; the guinea pigs on leashes belonging to the Weird Old Chinese Man; the buck wild ferret mothered by The Sorority Girls; and a rumored monkey that no one ever saw (apparently a ringtail—"the not-in-jungle-type, you know, the type the crazies by the sea get, the collecting money kind, like with vests, with two chinking gold music-makers, you know—but without all that, you know," claimed their building manager, a man they called The Pelican because of his unpronounceable Romanian name, and also because of his facial structure) . . . they had all walks of life, on every rung of the food chain, in Eden Gardens. But the *gorbehs* topped them all. They were the staple pet—everyone who didn't have something more exciting, something more far-fetched, something more

California-crazy, had cats, except the Adam family, who had . . .
nothing.

We have a pet Xerxes! (Xerxes deeply resented his mother's joke,
from age seven, when he first comprehended its casual insult.) *Animals anyway*, she would growl, *are dirty.*

Says Allah and Allah only, his father would laugh. *How ignorant your
mother is.*

What do you want from me? she would hiss. *A horse, a donkey, a hippo,
puppies, and rats everywhere?*

Maybe something small, his father would say quietly, spookily, his
gaze lost somewhere back in the spectacle of a stark boyhood dream,
maybe even a bird. . . .

Other than that Xerxes had never heard a word about birds—
any interest in them, any fascination with, any desire to rescue, any
sense of a mission for—not a single mention of them from Darius
Adam. And then with the blue jays' sudden arrival in May 1988
and their systematic serial slaughtering by June, birds suddenly
became king. *Dead* gave their ends too much dignity, Xerxes
thought, agreeing with his father that their aftermaths, the killers' nonchalantly relinquished evidence, all made the cause more
noble. The dead blue jays appeared splattered, flat, like ink-soaked
envelopes, stamped and razzled and bludgeoned and sucked and
maybe even left half-alive in some flatironing ritual of the grisly
cats, who all killed the same—*Unless it's one killer, one bloodthirsty
gorbeh*, his father speculated at one point, *but one is all it takes to spoil
the bunch—like racism, the whole race suffers when one raceman wrongs.* It was
true. Xerxes especially felt his father's pain, when he'd witness him
coming home from work those evenings, suddenly less lazy-eyed

and dazed from overwork, but instead disturbed and jittery at the doorway, rushing to wash his hands, then sniffing them, shuddering, biting his lip, looking downright rabid—those were the signs that his father had just discarded a dead one.

He did the deed only once in front of Xerxes, on the way to school one day, when Xerxes came within inches of a dead bird. "Stop!" yelled his dad, shoving him into a rosebush. Xerxes, furious, saved himself from mass-pricking and watched as his father yelled, "Don't watch! Turn around! Run to the car!" His father meanwhile crouched down—as usual, totally unversed in child psychology, telling himself his child had done just as he'd said, looked away or left—and reached into his pocket and pulled out a ready plastic Baggie. To Xerxes's horror, it was the same type of ziplock bag that his beef cutlet sandwich was always packed in. His father, by this point, was always ready for the recurrence of his waking nightmare with a few Baggies at all times in his pockets, plus a scooping instrument Xerxes also knew well, the plastic spoon—again, to Xerxes's horror, the same make and model used for the shoveling of his pudding snacks, also in his lunch box. He watched, mesmerized, as his father directed the bag's mouth open wide, sighed a few times, and with the trembling spoon, scooped the messy, bloody mass of feathers and disjointed bones into the bag. "Run, run!" his father yelled, when he finally discovered Xerxes spying behind him.

And Xerxes *would* run, as fast he could, past the car, past the Dumpster where his father would mutter some curse like an anti-prayer and drop off the anti-sacrifice, past the corner and all the way to the next street, where his school would be in sight about a half mile away, and then maybe all the way to the next corner, wishing there was a way to get lost, get really lost in his one and only hometown, or farther, always thinking bigger, frantically scheming until the honking and flashing lights of his father's Dodge Omni hatchback would corner him at the curb, and he'd breathlessly, shamefully get into the car, both males silent and awkward, ashamed, of it, of that, and of everything between them or *missing* between them, until they'd get to his schoolhouse, grumble good-byes, until suddenly Xerxes was free to hop out, skip out in fact, suddenly relieved to see people other than his family and his world. He would go through the motions of the day, living for lunch, then at lunch give his lunch away or throw it away— whichever came easiest, whichever ensured not having to look inside at the Baggie and the spoon—and run with the spoils of his family's laundry change in hand to the cafeteria counter for a crusty cold square of pizza and a warm can of Coke, like all the other kids.

✳   ✳   ✳

As Darius saw it, Darius was always right. The blue jays indeed stopped dying. If it were a game they would be in the win suddenly, but barely winning owing to their earlier losing streak, since no cats had died as a result of their living. It was amazing to see the *gorbehs* on their usual prowl, looking irritated but not that much more irritated than cats always looked, thought Xerxes, deciding early in life that he was not a cat person. They went along with their louder lives, prowling the apartment green with a newfound ruckus, sometimes a couple at a time in opposite corners, clamor against clamor as if their consciences were dialoguing. It was like a bizarre rude Christmas parody: everywhere jingled bells, and instead of Santa and his crew of reindeer there were only his father and a cast of bitchy cats. Once, in the early period of the bells, Xerxes saw Tabitha resting on a step; suddenly, at some sound she dashed off, her bells going nuts as a result, and forcing her to freeze up at her instantaneous cacophonics. From then on, Tabitha would creep around at most, playing a most ingenious game—*In what manner can I still walk around as usual, yet without causing myself to go off?* It took coordination, a light foot, a certain craftiness, and extreme mental and physical concentration, but if anyone could do it Tabitha could. Tabitha was smarter, Xerxes decided, the kind of cat who was aware of sitting on a time bomb, who was going to live with it and live well, making lemonade out of lemons, getting the most out of prison time by writing a memoir, learning Latin, perfecting her chess. Xerxes secretly wished Tabitha could thwart his father's cause by somehow managing, with her almost yogic conquering of the body's havoc, to silently devour a blue jay. He could see it in Tabitha's eyes sometimes, that very thought, as she watched the stirring burdened trees and listened patiently to the blue jays' boastful squawking.

It felt like forever, but Xerxes's stint as after-school-to-summer cat watcher was short-lived—just a couple of weeks that June—because the sound of the bells quickly became unbearable to him, and eventually to everyone, especially the cat owners. They caught on with remarkable lazy-Californian slowness. One evening, as the family lounged around the TV, avoiding conversation, there was a knock on the door, which as usual merited shocked looks on his mother's and father's faces—the look as if they were thinking *Oh my God, who would possibly want us to open the door, who could possibly have gotten the nerve to put their knuckles to our rented entrance!* Their social anxiety was a constant source of disgust for Xerxes, instilling in him early on a habitually peeved state that would overwhelm the spectrum of his emotional makeup later in life.

At the door was a woman: short, white, draped in black, tangled hair. She was a more recent tenant, Xerxes thought. She was holding a black cat under her armpit, clutching it like a handbag. In her other hand was a bell collar.

"So, hi, yeah, I'm in number six and, really, I don't want to waste any time here, folks," she blurted out in one speedy breath, before Xerxes's parents could even think of saying *Hello,* or more likely, *What do you want?* "See, for many days now, off and on, I keep finding these bell-thingies on my cat. I take them off, throw 'em out, and they come back on. Interesting, no?"

Xerxes rejoiced at the very matter-of-fact way his father nodded. This would get good, he thought.

"Yes, well, Castro is *my* cat," she said, suddenly speaking more slowly, perhaps picking up that they were foreign, Xerxes assumed, as usual, whenever any American seemed artificially polite, slow, or simple around them. "*Mine.* I don't like having strangers put things on my cat. I find that screwy. I would have said something sooner, but I couldn't figure out who had done it. And then I talked to another cat owner here in Eden, who had the same thing happen to her. And she had spoken to another family that had had the same thing happen to them. Eventually, we found an owner who claimed to have seen you take the cats into your home. So . . . we have a few requests. . . ." Still clutching Castro as hard as ever, she dropped the collar and produced a crumpled piece of paper from her pocket.

Xerxes's father looked back helplessly at his wife and son.

Wife and son both stayed seated on their respective couches, pretending to be absorbed by the TV commercials, feigning that they couldn't hear a word at the door, that it was none of their business anyway, that it was not their fault, they were not involved, that they were deaf, dumb, brain-dead, plastic. They just happened to live with the bad guy.

She cleared her throat and read her statement: "So. Our first request is to know why, just the basic reason—that's A. Our second request, B, is to know why we were not involved in your little mission. C, we need to know when and how and what was used to get the cats into your home. D, we need to know if you plan on stopping this now. E, what are you thinking, what's your fucking problem, what's your fucking name even?"

Dang, thought Xerxes, *double dang*. It was hard for him to pretend not to have heard that final, certainly improvised, incredibly effective arsenal-morsel. What Mrs. Cook, his last elementary school teacher, had once referred to as the "effin word" had suddenly surfaced naked, loud, and toxic in all its verboten glory, like a defecating bogeyman, perfectly and shockingly used by, of all people, an adult, an adult stranger, over, of all things, his father's mission to put bells on a bunch of annoying, bird-hungry cats. Xerxes was thrilled. He watched his mother's eyes close, felt the clench in her jaw, the deep breathing, he could almost hear the ghost of her mind control tapes bellowing, *I am an endless warm beach in the evening, troubles like waves brush against me and phooooooshhhhhh. . . .* She was mortified. It was possible, Xerxes thought, that his mother, having never been on an American playground, having watched few movies—and the few being Disney as far as he knew—had never even heard the word uttered out loud. For a moment he felt ashamed, recalling the boldness of his early youth, when at age eight or so—the age when he first heard it—he decided to present it to his mother at home, craftily phrasing it to her like, *So mother is the eff-you-see-kay-word pronounced fee-ook?* He was, of course, aiming for absolute innocence, as if hoping his naïveté would be curtly rewarded with a short lesson in why not to say that word, the frosting on top being possibly trapping his mother into having to properly pronounce it. She had instead said, *I do not know how, all I know is we do not say it, now get out, shut up, stop it.* That was all.

But now that he had heard it used so appropriately, he agreed that the word could really be a *terrible* word. Somehow it worked for comedy value when uttered by the fattest, dumbest, red-faced blond boys on the playground, was a word for the streetwise robber on late-night TV, a word that had magically escaped radio-bleeping on a rap song—but from this average, angry American woman, armed with an armpit full of feline, it was frightening.

Xerxes closed his eyes. "There is a child in the house," he could hear his father saying, "a child who does not know such words." He could hear his father lying, "and I do not think the situation requires the use of that word."

"What does the situation require then? The police?!" the woman snapped, pissed off. "You've kidnapped our cats and wrung their necks with bell-thingies! The police maybe, huh?"

Enter a long silence. Xerxes knew those, the ones that often came after a conflict, after the conflict's climax in particular, often between his mother and father—the worst one having happened at one Saturday breakfast when Xerxes's mother had hurled a croissant into his father's face for reasons that were unknown to their son but apparently very clear to her husband who had retaliated by strangling an innocent stick of butter. The silence had been very long. Xerxes had even had the chance to time it, it was so long. (Exactly 197 seconds, his digital He-Man watch revealed.) He had learned then that the best thing to do during such silences was to simply cough. Simple formula: loud noise→loud noise crescendo→ SILENCE→*cough!* maybe even *cough! cough!* When a student got chastised at school and the silence descended, Xerxes coughed. Often other students, a few, would follow his lead. It felt as if they had tapped into some social Band-Aid straight out of the pages of the tenets and anti-tenets of adulthood, the conversational rescue, the nonverbal reliever. Like padding a sentence with the soft fat of "um" and "like," it just lubricated the austerity. Xerxes found it very useful and once when he used SILENCE with his mother, he was terrifically tickled, not to mention intellectually validated, by a quick *cough-cough-cough!* triplet from his father, who was staying out of it but supplying some rope.

But he could not cough in this instance. He knew why: the danger with coughing was that it made your own presence known. There had to be the faith that the two or more players in the silence game were so engrossed in their static conflict that their concentration could not be broken by an outside accidental utterance. But here he was not sure. Who knew the degree to which the angry woman was invested in having just a showdown with Darius—she could be as likely to lash out at any target. No, they were all involved and to cough here would be suicide. His father would have to handle this.

In his own way, he *was* handling it. "First of all, my name is Darius Adam," he said slowly when he did finally speak, slowly but firmly, "and I did not do whatever you're talking about and also I don't know what you're talking about."

It was brilliant—shocking, but brilliant. He swore he saw his mother's face go from a clenched grimace to a sudden split-second ghost of the beginning of a grin, and then quickly back to clenched grimace.

The woman, obviously reasonably intelligent, didn't believe him. "Oh, okay. Right. You have no idea, no idea why something like this would be happening?"

His father shook his head in a way that indicated understanding, empathy for the cause, and utter condescension—as if to say, *What a crazy woman you are, asking me, someone who did not do whatever you're talking about and also who doesn't know what you are talking about, bothering me with questions. Okay, I will just humor you, how's that?*

"I will say this," Darius Adam offered, "If someone is doing it at all—for any reason—I would imagine it is because the person wants the cats to make a sound, yes? And a loud sound. Now why would someone do that?"

"Are you asking me?"

"No. Just know there is a reason for everything. Ask *yourself*, if someone wants the cats to be noisy, why? What benefit? Cats are quiet, yes? And what do quiet cats do?" He paused dramatically and Xerxes knew that what would come next would be good—his father had that deeply contented half smile that promised that his brain had just concocted an effective verbal punch: "They kill. *Kill well.*"

"Kill what?"

Xerxes's father took the opportunity to add a laugh, the hard laughter of adults that rarely expressed genuine humor, but rather cynicism, darkness, a sort of inner deadness. Somewhere deep inside, Darius Adam was ready to decapitate this woman.

"Oh, let's see . . . birds? Birds, maybe? Blue jays?"

This time it was the woman's turn to laugh. It was a witchy cat-lady sort of laugh. Even though his father was in the wrong in every way, it felt good for Xerxes to imagine the woman defeated.

"So you've gone out, bought these ridiculous thingies, put them on everyone's cats, so the birds can, like, get away?"

"*Someone* has done that, I believe."

"That's not the solution. To kidnap other people's cats and force them into these stupid things to save . . . birds. Please! *They* don't belong to anyone."

"You're right," said the man named after a mostly unconquerable Persian king, with a half smile. "They don't belong to anyone. They belong to *everyone.*"

The silence again. The woman looked disgusted; Darius looked triumphant.

"I don't want you touching my Castro or anyone else's cat ever again," she snapped. "I *will* call the police."

His father shook his head—additionally implying, *Why do you think it's me, so misled!*—as he shut the door on her and her cat's equally homicidal mugs, the way he had seen done on a million television situation comedies—a move she earned after her hostility, her profane language in front of his woman and child—and of course, the opportunity that came with it, the cherry on top of a grand-slam banana split like that, was the word, a single word, that both Xerxes and his mother knew all too well, his favorite word, uttered when they had crossed some sacred line with him too weary to say more, when he reminded himself that he, Darius, was born for the last word of last words: "ENOUGH."

*   *   *

It was many years later, when father and son were together in Xerxes's Manhattan studio, sitting in plastic chairs and drinking hot milk and eating dry Fruity Pebbles, that it all came back to Xerxes and he asked Darius, in a window of silence, simply, in total innocence, to talk about something that had been glossed over in the many humorous/atrocious anecdotes of his youth: his father and his mission with the endangered birds. . . .

New York, 2000

Hot milk?! Fruity Pebbles?! Darius couldn't believe it but it would have to do. Xerxes had run out of tea, he lied to his father (since he never bought tea, ever), although he did have a cup's worth of instant coffee (his father wouldn't touch the stuff, he told him, especially the instant stuff), so his father, expecting his own constant dismay while in his son's bare-bones new abode, finally dumped some milk in a pan, turned up the heat, and declared, like everything else, *it will have to do*. Outside it was freezing, after all, and

Darius Adam would not deal with the East Coast chill without *a warm inside* especially since his son's apartment was *a goddamn igloo* (*The heat is on, I swear,* argued Xerxes, to which his father snapped, *Always a liar of convenience!*) And as for food, Xerxes offered potato chips, which his father looked at as if he had never seen a Pringles can before, awestruck at his son's supposedly adult living conditions. Xerxes offered to make some pasta (*No sauce?* asked his father— *I prefer the other stuff . . . ketchup,* said Xerxes) or perhaps some canned vegetarian chili? Finally, his father, after rummaging through his mostly empty cupboards, pulled out the only product he found several boxes of: Fruity Pebbles. His father sniffed at it, shook his head, sniffed again, shrugged, pulled out a bowl, and the two men passed the evening sipping at slightly sugared hot milk—oddly, nicer than they could have possibly imagined, they both thought independently, although it was making them lazy, slow, more bored than before—and dipping for fingerfuls of strange pastel-colored sugar-crusted cereal bits.

"Strange indeed," said his father after a while, after their usual too-long breaches of dialogue, in which chewing, swallowing, sipping, a stray radiator chime, and an occasional old-tactical-standby cough from Xerxes were the only sounds punctuating that depressing institution of silence in Xerxes's apartment, "your life."

"It's okay."

"What were the places you lived in after college like? Certainly your roommates did not live like this?"

"Worse."

"You like being alone like this?"

"Yup."

"Awful."

"Whatever."

His son's first apartment alone was nothing like what he had said it would be. Darius Adam remembered the first letter he got from his son that called the place *spacious, almost one bedroom, high ceilings, wood floor, two windows, bath and shower, centrally located, only twelve hundred dollars a month!* He had asked what the big deal was for a "wood floor" when they had wall-to-wall carpeting in the apartment he grew up in. *Dad, everyone here wants hardwood!* His father asked him how he vacuumed. He didn't, he said. Oh. Twelve hundred dollars is a bargain then? *Practically free.* Oh.

"I could not live like this, son. I just want you to know that."

Xerxes knew he wouldn't understand—or would pretend not to, although he suspected that deep down inside his father envied it all. With his father it was always Opposite Day, his black-to-white contrarianism reminding Xerxes of the stuff of that wacky schoolhouse pseudo holiday: pants worn backward, fingers crossed behind backs, poker faces over untruths, et cetera. Kids loved that negation crap and so did his father, Xerxes had decided long ago. His "I could not live like this" probably translated roughly to *I would do anything to switch places with you and not live with your degenerating menopausal mother in our suffocating cultureless California life, where there is no such thing as central location.*

They had come to the point where they were both men, Xerxes at twenty-five, a man finally, supposedly; and his father fifty-five, a man still, thankfully, not quite an *old* man yet. They would have only a few of these years in which they were of a shared demographic, both men realized, never commenting on it, even as they knew it was one of the few safe commonalities, other than their surnames and blood, that they could discuss without controversy. For some reason, this idea brought Xerxes to the point of tears a few times. He was aging, his father was aging. Soon all they would have would be their past, all conversations starting with "remember when"—the only future for him being his own old-man-hood and for his father . . . death. *Shit*. Life was actually short. Most times Xerxes felt grateful for that, but other times, like this, his father's first trip to see him since he had moved out for college, he felt all the sadness of life's midget proportions like the dull throb of a bad knee on a rainy day: *we are all dying, we are all dying. . . .*

Maybe it was that sudden tenderness for the situation that had made him ask about it. It was the first time he had remembered the birds again, somehow for Xerxes one of the most moving memories of his youth, one of the only ones that didn't paint his father as a full-on asshole but just a confused, okay-hearted, perhaps bored man, trying, just trying, trying his and their lives away.

"Birds?" his father squinted his eyes at the mention.

"Yes, the birds, the dying birds," Xerxes lazily muttered, his stomach upset with the oppressive oversoothing of warm milk.

"Huh," grumbled his father, neither an acknowledgment nor a negation.

They were silent, both men waiting.

"Do you eat any vegetables?" his father suddenly asked. "Potatoes?"

Xerxes shook his head, brazenly.

"You look sick," his father finally raised his voice. He suddenly grabbed the bowl of Pebbles, walked over to one of Xerxes's two windows—both barely equaling one of the windows of the house he grew up in, Darius Adam observed, just two narrow slits, just giving a slight, dreary glimpse at the dirty brick of another complex next door, *hideous!*—opened the latch and dumped the Pebbles out into the street.

"That's for those birds you want to talk about," he snapped, and then lay down on Xerxes's sofa/futon and proceeded to take a nap. Xerxes knew well that the nap was just an excuse for his father to shut him out, his father who for unknown reasons was now in disgusted mode—although in Opposite Day logic his grumble could mean, *I am so happy for you and your new life, son.* Xerxes eyed his playing-dead pose and announced that he was going to go out for the paper, and went out, got a paper, sat inside the corner bar and had a Scotch on the rocks at five in the evening, alone.

Once the door shut, Darius Adam popped his eyes open and sighed. He did not sit up. The whole thing exhausted him: his son's life, the apartment, the East Coast, New York, the milk, the Pebbles, the bird shit. It was all bad. And to top it all off, he could not sleep. He hadn't slept a night since he had gotten here. Sure, there were noises outside, honking cabs, screaming humans, city stuff, but he had been sure that he would sleep once away from certain unsavory elements of his world: For instance, his wife— no more of her constant elbow jabs and hissing in the middle of the night, something she swore she did in her sleep, though once in a fight she admitted she did it consciously, to get him back for snoring all the time. And work—no more being at the mercy of the community college's odd hours—helming an Adult Education Chemistry class at 10 p.m., a Remedial Mathematics I class at

7 a.m., Beginning Bio for the English-as-a-Second-Language set at noon on Monday but 2 p.m. on Wednesdays and 5:30 p.m. on Fridays with a few Field Trip Saturdays of course, or the class he wished he could rename Slow Substanceless Science for the Senior Citizen Set which went on and on for two hours five days a week, 30 weeks a year; and no more backaches at the podium, no more having to listen to the sound of his robotic orator-voice for far too many hours a day a week a month years, correcting, reminding, answering, encouraging the hell out of them, over and over. Truly, he had plotted his vacation as running-off-to-evaluate-what-time-had-made-of-his-son, but it also had the merit of serving as a running away from all that low-level everyday knowing.

But no wife and no work, and still he could not sleep. Somehow in recent years he had developed peculiar discomforts with the very ritual of sleep. First of all, for the first time in his life, when he *was* actually sleeping, he was having nightmares routinely. Since Xerxes had moved out—he chose to blame it on his son's departure, another in the long list of Xerxes's crimes—he had had bad dreams every night, vivid ones, pure horror, that he always remembered. It was possible that he had had bad dreams before, but just didn't remember them. After all, he remembered being in his thirties and at an evening party in Tehran, where everyone, drunk as hell, was recounting dreams, and he realized he was silent with nothing to share because he had *never* remembered a single dream. When he finally confessed this to the rest of the guests, everyone laughed. *Oh, c'mon, yes, you do!* they insisted. *Not a single one,* he swore. *Oh, please, certainly you do, Darius, in your childhood!* He shouted back finally, *My childhood is blank white, dead black, no dreams!* and that shut them up. Sometimes he was sure people just made up their dreams for conversation's sake, especially at parties when there was nothing to say but something fantastic and wild and indisputable that would elicit a safe response: laughter, nodding, oohing, ahhing, life-affirming sour nothings.

That, sadly, was then. Add America to the equation and, like a live-in visitor who claims he'll crash for a night and stays forever, in came the dreams! Then add Xerxes, age eighteen, seeking out the farthest point from his family, the East Coast, and in came the nightmares—and always, always the worst sort. Whereas those guests had recounted their subconscious yarns as involving animals and abstract images and colors and foods, his dreams felt deadly realistic. They were real in that Darius—starring always as his very real self—was always involved in something fairly normal, enacted in a feasible manner, ending with a horrific outcome that was entirely possible in real life. No goblins, no demons, no hellfire. It was simpler than that. He was always in some highly authentic danger or, worse, helpless to assist someone in the face of danger. Eden Gardens was there, his wife, Xerxes, and . . .

There was a young girl, who came and went, the object of the bad dreams' worst crimes. In his dream life, there she was, a female that he assumed was the daughter he had never had—Xerxes's phantom younger sister perhaps, a nonbeing never contemplated by Darius or his wife because, especially in a life postexile, who could go through that again, put another being through that, even more so when this child's—a foreigner's—future would be even more unknowable to them than their own. But apparently they were nobler people in his dream life—they had bothered to have a second child. And indeed it had fucked up their lives, because this little girl was always in danger. She left nightmare material in every corner of Darius's mind that she roamed. She was a skipping little thing, often in a sundress in what Darius regarded as suitable girl colors (pink, red, orange, lavender, white), head adorned with what he envisioned as the classical Persian ringlets, although sometimes they'd rebel, haloing wildly around her face and down her shoulders, framing her golden skin, highlighting her bright brown eyes. She'd talk excitedly with her hands, constantly laughing, never pausing, nimbly dashing with those thin fragile limbs, galloping and skipping and acting out, being alive as if it were an art rather than just a given. She was *something*. Until some abstract nightmare villain would strike and suddenly there she was on a deathbed, in tears, skin gray and eyes foggy, sighing her last breaths—or in a dark room tied up, crying for parents who would always arrive too late—or in the car of a sinister silhouetted man who had offered her poisonous candy, offering her his lap—or in a disaster, a fire, an earthquake, in which she'd be the sole victim when the doorway collapsed—her screams, her final cry, the last thing for a father's ears until he'd snap himself awake and, like the movies, wake up forced upright, drenched in a cold sweat, asking a silent night what the hell he did to deserve *that*. Oh, his imaginary daughter and her many imaginary deaths. A perfect girl—and that was the problem exactly, because nothing in the world was more in danger than perfection.

His son was thankfully, painfully, imperfect and as he got older the imperfections became more cemented. Darius was grateful for the grim reality of his son.

He could imagine what she would be like if he was visiting *her*, in her first home. She definitely wouldn't be living in a place like Xerxes's but in a reasonably priced, say, $600-a-month apartment, with real windows and a real view—of Southern California, of course—and recently vacuumed carpeting, a teapot, vegetables, gratitude, and enthusiasm. *Thank you, Father,* she would say, in Farsi even, *for everything that you instilled in me, for providing a good example, for giving me ample love, which has now translated into me living a happy normal adult life in a home that I selected with your approval in mind, and thank you for everything, thank you most of all for having created me, even after what you went through with my brother, thank you for putting up with the bitching*—oh, this girl wouldn't even say "bitching," she'd consider that vulgar—*and the odd hours, and Mother's cravings and her fits, and the expense, because of course in conceiving me, it was a choice, and for you having made that decision I will live every moment of my life in tribute to my gratitude.* He would laugh and say, *Oh c'mon, you didn't need to say that.* She would say, *Oh yes, I wanted to say that. But I don't mean to annoy you with my effusions, so forgive me.* He would chuckle, plant a kiss on her head, and at her suggestion they'd take a long walk through the city, laughing at all the lonely, lost, loveless families, and all the while he'd be joking, *Oh, Shireen, sometimes I just want to slap some bad sense into you! Like, be bad, you good good girl!*

Shireen. He imagined that would be her name. "Shireen": *sweetness.* Even her name would contribute to the joke.

He was still thinking about that other road not taken, the daughter he never had but often lost, when the son he *did* have stumbled in an hour and a half later, looking flustered in a way his father had never seen before.

"I got the paper," his son muttered, tossing a section onto the floor.

"I see."

"What have you been up to?" his sole offspring had the nerve to ask.

"Sleep."

"You sleep a lot, huh, suddenly."

"As much as I can. It's my one freedom, Xerxes."

"I'm an insomniac," his son said, grinning wildly.

"I'm not surprised. Maybe if you ate better."

"Right," Xerxes laughed, sitting on the floor. He was suddenly more drunk than he thought. He had alternated Scotch with vodka gimlets just for the hell of it, and here he was very much on the border of that very hell of it.

"I am," Xerxes declared, and after the slightest pause, exclaimed, "great!"

He was focused on *great! great! great!* when his father killed the happy buzz: "What?!"

"Didn't you ask how I was, Dad?"

"No, no, I did not." His father's voice was like a chain saw cutting through the inconsequential.

They sat in silence for a few minutes.

His father wondered whether he should again say that his son looked sick, even though for once there was color in his cheeks. He looked messy but invigorated, wind-whipped, maybe even happy.

"Dad," Xerxes said suddenly, "maybe we should get out of here. It's nice out, cold but tolerable, pretty, even. It's Christmastime! Maybe we can take a walk through the city for a little bit?"

He was amazed—his son had channeled Shireen. He was for a second moved by his son. The outdoors had done him good and now here he was wanting to be with his father, wanting to share an evening with his father. There was nothing he wanted more at that minute.

But he strained the sentiment through their most commonly used communication contraption, the Opposite Day translation apparatus. "I don't really want to," Darius said, measuring out his response, "but I will if we *must,* if you are *insisting.*"

"Afraid so," sighed his son, understanding and thus reciprocating by sucking the buzzed joy out of his voice. He found them almost endearing, those moments when the old illogic still applied.

✳　✳　✳

New York: dry and icy when not wet and slushy, and steel blue when not dead gray—those were Darius Adam's first impressions of the city. The holiday element just made everything look glary, blurred, hasty. Scattered baubles of Christmas lights here and there arranged to scream their usual nonsense mantras, fat old men in red suits carrying giant bags full of padding, flying plastic deer with neon-red rubber noses, overfrosted dancing cookies and candy canes. The usual American nonsense, his father thought. He had lived well over twenty American-nonsense-Christmases and every year when it came, he'd realize it all over again: *this country is absolute glorious bullshit.*

Xerxes insisted they stop at a nut vendor, something he'd never done. "It's a very New York thing, they say," he said. Admittedly the hot cashews, coconuts, and peanuts raised a ridiculously good smell over the usual city stink, but Darius wasn't sure he trusted the whole operation. Who were these dark-skinned men with their steaming nut carts, with scarves wrapped tight around half their faces, with their Yankees caps, questionably clean fingers, and wretched accents?

But he was starving and knew he could not count on his son's apartment for sustenance. Xerxes ordered for them.

"Thank you," Darius said staring bleakly at his $1.75 worth of greasy hot nuts. He looked at the nut vendor for a good minute, just standing there, and finally asked, "Where are you from?"

Xerxes tried to suppress an eye roll—of course his father would ask that—he had already asked three cabbies (one Bangladeshi, one Tunisian, one Israeli—his father claimed all three were lying). Basically any man who was ethnic-looking to him, possibly Persian-looking, with a strong accent and a service job—which required he be polite and appease Darius's "curiosity"—was a target.

"I am from New York," the man gruffly answered back.

"New York? Really? No, I mean where are you *really* from?"

"Okay, New Jersey."

That was that. It was the second time during his trip that he had gotten an uncooperative answer. The first time was on the plane ride over when he had suddenly turned to the olive-skinned woman sitting next to him—attractive, his age, very likely Middle Eastern, probably a Persian Jew with her sternly made-up face, corporate blazer, and hard-hitting gold jewelry—and said, *Hello, my name is Daree-oosh. Daree-oosh Odd-damn. May I ask where you are from?*

I am from the United States of America, she had said, *like you?* It was chilling how she added that. He had no idea what to make of it, so he smiled and was grateful when she pretended to be asleep for the rest of the flight. *Maybe you shouldn't ask that,* his son had said when he told him about it.

"Maybe you shouldn't ask that," his son said after they left the nut vendor.

Darius grunted. New York. Hidden identities everywhere. Of course. It was as he expected and more, clichés coming alive at every step. Cabs pushing and shoving like giant yellow roaches, much in the style of a third world country, much in the style of *his* country actually, lawless and rowdy and efficient. The people and their attitudes, everyone constantly running into him and then insulting him, stepping on his feet, pressing up against him on the subway, asking him questions like what time is it but never waiting long enough for an answer. The bagels, hot nuts, black coffee, fast food, faster food, food on the go, whatever could be eaten while speed-walking. It was uncivil. And now throw the Christmas lights into the occasion—it was blinding. He could barely *see* the city, much less gather the resolve to hate it properly.

His father paused on Ninth Street; it was decorated with white-lit doves carrying banners that said "Peace." He squinted his eyes.

"Nice," said Xerxes.

"Strange," his father finally said.

Xerxes again asked, "Dad, the other day I asked about the whole bird thing. Remember?"

That was his son. Deathly stubborn. He turned so he could look his younger double square in the face, employing every intimidating facial muscle he could enlist.

"Xerxes," he said, "*I remember.*" He had no idea how his son even knew. It was one of the loose ends, one of the unfinished complicated parts of his past that he couldn't resolve, another enigma in his own world that could never rematerialize now, since they had lost their Iranian roots, something that would require not only a boat or a plane, but a time machine, and maybe an old brain, maybe subtitles for himself suddenly, to explain how the hell, how truly in the hell, he and his childhood and that old country could have wreaked such havoc.

We all have a topic that we avoid—the one that might keep us up at night should it pop up in our heads, the one we have spent a lifetime struggling to block, Darius Adam would write it himself just like that, if he could.

"So, yeah, the birds, Dad, the birds," Xerxes was saying, like a windup doll. "What was it about the birds. . . ."

It was no good—his son was making him lose control. If anyone could make him take that leap into the bad zone, it was Xerxes. He had, after all, rehearsed it many times in his head, he in tears, often hysterical and bowing into the tiny hands of Shireen, who worshipped *birds,* who wished on *stars,* who didn't understand her father's hardness, his fears, his dark old ways . . . he'd be on his knees apologizing to her, *Sweet sweet Shireen, this is something that makes a man unfit for kids, his own past kidhood and how he spent it . . . Shireen,* he might say, *at least I know what my hell will be like.* She would be in tears, too, and beg him for the full story, and he would say it in a whisper, not his, but some ethereal voice-over which would somehow soften the blow, perhaps even make the bad parts imperceptible, ultrasonic, subliminal, for the ears of his young sweet Sweetness— and now suddenly for his older harder Xerxes, though in a more guided voice that came closer, was more willing to be grounded, and yet more likely to crash down to earth, he spoke:

Here you go, you asked for it . . . so. Back when we were kids, back in the old country, we boys had some games. I was barely a teenager when I first remember participating, but a lot of us boys did it, from really young through high school. It was a neighborhood game and as far as I know, it never left our neighborhood.

And it will not leave this conversation.

It was more or less a game we kept secret from the adults but maybe they knew and maybe we even learned it from one of them. I don't remember. I don't even remember how long I participated. I really just remember this one summer, the summer when your grandfather died—I played it a lot then. It's funny, I'm saying "playing." There wasn't a lot of play involved.

In the old country, we had doves. For all I know, this could have happened in every neighborhood throughout time—except I'd say only we had the doves. I know here they're rare or seen like some big deal, but in the old country they were nothing, nothing more than white pigeons. They were everywhere. I'm telling you now, it was no big deal. We'd meet in this courtyard, late at night, in the summer. We'd capture doves, one by one. We'd shove them under our shirts sometimes—we thought this was hiding them, or else a good way to capture them, I don't remember exactly why. I did it because the others did it. Anyway, we'd be giggling with the tickles because of their feathers, all flapping like crazy. We'd get pecked and scratched in the belly. These doves might be doves of peace to you, but they were not so innocent. They could fend for themselves—they could fly, damn it—and they could hurt us, too.

Somebody would bring the cage, and somebody, the kerosene. Bear with me here. One kid was in charge of the kerosene. Sometimes the kid had gloves and sometimes, would you believe, he didn't. But that kid—he'd be older usually, a hard kid, a pro or something (but not harder than the guy I'll tell you about next)—he'd go around and slap the doves with a little oil. You didn't want too much, because with this type of thing you wanted it to last. There would usually be about a half dozen of us, boys and birds. The birds wouldn't do much more than flap a little. Sometimes it seemed like they liked it, the kerosene feel, like it was a lotion of some sort, soothing or something. I don't really remember though. Maybe they flapped more, maybe they knew, maybe they were just crazy from the smell. The smell wasn't great. You kids don't even know what kerosene smells like. Anyway, I can't remember how much time would go by because we were too excited at that point, in the dark courtyard. There were no lamps. We were the ones with the lights. We thought, I suppose, that we had no choice. We had to make light. In our thinking—just thinking, different than knowing, different even than believing—out of death came hope.

You can trust that sentence as much as you can trust any sentence.

Anyway, the hardest boy of all, not necessarily the oldest, but the boy who'd done it enough, would be in charge of what came next. He'd take the bird, pop open the cage, lift it in the air, take a lighter from his pocket, say Ready? *This might be the point where the coward of the bunch—and he'd be ridiculed for this forever (it was never me!)—this kid, often one of the younger ones but not the newest, though definitely one who'd seen it before and didn't want to see it again—this kid would go running out and away. (We'd find him later and threaten him and he'd never say a word and would you believe, sometimes he'd even join again the next year.) So we'd repeat,* Ready! *And that hardest boy would light the flame underneath the bird and the fire would catch—and because we'd put just the right amount of kerosene, not too much, it would spread with a certain slowness. You can imagine. You can imagine what was happening to the bird. The boy would open the cage door and the thing would go flying, madly, wildly, desperately, like all hell, like a star, a big big wow, off off off away into the distance. They were our lights. Sometimes if you were lucky you'd see the ball of fire go go go and then come down, still in flames—we called those shooting stars. It was all about stars, you see, hope burning bright and gone, a promise we made and killed. For once, it was in our very hands. That was it. Would you believe—*

And she would not. That would be Shireen's greatest gift to him, always. She did not see his ugliness. When it was blatantly there she insisted he was playing a role, just joking, making a point. For Shireen, like a cloud the thing would exist, then quickly disperse, then *poof!* disappear. He would be absolved. *Would you believe?* She would shake her head, laughing. What a kooky father she had. He would hug her. Absolved.

For his son this was not the case. "Would you believe," Darius muttered quietly, capping the tale with a cough, and Xerxes nodded. He was in fact nodding the whole time, as if it was a story he didn't know and yet sensed all his life. Darius could think of no other word for his son's expression than *glazed*. He looked deadish, in a neat, preserved, polished sort of way. He had seen his son look that way once before.

Several minutes later, Xerxes cleared his throat and said with an unprecedented carefulness—he was suddenly more sober than he had ever been in his entire life, he felt—slowly and quietly, with an additional softness that wasn't his, or any Adam's at all: "I wasn't asking about *those birds*. I didn't know about that. The blue jays and cats, that was my question."

His father felt a deep runaway train rush right through him, like an elevator of sense dropping deep down through his guts and landing with a thud into his pelvis—Xerxes had gotten him where it hurt most, in the zone of pure lunatic error. "Oh." It was a sensation he rarely let himself feel; it was the sensation of a man doing what manhood requires he avoid: admitting he was wrong.

"Oh, I . . ." He had made a rather substantial *wrong*. Of all the fuckups in his life, this one was bad, *but*. There was thankfully a *but*: it was perhaps the most necessary, for it was a fuckup that felt like a fuckup but had the slightly positive side effect of taking that proverbial load off his shoulders.

Darius tried to sigh but it came out like a moan.

"Oh, well, they are still causing problems," Darius rasped. "The cats. The birds. I mean. You know. The animals. The old trouble, still."

His son didn't seem to hear him.

His shoulders did feel relieved of some load, but it was as if he had traded that for a different type of burden—instead fangs, nails, prods, beaks poking into his back. He felt injured suddenly. Something reeked of his doom.

In trying to stay calm, in trying to think up instead of down, in aiming for fix-it mode, Darius Adam went ahead with what often happened when he had such intentions: the opposite. He exploded.

"What can I say?! You came out of it, from me, from my life, how can it all be so bad? How come it's all so bad with us? I'm not afraid to say it's *you*, Xerxes! You can't face that you were built of my past—hell, even the past before me—can you? You've decided to be of no past! Ha! Think you can come here and pretend there was nothing and I was nothing and everything of Xerxes-before-he-came-to-New-York is nothing? You think you can cut it all off, eh?! But it doesn't work, I am telling you! So for once in your life, your goddamn so-far-so-short life, face and accept it, all of it, then get over it, all of it, and, *enough*, let us move on!!"

But Xerxes couldn't move, much less move on. For the first time in his life, Xerxes felt nothing for his father, absolutely nothing. His own devastation shocked him. Was it the birds? No. He didn't care about the birds—at least, not like that. Perhaps it was his father's cruel and unusual past, a world forbidden to be spoken of, that Xerxes had always sensed intrinsically? Another reason, any reason, a final reason, to hate himself and his family? All he knew for sure was that the feeling had familiarity. This was one in a long line of his father's stories that he had unloaded on him, burdened him with, but, as often happens with what is saved deliberately for last, this one would have to be the worst. The past had come full circle; this story had pulled with it every other story; history had become theirs, just theirs.

"Son, are you hearing me? Your father is speaking to you—hello?"

It was too much. Xerxes felt his body grow cold and he shuddered, shuddered from the soles of his cold feet to his numbed skull, shuddered long and hard as if a ghost had taken residence in his body, and he looked around and sought something in the sudden quiet of his adopted city's streets, as if aware that something bad, something worse, was going to happen to them all. He suddenly felt like he could sense millions of panicked pulses around him, like the instability had become bigger than just theirs. The old phobia overtook him until he was sure the world around him wanted to explode and he blamed himself. He had let his father come to him, he had brought his city to his father; he had done the one thing that as a child he had learned never to do: he had let the worlds mix.

"Let's go back," Xerxes heard himself mutter, slowly scanning the infinite blocks of city, until his eyes had nowhere to go but to fall on his father.

They finally faced each other, silently, for what felt like the passing of many generations. It was as if their entire lives they had waited for the power of a single story to split them forever.

The world reveals its intentions in sick ways, ways livid with meaning, and Xerxes knew only time would tell why that story had to be the one. He turned around and began leading the way back to his apartment. Tomorrow evening, his father would be gone. They went to bed immediately that night. The next day Xerxes left a note saying he had errands to run all day, a note his father would get late, as he had been out running errands all day himself. When they finally met up again in the evening, a few hours before his father's flight, they stared at each other over an empty suitcase. "How heavy can a carry-on be again?" was the sole question he was able to ask of his son. Xerxes shrugged and muttered, "Heavier than you think." That was that, and he quickly decided it was time to get the paper downstairs. His father's flight was in two hours. He went out, got the paper, and patronized the corner bar for another four hours, until he was absolutely sure that his father would be gone, until he was completely certain he'd be sufficiently wasted beyond caring.

In their minds, they remained in true sync on one notion: they had both decided they would do their best to make that moment, the one about the heaviness of carry-ons, the last time the two men would speak ever again.

Part Two

Kingdoms

They were named after kings.

Try explaining that when they give him their confused looks, after just barely managing it with roll call, usually settling on what they assume was wrong anyway, a clunky absurd "Exer-excess." Sometimes they might risk the Z-sounding X's—"Zerzezz" being the most common mispronunciation, but rarely do they make it just a few nudges over to its rightful "Zerk-sees."

(Nobody was bothering to explain, of course, that the family had already made concessions, inside the home and out, by settling on the Hellenized versions of the old Persian names—try the actual *Khashayar* if you wanted a headache with pronunciation.)

It's the last name that they rush to get out, hoping it might rescue them from the insult-and-injury cycle, with its familiar American form—the simple, biblical even, "Adam"—not realizing it's there where the most damage gets done. In spite of Xerxes's secret and sometimes not-so-secret acquiescence to the Americanized

"Aaa-dumb," Darius Adam—whose first name fared well once he let go of too much *Dareeyoosh*-ing, blessed/cursed by American black men's fortuitous lease on a simple "Dairy-us"—would never once take what they could give on his last name.

"*Odd-damn*, please," he would correct every time.

"A-D-A-M-S, right, sir?"

"A-D-A-M. Zero 'S,'" he would grumble.

"A-D-A-M?"

"Yes, A-D-A-M. *Odd-damn! Odd-damn!*" he would shout, like an overzealous standard-bearer, brandishing his coat of arms.

"Okay, okay, sir! I just assumed A-D-A-M would be Aaa-dumb. . . ."

"No, trust me. It's my goddamn name. It's my goddamn *Farsi* name. *Persian. Iranian*—or *Eyeranian*, now you understand? Take my goddamn Odd-damn word for it." Now he was fuming—nothing bothered Darius Adam more than when jokes, puns, rhymes, et cetera happened without his permission.

"Ha, yes! Apologies, Mr. . . . *Aa-damn?*"

Just fuming. "To hell with you."

He didn't know how to make it clearer, that it had nothing to do with *their* Adam. He remembered a particular ordeal during young Xerxes's first season in kindergarten, back when he was cute and everyone was friends with everyone, even the foreign, particularly if they were cute. Xerxes had had a friend with his own strange name, *Ezra*—apparently plucked from the biblical baby name books by the suburban Baptists to whom the gold-cross-and-"Total Devotion!"-T-shirt-wearing five-year-old was born—and one day, when Darius was driving them home from school, came the precocious question that would define his very *Ezra*-ness forever in Darius's mind,

"Did you know, my parents wondered if you were Christians or Islams?"

Darius Adam was furious. The kid was five. What did he know about Islams? "Why do your parents want to know?"

"I dunno," he grinned and added rather brilliantly, Darius had to admit, for it did absolve him in a sense, "I'm five."

"Yes, well, you can have them ask me."

"Okay. Did you know, what's your last name?"

"Odd-damn."

He was five and brilliant and an asshole, Darius decided when Ezra then turned immediately to his son, with a giggle, and said, "Xerxes, what's *your* last name?"

His son immediately—this was the age before parent fearing, after all—answered him with a clear, bold, "Aaa-dumb."

Ezra giggled on. "Did you know, that's the first man!"

"No!" said Darius, immediately depressed that it had come down to just a "no," a desperate general negation, as in: *I negate you, little Ezra-asshole, and everything you are, your world, your parents, your beliefs, your America, no no no!* What else could he say? This was no time to chastise Xerxes. He wondered how deep he could get into it with this all-knowing baby Jesus-lover. "No," Darius muttered again and paused until he figured out the only calm, cool, but suitably astringent reply, "but I *was* wondering why, *did you know*, do you have a girl's name, Ez-ra?" He knew he was likely wrong but as it went in their New World, sometimes wrong hurt righter than right.

That evening he had a long talk with Xerxes, who had, as kids do, immediately forgotten the whole thing and moved on with his life. "*Odd-damn*, Xerxes. It is not an American name. You must remember that. You are Persian. If not Persian, then Iranian. Two choices."

"Yes, Daddy."

"Actually, you can call me *Pedar* or *Baba* if you want."

"Okay, Daddy."

"And when people ask you about Adam, of Adam and Eve, you say 'no relation,' got it?"

"Who are they, Daddy?"

Ignorance was bliss—no need to make the forbidden fruit sweeter for his newly irritating young son. "Oh, just Ezra's parents."

Routinely, over the next few years as their relationship grew more and more wordless, the silences becoming more their trademark dynamic than incongruous episodes, Xerxes, still too young to recognize the genius behind his annoying inquiries, would find occasional moments to pierce the dead air with his favorite questions: "Who is God's wife?" "Does everyone's caca look the same?" "How do ants make babies?" and sometimes, "What does our last name mean again?" Darius assumed he knew but was trying to trap him, hoping for the day he'd just give up and collapse into "Aaa-dumbs" and admit they were just stupid Americans, too.

"It means human."

"My name is Xerxes Human?" he would say, often spiking the question with giggles.

"No, Xerxes *Odd-damn*," Darius would snap. "You don't have to translate every goddamn thing on earth to the English, you know."

Usually Xerxes would stop there but when he got older and smarter, an older and smarter inquiry got tagged on: "Dad, does it interest you at all that Adam was the first man in Western civilization, and our last name Odd-damn also means 'man' or 'human'? What's your take?"

"Oh, Xerxes," he would sigh, long and hard, stalling in the universal annoyed-dad manner, while his mind raced for negations of an appropriately intellectual magnitude. He was smart, his son, but naïve, certainly. "You're still young apparently. One day you will grow up to see the world for what it is: disconnected and chaotic. Not everything is linked. You are what you are; they are what they are. Grow up already."

And so he did. And still, in Xerxes's head, there were theories.

For Darius, the Adam/Odd-damn fight never ceased to upset. It was he, after all, who had chosen the cursed spelling at the INS office upon their arrival to the country. An agent had eyed the snaky Farsi script on their travel documents—their nonsense curlicues that were supposedly script and scribbled from right to left, *the backward people!*—and demanded they, right there on the spot, come up with a spelling for their Green Cards. He had debated phonetics with the bored agent who offered them "Autumn," "Oddman," and "Adam." In the end, a neighboring Iranian in line had made himself known and said "Adam" was a winner, as it meant the same thing, *human really*, and Darius—immediately equating etymological shoulder-rubbing as infernal conspiracy theory, perhaps another way in which the West had robbed his East, taken his Adam as their Adam—had decided, *why, actually, yes, sir,* he would take it back. Only to be later more infuriated by the nonsense "S" tagged on to many American "Adams" families (insult-injury cycle further aggravated by the fact that *Adams* meant "chewing gum" in Farsi). Still, at the INS office he forced a smile at this new variation of his coat of arms and he adopted and embraced his Adam without ever considering the everyday phonetic battles that would make up a large part of his daily life in the New World.

But even so, to Darius, "Adam" was not the real problem. The first name was the source of their real problems, his and his son's, something the outside world could never fathom. On the upside, it was a small chip at the inherent claustrophobia of the closet-sized dismal father-son universe—they shared the name trouble. They had both been tagged, perhaps even cursed, at birth, each by his own father—who knows out of what spite or vainglory they did it, Darius would wonder, passing on the musing to Xerxes, who later, upon his severalth nervous breakdown, would also wonder about the possibility of socio-psycho-semiological-metaphysical curses, the fateful power of fucked monikers, the lifeless and nonexistent and mytho-historic-*inanimania* once again one-upping the living—something like that anyway, as during those periods when their names would come rushing out at him, this was how Xerxes would think, feverish from bouts of familial chaos theory and hived with ancestral existential smallpox. . . . The underlying problem, both men thought, was that from the moment of birth, his Xerxes to his Darius and his Darius to his Xerxes, was to create one hell of a highly flammable foundation for the mayhem dance of their joint kingdom of Adam.

Darius, King of Persia, Part I

Let me explain, he would begin, our history is a *his*-story, blood on blood, a hot one, and if you take the line and read that which is underneath the lines—*It's 'read* between *the lines,' Dad, 'read* between *the lines,' you mean*, his son would hopelessly correct, and he would insistently ignore, preferring his errors to *their* right—then you, you, son, even you, will see your own story.

Somewhere around twenty-five hundred years before my birth, born out of the royal family Achaemenidae, was one Darius, king of Persia. He died in the year 485 BC. Correction: he was assassinated. He was sixty-four. Not much time for me until my killer comes, if we are to believe the connections, and why not, in a world where it's more likely that crazy things happen than that things coincide perfectly?

I thought you thought things are never connected, that looking for connections is, Xerxes pointed out, *retarded*.

I say judge for yourself, his father continued. Darius ruled over Persia from 521 till his death. He was the greatest of men—how do we know? Largely from him, judging from his own inscriptions, especially the reliefs of Behistun in which he chronicled his life, having no choice but to face that *okay, fine, yes, I, Darius, am the greatest*. Cannot beat this bush around, son.

Cough, mustered Xerxes. *Cough-cough-cough. Cough.*

Listen, before him it was hell. It all began with suicide in a time of governmental corruption—the mad Persian king Cambyses, the second—and then his throne taken by the usurper Smerdis . . . but these men were not chosen ones. Darius observed all that hell and soon, with what he said was the help of Ahura Mazda—

Who the hell?

God, son, god. The Zoroastrian God.

Mazda? Like the car?

That is a stupid connection, simple coincidence.

But I thought you said that connections—

Enough, son—anyway, with his God's help, he secured his kingdom. Now there are legends, mostly by the bastard Herodotus, the Greek heathen historian who says that Darius, a man who was not most obviously up for the throne, left the decision of who should be the king of Persia to his ally's goddamn horses and they—the horses—decided.

Funny stuff.

It was clearly a stupid, possibly mistranslated, legend that I include here only to highlight that history is full of bullshit. Anyway, Darius didn't necessarily own the throne, because his father Hystaspes was still alive. But his father didn't vie for it; evidently he was courageless. A weak guy, but not a bad one. Hey, I get it: it's every father's dream, I would dare say, to be weak in the shadow of his son. It's a defeat, sure, but it's also a family triumph. Like how I let you win sometimes. I could just refuse to get off the couch, and say, I am old, I am tired, I am weak, here son, you are me, better than me, mine, my creation, therefore more me than me, but yet under me—here, you have a go. I find this part moving.

So to make short this longer story, Darius killed the usurper and won the crown. And he took the usurper's wife, Atossa. That's how things went back then. Of course. She was happy, by the way—she was okay. Find one like this, by the way—the ones you don't have to kiss up to or do big things for, the ones you don't have to fight either, or buy or force. Find an easy one—they'll look hard, and maybe only much later will they become that hard. Atossa, from what I can guess, didn't care too much about what happened as long as something *did* happen. Behind the scenes, she had more than enough control, as they often do.

It's the others you worry about. Because people being stupid jealous bastards like they are now, they rebelled. Everywhere in the eastern provinces, Babylon and elsewhere, usurpers ran for office, fakes claiming the right to rule, con artists posing as heirs of the royal race, and they gathered their armies. Darius, with only a small army of hard but good guys, shut them up, smoked them, and went undisturbed. Because he might not have had men's support, but he always had God's. He was king.

He was *the* king. He was known for his organization skills, for creating states, extending and drawing borders in total wilderness, forming governments, and for bringing civilization to the early world. He had no time for barbarous tribes. He introduced gold coinage to the world. He dug a canal from the Nile to the Suez. He expanded commerce. His ships sailed the seas on constant exploratory expeditions, all the way to Sicily.

He is documented in hieroglyphics, in Jewish scriptures, in the Vatican. He was seen as a high priest, a spiritual statesman. He is the reason all the Greek oracles in Asia Minor and Europe stood on the side of Persia in the Persian wars and told the Greeks to attempt no resistance. Their enemies couldn't even rest easy as enemies. This, son, is more power than power itself, you see?

He is documented in the Bible, if you want enemy evidence. Nobody is proud or ashamed, it is what it is, but basically it was his order that placed Daniel in the den of lions. Yes. It was Darius who made Daniel one of the administrators to rule over his 120 satraps. Darius's stupid but loyal satraps feared him so much that they did anything in their power to please their king. But when Daniel started looking too good—who knows, he was probably a kiss-ass or a fake, or perhaps good, I don't know, the Bible is written so you can't really figure out anything, sorry (don't read it, by the way)—it appeared that the king might appoint him as the only administrator and have him rule over his kingdom with increasing power as, say, an adviser. Well, the satraps, thinking they were doing good for the king, I guess—and who knows, maybe they were, who knows what history would look like if history had a nudge and tuck and rip here and there—they decided to find grounds for charges against Daniel in his conduct of government affairs. But they couldn't find a piece of his dirty laundry. Finally the satraps decided to pin him in a way no one could prove really for or against: in matters that had to do with God—on impossible charges basically. So the administrators and the satraps went as a group to the king and said their usual 'O King Darius, live forever!' and then they said Darius should issue a law that anyone who prays to any god or man during the next thirty days, except, of course, their king Darius—I guess in a move to symbolically free up God's time so God could just be one-on-one with Darius, not a bad gesture—anyone else shall be thrown into the lions' den. Well, Darius wasn't a fool—who would say no to that? When an intelligent man hears something that will work for him, why not?! And all it would take would be a break from God for his masses.

No biggo, right? Who would have guessed goody-goods God-obsessed Daniel would mess up his own life, and there, thoughtlessly, put one of the first dents in East-West relations, by making Darius look like a cruel, unusual dictator.

Ah, Daniel 6:1–8. But, Dad, isn't the moral more like—

Enough, checking facts, the nerve of you. . . . Look, Daniel doesn't learn a thing and is a biblical hero. And so what, Darius rules on. And even if the whole story is true, maybe it taught the masses a few things: people loved this man and his devotees would do anything to keep him powerful. He was a man of law and when laws were made, he went with them all the way. And lastly, he was a man of power and what a trap that is—*power*, of whatever nature, good or evil, in the larger scope of things, all amounts to the same. Remind you of your era? You wish. Your era thinks they're gonna live forever—they won't. Wait till burst goes that bubble and you see the ugly side of the real world—in every man's life the world's worst shows itself. Darius was all too aware and I think he feared death, like a normal God-fearing common man. You're not a full man until you feel that fear, and commit to live with it, and further, to die by it. For Darius *that* fear must have suddenly overcome him upon his great-dom, and it must have become like a shadow before him—a fear you can always see, especially in the sunlight, your shadow always at your side, sharpest when you are shining the most. To get by, the happiest of men are ignorant of their shadow, simply blind to its existence. But not the great, truly powerful ones—certainly not Darius. Fear is their fuel.

* * *

It was Darius's own father who taught him "Enough." His "Enough" however was a different "Enough." When he cut some-one's sentence off with an abrupt "Enough," it was about merciful truncation, the "Enough" that said, *Okay, son, okay, wife, let's just snip that sentiment off right there at its best, nicest, happiest point, before it goes bad.* It was Darius's father who would silently wander off just before he sensed a movie's climax would strike, not interested in the boiling point that would lead to the chaos and the danger and the misery —he would often walk back in for the last few minutes which he, without fail, always sensed correctly: a musical number, a final kiss, an end that was a beginning really. The old man was not inter-ested in the ugly things in life—he was interested in turning frowns, indeed, upside down. Bring up *death* and before you could add a word, he was "Enough"-ing it back to *life.* He would remind them that life was short, there was no time to waste dwelling on wars, nightmares, farts, earwax, tragedy. The old man even had dull brown eyes that were always comfortingly murky; young Darius imagined the fogginess was the mucousy film of nice dreams, the half-blinding blanket of goodness, an obscuring handicap that gave the world its more cordial tint. Darius's own eyes, flashing and black, were always desperately clear—he saw everything, and gen-erally everything was as bad. As bad, he would insist, as what his father seemed to be hinting with the enforcement of his adamantly benevolent, fascistically celebratory, false optimism.

Unlike that seething cartoon-cat scowl that Xerxes's mind's eye always equated with Darius, Darius's memories of his father were of him constantly mid-smile, smiling through everything. Apatheti-cally smiling at Darius's being sent home from school for sulking

too much: *He'll, they'll, everyone will get over it, that, everything really*—
insistently smiling at his first stillborn child: *God got him back, he is the*
lucky one, not us—deliriously smiling at a thief in their house during
Darius's twelfth birthday party: *Robber, I am sure you will realize what*
you are doing is wrong, and will leave shortly, otherwise I am sure you will take
what you will and leave us, and our lives will go on, agreed?—softly smiling
at his wife's inexplicable bouts of crying later in her life: *It is just the*
eyes, and maybe the soul, no difference, cleaning themselves out, perfectly normal,
woman—rigidly smiling at the news of his mysterious disease, the
malignant cells that were doing everything in their power to chip
at his aged anatomy, ultimately winning in a matter of months—
and what is the surprise in that, we all knew our lives were temporary. No regrets,
no tears, no needless helpless sadness, you hear me? Enough.

Darius secretly worshipped his father. But the worship was
complicated, sometimes by hate. How he would stuff Darius's
early silences with singing—the old man forty years his son's senior, bald and big-bellied, although still managing a lithe lanki-
ness with his towering six-foot-five stature—suddenly breaking
out into cringe-worthy off-key maudlin song, most likely songs
he made up, often snapping along with a rhythm only he sensed,
a seated jiggling that almost resembled dancing. It was too much
for Darius, who felt zero connection to any internal rhythm.
Sometimes to make him stop Darius would say, *Father, I have some-*
thing to say. For a second the old man would stop, Darius would
be silent, but then he would start again. *But Father, I have to tell you*
something. And so he would stop and Darius, unable to think of
anything, would resort to telling his father something terrible,
just to hear that comforting promise-filled "Enough" rather than

all the nonsense jigs—something like, *Father, I would like you to address something I think of every night, every day, namely that I am very scared of the fact that we all have to die.*

He would want his father to himself, but it would be rare. There were always house parties, when the old cottage would be filled with strange-smelling relatives all eager to kiss and hug and pinch him, all saying the same nice things, with their pots full of cold plastic-looking stews, their baskets of badly bruised apples and pomegranates, their fistfuls of stale almonds and cracked candy— all contributing to Darius's hating relatives and parties and most food for the rest of his life. But he remembered one house party in particular, the first time he had consciously registered his father drinking alcohol, finally old enough to understand drunkenness at fourteen. His father, as usual, was at the center of attention, but more so even with a few extra and sometimes punch-line-less jokes, a zanier brand of his usual unshakable tyrannical happiness . . . and he remembered a guest, maybe an aunt, or a cousin—who knew the difference between any of them?—making an announcement. Her voice had broken through the chatter with an elated shakiness, declaring, *It must be said, our host and his lovely wife are the best couple in our midst, by far!* Darius remembered his father applauding and then swaying a bit in his inebriated state, making it to the kitchen, bringing his flustered wife over, and asking the guest to kindly repeat the compliment so his wife could hear. She did. And Darius's mother—maybe drunk, too, who knew—modestly laughed softly and wiped an eye, taking her husband's hand, waiting for him to say what had clearly been on the tip of his tongue for several minutes, or maybe his whole life, yet another perfect proclamation, a near-proverbial utterance, one that would send chills down Darius's spine forever, whenever he'd think of his father—particularly years later at the old man's deathbed, when the impact hit more ironically and sadly than ever, oh, the deep poignant horror of the beautiful devastating declaration—*My friends,* he had announced without a moment's reservation in front of them, in front of them all, *You see, I would take the deaths of my very own children before my wife's—it is true, that is how strong our love is!*

And Darius sat with his sister and brother, both of them under ten, he the only child old enough to fully comprehend the atrocity and, apparently, the nobility.

Many decades later the old man's sentiment, by the powers of some cruel genetic osmosis perhaps, made its way organically into Darius's own heart. One early Sunday morning, with Xerxes still in that viscous sleep of prepubescents, Darius and his wife woke up immediately snappy, ready for a fight, any fight, somehow both of their belligerent moods coinciding. It was rare for them both to be so simultaneously invested in a fight, but there they were, whispering sharply, hissing like riled snakes, whipping insults at each other as they swallowed hard whole bites of their cold breakfasts in an unlit kitchen, until finally the episode required a climax, and he snapped *Enough Enough Enough!*, waved her away, readied his teacup and turned on the stove, and accidentally set the gas flames on his wife's stove-top-lounging hands. She screamed so loudly that Xerxes rose out of his cruddy slumber, in time to witness the spectacle of his mother's shaking charred peeling hand, sound-tracked with her animal moaning. That against his father franticly pacing in circles, searching for his keys, muttering, *It was an accident, it was an accident,* finally following his hysterical wife out the door, and slamming it on their son without an explanation. Later, in the emergency room of the hospital, Darius found himself turning to her, perhaps crazed to the point of involuntarily repeating some unhappy history, and saying something much bigger and much more horrible than an apology, something he felt had been in his system since that childhood house party, that he, too, perhaps, in the confusing moments when forced to evaluate love and loss had to face: *My wife,* he had said, in a voice that was not his, gasped it out, *My wife, when I accidentally did this to you, all I could think then and now is that I am so regretful of your pain, your pain ever, that I would in fact rather have it be my own or even my own Xerxes's pain—I feel it that much, do you understand me?* She had looked at him awestruck, and finally, when she could manage the words, warned him firmly that he had better shut the hell up or she'd have one more reason to wish him dead.

The Iranians, Xerxes thought, *were always wishing things dead, imagining death, wondering about the dead, ready to curse everything with dead-stuff. Death was everywhere.*

"Enough": it was not Darius's old man's last word, as many would have probably plugged into his voice, say, in the novel of his life. His last words unfortunately—*so so unfortunately,* all the family secretly thought to themselves—were a request for *a sip of marrow jam,* something that it was safe to say was utter nonsense, but forever emblemized in his family as a poetic man's final motion at natural poesy.

Darius was eighteen, and he thought stunted by it, because even at that point the idea of death, something that he obsessed over every spare minute of his adolescence without any resolution, never made any sense to him. He asked his mother, *So, where exactly—and if you don't mind being as specific as possible, I'd appreciate that—is Father, in your opinion?* And she, frail, tired, suddenly an old lady overnight after his death—turned to him each time and snapped, *Oh, of course, he is walking with God.* And Darius having heard the phrase before, understanding what a euphemism was—pressed further, *But what do you mean by that exactly, Mother, if I may ask? What does this walking with God really mean? Do you literally mean walking? Is he walking with God, like a friend? To where? From where? Are they speaking?* His mother, frustrated and tired, would agree to it all, and in playing along turn the abstraction awfully concrete—because it was always easier to render a world literal, since the possibilities of the figurative, rhetorical, and speculative were inanely multitudinous, the older Xerxes later rationalized—she'd agree, *Yes, he and God are walking. They began at this world. Now they are walking to the other. It is . . . a mountain. A long winding road up a mountain. They are talking about how much your father loves us. Your father looks good, happy. So does God. They are also talking about how much better it is to be where he is than where we are. They are having a good time.* And Darius would ask, *And so that in your opinion is the kingdom of heaven?* And she would think and pride herself on being able to quickly manufacture an apt conclusion: *The kingdom of heaven, as I see it, is a place we in our heads know to be the kingdom of heaven, but the dead, when in it, have no idea, so they wander with God through its roads and valleys and peaks, and climb endlessly, and only God knows they are not going anywhere, that they are just in it, that it is what it is. The dead are very ignorant. They have no need to know. The dead don't understand "dead." The dead are very happy.*

Darius became the man of the house. At the age of eighteen, on top of being a student—Darius had been accepted into a mathematics program at the local Tehran college—he became responsible for his sister and brother and even his mother. He took an extra job selling sour apples and iced sherbet on the streets to support them. His mother, resenting their lot in life, her husband's passing for no apparent reason, no explanation but some unnamed killer inside him that had decided to deprive his family for the rest of their lives—decided to mostly ignore Darius and pretend that he wasn't saving their lives. Darius believed that in those final ten years in Iran they had at most three longish conversations. The rest: single sentences, where both parties felt the resentment and blamed it on a dancing, singing, mysteriously summoned dead man dreaming of marrow jelly while traipsing around on a mountaintop with God. . . .

The older Darius speculated that his sudden distance from his mother around that time led to his low opinion of the female gender. *I have problems with my mother, I suppose you should know that,* he found himself often telling women he dated, knowing instinctually that it must be important information for women. Most women would giggle it off and even pretend they were relieved, and then in a matter of weeks or, at best, months, dump him.

Until he met his wife—with whom he found himself taking it further, *I don't like my mother at all really, what do you make of that?* She had shrugged and so he had added, *Or women, most women really . . . ?* She had looked at him glumly, eyes as dimly lit then as ever, and muttered, *Neither do I. Except I hate men, too.* When Darius thought about it some more, he felt he agreed.

During their courtship, nothing meant more to him than their common misanthropy. How relaxed he would be when they would go out to a popular Tehran eatery and he would notice its flaws, and then she would suddenly voice them, or else it would be she who would be visibly jarred, and he'd manage to pinpoint her complaint and moan about it. They would bitch and outbitch. They would go out dancing and instead of actually dancing they would have conversations about how all humans looked stupid dancing. They would share a bottle of wine and agree amid their drunkenness that feeling drunk was miserable. They would have sex and chastise themselves for not having waited to do this really overly championed thing when you thought about it—what a ludicrous, monkeylike, nasty, clumsy, ugly act it was. He would point out that she had the typical bumpy too-big Persian nose that he, unlike most Persian men, did not fetishize at all whatsoever. She would point out that his bony furry back repulsed her.

He warned her after proposing that he could see already that their marriage would be plagued with misery, that he was not his father, he was not blind and happy, he would not in that same meaningless way leave a family—he would rather control the family with a fist, he would expect things, maybe even demand things, and perhaps could go as far as not being trusted. She said she did not care, because obviously, in loving such a man, she deserved it and that she didn't really care, just needed something to pass the years.

They married.

And they both thought like this on and on until the days when the Iranian Islamic revolution became a reality and took over their worlds, and turned their entire ungrateful existences upside down. Like much of their class, alarmed by the dark wave of new "R" words—reform, revolution, religion—they felt their old lives turn unrecognizable overnight. It was hard to tell if the nation was crumbling or building itself—agendas were traded for agendas, crass capitalism was melting down into austere theocracy, paranoias of the secret police were evaporated by the confusing darkness of an old God's newest incarnation. Action dethroned thought—all their people knew to do was to move and move fast.

And so on a train to Istanbul—fleeing, seeking neutrality, anonymity, normalcy, suddenly, both seized with the alarming reality that they were running away, fleeing from their homes, maybe forever—they looked at their young son, humming obliviously on his mother's lap, and she brought it up with tears in her eyes, and he agreed instantly, that of all the naysayings they had done in their time together, perhaps the one they feared and regretted and hoped hadn't cursed them the most was the one in the time of their dark courtship, where they had both agreed that if they ever had a child it would be miserable, untalented, ugly, uninspired, a nothing of an offspring, the end they would both deserve: an error even, at best.

Darius, Part II

Every great man makes some mistakes. This was his first one: in 512, Darius decided on a way to secure peace on the northern frontier of the empire; he would launch a war against the Scythian tribes. Wrongly, the army went to the Black Sea, where the Scythians were not, and the whole army got lost and frustrated and it came down to chaotic nothing. The catastrophes of geographical errors. Darius was haunted at the very least—he had to be. Herodotus, the over-eager historian of ancient misfortunes, is all too happy to tell his tale; as for Darius's own inscriptions, generally he wrote it all, the good and the bad, but this episode is the only chunk of the inscription he left on which most of the tale has been destroyed. Who knows?

Son, I hate to tell you that bad fortune in life is often answered with more bad fortune. The age of the Persian Wars had come. He made the preparations, took the meetings, laid out his plans, knowing well that it would be a trial larger than his lifetime. The world was in a state of chaos: Egypt uprising, Greece restless, Persia suddenly insecure, the pagan tribal world hungry. And so it came that after a rule of thirty-six years, with much unfinished business, Darius was killed—his murder nothing to ponder over, no biggo, as back then no great men died of natural causes, killers just appeared to assist history when they perceived these huge men's pathetic ends, as if it were their natural duty—and there the bulk of the problems began for our people. Forever, really.

In the year before his death, when he sensed his end—great men know confidently their descents as well their ascents—he had come to a time when he had to decide which out of all his sons would be his successor. He had the elder of his sons from a first wife, which a world law of sorts would dictate the crown would rightfully belong to. But he also had Xerxes, the first son born with Atossa, after he became a king, remember—Atossa, who had already paid great dues, wed constantly to the wrong dead men, from Cambyses to Smerdis until Darius (and he had to marry her in order to confirm the legitimacy of his taking the throne from her ex)—Atossa, who, sure, maybe he loved, but to whom we know he owed, must have felt so at least, because without pointing any fingers, they—history—gently tells us that she, unlike the wives of that age, had power over him and perhaps too much—Atossa, who didn't know any better when she insisted that he choose her Xerxes . . . and since all children at a certain age, we can agree, are the same, well, he didn't know any better either. Xerxes would be king.

*   *   *

There is an old saying that exists in every language, including Persian, that translates roughly to this: "Every man is king of his domicile, but it is secretly his wife that really rules him." In every man, this semiproverb lives, although precariously—it is seldom publicly acknowledged even between men, for they either A) dismiss it as cliché and prefer not to repeat it should their wives take it too seriously, or B) recognize it as true and prefer not to repeat it should their wives take it too seriously.

Lala Adam knew it well. It equaled vengeance, the vengeance which she imagined must be a given in all marital unions. That was what you got for tying your life to this one person, chosen on some sort of essential whim, like picking a pebble on a pebble beach. They were all the same, and yet were they? Who knew?—Lala Adam gave it a rating of *shrug*. Darius had been her only lover, her one partner, and while there had been a few suitors, she really had no experience with romantic unions. She barely had a chance with herself.

She blamed it on *literally* having had no model, no parents that she ever knew of, just aunts and uncles and grandparents and family friends and a brother, because her own parents were too busy spending the entirety of her childhood somewhere unimaginable, yes, walking with God perhaps. Among mountaintops indeed, she guessed, cold, icy, dark—just where they had left her.

Lala's parents had lost their lives in a car accident when she was five. She was in the car. So was her older brother, who was nine. There was an ice storm in the hills of Mount Damavand, and her parents—the wealthy weekend traveler type, that was what her memory preserved them as, two people ever in love, always in a car, eternally on the go—were driving. It was night and apparently the roads were icy and unsafe—unsafe for cars, unsafe for a family, a family with small children, helmed by young adults, four full futures ahead of them—when the car, apparently taking them home from a family gathering at a second or third cousin's country home, deep in the thick unlit Iranian countryside night—a sky she remembers always possessing a blackness that was like negative space, a trick presence that was a true void, an infinity that was all dead-end—suddenly collided with what was described later as a jagged rock, causing the car to overturn and topple down into wilderness. The couple died; the children lived. In the following days, the police and the relatives repeated that their deaths had to be instantaneous, but who knew? Only her brother bore the burden of pure memory, the night in which he and his little sister—too little to fathom anything but a vague entrapment in an icy silent darkness—endured twelve hours in a car with dead or maybe slowly dying mostly mutilated parents, until finally well into daylight a farmer discovered the wreckage.

The Iranians, Xerxes thought, *it's like they were made for tragedy, always trapped in some sad dramatic past, generational pain, familial anguish, personal turmoil, a collective tragic disposition, an almost genetic mass pessimism. Tragedy, everywhere; blood always in the air.*

Lala had many things she did not want to think, much less talk, about. One was her brother. Her parents, she would talk about them without pain, for luckily her memory kept them enstoned as the gorgeous young couple of family photos, with their expensive coats and wild smiles—but her brother, very much living, somewhere, anywhere, was a loss she could not bring herself to face anymore. For most of her childhood he had already been a bit lost, as much of a stranger as a brother could manage to be—always behind closed doors, in a private torture nobody could really grasp— and just when she felt old enough to face him, he packed his bags and disappeared without a word to her or the aunt and uncle who had raised them. It was on the night of his high school graduation. No one went looking for him really; it was expected that he would be off, *gone* seeming like his natural state. She heard about him more than once, much later, from the occasional relative who would call to check on her—still out of the pity-reflex, feeling eternally responsible for her, still considering her *their* family tragedy, the little girl who was practically born out of the consummation of a dead couple they seemed to imply, to her disgust—and they always had some vague word that he was "out there." Where, they never seemed to know for sure, but the family gossip always added up to some blurry black-and-white sketch of a sick man very much alone, his madness multiplying with every year. There were rumors he lived in Europe in a huge house and was attended to by many nurses; there were rumors he was deaf and blind and penniless and in Asia; there were rumors he was in the States, involved in drug trafficking; there were rumors he was in Iran all along, hiding in the rural bits not far at all from where his parents took their last ride. Lala never listened much to what they had to say—she never even asked. Eventually time fractured any contact she had with her relatives. She lost their numbers, neglected to keep track of their migrations, never learned the names of the new nieces and nephews and grandchildren and in-laws. Soon even her aunt and uncle became ghosts to her. They were there somewhere, but it would take something like foolishness for her to rouse them, she had convinced herself.

There were other topics also: she had no comment on her old homeland, for instance. She wanted to break away from it, pretend that when they fled, all the everything that they left—a child's nursery full of toys, their books, their clothes, their furniture, their lease, their families and friends, everything but two suitcases mostly full of photo albums and letters and some winter items for who knew where they would end up—all the loss helped make it over for her. She repeatedly claimed she was not interested in discussing that particular past, because, *You cannot change it, you can't even understand it, talk and thought doesn't help, what's done is done, and I think all I and my people want—if I can talk for my people, ha!—is a chance to live again, start our lives from where they were cut off midlife really, early life really, because with all that loss, I tell you, if I were to really spend my days facing that hell I would in a second put an ax to my neck. I'll give you Iranian tragedy. It's all there. . . .*

She was happy in America, she claimed, America with its Disneyland and Las Vegas—her two favorite destinations—home to ignorance and bliss, a land unloaded, haven without baggage, a fresh starting point for people *to lose their minds!*

"You mean," young Xerxes interjected, carefully considering his mother's nonsense handling of the English language, "to forget their pasts? Let go of their memories, yes?"

"Yes, lose their minds!" And so she did, little by little, carefully find ways to banish the old from the new, hoping the body might influence the rest of her. Her first change in the new country: dyed hair. Her dark classic black became an orangey-brown that she announced was "tawny honey," pointing to the label and its overly tickled chestnut brunette. Her next move: the language. Never a bright student in Iran, never one to study much—certainly not enough in the many years of required and seemingly superfluous English classes—she suddenly began spending all her time and money in adult English classes, at one point taking two, insisting one was more conversational, the other for reading. She learned. She began having chats with people in the supermarket and the post office. She began mimicking their lazy pronunciations. It inspired her next move: the changing of her name from *Laleh*. After months of dealing with being called "Lale" and "Lah-lee" and at best "Laa-ley," the answer finally came to her in the form of a credit card solicitation. Her first name, as usual, was misspelled, but somehow more kindly so. "LALA," it said. She immediately liked it and showed it to Darius, who burst into hysterical laughter.

"Lala?! *Lay* or *Law*? It looks 'la la la'!"

"What do you mean?" She asked, perplexed. The *la*'s didn't translate—in Farsi, the sound for song was, after all, *na-nye*.

"Oh, Miss English speaker doesn't know her *do re mi fa so la ti do*! Ha!" Darius continued to mock, in no mood to throw her some rope. "La la la la la!"

"What are you talking about?" she snapped.

"*La-la* is American-nonsense-tongue for scales that are meaningless, children's chorus stuff, like song filler. It is like *tada* or *ching!*"

"Ching?"

"My point is," he enoughed, "it is not a name."

She scowled at him bitterly. *Typical,* she fumed as he walked off without the patience or care to get her to understanding—*Understand what? understand nonsense?!* he shrugged it off—but she understood, all right. Apparently just for the royal hell of it, in the kingdom of Darius Adam, there would be no "Lala's." Even if it did mean song—which now that he mentioned it, did vaguely ring a bell, like something she had sometime in the nebulous past heard on TV—but even if it meant just that, how *like* her bossy parade-rainer husband to denounce *that.* Oh, *Laleh*-the-Persian-flower-that-does-not-exist-in-America is fine, but *Lala*-the-sound-of-happy-children-singing-who-maybe-aren't-paralyzed-by-their-family-tragedies-for-whom-not-everything-has-to-be-ancestral-and-plagued-and-deep, *that* Lala, no, it cannot exist! Not a name!

"It is my name," she announced to an empty room, loudly. "From now on."

To prove it she got a lawyer, paid him from their joint account, signed some papers, and came home one day to an unsuspecting at-peace Darius Adam and informed him *Laleh Adam* was dead and that there was only *Lala,* and if he did not recognize her he was breaking American law and could go to jail—she knew the last part couldn't be all that true, but she thought it could at least seem somewhat feasible in a country so obsessed with all sorts of strange freedoms. Darius Adam refused to let his peace appear as disturbed as it truly was, so he shrugged and said nothing, and she stomped off, annoyed at his best tactic—the simple, anticlimactic nonanswer —but for the rest of their lives together, he stuck to *Laleh* when he absolutely had to say her name, making her cringe every time, once past the era where she would actually bother to correct him. Usually his preferred tactic was to call her "Woman," or nothing at all. For his own reasons Xerxes Adam also automatically participated in the boycott of the oral pronunciation and thus active recognition of his mother's new name—the Americanized change, yes, being shameful on one level (and her out of all people in their family with the simplest name!), but furthermore the meaningless tenor and his mother's clownish sense of triumph over such a humiliating victory, it was too much, and just another example of how every man's greatest embarrassments would be indelibly linked to his most immediate creators.

Xerxes, King of Persia

Fact: Darius was a solid good guy; Xerxes, while interesting, ruined everything.

Xerxes, child of Darius and Atossa, ruled 485–465 BC, until he was killed in his own palace. Imagine that. He was known as the Persian king despised by the Greeks. He was the king who reigned over ancient Persia's decline from mighty power to fading empire, would you believe? He was the way down, while his father was the way way up. Ahem.

While Darius was regarded as a natural leader, a self-built man, Xerxes was spoiled and rottened. Easy to go for great when you have Dad's successes to feed you, no? He was raised in the very nice rich Persian courts, among slaves and women. Blessed and cursed. Had it not been for his father's glorious track record it may not have even occurred to him to follow through with the ultimately disastrous Greek expedition. They say it was his vain ways and the prospect of topping his father's fame that fueled him so crazily.

And why am I named after this total loser?

Because after Darius, Xerxes comes next, no stopping it, son— enough! Besides, some call it a kind of greatness—Xerxes became a legend in his own way. Herodotus tells us that after a storm on the Hellespont delayed Xerxes from crossing into Greece, Xerxes ordered that the waters be given three hundred lashes as punishment— yes! It was said that his army was so huge that it took the entire population of a large city just to feed them each day, while whole rivers and streams would run dry from their thirst—whoa! Old Xerxes was full of good story food, but even just *that* says something— when a man has this much fluff about him, this much head in clouds, this much smoke in eyes, what does it say about the man? Poor Darius was rewriting his life plain and simple on walls of dirt and rock, reliefs he knew were destined for nothing but ruins. Xerxes meanwhile was stimulating the imaginations of bored historians with fog and fairy dust. Big-wow guy, I guess, but in the end big wow does not pay the rent of a nation, you know?

You got that from me.

Oh, big wow for the big wow, son! Anyway . . . you can imagine that he had his father on his mind. So much so that ten years after Darius was defeated by the Greeks at the Battle of Marathon, Xerxes got together a big army to invade Greece and get revenge for his father's loss. Good boy, but of course he did it his way. His troops of ten thousand were fancy in dress and weapon, more fit for show than battle. It was in the ways of their leader—foolish boy—what could they do, these grown men, rough soldier types, all suddenly draped in heavy golds and gems, done up, weighed down. Xerxes: all showtime, and what a show. It gets worse: he's telling his men they can't cross the Hellespont by ship as that would have been too easy, of course—no, Xerxes wants a symbolic link that would bring worlds together for him, having his men work for years to build bridges that would connect the continents! Would you believe?! Where are they now? Absurd waste of all humankind's time—we would have been at least a couple years ahead if it hadn't been for the wastey ways of your namesake. Anyway, after Xerxes crossed the Hellespont he took over Greece. He won a costly victory at Thermopylae—the famous battle which ended with three hundred Spartan warriors creaming the entire Persian army in a last battle to the death—and finally reached Athens and captured the deserted city. There is a fine line always between victory and defeat, one must always be aware of the edge and know the boat can be easily rocked, but apparently Xerxes thought he was riding high. Suddenly, the Persian navy was routed by the Greek fleet at Salamis and hundreds of Persian ships were lost. The invasion ended in this disaster. The Persians, just barely past their moment of glory, had suddenly fallen—at the high point where it hurts the most to fall. Xerxes was left to retreat to his palace in Persepolis. His army was defeated by the Greeks shortly thereafter. And in spite of the defeat, Persia remained an important nation. *And* in spite of Xerxes suddenly withdrawing from his duties and, according to Herodotus, finding more interest in "the intrigues of the harem." Yes, oh, yes. Fifteen years later Xerxes was stabbed to death, probably by the order of his son who succeeded him, Artaxerxes; or the captain of his royal guards, Artabanus—in any case, by one of the men closest to him. Assassins, like I said, were no biggo back then, but to die by the hand of those close to you—well, there's a certain type that gets that end. That is how it is when you walk the line between famous and infamous, genius and madman, leader and dictator—the first thing to go: your mind; the second: the men closest to you. The women, the children, the riches, it takes a while for them to break off. But the men who were by your side, who saw it all, who can read you, who are your only true reflection, those guys, with a swift stab behind you, they're out for you—oh, when everyone is out for you, hell, be thankful for when the curtain drops, when the end ends, because, son, at certain points even nothing is better than nothing.

*   *   *

For most of his formative years, like those of his gender, Xerxes generally found himself in the company of men, or rather, boys. Boys with names like Chris, Ryan, Brian, and Joey, although even Ezra and Yukio would appear. In California, a "Y" name they could do but an "X" name—no, that was subversive, somehow off, subject to all sorts of avoidance, fun-making, and ill-founded investigation.

The hardest friend to make was, for obvious reasons, a boy named Adam, who, in spite of it became Xerxes's best friend through much of his single-digit years. As if to further taunt Xerxes for his name with its odd "Adam" surname and socially unacceptable "X"-y first name, teachers routinely took to accidentally calling

Xerxes "Adam" when they meant "Xerxes." This was of course embarrassing on both ends, and soon what began as a minor annoyance turned into a major one and eventually something adding up roughly to a Problem.

The real Adam had many odds against him, odds which only multiplied in those awkward years—he was fat, prematurely pimpled, perpetually smelling of an already overripe boy-musk, cursed with a constant supply of unfashionable hand-me-downs, and of course incredibly untalented at sports—the sum of which spelled total doom in elementary school terms. And befriending Xerxes made nothing better. Soon, kids—catching on that Xerxes's insistence on his last name's proper pronunciation was wearing off a bit, that it was breaking down from the defiant revolutionary "Odd-damn" to the watered-down, half-ass "Odd-dumb," which had to mean very soon it would land as its normal, rightful "Aaa-dumb"—decided it would be funny to spread the disease to Xerxes's tiny empire of two, by disgracing his dumpy sad sidekick with the apparently correct pronunciation of his better half, "Odd-damn." Soon, agonized Adam grew all the more angst-ridden as the handball mafia and the jungle gym elite derided him with "Hey, Odd! Odd-damn!" Sometimes a clever wormy girl or two would hiss at him, "*Damn*, you're *odd*." Somehow it was Xerxes who came out unscathed through these interactions. It was a truly *odd* thing to have the object of another man's insult be *you*, *odder* to have that insult in no way touch you. Xerxes was amazed at the linguistic ingenuity of his peers. Kids had a way with saying *fuck you* to everyone, no one, and still one or two, all at the same time.

One day Adam decided to bring it up to Xerxes. Inspired by boredom to become unusually expressive as he and Xerxes spent their longest recess in unambitious rockings and lazy circles, idly, on the swings, he cleared his throat and let it all out, "Hey, why don't you just say our name right, jerk?"

Xerxes rolled his eyes. Already by fourth grade he was phenomenally bored by the subject. "Your name is not my name, fool."

"You're wrong! It is! Wake up! You're like everyone else! What, you wanna feel special or something, dork?"

As a matter of fact, Xerxes at that point subscribed to the deep conviction that he *was* special. For starters, he was *quite* different and he had the suspicion that it was the better sort of *different.* He was well aware of extreme potential if not a guaranteed exceptional future. Never mind that his parents and teachers fed him that bullshit constantly, but he just felt *better.* Somehow it didn't irk him to be stuck with fat loser Adam for a sidekick or to be constantly greeted by girls' stuck-out tongues, or to be endlessly picked on by teachers who could maybe tell, too, and resented this better man disrupting the lowbrow harmony of the communistic classroom society. In spite of looking at who his parents were— their foul-smelling past, his hodgepodge nightmare heritage, his unclear place in this or any world—Xerxes back then *did* like himself. He believed himself to be an honest clearheaded young man who had perspective, a good grasp on objective reality, and deep trust in the truth. And so all he could say to Adam at that point *was* the objective truth:

"Sucks to be you, asshole."

Adam said nothing. But months later, Adam's retort came in a particularly graphic form.

It was on the day before their holiday break, during the routine card-swapping/gift-giving nonsense that teachers filled the final day of a semester with. . . . Xerxes was going around numbly dishing out Lala's hastily-bought supply of plastic-wrapped cracked candy canes, when Adam suddenly approached him with a card and particular sort of smug smile. Naturally, once he was seated, Adam's was the first card he opened.

At first glance, it was simply confusing. It was not what he expected, clearly not the kind of card that came from supermarket or mother's hand. Adam had made the card especially for him, it seemed. It was something quite different; it was, in fact, barely a card.

It was nothing but a simple index card with a wobbly animal drawn in underneath a scrawled "MERRY X-MAS. Adam." He looked closely at the penciled creature. It was a horse, he thought. But not quite. A cow? Not cowish enough. Bull? Deer? A unicorn? Possibilities. But when he looked closer he saw that those were no horns. . . .

They were *humps*.

He swallowed a few times. No, he knew . . . there was no getting around it . . . it *was* that dreaded *that*. Adam had drawn him a camel.

What haunted the future adult Xerxes the most about this was how clearly he understood, as just a young kid, what the camel symbolized. It had left him in a daze for the rest of that day. He avoided Adam like the plague, hid in the bathroom for recesses, and at 3:15 when the final bell shrieked, he sprinted into his father's car, instead of taking his usual sheepish after-school stroll.

"What happened to you?" Darius Adam asked, alarmed at the sudden display of energy.

"Nothing," Xerxes answered breathlessly, slamming the door shut with all his little might. He had decided against showing his father the card. He was sure it would make everything worse, somehow, in some way, as everything that involved his father suddenly took that turn. He had decided, anyway, that it would be best to forget the whole thing.

"C'mon, son. I'll keep asking and it will keep annoying you so let's get it over with, what do you say?" Darius insisted.

The resolve of children, especially if they are too young to realize "adult" is not so different from them, is often flimsy. Xerxes, with a groan, with a mental middle finger—given to everyone, Adam, himself, his father, his family, Iran, camels, everyone—took the crumpled "card" out of his pocket and handed it over to his father.

He knew it, too, immediately. "What? *Shotore!* It's a *shotore*. A camel. Is it a camel? It is, right?" He was smiling, as if it was a recognition game and he'd get a cookie for seeing a thing for what it bloody was.

Xerxes glared at his dad. "You know what it means."

His father ignored him, put the card in his breast pocket, and whistled all the way home. Just like that. When they got to the garage, he turned off the car and turned to Xerxes.

"Camels have nothing to do with us," he began. "Do you understand? Just you making a link with us and camels is the problem, you see? This kid, he drew a beast on your card. That is all it is to you. Got it?"

Xerxes suddenly felt his face grow boiling hot, and the humiliation of his father's eyes beholding the raw redness only made it worse. He got that taste in his mouth and felt the dull sting in his eyes. He was about to. Oh, he was close. He hated that. Sometimes, especially at that age, Xerxes would get dangerously close to full-on bawling, but would by some masculine miracle be reined back and rescued at the final moment.

He nodded. He wanted the conversation over with and so he nodded many times and the conversation vanished obediently.

And he never spoke to Adam again.

By junior high, Adam thinned down, acquired flawless skin under a successful oral-plus-topical-antibiotic regime, suddenly took on tennis which he was remarkably talented at, played lead sax in the school band, made the top five lists of the female oligarchy of their grade, and thus, against the old odds, became the most popular boy in his grade. He wasn't a one-off—Xerxes had a highly impressive track record for attracting the most unappealing sorts who would eventually, after an awkward incubation with him, inherit that intangible cooldom as an out from their temporary friendship and an entry to their successful new beginnings. His friendship was like a halfway house for loserdom's last dance. Xerxes was . . . *proud*, he liked to joke. To himself.

"Are you what they call popular?" his father would ask. "I mean, you have friends?"

"I am popular; I have friends," said junior-high Xerxes in his favorite new persona, the auto-programmed robot that played questions back in statement form, that only affirmatived or negatived, that came out of life unscathed because he'd chosen to exist outside of life. Yes. This persona was one of the few that he found very useful later in his adult life.

"I thought so," Darius always answered.

Of course, secretly Darius was suspicious of his son's social adjustment. And he never forgot the camel card either. He kept the card in his files forever. Once in a while he would accidentally find it when looking for something else and it would make him pause and suddenly forget whatever else he was looking for and think back to little Xerxes, age nine, pretending he was not about to cry, getting this sick bullshit from a kid his age, a disgusting American slob-freak—how did any of these boys understand what *that* meant? How did kids know so much?

What haunted him the most was his admittedly bad handling of the situation; on occasion Darius got so honest in his self-evaluations that the analyses punctured that generally unused pseudo organ of his, the alternating hardening-and-softening pulsating blob of *conscience*. Many decades later, after that landmark first and only trip to New York City to visit his son, Darius, bored on the plane ride home, found an empty pack of Camel cigarettes in the seat pouch in front of him. With Xerxes always somewhat lurking in his subconscious, he was suddenly reminded of the camel card and Xerxes's reaction and his treatment, and he thought it was possible that his son's grievances with him began back in the time of Adam and the camel card. Forget birds, when you had the camel and the intimidating menagerie of ugly anti–Middle Eastern sentiment that it opened a door to, in a new land where you were the most freshly foreign and thus victim to such hate, with the uprooting from oldness to newness where hate like a reflex likes to precede understanding, all from an Islamic Revolution that made escape more necessary than ever fully possible, after decades and centuries of corruption and exploitation and manipulation by the West's shining gold and East's dusty gods that put the capital R in "Revolution," and all of their ill-founded dynasties and incest-maddened emperors and the backward invasions and the shaky kingdoms built by homicide and suicide and even infanticide that directed the baddest karma like well-trained bloodhounds, all the unsound blood in the sand and restless spirits behind the sun from Before Christ, destined by history's tireless cyclical soul to derail all the AD to come. . . . *Yes, no, see, see!* the older Darius wanted to explain to the older Xerxes. *It was nothing personal, son! Birds, camels, please! It was always about other things, no? Things bigger than us! We, we would have been okay! It was everything else that wouldn't let us! Trace the trouble, look deeper—and it's all there! How could we, small us, really stand a chance against civilization, history, and blood, son?*

"I never knew about that," Lala said, as Darius just barely explained why he'd been compelled to bring home an empty pack of Camels as a souvenir of parental failure. "Why didn't you tell me about the camel card?"

"I could not speak about it. I meant well. I didn't want it to be a big deal in Xerxes's eyes."

"Who was this Adam?"

"Nobody," Darius said—but what was he saying?! He gruffly addressed the truth, "I think he was that valedictorian kid on the football team who went to Princeton, maybe. . . ."

"Oh. I thought you said a fat little kid—*he* was not fat at all, tall and thin actually. . . ."

"So goes life."

"I don't think that's what caused whatever it caused on your trip," Lala insisted. "I am sure Xerxes doesn't even remember that card."

"Every time I see him about to cry, he's thinking back to that first time I saw him like that, with the camel card. I know my son."

"He never cries," she said, not being able to recall an instance outside of his infanthood.

"Shows what you know, woman. He is a soft guy. He is constantly about to." The truth was Darius Adam was not sure. He knew him then less than he had ever known the guy, but he assumed he was filled with some pain, possibly enough pain to force him into that—softness, susceptibility—because that was the business of pain, to conquer, not kill.

"Well," Lala snapped, frustrated, "maybe you should do something about all this! I don't know! Turn back time! I don't have these problems with any of you . . . leave me out!"

So he did, and so did *he*. For a while, both men left Lala out of their cold war. And both of them, in inevitable father-and-son sync, wondered if this was just how it had to be, over and over, offspring after offspring of good and sometimes great men, stuck in sticky cycles of silent wars and emotional massacres over their ever-finite, eventually invisible, inherited kingdoms. . . .

The Iranians, thought Xerxes.

The Iranian men, thought Xerxes.

Shit, thought Xerxes. Unlike their long-gone namesakes living on in reliefs and ruins, on some level *they* were just words with problems inherent in their own etymologies, still burning through whatever tongue, however foreign, however safe. . . .

Part Three
Heavens

In the only residential district built entirely upon a hilltop in the southern end of Pasadena, California—a city *known*, in a sense, for its Rose Parade, Rose Bowl, Rose pageant, and little old ladies; a town tagged heavily with descriptors like "fragrant," "suburban," "oblivious," "heavenly," "oasis-y"—there is one main windy road, Linda Vista, that entangles itself like an out-of-service noose, creating curvy little substreets with the names Mockingbird, Elysian, Glenwood, Sherry, and Arcadia. At the highest point on Arcadia Drive sits one of the smallest of the larger apartment complexes of its sort. This is Eden Gardens: thirty-some units of pastel pink stucco, wildly shrouded by an imposing green. Thanks to the poor Mexican gardeners, more than two of them unfortunately going by the name "Jose"—perpetuating the casually Californian, ignorant assumption that all Mexican migrant day laborers are named Jose—thanks to them, Eden Gardens, to the pride of landlord Pelican and his residents, is at the very least superficially extraordinary. It is not uncommon to have visitors refer to it, upon entry through the glass French doors—always open and apparently irreparably broken—as "unlike any other" and "out of this world." Eden Gardens, for instance, may not be alone in featuring a pool, but what pool could boast the extra fauna, natural water lizards, water bugs, the occasional skimming bird, and an occasional common dead furry or feathered thing bobbing in the anemic tide? The animal presence is strong, from field mice to garden snakes to the strange California pets, all in abundance. Constantly—4 a.m., half-past midnight, perhaps every hour—to wake one up, to coo one to sleep, birds erratically release aggressive, exclamation-point-heavy sirens through their rather vast slice of the cosmic fabric. And not just any birds, but often the neighborhood's native parrots—the offspring of the avian underlings of a mad old millionaire, they say, who lived in the neighborhood a half century ago when the entire hilltop, on the upswing, flourished as one luxurious minor-celebrity-ridden hotel. Legend had it that it was he who had decided one day to set his dozens of pet parrots off back into the sorta wild, and thus parrots survived enough to create the new batch of ever-shrieking first-generation outcast aerial animalia for the neighborhood. As native as anyone, green and gold and ungodly, they have become the least celebrated symbols of a township just fifteen minutes from an ever-bustling, amicably toxic, pink-and-brown-sky-lit downtown LA.

Lala Adam always took note of her great LA outdoors . . . only because she was one of the few nobodies who walked in LA. Not just because she could not drive, but because she had downtime. Over and over, she became house-ridden, flunking several different jobs in the New Country. She didn't mind. She let them give her the boot without much upset, unemployment checks tucking her back in nicely at home, a place where she apparently belonged yet was constantly fantasizing about leaving. To battle this conflicted confinement, she took walks. She never got far. Usually just the pathways surrounding their complex and maybe the winding stretch of Arcadia Drive was enough. She walked, watched the birds, counted their omnipresent poopings, *tsk*ed, dodged bees, idly picked the state poppies, and gazed out into the heavy death-tinged Los Angeles skyline. She was happy there.

I am Eden's Eve, she once christened herself. *The Adam Eve. Ha!* Like most women with inconsistent impulses toward humor, she found flickers of entertainment in the cave of her sober mind by repeating her few witticisms back and forth, smugly, immaturely, like the guy who invented the word "invention". . . .

For Lala Adam, just being alone in her mind all day was usually three-quarters blessing and just a quarter curse. Done with the always-off household men, done further with a country she couldn't even imagine anymore, done with the fragments of an old family scattered like tears, just done in general with the past that at its worst had somehow half-claimed a brother she had resigned herself to having lost like a severed limb you are aware of daily but no longer feel for—for Lala Adam this was what freedom in America really meant: *being rid of things.*

Then, only once in a while, the feeling overdid itself and Lala Adam was confronted with her humanity—the loneliness that only those who once had and then lost companions can feel. At those times, she'd feel like a husk of her former self—dry, apathetic, automatic, pulseless. But usually she knew better. Often before that anti-feeling could creep in she'd remind herself that it was all shit and she'd snap back with a triumphant *Oh, thank goodness for ridness!*

For instance, she didn't call when Darius Adam was out visiting their son in New York, the first time she was in Eden without him. She thought of them, often, but never called. Let them call her, she thought, knowing they wouldn't. And they didn't, of course.

✻ ✻ ✻

One of Lala's favorite Americanisms was "get a life." The first time she heard it muttered on TV by a fat blond kid to a skinny blond kid, she did something she rarely ever did: laughed, and *hard.*

"What?" Xerxes, thirteen, snapped.

"What is that, 'get a life?'" She couldn't stop giggling.

"You haven't heard that? It's like *bad.* It's like 'get lost.'" He tried to explain clearly and quickly, disturbed by the notion of depriving the home of its usual somber feel by this unprecedented emotional response, from *her* of all people.

"A *life* equals *lost?* I don't think that's right. . . ."

"Mom," he sighed, knowing how to win it once and for all, "who's the American here?"

Since then, she had thought of it often. Used it secretly, sometimes in a murmur, more often in a holler just in her head, almost always at Darius. Lost Darius, life-less Darius.

Because she was on her way to one, she knew—it would take over a decade from when she first learned the phrase from her son, but eventually she would have it—*and yes, here it is, oh yes, a life, a big normal crazy American life!*

Best of all, the life came to her. One afternoon as she was doing her laundry in the unit's laundry room, she faced it in the form of another woman.

"My name is Gigi, apartment thirty-four," the woman declared. She had a slight accent. Mexican, Lala could recognize by that point in her Californian experience, although it was still something that Lala dubbed as "Espaniai"—which was Farsi for anything from Spain, Latin or Central America, maybe even Southeast Asia.

This woman, Lala noticed, was not *that* unlike her. She had her height, her weight, most likely her age, her class maybe as well, also doing laundry when she was doing laundry—she could be taken as her Espaniai equivalent, she decided to conclude.

"Hello, my name is Lala," she said quietly, robotically, embarrassed at an interaction that was a first for her but clearly second nature to her newfound twin.

"Lala?" Gigi exclaimed, with a laugh. " Hello, Lala!"

Lala had no idea what was so funny. *Her* name was Gi-gi. Still she didn't want the encounter to end, the potential for whatever may come with this woman to dissipate, so she just smiled and nodded.

"So you live where?" Gigi asked.

Lala pointed outside, to the top floor of a visible stucco tower.

"So, you do what?" she asked.

"I," she paused. She hated the question. It had always followed her, as even in Iran she did not know what she wanted to be. In America, she still did not know what she wanted to be, so there she was, putting it the only way she knew how, resigning herself to its reality, yes, she did, "keep house."

Gigi hooted—a literal hoot. She could not believe this woman, Lala thought, smiling politely, mesmerized at what she'd done to deserve it.

"No, no, no!" Gigi burst, hysterically, clapping her hands even.

"Yes. Yes, I do."

"We are the same!" Gigi cried, pointing to the four enormous laundry bags at her feet. "I am a housekeeper, too!"

Lala looked at the laundry and back at Gigi fully digesting the meaning. No. That bag of laundry, that was not her life. She hadn't meant it, of course. "Housekeeper" was different than "housewife," a word she could not recall then, damn that slippery English and its subtleties! She shook her head at the laundry: *no way*. Gigi was in fact insulting her with the misunderstanding.

"No, no, I live with my husband and before with my son, too," she tried to explain, "and I am at the house. I am a . . . housewoman!"

"So am I, sister, so am I," said Gigi. "You don't think I made some babies in my day, girl? Ha!"

It took days, a few conversations later—as suddenly Gigi was everywhere, constantly bumping into her outside, on the steps, once even eerily outside her front door—until Gigi *got* what she did or rather what she *didn't* do.

"So?" was Gigi's reaction, when one day Lala's remembering the word and remembering to tell her all happened to coincide perfectly.

"So, that is who I am. Housewife, usually. That is all."

"No big deal!" Gigi snapped. She got quiet, which made Lala nervous, and they proceeded to take a tense walk together.

"So you *need* a housekeeper, or what?" Gigi asked her at the end of her walk, the first of many times she would ask.

"No, I am sorry," said Lala. "I am—I mean, I do it myself."

"You housekeep. Yes?" Gigi's eyes looked ready for a laughter that Lala couldn't quite tell to be good or evil.

"Yes, well, no, I mean well, yes, for my family. For no money. You see?"

"I feel sorry for you, sister!" Gigi raised her voice, suddenly. "I get paid, I have a family who lives far away where I don't have to keep their houses, I live alone, for myself, *and* I get money!"

Lala couldn't argue with that. "That sounds good." She thought about it. "It really does."

Gigi laughed, hoots riddling the still air. "Right, right! But whatever, we can be the same, we'll be friends? Yes?"

Lala was touched and frightened simultaneously. The woman was overbearing, impenetrable, and yet interested in perhaps rescuing her from her unbearable nothing existence. Enter conversation, laughter, mishaps, insults, teas, walks, pokes in the ribs, et cetera, all the et cetera she could never predict, into her usual vacuum of daily existence. Bad or good, her standard of living was on the tip of a potentially dramatic shake-up.

She didn't ask, didn't question it; nonetheless Gigi, obesely equipped with replies for everything, felt compelled to kiss off the silence with her answer.

"'Cause you need a *life*, sis!"

She didn't immediately tell Darius about Gigi—until she was forced to casually introduce them in the courtyard, but she could see the brief awkward interlude vanishing from his consciousness without a second's staying power—she didn't know why but knew he would somehow disapprove of her life-getting, somehow see something threatening in it. But in the week that Darius was in New York, she saw Gigi constantly—day and night, they took walks, made soups, watched soap operas together, told stories about their lives—often the truth, sometimes the truth tinted—and even had a good time. Gigi was Lala's first American friend. In her week of total freedom from keeping house, indeed—she was suddenly agreeing with Gigi that she *was* essentially a house-keeper, but while Gigi had the more exalted role of freelance, she was on the lowest rung, an intern, a slave—she not only hung out with Gigi, they went out. They saw a movie, had dinner, had drinks. Gigi bought her her first American drink, an Espaniai one surely, Lala decided, all pink and fruity and icy and tasting like an underage bad girl. Once they even met up with Gigi's only other friend, a tall black man in a shiny shirt, with a sweet growly "hello" that sounded like granola-in-the-throat. He was black indeed, and tall like a basketball player, which Lala assumed he might as well be—either that or a singer, a jazz musician, an entertainer possibly, no?

"Marvin, at your service," was his introduction, with a firm handshake and huge smile. He was like Gigi: happy. Happy and strange.

Lala smiled and shook his hand. They all got very drunk: Gigi after a whole rainbow of exotic candy-looking scandalous drinks whose umbrellas and flower by-products were used as weapons to assault her companions; Marvin after about a dozen shots of some-thing clear and undoubtedly lethal; Lala after three of the same dirty-girl drinks.

"You're like Gigi. But not!" he laughed, causing Gigi to hoot.

"Isn't that right, sister?! Hoooooo!" Gigi hooted.

Another round, they decided.

"You dance Persian?" he finally asked.

She shook her head. At gunpoint she could, but would she? Never.

"Belly dance? Genie style?"

Marvin and Gigi were beside themselves with laughter. Lala joined in: oh, yes, her country, her Middle East actually, *was* hilarious, yes, she'd agree!

"Never mind, another round, waitress!" he shouted. As the round came and they simmered down—Lala softly giggling into the bar's smoky air, so grateful to be alive in the night, even if it be with these strange and maybe ultimately undesirable people, but people nonetheless, and people who had some investment in her, something, she sensed—she was confronted with her own name in a new voice: "Lala," Marvin, leaning, said in a faux-secretive-sounding whisper, "from tonight on, we three are a team, you hear me?"

She did. And the next day schemed on how to keep this new world under wraps when Darius would return. She was suddenly invested in her new friends' air of reckless optimism—she could see Marvin laughing at her worries, and she could hear Gigi saying, *Oh, sister, everything will work out, cool it!* It was worth the cover-up. Because she knew it when she saw it . . . there it was: suddenly more than she expected, after a couple decades worth of hardly searching in that barely–New World, the goal miraculously had been wholly met—she had gotten it, *A Life,* and maybe it was good.

*   *   *

Once, he left his life and it was bad. But it occurred to Darius Adam, waiting at his departure gate at JFK International for the flight back home to LAX, that it could get worse—for one thing, he had not called home, not once in the last week in New York. He considered how angry she must be, how much she must have missed them, how panic-struck Lala must be by now, and eventually decided, against his better judgment, to face the painful call.

"I don't care," she grumbled, but added softly, "but it would have been nice, maybe once or twice."

"Why does it matter how many times I call? It was a week and I am calling now," he said.

"Oh, what do I expect? That you two think of me? I know what happens to you men once you leave this place."

Darius Adam uttered nothing but a heavy breath to let her know he was there, but that he had nothing to say to that.

"Well, how was it?" she finally asked.

"I'll tell you when I see you," he retorted.

"What is the point of this call, Darius?"

"To tell you my flight is on time and I'm coming," he snapped and moaned. Why had he, why . . .

There was some silence. Finally she asked, "How was he?"

"Terrible. Fine. You know. The same. I don't want to talk about it." He was not prepared to answer that.

"And you have nothing more to say than that."

"My flight is on time," he repeated, "and our son, maybe the only difference is that he is more *himself* than ever. As in, he did not hide his hatred of us. Are you happy?"

86

"What do you mean?" she gasped.

"I don't want to talk about him. I just spent a week *living* him, the last thing I want to do—"

"Well, I'm calling him. Maybe he can be a man and tell me something." It was her greatest weapon: challenging his manhood. She could sense his fury throbbing through the receiver. "Then, soon, you'll talk, I promise."

"When I say I don't want to talk about him, woman," he snapped, "I mean, *not at all.*"

She hung up, as she was prone to do, and spent the next several months leaving messages on Xerxes's answering machine without a word back from him. Apparently their son had nothing to say about it. Meanwhile, back at home, Darius Adam, to her surprise— *like a man, indeed, a big stubborn fool-headed man,* she thought—stuck to his word completely.

* * *

Although nobody ever saw them—nobody saw anybody; this was suburban California after all, and occurrences like the meeting of Lala and Gigi were classified under "miracle" in the context of antisocial LA apartment units—there were secret immigrants everywhere in the neighborhood. In Eden Gardens especially. The Pelican had done quite a decent job of housing those not from "there." If someone were to be creepy enough as to put a glass to their doors, in nearly every unit they would hear the always-angry-sounding coarse garble of a language that was not the reigning tongue of the land. The foreigners lived their old lives, each family thinking they were the only odd one out.

For all they knew, the Adam family were the only Iranians in Eden. And, in fact, they were right.

For them, as for every foreign family, it was all up to this first generation—the ones maybe not quite born here, but close enough, who maybe went through only a few months of tackling their way into the tough putty of a new language. But how did theirs do it— the young oblivious things constantly exposed to the Old World linguistics of a lost mother culture, at best subjected to their parents' broken imperfect attempts at assimilation? How did the kids manage it, cultivate those smooth form-fitting American accents, when just to hear them was to imagine some T-shirt-wearing, baseball-capped, freckled run-of-the-mill American *kiddo*? Only their names, and sometimes the pronunciations of their names—if they didn't immediately give in to the assimilatory meltdown of their oddball appellations—made them something *other*. But for the most part, through the vehicle of language, the youth of Eden Gardens became the Americans-in-residence in every way.

For Xerxes Adam, American English came to him effortlessly via only two vehicles: A) school and B) television. Especially the latter, for that was how he contextualized what he heard in the former— that was his dictionary to look up playground insults, and to discover new ones to try out the next day. Television was the icebreaker, the playground unifier—if there was nothing to say there was always TV talk. There were He-Men and She-Ras and sitcom dunces and cartoon villains and commercial quips and the dumb stuff their parents watched, to bust out and congregate over.

The only hole in the *kid+TV→school success→English proficiency = a future of adult American normalcy* equation was the one only Xerxes

Adam was, of course, doomed to the trenches of. What happened if your kid—your not-a-freak kid with two legs and two arms, average looks, acceptable clothes, a good disposition, above-average learning aptitude, an eagerness to people-please—happened to not watch the *right* TV shows?

Xerxes Adam actually did watch all the right shows—he skimmed them like a book that was good for you but in the end action-and-dialogue anorexic, full of long descriptive landscape paragraphs that practically pleaded for ADD eyes. He knew—*somewhat*—the shows the kids liked. He could smile and nod at their references, *somewhat*. He knew a catchphrase, a scenario, a superhero, a punch line here and there to drop at emergency points in kid talk. But it was not where his heart was. For Xerxes Adam, there was really only one show, THE show, a show that was so before his time and out of his universe—and in fact out of all universes, almost implying a societal disregard, part of its beauty for Xerxes—the show that he could thank for filling his ears with edifying English language lessons, but really a show that shaped *him,* his character, his future aesthetic sensibility, his sense of not just the world, but its possibilities, a show that made his everyday hell in this supposed Eden a heaven, a show that was less *show* for him than the one livable half hour of another long lost day—thank God for cable channels and syndication culture!—a show known as: *I Dream of Jeannie.*

Although not quite godhead, it was, it had to be admitted, a reasonable television milestone of its era. Inspired by the success of rival network ABC's occult farce *Bewitched,* about the domestic life of a married "witch" (debuting in 1964 as the second most watched program in the United States), Sidney Sheldon wanted something to compete on his network, NBC. By 1965, Sheldon had his situation comedy: *I Dream of Jeannie*, which ran until 1970 and revolved around the conjugal mishaps and sexual tensions of one blonde genie (Barbara Eden) and an astronaut general (Larry Hagman). The story lines were as simple as TV convention, once you got past the premise: that an astronaut has to abort a space launch and crashes on a desert island; he finds a bottle on the beach; he opens it. A genie is stirred from a two-thousand-year imprisonment. Since the liberator of a genie thus becomes its governor, Captain Tony Nelson reluctantly accepts the role after insisting the genie can go free, upon his rescue. But Jeannie the genie has fallen in love with him, the first man she set eyes on in two thousand years; she follows Nelson home to Coco Beach, Florida, where she goes from the cutely antagonistic household "help," to Nelson's fiancée, and subsequently becomes his wife in the fifth and final season. "Master's" challenge is keeping her supernatural talents a secret, while very often relying on them to rescue him and Jeannie from the very sticky situations the mischievous outsider is also capable of conjuring.

"Dang, genie!" Xerxes would exclaim, shaking his head with a flummoxed grin, sometimes even jumping out of his seat with the entranced gusto of grown men deep in the realm of a televised sporting event. "*Dang!*"

It was the first time Darius and Lala Adam realized that just because you create a thing, doesn't mean you will understand or even recognize it. The question *why* was not even a fair question. It just was. And they could do nothing about it. *They talk about a can of worms opening,* Darius thought; *this is the first time I found my son's worms outside the can.* Lala actually agreed. It made them uneasy, forced them to analyze it, to try to put it in a larger context, to somehow try to come to terms with their son's first unlikely obsession. *It's just that it's not normal,* Lala thought, *that's all. Isn't that all?* The mystery made them uneasy and then, further, made them question their mysterious uneasiness.

The speculation of the creators went on for years, and never really ended.

DARIUS: I never approved of this, so in a way I am not evil to say, hey, her fault entirely! I believe in supervising kids. I believe if your son likes *Planet of the Apes,* which he did for a while, or *Star Trek,* which he also did, okay, so they are weird impossible shows, but harmless—TV is what they do when they're not doing other useless stuff. But if your boy likes a show that is for girls, that's where I draw the line. But this is the tough part with that damn show: so the main character is a girl—is it a show for girls? Because sometimes guys like girl shows, for the girl. I can live with that: he loved it in the guy-way. Any of us could be guilty of that. Fine.

LALA: At first I said, oh, he thinks she is from our country. Genies. Better than terrorists!

DARIUS: She is Arab—get that straight. There are no Persian genies. None! *Arabian Nights,* got it? No belly dancers either. This Jeannie is just an Arab woman, with a low self-esteem who dyes her hair blonde, with a white man husband she calls "master." Ha! That sort of disposition is unheard of among the hard—I'll say it: bitchy—females of Iran.

LALA: Very early on he asked me what her real name was. "Barbara Eden," I said. *Look, Mother, Barbara Eden is on!* he would say. Maybe he thought she owned Eden Gardens?

DARIUS: I'll admit it: around that time I bought him his first toy gun.

LALA: But what is the problem anyway? Oh, your shows about robot armies and things that blow up and crazy killing sounds, that is normal! Oh, sorry, cartoon is normal! What the hell is cartoon? You know, sometimes I have liked it. Nice colors, fun music, everything works out. [*Pauses.*] It bothers me, yes. I mean, will my son ever wear a tie? Have a car and house and kids and a wife? Or . . . ? *Or.*

DARIUS [*with fingers in ears, eyes closed*]: If you want to know the truth, I trace Xerxes and my problems actually to this, the moment I realized my son was *really* off. It's not impossible to say this is the real reason that Xerxes and I were destined to stop talking altogether one day. Barbara Bitchy Eden, you don't even know us, and look!

LALA: It was in our early fights that I think Xerxes first saw that married life was all war. With us being us, of course he took a genie! Even I liked her more than *us.*

DARIUS: Anyone would wonder it. *Is* my son? Can he *be?* Will he *be?* Well, of course not, I say today. But sometimes when it comes up the old fears arise.

LALA: He is human first—*adam,* yes—then boy. He can be whatever he wants to be, like whatever he likes. You know. But *that,* of course, well, *that's* difficult.

DARIUS: In three letters that start with a G, and no it's not God, the opposite of God, God's greatest nightmare, another curse that comes with the territory, only in America!

LALA: We never talked about it with him. Why give him ideas? In Iran, they don't exist.

DARIUS: Sure, in Iran they are there, but they hide. They are considered molesters, boy-child-loving perverts. Once, in America—oh, the black-and-white one of my youth, with its musical couples and family values that made all of us want to come here even before we had to—it was hidden, too. Now everything here, it just all hangs out.

LALA: You want foreign? Call us foreign with this. We are happy to be, in this matter!

DARIUS: In America, I am told it once meant "happy." There you go. America's heaven: our hell. Their Edens: our *jahanam.* Happy! If by happy you mean, *pedar sageh antareh goh!*

[*Pause*]

XERXES: You don't want to translate that.

LALA: Eventually he grew up; it went away. By that I mean: we stopped talking about it.

DARIUS: In the end, there was *Enough,* and enough was enough—and okay, what if enough *wasn't* enough, well, thank God, I have only about three more decades of life—I did what I could, let him, that strange stranger my son, learn in spite of me—and what I can't see won't hurt me—if he *isn't,* okay, if he *is,* if that is his happiness, damn us all—

LALA: Maybe. Sure. But certainly no. At the worst . . . what are we talking about again?

XERXES: It was a very difficult childhood. It was the best time of my life.

* * *

Of course, Xerxes attempted to explain his fixation at several points in his childhood without ever getting the chance to get into it uninterrupted—they with their alleged Persian nationalism not even bothering to ask the right questions, not even bothering to probe whether the interest could be, in part, a young boy's investigation into an American rendering of a Middle Eastern myth, the genie—surely there was something to that? It wasn't the whole story, but Xerxes wished, at best, that they could see it that way, if they saw it in any way at all, the dullards!—because Jeannie's dog after all was named "Djinn-Djinn" (Farsi for "demon-demon"), and the enigmatic Chief of All Genies was called "Haji" (Farsi for something roughly like "Dude"), and ancient Persia was even re-created—poorly—in Episode 2 . . . *What do you make of that, any comment on that, O Iranian progenitors?*

Do you ever see what I see?

What Xerxes did not attempt to point out was that his love of her also involved what she was *not*. For instance, dark, doom-loving, heavy with the weight of history, harrowing to a western community, a regular on the nightly news circuit, a part of the map they'd teach them to color black, if not blood, if they could—no, these things she was not at all. The happy blonde genie was instead an escape, an impossibility, an out from the realm of heartache and sighs and moans and bawls and screams and breast-beatings and hair-tearings. She was the laugh track laugh that translated roughly to real laughter; she was a network's whim—some tired, white, under-paid male team's cheap mindless fantasy, working her way into America's family time effortlessly. Oh, Xerxes would have taken her "life" story, the episode outlines, his own explorations on theme and character and historical significance, et cetera, and filled the textbooks with *her* stuff instead of the yellow-and-black 1970s photographs of dusty tanks and soldiers, and emaciated palm trees against flashy murals of turbaned prophets and machine guns, and mustached men whose dirt-powdered faces looked lined with an-cient secrets as they guarded their women who, like black-draped ghosts, had the appearance of mourners on eternal parade, the nega-tive space of their dead olive faces speckling the blackened city streets like holes that have long riddled a conscience. If he had it his way, the textbooks would be animated in pink and purple and gold and glitter and bliss and other imponderable arabesques, es-sences he didn't imagine belonged to his people. Because above all things that Jeannie was not, she was of a brightness that did not burn.

✳   ✳   ✳

Lala began agreeing with Gigi: *Yes, you are my sister, sister.* Why not? Gigi was not only her first American friend, she may have been her first friend ever. Sure, women had come and gone back in her old life in Iran, but they were mainly school chums, friends of the family, distant cousins, ladies who spoke in formalities and house-warming presents and were known only by their husbands' last names. Gigi *knew* her. They had secrets, inside jokes. Once she even went as far as bringing Lala a gift—"panties I thought you probably wear," she shrugged as she handed over the brown paper bag full of silky, lacy, flowery thongs, apparently the fruits of a day of bargain shopping in downtown LA discount stores. Lala thanked her, and threw the bag into the garbage once she left, of course— *that* was too much. But still she recognized it as one in a long line of her many gestures of sisterhood. Gigi was her friend.

And so the time had come for a good story to back this life, mainly an excuse for Darius, who was bound to smell a rat soon, especially as Gigi was starting to put on the pressure to "hang out" more in the evenings. She tried to explain to Gigi that it would be tough—that Darius wouldn't understand, that she was a wife and mother, that in her country family women didn't go out traipsing around in the night.

Gigi, of course, didn't like that. "Do you think maybe he is, I don't know, abusing you?"

"Abuse?" Lala let the word roll around in her head, evaluating its every angle and crevice through the English language converter machine. No, she thought, she was not getting beaten or forced into sex. No. "No, Gigi."

"Oh, I see, being too afraid to go out with your best friend when he's home, oh, that isn't abusive?" she snapped, rolling her eyes.

"He just wouldn't understand," Lala muttered.

"And what is that which he wouldn't understand?"

"I don't know. Going places. Drinking. Hanging out."

Gigi gave a sarcastic hoot. "Bring him along!"

"No way," groaned Lala. "That wouldn't be fun for us anyway. I'd worry."

"About what?! It's just life, sister!"

"Maybe it isn't him," she said, then paused, having thought of it only once she'd uttered it. "Is that what you want me to say?"

"It's you!"

What a can of worms, Lala thought, but it had some truth, some truth that could help her off the hook. "Maybe I just need to keep something in my life to myself."

"There you go, sister! You don't want him all up in all your worlds! Good! Then do it and keep it. That's my girl."

Being Gigi's girl reminded her of the lifestyle of schoolgirls, how she'd eavesdrop on their talk of all the things they did behind their parents' backs. All the fun in the world was about violation, deception, hidden things, lies, things kept to oneself. Lala had never gone there. With dead parents there wasn't much to hide and with substitute parents you can't quite muster the heart for disobedience. In life, her main goal was to live in whatever mediocre manner was her lot, but to do everything possible not to be abandoned. She had used up her emotional capacity for abandonment.

So she conjured up a story for the nights that the Gigi impulse won: Lala was going to assist Gigi with the babysitting portion of her housekeeping business.

"But you hate babies," said Darius when she announced her first nightly engagement of what she planned as a series, "or was that just ours?"

Lala took a deep breath. "Look, you, my life is dull. What, do you want me to go out there instead, get another job, get another world, another life instead?"

Darius thought about it. "No, not really. . . . So you'll be in the complex, with strangers' kids, that is what you want?"

"Yes," Lala said. "If by strangers you mean our neighbors."

"Whatever," said Darius, "but I will say this, don't think I don't notice you have been acting weird and don't think that I didn't put together that it's been ever since you met that Gigi monster. I see everything, woman."

"Don't start with me," she said, with exaggerated outrage, grabbing her keys, smoothing her hair, taking a deep breath for a long night ahead of her that she wasn't sure even merited this tricky campaigning. . . . "You and your abuse!"

She left Darius sitting there to contemplate the very American word "abuse," which he heard all the time, a word designed for criminals on each end of the spectrum, which he suspected meant nothing, which was why he missed the moral of her jab, as usual, attributing it to her new cardboard Americanism. Instead he thought about her going to "work" in those jeans, suddenly wearing jeans all the time—his wife who first set foot on this soil in a suit of perfectly pressed tweed, panty hose, and heels, and a mask of makeup. And here she was over two decades later, still beautiful—well, as beautiful as any man could consider his wife of twenty-something years—but conspiring with time to break down beauty's last remnants. T-shirts in the house, then jeans outside. God help them and what they had become.

Outside in the parking lot Lala met Gigi and they hugged, like those very schoolgirls giggling breathlessly and then hushing each other, all red in the face, as if Darius the Dad was lurking just around the corner. They dashed into Gigi's Honda and sped off to a pizza place/bar where dollar pitchers and jukebox music of whining cowboy men carried them through a night with Marvin.

It was a nothing night, nothing much but eating and drinking and talking, and, of course, laughing—she laughed at jokes or sentiments she didn't understand, or fake laughed at things she did get but couldn't really get a real laugh out of, or when she felt the urge to put something into the group dynamic where she couldn't fit words—*Oh, never mind*, she thought again and again; she was grateful for this life she had gotten.

It happened that one evening when she strutted out of the house in her jeans, into the parking lot, Gigi's busted Honda was not there to meet her. Rather, there was an SUV, pulsing with a low bass, presumably from a sound track, hinting of a night out. Inside, a man—dark, obscured by tinted windows, just a silhouette of a large man in his large car—waved at her. She stood frozen, terrified, tried to ignore the driver who had undoubtedly mistaken her. The car honked. She closed her eyes, hoping it would go away. She heard the buzz of rolled-down automatic windows, and the familiar call, "Hell, Lala, it's me, girl!"

It was Marvin. She was relieved, and yet . . . not relieved at all. He had never picked her up. She had never seen his car. In fact, he knew nothing of her pact with Gigi and their secret outing agreement—hence the blasting of music and honk and holler. She waved back hesitantly, and he laughed and honked again, motioning her in. She walked reluctantly over, worried that Darius might somehow psychically or just plain *physically* discover her secret in an incarnation she never anticipated. . . .

Inside, Marvin was laughing to himself and shaking his head at nothing at all.

"Hello, Marvin," she shouted, inside, trying to rise above the party music, putting on her seat belt. She was on autopilot suddenly, fatalistically resigning herself to whatever it was the evening had in store for her.

He slapped her thigh hello, with a chuckle.

"Where is Gigi?" Lala asked, inevitably.

"That's the thing," he said, refusing to turn the music down, forcing himself to shout back, "Gigi's home sick. But she didn't want you to miss an outing! Now that's a friend!"

"Oh. Well, you didn't have to . . ."

"Now why did I know you would say that, girl?! No worries, Lala, I love hanging out! Hanging out with you!" He poked her ribs and laughed at her cringing.

Hanging out, Lala thought. Suddenly it took on a bitter taste. Oh, what the hell was Hanging Out anyway? What did he mean by that? Another bad restaurant, another junky meal, another few rounds of dirty-tasting alcohol and some chatter. What was it about this life that made her want it? Did she want it? Was Gigi another Darius?

She shook off everything in her head and told herself it was just one night, that she could make it through this one particularly awkward hanging out session. She just wouldn't reveal her feelings. She would let him talk. He *would* talk. Maybe he, too—at the worst—would find it awkward and question their hanging out time. At the very worst, he would tell Gigi she was out. At the very very worst, Gigi would stop talking to her and she would lose her "sister." At the very very very worst, she would go back to her old life with Darius and, she supposed, survive.

Suddenly, she worried that it would not be possible to survive back in her old life.

Marvin interrupted her anxieties by announcing the plan: tonight was "Chingo 2-for-1 Sushi Nite." The disaster was growing richer, Lala thought, for she had never had sushi, had only heard about its raw, gelatinous, bacteria-ridden primitive horror—oh, she didn't even know how to hold a chopstick.

"I'm no good at this," Lala told him at the entrance to Chingo's, "sushi, you know."

He slapped her hard on the back as he opened the door for her, whispering in an inappropriately overjoyed fashion, "Who is??!!!"

Once seated, as Lala expected, Marvin did the talking. And the ordering.

"Please, nothing too, too raw," she urged him as he paused with the waitress.

"California roll, how's that? The crab is raw but it's also fake," he told her.

She looked up at the waitress, who had nothing but total indifference for them.

"Sounds all right," Lala nodded miserably, although the only thing that sounded worse than cold raw fish was maybe fake cold raw fish.

Another problem with Marvin was what she suspected was simply the pitfall of being the talker. Eventually any extrovert had to run out of steam, but the hardest part had to be covering these lapses of conversational impotency with the insertion of randomly generated questions—this was what Lala assumed happened to Marvin when his loud nonsense anecdotes about his day at work, his coworkers, his insurance, his previous jobs, his dream job, et cetera, would suddenly come to an abrupt halt, and there, jarringly, he would insert a question, often highly personal, aimed right at her, so fast as if to trap her in a moment of total inattention, which she was often deep in, but easily enough snapped out of, always somewhat ready for the shotgun turns of his conversation.

"And it's all about the 401(k)—you put some years into a place—and that and your health insurance, and I got a PPO—I tell you—and with my exemptions, you figure the state tax, social security—say, Lala, are there any black people in Iran?"

The question, no matter how scary, felt as though it had been coming, she had to admit. She swallowed hard. When she first met him, she had to admit, the first thing she thought was, *Here is a Black Man. I don't know many blacks. I've seen them on TV before and now on the streets of America. In Iran, I did not see them ever. On TV, but only Sidney Something and Sammy Something Else. Here is the first Black Man I am expected to talk to and befriend. I don't think I have ever befriended one or thought about it. My. How do I act normal and not let the Black Man know I think and feel this way?*

Lala did not know how necessary it was to be honest, but could not muster the energy to lie either.

"There must have been," she said, "somewhere. . . ."

"You didn't know any," he said flatly, without much surprise in his voice.

"Not really."

"None in America either," he stated.

"But I don't know anyone in America," she piped up, happy for that truth suddenly.

"I'm your first black man!" he declared, with a small smile and his fist softly pounding the table.

"Well, if you put it that way," she tried to smile back, uncertainly.

But his beam grew to its usual epic proportions. "Congratulations!" It was of course possible that it was mocking or mean-spirited, she sensed, worried. He looked upward and laughed, as if into the face of a slow god. "*Shit!*"

He got quiet again, though he capped his reticence quickly by plastering on a wide smile over his silence. The fish came. It was delivered on blocks of damp wood, in a nine-piece tic-tac-toe of rice filled with colorful green orange yellow, secured by a crusty bandage of green seaweed holding each motley monstrosity in a tight bind. She looked at the chopsticks and watched Marvin expertly break them apart from one another, rub them together, and then trap them in his fingers in a way to naturally create a graceful picking-up device. He ate effortlessly. She chose the moment he looked down at his food to reach out and stab a roll with her chopstick, stuffing it quickly into her mouth before anyone noticed. It was, as expected, cold and wrong. Surreal even. She swallowed most of it whole and then did it again.

"How is it?" Marvin asked.

"More than I imagined!" she said, picking a few rice bits off the roll.

He ordered some drinks, plum wine, and Lala drank it like water, thirstily, grateful for its going right to her head.

He went on with his usual babbling, "This place—it's amazing— Japanese food, what history, sushi, sake, soba, sashimi, tempura—I tell you, culturally the country is about as daunting as it is economically, I mean it—" and then like a shot in the dark, of course, it came—"so, Lala, *you* like black people?"

She nodded immediately, but worried her nod was a lie. What did she know about liking a whole people anyway? She never liked anyone, really. Nobody was okay, she liked to think, until they *were*.

And perhaps because of the misleadingly weak-tasting plum wine, which she had immediately had a second then third glass of, she decided it was safe and perhaps a good intimate move for her to tell Marvin about an incident she had not thought about in a long time, namely the first time she saw and interacted with a Black Man—long before him, before America even. . . .

He raised his eyebrows and motioned with his handheld wooden crane to *please, girl, continue* and suddenly all the evening's talk was hers:

☆   ☆   ☆

So it was in Paris. Now don't think anything of that—we had been on the run, fleeing, we had just run away from our own country, over to Istanbul, ready to be accepted by anyone who had trust in our flimsy passports, waiting for The Great American Green Cards, killing time with makeshift vacations, and we had some relatives there, and thought why not, it may be our last chance—and it was—so: Paris. He—my husband, Darius, who you don't know, and never will actually, better that way, trust me—was out as usual job hunting, seeing what may exist for us out there after all the running, uncomfortably eating off our distant relatives, trying to carve a future for us in a very daily hope-filled way. It was a hard time. The days had no structure, sunup to sundown, for me and little Xerxes, barely six, so we roamed through the beautiful city. We did not know the language, we did not know our way around. We just walked like two characters out of a dream suddenly finding themselves existing in a real world. We would go to cafés and we would spend almost entire days there—we would start at lunch at, say, one and stay all the way till dinner at, say, six. Our day was one long stay at a single café. There was less risk in that and Xerxes could be managed, fed, contained, entertained, and fed again: bathrooms, snacks, water, people-watching. It also felt like something one would do in Paris. It was pleasant. So there we were at a particularly nice café I recall, too nice for us—we were immigrants now, we had to save, just all that eating out today even shocks me—and anyway Xerxes was eating some fries or something, deep in his own little kid head—who knows what they're thinking and do we even want to know—you laugh, but you don't know my son, what my son has become—anyway, suddenly his attention went outward. To the people. To a person, I should say. Before I knew it, to my horror he was pointing at the person, pointing and smiling, like he found an old lost friend, crying "Look, look, look, over there, look at what I see"—and here I was trying to put his finger away, trying to hush his laughter, telling him, "Okay, Xerxes, I will look, I see, I see," and struggling to see in the crowd what on earth could have possibly gotten his attention, when I realized it was right in front of me, at the café. A waiter.

A black man waiter. Yes, the first.

I said, "Okay, Xerxes, so what, it's a waiter"—but even I couldn't take my eyes off him. He was striking, very very black, very African, wearing the dark red uniform of the café and smiling and waving back at Xerxes. Xerxes was overjoyed. Because you see, in our country it means something else: the Black Man, that is. This will sound silly—trust me, I am embarrassed at many things in my culture, add this one to the list—but he exists in our culture as a character, let's say. See, our New Year's is like your Christmas in many ways. The biggest, most important of holidays. And we, too, have our own fake things and fake people like your reindeer and elves and Santa. We have a man we call Haji Firooz—which actually means Mr. Festive or something, so I guess he's like a Santa. Except, he is . . . black. Well he's not black-black but his face at least is painted black. But I mean, he is black not out of race, but, well, because he is dirty . . . oh dear. I mean, coal, his blackness has something to do with coal, you know, like your Santas and their chimneys, perhaps, except he more realistically gets really dirty. Oh my. I know, it sounds bad. What can I do about this tradition? He is a good man to us. He laughs, dances, sings, he is everyone's favorite outsider! Maybe he is black? You know what I mean. I mean, the tradition is so old, so who knows? Do I think it's bad? I don't know. Could it be? Maybe. Look, there are no black people in my country and we have this black Santa guy and, sure, he resembles you people but there are also explanations like . . . dirty. Oh, I wish dirty didn't mean dirty. Well, you know, right? It's just language and tradition and old stuff? Who knows what to make of it? Anyway, my son thought it was Haji Firooz and he was overjoyed and eventually so overjoyed that the waiter could tell and came over and played with Xerxes a bit. And I tried to explain in my barely English and barely-even-less French that my son had mistaken him for someone else. And the waiter had smiled and said, "Are you looking for someone?" I had to tell him back, "Oh, no, my son thought you were someone, someone we aren't

looking for at all, someone who doesn't even really exist, pardon me."
I must have seemed a madwoman. But this is the problem. Not everything is translatable. My country is not bad or wrong, just different,
and I knew at that point the rest of my life would be one long chain
of meaningless untranslatable unutterable perhaps offensive perhaps
excuseless explanations for my existence, mine and my family and
my heritage, all best left to silence and maybe apology—

✳   ✳   ✳

"Hey, no need!" he had laughed, with a stop-sign hand, banishing
the whole thing off to the suddenly desperately tense, sound-sys-
tem-less silence that became their whole ride home.

It felt longer than it was, of course. In the parking lot she tried
to mutter her good-bye, when he suddenly grabbed her arm, and
said with an unprecedented earnestness, "Lala, I want you to know
I like you very much." Before she could even attempt a smile, he
unbuckled his seat belt and reached out and hugged her stiff stunned
torso for longer than would seem comfortable to any human, much
less one who had just spent an hour or so steeped in the most sticky
of racist guilt. *Black Santa, my God,* she replayed in her mind. She
didn't know what to make of it, but she tried to comfort herself
by recalling that *they* had made Blonde Genies, so there. . . .

The next day she ran into Gigi, who seemed fully recovered from
whatever illness. Lala told her about her night "and at the end, he
hugged me and for longer than was comfortable, let me add," she
declared.

"Oh, sister!" In came the hoots. "What are you saying? Are you
saying . . . ?"

"I am saying nothing," she snapped.

"Well, don't worry about Marvin," Gigi said. "He's not like *that*."

Lala nodded the conversation away, as if she knew what was meant by *that*. They went on their walk silently until it occurred to Lala that there was no benefit in pretending she understood what Gigi meant by *that*. What *that* was that?

"Oh, you know," Gigi smiled mischievously. "He isn't about us!"

Lala squinted her eyes in confusion.

"About us *ladies* I mean!" Gigi grinned.

"Hmm," went Lala, absently stalling, the part of her brain that was so good at piecing paranoid factoids suddenly disabled. She suspected, but wasn't sure, but she wanted Gigi's bluntness, did she mean he was, he was—

"Fag!" cried Gigi.

Lala stared blankly, puzzled at the foreign word that just maybe sounded like, that maybe she had heard, that perhaps meant he was—

"Homo!"

—that also sounded like, that indeed could be, perhaps she did mean he was really and truly—

"GAY, girl!"

They walked on. Lala felt relieved and yet, not relieved at all. "So many of those kinds of people in your country," was all she could think to make of it.

"They're everywhere! Not just popping up but they've been there all along, sister!"

Lala nodded numbly. Gigi was able to live in a world like that and worse, Lala imagined. *They've seen it all*, she thought, *the Americans*. As she let all the new bad ideas have their way with her head,

Gigi pulled Lala in conspiratorially and added with a widening grin, "Oh, I am sure they exist in your own complex even . . . !"

*　　*　　*

Their son relentlessly worried them. In the time of commonplace resolutions, in the time when their family's least happy of endings still made the ranks of happy endings—the only time that Xerxes believes he was close to happy, when life existed in a box you could turn on and off without leaving your couch, when dilemmas would relieve themselves with laugh tracks strung together in the neat span of the miracle half hour—his parents watched him with worried eyes constantly.

Who was their son? How was their son? *What* was their son?

He was a kid. His routine was quintessentially kid-ish: get dragged up to go to school, dread home life so much that the ride to school with Dad would appear bearable as an ephemeral gateway to the school day, have such a generally terrible day that suddenly going home took on the desirable role, get picked up by Dad, get reminded again that home is no better after an annoying conversation or nonconversation with Dad in the car, the routine follow-up questioning by Mom as a price to pay for after-school snacks, watch TV, do homework, eat dinner, watch TV, get forced into bed, lie awake contemplating all the TV, and dream, dream, dream of a nonreality of a nonera with a nonperson named Jeannie. . . .

Back then, in between all the being-a-normal-kid stuff, he neglected to recognize their relentless picking and probing as, say, early psychologically destructive hurdles fit for a good lifetime of therapy sessions.

"Xerxes, say, what do you want for your birthday?" they would ask.

"Toys!" he would naturally reply.

"I know, but say, a train set or . . . a teddy bear? Monopoly . . . or Candyland?"

"I want a He-Man."

"A He-Man *doll?*"

"A He-Man . . . action figure?" he'd reply, not on to them at all.

"Maybe He-Man's spaceship, is that what you want, Xerxes?"

"He doesn't have a spaceship. Just a He-Man and . . . Skeletor. That's what I want."

"Maybe. No promises. We'll look into it," they'd gingerly offer, but always going further: "So explain He-Man's relationship with Skeletor."

"Mortal enemies."

They'd give each other the facial equivalents of high fives in relief. "Oh, good!"

If he had lived in the time of Jeannie when there had been plastic Jeannies to be had, maybe, he thought later, just maybe, he would have wanted her . . . because what they didn't understand was that Jeannie was no different than another boy's superhero. *Honest.* Instead of being a flying muscular guy in tights and a cape with boring predictable dialogue, Jeannie was a pretty, funny, magical, blonde pseudo-Middle-Eastern sprite. *Cool.*

Darius would try not to question too much lest he give himself entirely away but eventually during his occasional supervisional drop-ins on TV hour, he'd take the commercial break as an opportunity to investigate further, on his terms:

"So, where the hell did she come from?"

Xerxes would flip open to his *TV Trivia Time!* encyclopedia's only bookmarked section and reword naturally as if it required translation for his father. "Well, Dad, in the first episode 'The Lady in the Bottle' —1965—we see Nelson, the astronaut, in his space capsule landing way off course and onto some deserted island where he finds a bottle. He rubs it and there she is, the two-thousand-year-old genie Jeannie!"

"Fine. Why does she make that sound all the time?"

"Well, Dad, it's the sound of the Jeannie magic move—the crossed arms, the nod and blink." He actually did his best impression of it, much to Darius's dismay. "When she blinks we are hearing the sound of a Jew's harp—when the trick fails, that's a warped chord on an electric organ."

"Fine. So who is that annoyed man in the suit? Her husband?"

"Well, good question, Dad—not in this episode, he's just Master still. He's Tony Nelson, an Air Force officer who works with NASA. At home, he's the genie's master. But eventually—'The Wedding' episode . . . December 1969, yes—Jeannie and her master do get married!" He looked almost too ecstatic, over-the-top iridescent, Darius worried—he was like a knitting circle propagandist, a butterfly-chasing toy puppy, a snowman made of ice cream!

It would always get him down. It always pointed to that biggest fear. Is he? Isn't he? And so he'd have no choice but to change the subject, to a subject that just seemingly forked off his investigation,

"So, son, what's your favorite color these days?"

"I don't know. Red, black."

"Red or black?"

"I don't know. Maybe red."

"Red, huh? Hmmm. Red like a fire truck? Or red as in . . . strawberries, cherries? Fruit?"

"Red like . . . I don't know." He thought for a moment, blinking. Finally he said with a shrug, "Blood?"

The obsession was graphable, peaks and valleys, cosines and sines. In the summer between eighth and ninth grade, though, they noticed a seeming drop in his interest—no more incessant humming of the theme song, no more *did you know Fritz Freleng who did the Looney Toons cartoons and Pink Panther did the opening IDOJ cartoon?*, no more useless facts, no more collecting of weird bottles that might contain genies (often just empty wine cooler bottles or malt liquor jugs left in neighborhood Dumpsters and immediately returned to them by his irate germphobic mother). He was getting over it, they thought. Perhaps that was what junior high did to them: in the name of cool and fitting in, preteenagedom burst their obnoxious candy-flavored youthful bubbles.

Or so they hoped. But then came autumn 1990, and they could see it in his eyes: TV once again gaining all-importance, TV meaning one thing certainly. . . .

"*Dallas*??!!"

A little older, Xerxes to his credit gushed with a pinch less enthusiasm in his voice when he revealed it: "Well, Barbara Eden is going to be on *Dallas*—you know, Larry Hagman aka Tony Nelson's show. She'll be taking over his oil business, as his boss, in a pretty cool reversal of their old *IDOJ* roles. It's an, um, pretty monumental TV milestone, if you don't mind."

He did mind, Darius told him. So did she, chimed in Lala. This was ridiculous. What was his deal? Who the hell watched *Dallas*? Darius grabbed the remote and announced he had to watch the news that night, very very important nightly news, and told his son with doomsday frankness to get lost.

Lala sat him over by the couch and distracted his stunned self with questions,

"Xerxes, so you're getting older, and you have girls in your class . . ."

"So?"

"And boys, I guess?" she said, avoiding his eyes, not being able to bear it.

"Yeah."

"You like them?"

"Who?"

"Well . . . girls! Yes?"

Xerxes was fifteen. The female species—Mother included—agonized him. "Oh, God."

"Oh, God? Listen, Xerxes, it's normal, as you get older, to not hate girls so much. I, your mother, was a girl once! And boys liked me!" She plastered on the smile of good mothers in classic cinema. She paused and went ahead with it, "And what about boys?"

"They're . . ." and he shrugged it out, "*Okay.*"

"You're a boy, Xerxes."

"And I'm . . . okay. Okay?"

He never saw the *Dallas* episode with Barbara Eden in it—when it was originally broadcast, that is. He did see it taped, later. Courtesy of a scrappy, skateboarding, always gum-chewing, teen-years best friend named Sam, who also had an *I-Dream-of-Jeannie* thing, who brought Xerxes out of the closet with his fixation, confessing to the same, and knowing just how to add the cherry on top with a delectable justification to Xerxes—"You know, fuck that mainstream crap, we're supposed to be fucking watching *Saved by the Bell* or *Beverly*

Hills 90210 or some shit, well, we can rebel against their fucking expectation and watch *their* shows, the fucking p-rents!" They'd argue about whether Samantha's nose twitch or Jeannie's nod was more potent (both coming to Jeannie in the end, of course), which Brady would really be Most Likely to Succeed (Sam: Jan; Xerxes: Bobby), which *I Love Lucy* episode was the last one in black-and-white, and how the theme song from *Get Smart* went. They were stealing their parents' past, they argued. This of course left Xerxes a bit uneasy— he never got into it with Sam that it may have been *Sam's* parents' past and his parents' *era's* past, somewhere, but it had nothing to do with *his* parents' past. Theirs was something beyond them, beyond TV, beyond any American imagination. . . .

✳　✳　✳

And of course, Xerxes often fantasized about telling them about Sam—although he never did, because a secret friend was best kept secret, and Sam, well, Sam was pretty unpresentable, with the ripped jeans and profane caps and cuss ticks and the always ready middle finger and the terrible grades in school—and his Sam was a *girl* Sam, and maybe even his first girl crush.

XERXES: You heard me. Yes, girl. I liked—and like—girls.

Girl! they would have clapped. *Girl* as in not *boy!* they would have cheered—had he allowed them their victory, that is—until they'd have decided to go on to something else to pick at with their son and the country he was painting for them, like, say, race or class or the million other problems of identity that loomed even more menacing than gender and sexuality—for them especially, there was always something more to grip.

*   *   *

There she was, suddenly bawling in Marvin's arms—his safe, non-woman-loving arms, she reassured herself. One day, with Gigi absent again, Lala had gone too far, told him everything. It was his fault—he had gone on about his own lost brother, a brother who had succumbed to illness overnight running down an empty school-yard track field and just like that, given in to thin air, collapsed, just like that. She had lost it. Lost it entirely, suddenly going so soft there in his arms, in the darkness of his parked car, that he had no choice but to help. He began asking questions, taking notes on receipts, and stuffing them one by one into his wallet. Her maiden N-E-Z-A-M-I was certainly not as common as she thought it was, he was insisting. He said he knew people, people who could do the job, find anyone, anything, in this small—*definitely small*, he assured her—world. She had looked at him with wide eyes. He had said something about private investigations and other things she didn't understand, but all she knew was he had ins. She gave him all the information she had. It was, after all, her only immediate relative they were talking about. And this Marvin, with his suddenly comfortable although foreign arms, with his strange ways and untappable background, with his perhaps even empty promises, with his way of not questioning if her brother was even alive, just trusting that when you know you know, for a second gave her something: a flicker, a nudge, barely a taste of something she found as golden as it was toxic: *hope*.

✳   ✳   ✳

Almost exactly eight months after his father left him in New York, Xerxes Adam was awoken to the hottest summer day of the year by the invasion of a rather unwelcome mental slide show: visions of that distant prime creator, his mother. Maybe he dreamed of her all night, every night even, who knew? He hoped not. He hoped it was just his conscience in calculation mode, sending the alarm that it was time: *Xerxes, time, your mother is waiting.*

His mother had now left what he estimated must be one-hundred-and-something messages in thirty-something weeks. The first third had been desperate and urgent and worried. "Please, Xerxes," she would say, adding, "my son" in a shaky voice that made him feel as if his entrails were melting. The second third: angry, annoyed, acerbic, trickling eventually to a just-pissed snippiness—"And who are you mad at exactly?" she would snap. The third third: cheery, oblivious, delusional, often delivered in the form of five-minute-plus-long diary-entry-like recordings that chronicled her day, just disjointed spewings of whatever was on her mind at the moment, only at the end perhaps tagging on "Maybe you will call" or "This is your mother, wondering how you are, but not wondering too hard, bye-bye," or like the last one, "Here's to you being all okay or whatever, *shabb-khosh.*" It was the type of "good night" that you'd leave a stranger.

She would slam the phone down and turn off the lights. At some point she had decided that calling at her bedtime would be best—they were three hours deeper into the night and so he'd certainly be in at one in the morning, maybe two, *hell, three!* until midnight her time and she'd give up and force herself to sleep. But not without giving the possibly-pretend-sleeping mass of husband next to her a sharp nudge and lecture. "This is getting crazy, Darius," she would hiss into the darkness. "What the hell did you do to him? He's our son. This is something you did, now you get him back. You hear me? He is your son, too, sorry to tell you! You try for once! *You* call him! And don't waste it—apologize! Lie even! I don't care! Just bring him back to life!" He'd mumble incoherently and toss and turn as if to signify some grand struggle. "I am telling you," she would continue, "some other parents would call the police. How do we know he isn't, you know . . ."

Xerxes wondered how she would possibly know if he *was* dead. She wouldn't. This was one thing about New York he realized immediately: that to die in this city was to *die*, the end, click, exit human. No one would gather, no one would fight it or interfere, no one would even notice. No one was looking. And if someone found you, well, fine, you were just another one of the many who died in the city daily—mysterious, natural, unsolved, homicidal, suicidal—whatever, you were a number, and if you didn't like that, you could leave.

He did not want to leave. These were sacrifices worth making for the city, he had decided long ago. But it did alarm him that perhaps she had resigned herself to thinking the worst, in this third stage of messages—perhaps she did assume he was dead. And perhaps she noted any clues to the contrary—a changed message greeting, at best—as simple surprises, grains of evidence for an alternate universe she had once fought for but eventually tired of. Maybe his mother had done what no other mother in the history of the domestic matriarchy had done in regard to her offspring: abandoned hope.

This barely conscious reflection on his two-thirds of a year's worth of inhumanity, combined with the sickly stickiness of a peculiarly oppressive 9 a.m. heat, jolted him fully awake, as if from a falling dream. Of all people, why had he shed his mother from his life?

He remembered being a child and being mad at her, *her* so much more often than *him*. Because it was she who was constantly stepping into his world, combing and gelling his hair when all the boys wore it messy, wiping his face, fiddling with his shirt, tying his shoes for him, always hollering annoying reminders as he was on his way out, always checking up on him at friends' houses, always tucking him in with embarrassing, often untrue, admonitions or reminders. *You are growing up, you need to think about smelling good now that you are growing up—showering regularly to begin with, because I am about to vomit, and I am your mother.* Or the most dreaded: *Imagine yourself in the future and think, would my silly behavior today get me there? What would a future wife think now?*

Once in a while, in a rage, what would be on constant repeat loop in his head would want to leak out. In his head, the answer to everything, everyone annoying and adult, was the sinister kiddie staple, *I wish you would die.* Once, to Xerxes's own adult embarrassment, he remembered being pushed, pushed to say it out loud, though at best in a weak whisper.

What did you say?! she had snapped furiously.

I wish you . . . he had paused, sure he could see a glimmer of tears in her eyes, although in retrospect he thought that any human's eyes, naturally slimy and liquidy, could look tearful if guilt steered you in that direction—and he had rephrased . . . *I wish you guys would die.*

Psychologically it was better for him, but its true genius was in being better for her as well. *You guys* became the great equalizer. It was suddenly more like, *I wish the whole institution of you, parenthood perhaps, would "die"—not you personally.*

All she had done was shake her head. She had still tucked him in.

And so he wondered now, too many years later, how at 6 a.m. their time, in their other heat, their dry dull warmth of the West Coast versus his merciless wet dirty big city tropical wave, how he could reach her and soften his blow. He had basically, in his silence, in his refusal to reach out, said to them, *I wish I was dead to you.* And he had gotten what he wanted: he might as well be.

Plus, this time, his *I wish I was dead to you* meant *to her*, not *to you guys*. For *him*, he had a whole other style of *I wish I was dead*. It was more like *I wish I was dead, so as not to have ever existed by you.*

So when he finally did it that morning—did the dreaded dialing of a number he grew up with, which still seemed so natural with the automatic sequencing of otherwise illogical numbers that he had worked so hard to render unnatural—he didn't even consider that she might not be the one to pick up.

As life goes, it had to be him. His father, with his usual gruff reluctant "Hello," that put the emphasis on "hell," which he was probably conscious of and probably found funny or else apt.

There is no God, Xerxes sighed. Xerxes slammed the phone down, shoving it deep into a drawer as if to pretend it had never happened. He closed his eyes and buried the day back into his pillow.

Three weeks later—a day after the first one-third of September, 2001—he finally called, when life finally gave him a push to put whatever pettiness between him and that number aside, if only for a day, when he knew risking him could no longer be an issue, that he had to, had to more than ever announce himself as living, as one of the many who that day felt like a few, who had lived through it, so far, at least—and through the few dial tones, he said to himself over and over, *There is a God, there is a God, oh please let there be a God,* and suddenly there she was, answering, without even a "hello," just that mystical all-knowing mother's "Xerxes?!" and the first thing he could think to say was the only thing that he knew true in that surreal hell of a day: "Mother," he declared breathlessly, "I am alive."

Darius was of course at her side, just barely making out the sounds through the receiver at his wife's ear. His son's voice was that usually tinny, high chipmunk garble that phones rendered voices—*it could be anyone's voice,* he thought, *it all sounds the same, except that it is my son.* His son, calling from the heart of a danger he could not comprehend at the moment. He drowned him out, and drowned out his wife's overcompensating awkward coos and exclamations, and turned the news louder until they both disappeared into the unrelenting dissonance of disaster. On the television, they crumbled over and over, two tall, perhaps too proud, totems of a city, two towers erected to be each other's image, indistinguishable, somber doubles each dying the same death, neither intolerable when it came to the supposedly inevitable. Over and over, it replayed: one went down, the other stood solo—fast-forward to a new clip: the other goes down just as the first, and nothing. Where his son was it was sunny; it was also sunny where he was. He squinted out the window and imagined the entire sky over America smiling heartlessly. He imagined in his homeland it was almost dark. He thought there was at best only a moon over Iran and he thought how nice that was. He closed his eyes and gone were the repeating images on the television and gone was that blinding brightness and he let the just-so-dark wall of his eyelid melt into the image of the twilight Tehran sky. It was time to go home.

Part Four

Hells

One of the first lessons of adulthood for Xerxes Adam was the function of memory, and how the key to happiness was learning to detach yourself from its many machinations. It was the reason humans were more ghost than mammal. They couldn't come to terms with memory's devastating systems: how all things were connected, how one thing was important only in that it would remind you of another, how when things would happen it was not the thing happening that one realized but what the thing reminded one of. The world of things, whether animate or inanimate, past or present, scientific or phantasmagoric, et cetera, was all absurdly incestuous and painfully codependent—many worlds within a small word and too many words within a small world, and so of course there was mostly "hell" in "hello," of course "eat" lay sandwiched perfectly within "death." Add human minds and anamnestic faculties to the equation and it was a mess. For instance, whenever he uttered the word "window" he was overwhelmed by thoughts of cotton candy, most likely, he theorized, because the first time he used or heard the word coincided with the first time he tasted cotton candy. Maybe, at least. Sometimes the two totally distinct concepts got so muddled in the fucked-up filing system of memory that they were almost interchangeable—he was gazing outside a cotton candy, in his mouth melted the hairy sweetness of windowhood. This was a *good* example, he reminded himself—there were *bad* ones, too. For instance, when someone uttered the word "apocalypse"—or perhaps thought it, while watching the news, inhaling it all and exhaling *holy shit, good God, apocalypse!*—or when stumbling on the wrong AM station and suddenly there, amid a doomsday sermon, casually, nakedly, just another noun: *apocalypse*—or when stirred from a potent nightmare of anonymous mass mayhem, the very essence in the subconscious's manufactured sights and sounds—whenever the notion came up, it was never *it* that came up, he realized, never just a definitional dead typefaced "apocalypse," but a chain of its living breathing siblings, literal personal anecdotes, ones he had managed to live through, one at a time replaying themselves like those movie montages that attempt to cinematographically re-create "one's life flashing before one's eyes" with their collage of ricocheting images, spliced to some seemingly all-unifying finale song, while flapping through a simulated mind's eye. This, too, was how it was for him: relentless, automatic, concise, systemic, finite, his apocalypses, entering and exiting at some anonymous prompting, off and on to the beat of their own humanly imperceptible rhythm that was no less random than whatever human membrane, whatever conspiracy of synapses and soul created the dangerously tenuous yet steadfastly elastic daisy chain of memory that always took over the thing, The Thing, itself.

He imagined that one day his memories of Darius would out-number his actual interactions with Darius—they would grow and multiply and refold and unfold and remind and tease and taunt and poke and probe, until one day sufficiently far away, Xerxes the old man would laugh at them the way adults mock the old car-toon villains of their childhood, he thought, for hopefully one day he might be able to say he was separated from that final interaction—two men in a New York apartment, speechless—by a half century. *One day the cases will be closed,* Xerxes thought, *there will be no need to dish proofs, to footnote fucking nightmares—it will simply stop affecting me.* But in the meantime there they were, like eternally preserved crime-scene evidence, particular passages of the deathless past that had been highlighted in the crumpled diary of the mind for so long that, he hoped, all future reality would pale against them.

✳   ✳   ✳

His first memory came, according to his parents, from an episode experienced by himself as a five-year-old:

Night, and they were on the patio of the home they envisioned an Iranian-raised Xerxes as inheriting. Their neighbors were out in the streets as well. The whole city of Tehran was outside their homes, patiently gazing at the sky. Xerxes was in his mother's arms—it was a shaky place, her arms adjusting and readjusting, both rocking him and just rocking nervously. His father was at their side. But what stuck to Xerxes the most was the black night sky, perfectly black for star-showcasing back then, because Tehran, as industrialized as it was, was still a long way from sharing the always-lit pink-black of American skies that he would know later. Interrupting the thousands

123

of individually held breaths and eyefuls of aerial black, suddenly the sound of choppers and their respective artificially created initial breeze, and moments later a circle of pink lights, spiraling around themselves, in perfect formation. And then on top of that add the tone and vibrations of his mother's sobbing and then the echoes of people in the streets, waves of gasps and shouts and moans/groans/something, something defeated-like. . . . He recalled the sound of women overlapping the sound of men. He remembered his mother choking her way through chants, a strange guttural song of some sort—with repetitions it, too, spun around itself over and over in the breathless utterance. And then just as they came, the lights disappearing right back into the sky . . . and then the memory folding over itself, until all Xerxes had, years later, was the existence of himself as proof that things went all right that night, in the end.

Several times in his youth, when prompted by schoolteachers with their "first memory" exercises, Xerxes Adam recalled this scene. It wasn't until he was fourteen, bold enough to question whether it was real or some nightmarescape his strange child's head conjured, that he asked his parents.

"You can't remember that," Darius Adam decided.

"How else would he know?" Lala Adam reminded him.

"Somebody told him," Darius snapped.

"Nobody could, not here," Lala snapped back.

"Parents," Xerxes interjected, sighing with the patronizing faux patience he had learned adults spoke in, "what was it, what am I recalling?"

They didn't answer until years later when he asked again and his father gave up and rattled off as if it were meaningless, "Anti-aircraft missiles. War. Revolution. So what? None of that means anything to you, so, enough."

✳   ✳   ✳

The first time he was reminded of that first memory, he was nine, and again faced with a horror that with time *was* extinguishable— no pun intended—in that it was *there*, before him, close to him, seen, witnessed, and yet left him unscathed. Some apocalypses, he learned, were like this—and maybe these were even worse than the worst ones, because nobody would live to remember the very worst ones anyway.

While many of his hells were easy to automatically blame on Darius Adam, this one actually *was* his father's fault. After all, it happened in another summer of Darius Adam's extreme seasonal restlessnesses, when he'd spend empty hours flipping through the few old pictures they had of Iran, not just to see them, but to inspect them: the background minutiae, scraps of homeland foliage carelessly captured, blurs of background people caught in their own frozen moments unaware, a sidewalk, a storefront, the sky. He'd observe how it was different, or how it was not really different and how annoying that was. He would try to inject himself into that world and imagine himself then, and there, but this time with the awareness that it would all be lost. Only once in a while would Darius Adam allow the feelings to bubble up and take him over, make him drive to a Middle Eastern convenience store, ignore the helpful Arabs, rush for the packets of saffron and sumac and hold them hard in his hand, sniff deeply, and stumble out, like a madman in a nonsensical dream, feeling mildly shitheaded at the stunt but somehow satisfied by another scratch at an inconsolable itch.

It was his alone—Lala had rid herself of longing somehow, perhaps by her talent for never thinking too deeply, he thought—but he, he was stuck, and what isolated him further was the knowledge that that sickness, that deep aching lust for something as complex and impossible and maybe nonexistent as a homeland, was something his own child would never understand.

At those times the only relief would be to divorce himself from the self they knew—father, husband, teacher, whatever—and become the most abstract thing of all: an Iranian. His national identity, he would work to become that and that alone, a part of a nation, a patriot—he would work to shed any and all individuality and concentrate on what he could do to link himself with a pulseless, purely conceptual thing. He became *it*, high on a pole, far far away in his native wind, waving—he was red, he was white, he was green, he was the gold lion, he was the gold sun, he was the gold sword—and it was *enough*.

Xerxes Adam never had any knowledge of this mania that made his father suggest the protest in the first place. All he knew was that it was another season of consistent uneasiness and upheaval on his father's part, when Xerxes and his mother would have to fill the dinner conversations with idle chatter, back and forth, volleying blank statement for another blank reply, question and answer, laughter and coughs, anything to avoid a window of silence where Darius Adam could enter with something horrible and demanding and beyond them.

Like the protest. It came on one of those faceless all-vacation summer mornings, he remembered, when his father came to breakfast in a tie and dress slacks, very very awake.

"Okay, then, go ahead, tell us what this is about," Lala snapped after a moment, sick of waiting for the tense Darius, who was restlessly thumbing the hard layer of his toast, to give in.

That was all he needed. "Eat but then get dressed," Darius rose suddenly. "We have somewhere to go."

Lala and Xerxes both involuntarily glanced at each other. It was going to be bad.

"Would you like to tell us where?" she dared ask.

Darius Adam cleared his throat with an unsettling formality. With one hand in a ceremonial fist, he said it: "A protest."

If it had been uttered in English, Lala Adam could have used the opportunity to shoot her usual venom, make a joke about "protesting" (her protesting that idea, that the only thing she had to protest was him, that did protesting a protest cancel them out, ha, ha—*ah, language*, Xerxes thought), but unfortunately he had said *tazahorat* and the Farsi word for *protest*, as in *dissent*, was altogether different from the word for a rally in which an assumedly large mob gathers in the spirit of some professedly necessary negation of something definitely larger and more necessarily negative than them.

The young Xerxes was at an age where even the slightest aroma of violence had some inexplicably potent allure—even though this was a kid who was watching a 1960s genie play wife, not playing military video games—so somehow the notion of a protest, something he had only vaguely known from history books and the news, *did* hold a secret appeal. His better judgment—his *self* self—told him that since it was so adamantly endorsed by his father it could very well be something he would not like, but his plain self—the generic surface one, the one that made him eat candy and hate vegetables and resent math and fear girls, like everyone—that one wanted it.

"It is up to Xerxes," Lala had announced. Deep in her eyes Xerxes saw that she did not want this thing in her day, a day that could be pleasantly, uneventfully spent at grocery stores and malls, in the dumb lull of errands. Between event and unevent, Lala always chose the latter. So she shut up and shrugged and looked to her son, nervously.

She was always tossing the ball into his court, setting him up, wiping her hands of things by wiping the shit on him, his fucking mother. Xerxes, disgusted yet somewhat excited by the illogic of masochism and the thrill of self-defeatism, cleared his own throat and said sweetly, "Sure, Dad."

The first tip-off that this could be a bad day was that Darius Adam showed no visual signs of pleasure at his son's uncharacteristic acquiescence.

They went. It was more than Xerxes had imagined. For two hours they stood among screaming dark-haired people that, yes, looked like him, maybe even sounded like him, but were strangers and *strange* strangers at that. Every few minutes Darius Adam would grip his son's shoulder, and with a proudness that Xerxes found embarrassing, utter, "These people are more like you than anyone on this earth. These people are *us!*" It was a thought Xerxes found overwhelming as he glanced at the veiny old ladies with beak-like hooked noses and hunched backs but with raised fists bobbing in the air next to the even higher raised fists of men his father's age, men with animal passion and ferocious barks, flanked by whistling wives waving their homemade Iranian flags, egging them on. Underneath them all there were others like Xerxes: clueless, numb, suddenly mute children, who, even though they understood both the Iranian chants and the precarious English doggerel of "Uni-ted Na-tions / pay more atten-tion," were doomed to a counterfeit feeling, like uninvited ghosts, extras, like real people interrupting a world of Technicolor animation. This was not theirs. Xerxes amused himself by contemplating the nature of the role reversal—his usually rabble-rousing brethren suddenly turned into the reserved, composed grown-ups in a world where the adults were suddenly cussing, crazed, practically rock-hurling exhibitionists. No, there were no rocks thrown and what cussing there was they didn't fully understand—their parents never taught them *those* words—but the craziness, the exhibition, it was there. His parents immediately took their roles: Darius roaring along with the crowd, wearing that strange adult facial expression that was both grin and grimace; his mother nodding, laughing in a way that looked like crying, mouthing the shouts with closed eyes. Cars, full of oblivious Americans, drove by them, slowing down—the occupants with craned necks, reading signs, listening to slogans—and then speeding off. Occasionally a car would honk and everyone would turn and cheer the car on, the driver undoubtedly one of them. It was a strange world, the universe of the protest, with its undefined urgency and muddled messages and aimless energy. He thought about asking his father, *Dad, what the hell are we Iranians protesting anyway,* but he thought he knew the answer and that it was something vague but important like injustice, unfairness, dying, wars, et cetera. Even at that age, he knew a way of dealing with it was to just not hear it.

That was the first hour: consuming at least, and at best, Xerxes thought. The second hour things changed—a man with a microphone got up on the Federal Building steps and spoke on and on about specific problems that Xerxes had heard enough about to at least be able to stomach, about the tyranny of ayatollahs, about Islam gone bad, about American indifference, about revolution. "I am tired!!" he would say in Farsi; "I am tired!!" he would then say in English. He was buried among the mob of dark nodding heads— Xerxes tried to see him at first and then just amused himself with the disembodied voice's invisibility. "We are nothing to them!!" he would shriek in Farsi; "We are nothing to them!!" he would shriek in English. For a while Xerxes tuned him out, a bit bored, and thought about school and what TV shows were on then, and conjured a particularly incredible Lego blueprint for a space station in his mind, and suddenly couldn't wait to go home. But on went the voice: "Do you hear this?!" Xerxes tugged a bit at Lala's sleeve, and she ignored him. "Hope!!" The crowd roared back, "Hope!!"—enchanted by this man and his bilingual rants. Xerxes, frustrated, finally tried to get on his tiptoes to take a look at this guy—maybe that was part of the allure for the entranced adults, the guy's visuals—and at the very moment Xerxes caught a quick glance at the man's sweating swarthy mustached face and balding head and red, red T-shirt—he remembered the appropriate red, remembered trying to imagine the man picking out that shirt before he went out that day, the calculation and symbolism and visual effect of the red, chilling—at that very moment, the man raised a bottle full of something that everyone thought *okay, sure, maybe water*, but wasn't, and poured it over himself and then with the same hand fingered a lighter, and went *flash*—lighter, then shirt, then man—and in a hissing *phoo-phoo-phoooooosh* of white and red and black, was gone: lion, sword, sun, a man in a split-second flick become flame, to the paralysis of an audience of good citizens, in that unfortunate moment when Xerxes had to look—just moments before Lala's motherly reflex made her drop a trembling hand to his eyes—just in time to look and see man become a flamboyant zero like the magic trick of his dreams. Those seconds so thoroughly pierced themselves a slot in the easy mold of a child's mind that off and on for years he could not escape the thought of the man, his impassioned auto-cannibalistic *tada!* and the old anti-lesson of what happened when the world cared too much: it burned, it crumpled, it disappeared.

"What did you see?" his mother demanded on the ride home.

Instead of saying nothing, he professed everything.

Darius attempted to console both of them by saying it was nothing they hadn't seen before—and, well, he was right—the news, movies, cartoons, nightmares. "So this was just live. It was no realer. "Forget it," he said, "like everything else we watch, just forget it."

*　　*　　*

None of it was news to him, that these bad things happen—that wasn't the part that got him. After all, it first occurred to him on one of the days of his early childhood, when America was still new for them all—at one of the moments when he had spied his mother sobbing in the kitchen to no one but a running sink, while on TV Lucy bawled into Ethel's armpit to the laughter of some invisible audience—the new world, while a very demanding place for *all* of its inhabitants, held a functional, almost laughable misery for its own, and a possibly unconquerable one for the others. *Here, the older your world,* Xerxes-the-child contemplated, trying to make some rules out of it all, rules that even Xerxes-the-adult could not fully argue with, *the sadder and badder your days.*

✻   ✻   ✻

Once, when he was young—late single-digits, he'd guess—on one of those weekends when Darius chose not to participate—his "out for the day" meaning an exhaustion and antisocial feeling that demanded he lie sleepless under the covers with the curtains drawn until the day was over, or rather meaning he was feeling restless and therefore all the more antisocial so he'd silently slip away and seek refuge in the bookstores and research libraries of the local college—on such a mother-and-son day, Lala took him on a drive through the nice parts of Los Angeles. That was how she phrased it, "nice parts"—which ended up being a tour of wealthy Beverly Hills and eventually just Rodeo Drive, just a long afternoon drive back and forth, up and down its pathetic glittering length. Thirty miles or so but worlds away from their hometown, this Rodeo Drive was supposed to embody what his mother thought of "niceness." She told him it was a street for "the best people" which he translated to rich and famous, and so like a dream come true, after she finally parked—deciding that they, too, deserved a walk down this strip of gilded if not golden Los Angeles perfection—they encountered their first celebrity. Out of a slick black limousine stepped a black-suited, burly, silver bear of a gentleman . . . Ed

McMahon! Since this television personality was one of the few celebrities Lala Adam would even recognize—after years of savoring McMahon's "Heeeeeeeeeere's Johnny!" roar as *The Tonight Show* announcer in the 1960s and 1970s, not to mention her deep admiration for his stint in the 1980s as the presenter of American Family Publishing sweepstakes who arrived unannounced at the homes of winners—she began waving and panting like the teenagers in old concert clips. She urged Xerxes to go ask for his autograph, and when her son refused she realized she had to do something, so she loudly uttered a joke about whether or not she had won a million dollars, that he either didn't hear or ignored, and before they knew it, he had disappeared through a dark door on the strip. They just stood there meditating on his appearance. It was anything but nice for Xerxes, Ed McMahon for some strange reason giving him chills, horrible very real shudders creeping up and down his spine—Ed McMahon making him tense and afraid, downright sick. He didn't figure it out until many years later when reruns of the 1980s talent competition he hosted, *Star Search,* did the same thing, making him aggressively thumb the remote. At some point he realized that it was just that Ed McMahon for him reeked of apocalypses—it had to be because the first time he ever saw Ed McMahon and his dark suit and heard his booming tenor was on a night when he was very young, when he used the vision of the man on the screen to block out the sounds of his parents, behind their shut door, arguing more loudly than they could imagine, about unsolvable big things, like wars and dictators and regimes and military and mass deaths, one of their many but first-witnessed homeland fights. Ed McMahon had clapped and chuckled and introduced over and onward, over their cries and snaps and screams and bangs, but he could not outdo them—not only was the man useless, trapped in that blaring box, belonging to that applause-and-confetti realm; his world existing just side by side next to theirs somehow had the effect of making Xerxes feel less safe than ever. He was alone—the voices behind the bedroom door, the voices behind the tube, they were all voices far removed from his own small, high, cracked one. How would he ever explain a phobia of a man, a thing, an institution like Ed McMahonness? The older Xerxes adopted the illogic without a fight: window equated with cotton candy; Ed McMahon equated with the stench of a simultaneously foreign and native burning taking his parents and threatening himself. He imagined drilling a hole under the glossy platform of *Star Search* where Ed McMahon, for thousands of hours of his life, judged painted neon baby entertainers, drilling a hole so deep it would go through the smoldering center of the earth and come out the other end. On the opposite end of McMahon's shiny designer shoes, through the wailing volcanic fodder of the planet's core, would certainly be other feet, and maybe knees and maybe hands and, hell, torsos of the perpetually aching, ailing, hurting people of the other world, most of the world, that looked somewhat more like Xerxes Adam, looked at least more as he was supposed to look, that shared with him something he could never quite get in touch with but clearly had to have.

* * *

For a long time, his friend Sam was the closest thing to him that he had, the first human he had established a deep bond with. *Don't even fucking say it, I know the shit you're thinking,* she was known to say to him with a god-haughty grin. He, who never knew what he was thinking, had this, this girl friend—*not girlfriend,* they'd both have to wearily remember, *no way, fucking hurl city!* she'd snap if anyone dared—this ungirlfriend of his very-young adulthood, to always understand, to steer him, to set him right, to know for and beyond him. As Xerxes hit thirteen, Darius and Lala suddenly took on the appearance of fools in parent drag—phony, annoying, embarrassing —and suddenly Sam was his *real* family. She was all he had to grease the wheels of the ever-clunky initiation into teenagedom.

With her steel-toed Doc Martens and black department store denim that had been legitimized with Wite-Out scrawlings of anarchy signs and profanities, Sam was the type who identified with anything that the mainstream did not accept. And so Xerxes was it. Even when Goths, like the powdery black-frocked ghosts of the old shy weird kids, began to proliferate, Sam dismissed their dress-up and cultlike clustering. She maintained Xerxes was better. *X doesn't belong to shit, get it? X, I got you, you want me to fuck them up or something?*

High school: they began tempering old movies and *I Dream of Jeannie*—well, they still watched their share of *IDOJ,* but ironically of course, Sam maintained—with Sam's death metal and gangsta rap. Hours and hours went by after school when Xerxes's parents thought he was at band or choir or some music-thing practice (*Does he even play anything? He better not be putting his mouth on other kids' instruments,* Darius would once in a while wonder), when really "X" was just lying on the lawn with that strange/wonderful adolescent blessing/curse, the best-friend-of-the-opposite-gender, listening to what he liked to think were the sounds of her people: screaming, roaring, shrieking punk rockers and roughnecking, riffing, effing rappers. Without offering him any of her cigarettes—not that he would have accepted, Xerxes knew he was too scared of being caught—she would smoke as if she was inhaling something hallucinogenic, closing her eyes and smiling as if in some hazy bliss, once in a while snapping out of it to explain the music as if they were a foreign tribe of hers whose chants she had to translate for Xerxes. He was glad to belong to all that; he was glad somebody so bad could have it in her heart to *love—that word blows, X,* she'd always have to explain if he accidentally uttered that four-letter word, even in regard to a flavor or a brand or a something he more than appreciated—*like, I meant like,* like him.

They would clash over only one topic and that was his guardedness, his boundaries, his ultimate compartmentalization instinct. After all, Xerxes Adam believed he lived in two worlds and part of the dual-citizenship agreement was that he could not allow those worlds to mix. He could not risk having Sam even skim his home life, he had decided early on, and this infuriated Sam, who thought *Persians are fucking badass* and wanted to eat *kebabs and shit* and ask his father about politics and how *the white devils fucked the brown race.* What would they think? Just her manner of speaking would be an attack to them; her style of dressing an outright declaration of war against their God; and her relationship with their son an absolutely unpalatable impossibility because as far as they were concerned boys and girls were never just friends, and boys were certainly *never* more-than-friends with girls like *that.* On the flip side, he had no way of explaining them to Sam—he could imagine Lala dusting anything Sam touched as if her roughness of demeanor would certainly transmute into actual germs and scum; he could imagine Darius *Enough*ing at her over and over until he'd storm off with a slam of the door and refuse to see her ever again and perhaps even calls the cops— how would he tell Sam that it was okay, that was just how they were, that coming from a foreign country did that to you, that it was entirely normal in the context of abnormal things?! But not only was the opportunity for rejection ripe on both ends, how could he maintain his double agent status in the face of the two worlds colliding like that? He could not be two opposite things at once. How could he bear to reveal to Sam that he was not the badass, or even worthy of being the *real* badass's sidekick, that when his father snapped he cowered, that when his mother looked upset he had to console her, that he would have to talk about her with them behind her back in Farsi—and then at the same time, how would he have the heart to let his parents see that he related to the lonely misfit kids, that he liked abrasive music, that bad words were comforting to him, that inside him there was a dark weird soul that only Sam could access? And what if he slipped up, what if he became the apologetic-weak-cowardly Xerxes with Sam by accident, agreeing in soft murmurs until all the conversation in him melted to simply less-controversial silence—or the other way around, what if he became "X" with his parents, letting a curse or two out, slamming a utensil, kicking a rug, snorting at their outcries! After all, the slipups happened: in school, the Farsi words in his head had sneaked out once or twice to the snickers of his peers, and at home he had *almost* eff-worded them but had been able to massacre the clause into a coughing fit. It was always hard work, getting the sides of himself straight, he thought every time he adamantly insisted to Sam that the worlds simply could not mix.

I've been grounded all week, were his exact words in translating the dilemma to her. *No friends over.*

That's what you said last month, X! Sam, never a fool, would snap.

What can I say? Xerxes would grin, assuming that on some level the excuse always ensured a somewhat win-win outcome in scoring bad-kid points with his cohort, *I'm always getting into fucking trouble, you know?*

But Sam, being Sam, eventually had to get her way and so he compromised by having her come one evening when he knew they would be away, on one of those nights when Darius was giving Lala driving lessons. The entire hour she was there Xerxes was nervous, watching everything she touched and rearranging it when she was done, worrying that every car he heard outside was his parents coming home.

She admired the Iranian flag posted on one wall, cooed at the alien Arabic script on the book spines, took extensive note of the Persian carpets and old Eastern china on display in the cabinet . . . but she stopped dead in her tracks for just one object: a framed family photo on a shelf by the hall entrance.

For the first time, Xerxes *really* looked at it, too. There they were, Darius, Lala, and Xerxes at age six or so, flanked by two additions to their trinity: a giant mouse in gloves and a giant duck with a hat. They were clearly at what was known as the Happiest Place on Earth. Mickey had one hand around Lala, Donald was resting his hand on Darius's shoulder, and young Xerxes was in front of them all, right in the middle. Darius and Lala were grinning in the phony way adults act happy for their kids' sake, as if they were wholly invested in the word *CHEEEEESE!* The only being that was smileless in the whole mess was the kid all the smiles were supposedly in honor of, ol' X himself. Xerxes recognized the look on his younger self's face: it was sheer anxiety. He looked completely out of place, claustrophobic, wanting out, existentially terrorized, as if about to get shot by a gun instead of a camera. He had never noticed his expression before.

Sam was clearly noticing it. She tilted her head at the portrait, as if trying to take in all angles. Eventually she went ahead and held it. Xerxes almost asked her not to, but stopped himself as he watched her. She seemed lost in it, totally absorbed by it, and for the first time Xerxes saw Sam's face go completely soft. If he didn't know her so well he would have sworn she was about to cry.

She looked from the portrait to the apartment periphery, to him, and back to the portrait again as if to put it all in context. She looked sick, sad, as if she felt sorry for it all. As if for once she was understanding that he was an altogether *other* type of "other."

"I don't know," she suddenly said.

"What?"

"Look at you," she said softly, and he thought that she meant the "you" he used to be, the one in the portrait, but she was looking dead into his eyes. He couldn't be sure.

To get in the way of that moment, Xerxes decided to move the tour onward until they got to his room. To try to cleanse the subject, he asked her what she thought of it all.

"It's a small place," she said, politely adding, "but I do like it, X."

He began fiddling with his books and his music collection, frustrated at why he didn't have a single thing she would like, when he realized she was staring at him again.

He tried to say something he thought she could appreciate. "Got a fucking staring problem, Sammy? Dang!"

She gave him the finger and he assumed it was *all good*. But soon her face went strange again and she said in a smaller voice than usual, "You know what would get you in that old photo out of my head?"

He was shocked. She was really thinking about it. "Uh, no idea."

She moved closer to him, as if about to tell a secret. "Well, brace yourself, dude, and don't be fucking weird about it either, okay, Xerxes . . ."

She had called him *Xerxes*—how could he not be weird? She never did that! But before he could consider what the hell she was getting at, one of her hands was clutching the back of his skull as if his cervical spine was in danger of crumbling into dust. Pause. The other hand made its way onto his thigh. Pause. Her face began getting bigger, moving to his, her eyes began closing, he could feel her breath, he could smell the whole of her, and holy Satan, *POW!*

Her lips ran right into his, a bit hard and for a bit long, and it was very horrifically wet. This was how he remembered thinking of it, maintaining that it had to be an accident, sure that she would never do *that*, and then worrying that the wetness was somehow his and that now she was mad.

But she wasn't—she was in another world, it seemed. She was suddenly gazing out the window, well beyond it, to something he couldn't access. She looked younger or maybe just her age—suddenly he saw their teen age for what it was. It looked lost and small and delicate.

"Fuck," she whispered, in her dreamlike state, still staring outside as if for answers.

"I'm sorry—" Xerxes immediately began, the apology seeming like the logical thing since he simply could not think of what else to say.

She shook her head, annoyed—the old Sam was immediately back—and she got up, brushing herself off a bit. "Your parents just pulled in."

"Fuck!" Xerxes echoed and got up, too, and for a while it seemed like they were just panicking in place. Before he could process it all, Sam was out the door and down the stairs and around the side behind the parking lot, leaving Xerxes to also run for the door. Instead of the door, his frenzied state caused his limbs to get so careless he tripped over one of the very rugs Sam had examined, tripped right over it and right onto the shelf holding that very family portrait Sam had been so taken by. And thus the shelf, also panicked, let itself go and tipped just enough for the frame to fall flat on their faces, everyone of them, mouse and duck and Adams. . . .

And the fall was fatal: the frame lay cracked into two pieces, barely maintaining the integrity of the photo it was meant to protect.

Outside he could hear the first of their footsteps on the staircase, just as he sat there, sweating bullets over the photo with its critically injured encasement in his hands. He was fucked and there was no time—it was a bad combination. He quickly set the shelf upright and tried to prop the frame back up on top of it, but it was no use. The frame, in two, could not stand up as one. *Fuckedfuckedfucked,* he thought, as the footsteps felt seconds away from fruition. He was a dead man. He let the frame lie on its back, like a pathetic paralyzed thing just waiting to be noticed.

By the time his parents made their way up, he was able to extract himself from the crime-scene evidence, which was located quite dangerously adjacent to the entrance. The door was still open from Sam's escape, and Xerxes, numb from all the layers of chaos, was left dumbly standing like a doorman welcoming patrons when his parents finally made it home.

"What are you doing here?" Darius immediately said.

"I live here!" Xerxes snapped, stupidly, and speed-walked off to his room. He slammed his door shut and lingered there, holding the lockless knob, listening for clues in the unsafe atmosphere.

On the other side, they of course talked about him. His mother was trying to say being at the door was no crime, and his father was going on and on about how something was off and how that son of theirs was up to something. Then there were several minutes of very tense silence. He heard something go *clink* and then *clink* again—possibly glass—but he was not sure if his paranoia was making it up or if it was real. He felt his eyes sting, he was hot, he was angry, he was frustrated, he was *frightened.* You did not let the worlds mix, you never let the worlds mix, or else-else-else-else—

Hard footsteps. He could hear him breathing on the other side of the door, pausing as if he was listening for his son as well.

Hard knock on his door.

Xerxes tiptoed away from the door, backing up until he was on his bed, as if he was there all along. "What," he tried to answer in the most normal voice he could muster.

The door opened. As expected it was Darius. Darius with his Angry Face, with one hand holding something behind his back. "Anything happen when we were gone?" he towered over his son who was kneeling, in what he hoped was a casual pose, atop his bed.

Xerxes lied not because he was any more afraid of the truth— at that point, he figured he was dead no matter what—but because a lie was quicker, shorter, easier. Two letters: "No."

One of Darius's hands clenched. "I smelled the rat." His other hand came forward to reveal, of course, the broken frame, with its ill-encased photo looking bent up underneath. Xerxes made out their old smiling faces now suddenly looking absurd, mocking, sinister. Only the young Xerxes's expression seemed appropriate, wise beyond his situation, oracular even in its anxiety.

Xerxes tried to think: what was the worst part for Darius? That he had broken the frame? That he had broken that particular frame that held a picture of them as a family? A picture of them as a family in happier times? Or was the bad part that he had had the audacity to *touch* things when they were gone? That he stirred in the house? Or, perhaps, did he see it as a sign of something bigger? Did broken frame = nervousness = illicit activity = someone had been inside = a girl = a girl like *that* = a girl like that who had kissed him? Could it be that the faint smell of Sam's after-school cigarettes were lingering in the house (as it was a smell Xerxes was so used to he could no longer perceive it)? Had his father perhaps brushed shoulders outside with the tiny black ball of girl that wore the scent of his son's lips? Was it just the look of his lips, were they somehow marked? (He rubbed his mouth absently.) Did fathers just know? But what was there to know? That he had lied? Was this all to showcase his dishonesty—that first he had sneaked home a friend, a girl even, and then he had lied about it, and then he had tried to pretend that frame killing had never happened when interrogated? Or was he just in a bad mood and had found Xerxes victim-ready—was it just one of those times when it could have been anything and nothing alike?

And why did his father towering over him like that make him feel so scared if it was really just a broken picture frame? What the hell had he done, Xerxes wanted to know, which crime was it?

"One of the few times we are not home—*and we are almost always home*—and this!" Darius shouted, letting the frame drop to the ground, adding a fracture or two.

It was beginning to add up to a threat, that was for sure. The man was making his transformation into monster.

Xerxes had few choices. He took the first one that came to him and got up from his bed and tried to dash for his door, to dash out and away, from them, forever, to the outside world that in not too long he would belong to, to the girl even, yes, *girl*, who had just dared to bring him one step closer to becoming a man, to anything but him—

He fell into Darius's grasp like a blind mouse who runs into a cat's open mouth.

He wondered if this, just like Sam and him bumping lips, was more than an accident—was he running out to run *to* him? Was it an escape or was it suicide? Or was he trying to strike first? He could not understand it. What made him think he could topple the Empire of Darius at that moment, he could not fathom. . . .

Darius had him helpless. One of his hands was tight around his wrists and Xerxes could feel his father's hot furious breath on his face. "NEVER," he was saying again and again and the more Xerxes struggled to break free the more his father struck him. Again and again, like the fists in movies, they moved that fast, and he could not tell if he was hitting back, except something had to be making it continue, something had to be doing it, why else would he, would a, would someone who was, why else would a—

"*Dad!!!!!! STOP!!!*"

Xerxes could suddenly hear his own voice screaming like a madman, as if separated from his entire body and self, a runaway scream that was never-ending. And like the movies, the cartoons, just as it got really bad, just as his eyes took the worst of it and turned his scream into a howl, just then he got that famous break: he saw stars. Stars, as if some absurdist reward. Not like the ones in the sky, but the way they would look up close, just right in front of you, he thought. All white-hotness, a vacuum of light, the color of fire. He was grateful for it because it was around the time of the stars that it stopped and he was alone in his room again.

They did not speak about it. In the future, he was again left alone at times but never again did he mix worlds, and never again did he see stars like that. He promised himself he would just endure the next little bit of high school, do the very best he could, be scholarship-worthy, grant-worthy, worthy of the help of strangers with resources and institutions, and when it was time, when senior year and age eighteen would arrive with the promise of conventional outs, he would *run* out, run as he did when he was a kid out of the passenger seat of Darius's car and into the playground where he could lose himself, lose them as well—but this time he would run farther, run as far as the stretch of land that created the length of the country made possible.

In the meantime, he pledged to take the hard times like a soldier, but a soldier whose term was dwindling. And for that week after his first kiss, after the stars, when he walked around school with the very wrong misplaced badges from that experience— two tender dark purple bruises around each eye—he made the best of it. He tried to humor it in the gym mirror, tell himself he finally looked like a tough guy. A man. But he knew that while a few kids and a teacher asked and bought his bullshit answer— *Oh, just play fighting with a cousin got out of hand*—Sam did not. Because Sam, whom he spent almost every free hour with, as much as she did see, she knew not to ask.

*   *   *

In Farsi, the insult *pedarsookhteh* means something like "bastard" or "asshole," but literally translates to "father" (*pedar*) + "burned" (*sookhteh*), or "burned father."

The one time Xerxes saw his father hit his mother, he remembered it was the only word she uttered, as she just barely attempted to back away from his sight, like an ambivalent animal, in something like a whisper, after the blow.

＊　＊　＊

Then there was the memory that was all about Lala, the veracity of which she fought tooth and nail. As a rule, she emphatically bowed out of any notion that implied she was a coconspirator in the early screwing up of Xerxes's emotional health, but this one especially irked her. *You think I am one to deny bad things? I who was brought up and out of the worst thing possible? Don't forget.* This was her most potent point.

She seemed to imply memory was a realm much like an Opposite Day masquerade ball, where dreams dressed up in reality drag.

But to Xerxes it couldn't have been a dream because A) too many senses were employed B) his mother was never in his dreams, thankfully C) his dreams never involved linear narrative D) he did not like to replay bad dreams—what was the point—particularly when that particular space in the head/heart/whatever could be more than occupied with all the very bad *real* things in life.

And this memory replayed in his head a lot.

He didn't like Lala denying it because he saw the moral he extracted from the incident as highly central to his emotional underdevelopment. The moral was in a sense Lala's, ironically. This was Lala's lesson in metaphysics, Lala's lesson in super-psychology— Lala who had warned him of the dangers of the too-potent imagination, the recklessness of phobias, Lala who had said the words audibly, with ample premeditation, almost rid of her usual accent, lucidly, truly, intensely deliberately enough for the words to be forever etched in what should have been stone, but instead was just a child's paper-thin origamic conscience.

CLIMAX: *Look what your fear has done,* those six words the mother had said, and again, *Oh, look yourself, you, you, look what your fear has done, look what your fear has done to us!*—leaving the child wondering how many other times that sentence had been uttered in human history and how many more times it could afford to be uttered again.

BACKSTORY: When he was very young, even younger than when the story began, he used to be very scared of some things and at the very pinnacle of those feared things: bright things in the sky. Helicopters, planes, fireworks, a particularly vivid moon, leftover gashes of a particularly toxic LA sunset, supposedly natural glowing errata of the sky (*Perhaps aka UFO's?* he often wondered), et cetera—no, he didn't like them one bit. Darius's theory was that it reminded him of his early infant memories, perhaps those air raids in Iran, et cetera —he was a child of war, after all. It was no excuse, Darius would tell himself, but the child had to have gotten such a stupid phobia—*ah, annoying, the phobia of a light in the dark, whereas most normal kids just have the dark!*—from somewhere after all. Lala didn't theorize, just disapproved very passionately of anything she felt could be above her theoretical talents. She questioned her son again and again when he would suddenly burst into tears, pointing, then covering his eyes, at the most innocent of all things, truly, just an interruption in all that night sky.

What, you think the sky is shot or something? she would ask. *Please!*

Oh, is the beautiful perfect black blanket torn, is that it?

Uh-oh, somebody lost a killer diamond in all that murk?

Oh, look, I'm a little speck of alien and all I'm going to do is hover at you, right? Ha. His earnest gaze drove her mad. *Laugh!*

He did not like the condescension one bit, so after a while he did not explain. Usually, that is. But one time that he did, that he felt he had to, he cleared his voice and said to her, employing every sprouting grain of premature adulthood that he could enroll: "Mother, look, as inconceivable as it may be, I am only worried there is an aircraft of some sort, perhaps hijacked, perhaps experiencing mechanical failure, that is perhaps on fire, and perhaps just erratically flying due to being in the wrong ill-conceiving hands, that may be headed for our city, the greater Los Angeles area, a prominent one, or one of our city's major monuments or symbolic structures, and may accidentally hurt us in its crash, or at the very least, someone we know, or even at the very very least just happen to happen—isn't that, my current worst nightmare, bad enough? That is all."

She gave him a parent laugh, a laugh that said, *Oh, children and their absurdities,* but then in a lowered voice added that there was no point in thinking such crazy things, because what if the crazy things did happen, what would he do with himself and his head then, had he ever considered that?

He hadn't.

STORY: He was young, head at best just reaching his mother's hip. It was night and his father was away, as he usually was in the early evenings of his childhood—night classes to teach, errands to do, away in some other world desperately annexed to his work world to add some dimension beyond father and employee. Mother and son were alone, after dinner, both curled numbly by the TV, eating snacks, flipping channels, Lala often nodding off during commercial breaks, he fake coughing her back to life, she sometimes asking an idle question about school or friends just to let him know she was there, him grumbling and mumbling answers back. Back then life was very boring, he remembers recognizing even then. But after that night, when life said *Ha, you find me boring, do you, then take this, O bored ones, I'll show you what boredom looks like with its entrails pulled out of its anus with a neon stick, take that, you want boredom, I'll smear you in the toxic shit of adventure, you want that, I'll give you a supersonic nuclear urine-flushed swirlie down to the scatophilic-dream-depths of thrillsville, O too-content human*—after that night, should the night have truly transpired, he was destined to long for the comfortable vacuum of anti-event for the rest of his life.

It was likely that they were watching *I Dream of Jeannie* and that Jeannie had, perhaps in that same moment they were distracted, done something to annoy Master very much, something that Master by that point, after years of living with such a magical woman, must have known was fixable, but something that nonetheless merited his boiling point at the climax of that half hour of their fake lives.

In any case, as if on cue, they were suddenly both turned to the window, mother and son. He was pointing, one hand covering his face, but eyes still peeking through the slits of his fingers. He was saying, *Look, look, look, it happened, Mom, look what happened!*

She had said something like *So?*—an Americanism she had picked up from him, that implied not caring and annoyance, but was closer to the latter than the former, and in some cases, like this one, meant the very opposite of the former, a short verbal front designed in the tradition of juvenile Opposite Day philosophy, that the adult world often had to dip into to stall the oncoming horror of . . . horror.

He resented that *So?*

He remembered a dark sky, more purely black than Los Angeles usually mustered, a pure velvet ebony designed possibly to showcase that imponderable imperfection: a thin white streak, which with its ever-elongating streakhood became more and more jagged and appeared almost feathering—if something white-hot and clearly burning could ever be described as possessing properties of feathering or flaking things even—at least coming apart, a disintegration that topped the thing's own creation in its brilliant horror . . . oh, Xerxes, it *had* happened. In the sky, there it was, his fear, certainly— if not a spaceship or some combustible planet or God, hell—an aircraft was bursting into flames.

Look look look! was all he could say.

And she was looking silently.

He imagined the silence punctuated only by Jeannie's laugh track, the dumb jingle of miracles via her bobbing blonde ponytail, the holler of the ever-irascible Master.

And then something set her off—maybe a child's routine madness now finally taking the form of a most distinct clairvoyant sanity, the TV's obliviousness, the silence of the aerial holocaust outside, their utter loneliness in its beholding as if the thing itself had appeared just for them—something set her off and that something made her say it. And because Lala would not admit to the event, much less the utterance at the time of the event, we will never fully know why.

She said, *Look yourself.* And she said, *Oh, look yourself, you, you, look what your fear has done, look what your fear has done to us!*

On the one hand, it was true: what else could create the actual actualization of a half-developed being's worst nightmare—what could render rationally existent the most irrational of dreamscapes? He *had*—somehow—done it.

On the other hand: sometimes the worst nightmares of children exist because they are pieced from the larger-than-life realities of human existence. He had imagined it because it *could* happen, because it was inevitable even, because why not? Probability dusts the glitter off coincidence's shoulders.

On the other hand: the odds of *their* actually witnessing it, the son and the mother with the son with the vision—that was a bit much, no? He had done it—he: psychic, evil, prophet?

One the other hand: what an evil, sick thing for a parent to imply! Whether he had or hadn't!

On the other hand: it had never happened. Children have remarkable imaginations, so remarkable that not only do they imagine incredibly horrible things, they can imagine themselves imagining incredibly horrible things, and these visions are so real, that later, in adult life, they still suspect them to be true. In terms of magical thinking, one can then infer that the vision (as a concept) continues to haunt the unwitting accomplice (mother) just as much as the possibly delusional vessel of those visions (son), as if to reap some vindication in the potentiality of some osmosis between the young human imagination and horrible global cataclysms. It was therefore possible that it never *actually* occurred, but was rather something he had inflicted on them, just an imitation of life that, like cigarette smoke, hovered vaguely in and out their minds, insubstantial but intoxicating nonetheless.

On the other hand: he knew *something* real had happened by how tormented he still was by the piercing hold it had on his mental life, and he knew, further, by how upset it made Lala to even hear about it, that whether dream or reality it was a very bad event/very bad dream, and that because in the world these two things can be considered just a backslash apart, so interchangeable, so almost synonymous, and both divisible by that common factor, memory, the episode was validated as a milestone in his mental life.

*   *   *

Lala's parents met in the cafeteria of the Atomic Energy Corporation of Iran, which employed all of Lala's employable relatives, she told him once. That was one of the few times she ever mentioned them to Xerxes. She stated it factually, without emotion, without insinuation. But this only added to Xerxes's nightmare of these two perfectly frozen twenty-something sweethearts, these stillborn grandparents of his, locking lips in a sterile auditorium meant for a food break, intoxicated by love on top of an unimaginable ticking monster that he had to consider, that although no one would be able to guess what generation—not children, maybe not grandchildren, maybe not even great-grandchildren—could one day kill or harm at least one of their descendants.

*   *   *

If they could have forbidden her they would have, but thanks to Xerxes's knack for covert operations—always outside the House of Adam, he made sure—Sam remained a ghost to Lala and Darius Adam. But before high school graduation would force them to part, she would become a ghost to Xerxes Adam as well.

He drove Sam home for the last time, on one of the rare occasions of Darius's day off when Xerxes got to drive the family car to school.

It was a day when Sam seemed fragile. She quietly took out some matches.

"You can't smoke in here, you know that," Xerxes said more gently than usual.

"I know, dipshit," she snapped, "I'm not going to smoke. I'm going to. . . ."

"What?"

She struck the match and produced just the feeble flame intended for her to nudge with a finger—*so what, a kid's trick,* he told himself—then a hand—*stupid Sam, she'll stop,* he told himself—and then down to her wrist—"Sam," he cried, "Sam. STOP."

"Kick me out then," she said, "It's my fucking life, X."

"Sam," he sighed, not knowing what exactly to add. He tried to slow down, after he ran a fresh red that he could have sworn was still at the tail end of yellow. He settled on a grumbling, "That's such a cliché anyway."

Since they had gone deeper into their teenage years Sam had started to get miserable all the time, talking like the bad youth of bad TV movies, quoting lyrically destitute rock lyrics, even referencing old dead depressed French surrealists she had never read. And so it became a matter of time before their friendship was at a sad dwindle. She became the last thing he needed, one more school friendship lost, one more person he had lost all hope of communicating with.

Years later, he wondered what telling her he loved her would have done to that equation.

"I don't deserve fucking anything," she would tell his rolling eyes.

"Sam is dead," she would declare to his firmly turned back.

"I see myself and I don't know myself," she would whimper in his car to ears that would shut then if they could. It had become a mantra of hers and mantras did not suit Sam.

One good thing: she didn't kill herself as everyone seemed to expect. She burned a floor of her family's house in a strange rage one early morning but no one was hurt and it was ruled an accident. She threw a glass vase at her mother's face and shot her sister in the leg with a BB gun. She called her gym teacher "bitch" to her face. She saw counselors, social workers, therapists, psychiatrists, coffee shop sages. She got suspended, grounded, expelled, fired— she dropped out, quit, went back again, got out, cut corners, jumped all ships, everything, eventually, every time.

Meanwhile he dealt with his friendlessness by thinking forward, sweating bullets for the future, studying like someone who cared about his studies, forcing himself well above his natural averageness to honors with punishing hours, committing himself to all-nighters over trigonometry exams and SAT practice questions as if his life depended on it—*because it did,* he reminded himself. And when it came time to apply to colleges, he applied Early Decision to one that could have been any one, good but not great, small but not exclusive, liberal arts but not artsy, but the one he knew would take him, the one he knew would offer the most money, the one who wanted his sort of minority, the one he knew was the farthest away. He got in and when it came time to share the news, he walked the acceptance letter over to his parents, prefacing it by letting them know it wouldn't cost them a cent, emphasizing that it was Early Decision and that was *final.* They received the news with glum faces, confused, maybe even shocked that he had been able to pull off an escape without their suspecting it. In that moment, he missed her, the best friend he had shared all adolescence with, whom he had even dared imagine a future with—he had imagined her still being there, the *old* her, and how they'd jump up and down and make gleeful air guitar *you rock* gestures over his acceptance and how Sam would no doubt conjure a plan to piggyback his move and he would have her some more. Instead, he had let her get lost, somehow he had allowed her to lose herself as well, and there she was like she almost *wasn't*, alive to him in neighborhood gossip alone.

They never had anything in common, he tried to tell himself, except for something outsiderish. *What are you when you are outside even the outsiders?*

But in her nihilism there had always been an indelible wisdom that hit home for him, because well after he dropped her off that evening for the last time, dropped her off and lost her forever, her mantra *I see myself and I don't know myself* this time somehow stuck in his system for too long a time, like old gum in the gut. He shut himself up in his bathroom and looked at himself in the mirror. For the first time, he *really looked.* Literally, *saw himself.* And separated himself from his reflection, the idea that he was even human, and just looked at the form, what the form was, what the form had become, how the form existed. *And did not know himself:* the tentacle-like fingers, the arbitrary length of the limbs, the jelly quality of the ass, the hard musculature of the abdomen, the on-and-off flashing blue veins of the neck, the craters and cracks and pinpoints of the maddeningly imperfect epidermis, the oily wiry growths of haphazardly sewn-in hair follicle, the shell-less mollusks that were the ears, and the two lockets of white slime that held—*ughhh!!!*—the element he had no choice but to recognize as *his* . . . the exact, dark, flashing, no-doubt-about-it spheres of his closest double, the very eyes of Darius Adam! He turned off the lights and ran out.

Damn that Sam! He promised himself that he would never ever consider his existence so comprehensively again.

✻ ✻ ✻

They did not talk. But several months after 9/11, his father wrote him a letter, his first attempt at reconnection. It was also the first time he had received a letter from his father, ever.

He read it only once. It was all he could bear, and then he folded it up back into its envelope and put it under his bed, just as he did when he was a kid with terrifying things like Ouija boards, that he didn't want to deal with but didn't have the peace of mind to discard.

The letter did not acknowledge anything. Not their breach in communication, not the global events of the last several months, nothing. It was full of the irrelevant and unpredictable, as he would expect.

He said, *The weather is good here. It always is. I assume right now it is not where you are.*

He said, *I have contemplated adopting a dog.*

He said, *Well, what can I tell you? Maybe you will tell me what you want me to tell you?*

He said, *You see the drawing on this stationery? It's Zoroastrian, did I ever tell you about it? I used to consider becoming a "moobad." That is a Zoroastrian priest. There are temples in Southern California. Zoroastrianism is the oldest religion in the world, origins in ancient Persia in 1000 BC. The symbol for Zoroaster was popularized by King Darius—it's a sun disk—a sun with wings—attached to the prophet's image.*

He said, *Have you spoken to your mother? She has news. It's big stuff. I will let her tell you.*

He said, *I have dreams about a daughter born after you.*

He said, *I resent writing you this letter in English. I hope Farsi is in your plans soon.*

He said, *I am planning on going to Iran. It would be a good place to meet. Your mother is not interested.*

He said, *That is all. Feel free not to respond, as I predict anyway.*

It was a challenge, of course, he knew, the entire letter was, and he had already made sure he had won with the last line, because if Xerxes were to act according to his will, his father *would* be right. He decided he would let his father win. He had learned to choose his battles. He consoled himself by considering that a win in itself.

The stationery was from a Zoroastrian temple in Westminster, California, it said. Indeed, there he was, the figure of a bearded man with wings, encircled by the sun's beams ostentatiously starbursting around him. Xerxes had seen this before—while his father had never mentioned wanting to be a "moobad" before, books on Zoroastrianism did exist in their house. He had never asked. Underneath the prophet's feet in feeble script it said the words "Eternal Flame." It had some resonance for Xerxes—all he remembered about his father's occasional mentions of Zoroastrians was that they were fire worshippers. The key to salvation for this winged prophet was apparently fire. *Beautiful*, he thought to himself. . . . *Terrible*, he also thought.

He kept his father out of it for a moment and imagined the prophet with the drama of his Z-name and his headdress and his robe and the staple elaborate beard and his wings. He imagined him waking up one morning, no older than Xerxes, seized by a definite madness but a madness that made him feel more *him* than he ever had, that cool righteous madness of chosen men, causing him to rise with an endless chain of revelations on his lips, unable to live a man's normal life with the sudden implanted genius, thus gathering men and women from all over his village, leading them through expansive deserts, teaching them that instead of seeking shelter and shade and water, their true life force would be found in . . . *fires*. And then, there under a blazing sun, amid unforgiving dry duneland, in the dehydration and the heat, these mad laughing men lighting fire after fire. No need for rubbing sticks—this prophet would maybe point, extract a wisp of flame from the earth's star, and there suddenly they would have their lifeline in a paranormal beacon. And not only was it *not* the last thing they needed, in their location and climate, it was apparently the only thing all along.

Part Five

Nights

There is fire as well and there is desert also but this hell wasn't *his*, and it isn't his either. Whose exactly it is, he isn't sure, but he's lost, the classic nightmare: man alone and desperate, equipped with only the useless knickknacks of civilization—clothes, watch, pockets, wallet, change, nothing. Plus a small amount of hope that he will continue to have the strength to walk on and eventually get somewhere to something.

As it goes, it is very hot.

As it goes, he is thirsty.

As it goes, he has been walking for miles and is exhausted.

And as it also goes, *he* doesn't get to that something—something gets to *him*.

Desert bandits. *Of course*, he thinks. *Naturally*. They are men who look like Darius Adam—his race certainly, but different: they have heads bound in white linen wraps and their wiry bodies are draped in white tunics. They ride horses. They speak a tongue that is like his but not his exactly—he can pick up a few words, but not every-thing. But when they clutch his wrist he understands, and doesn't care—the watch, *fine*. In his situation, time exists bitterly only in that infuriating adornment, he realizes, handing it over. He'd give them his pockets, too, if he could.

Through a brief flash of survivalist optimism, the kind of con-solation that comes only to the direly endangered, Darius thinks to himself: *in a situation like this, the proverbial pits, there is no direction to go but that which is up.*

Instead of death, he gets to be dragged atop one of the miser-able horses and tied to one of the riders for hours through the desert. There is no sign of sunset—the invisible sun exists only in its force: high and angry and relentless. Eventually there are some tents, then some people, a few herds of animals, even some houses built of something resembling melting clay. Finally, they get to something: an artificial-looking hilltop, where stands a pal-ace, a perfect ivory palace, lined with palm trees and guards, bulbous tower tops gleaming on its shoulders—a classic place of kings.

They take him inside. He is glad to go. He knows better, but it relieves him to see it: the state. A place of laws—at the very least, a place of decisions. In spite of the dying sensation inside him, he has his curiosity and it soothes him to know he can still feel such a trifling emotion as that.

Inside, on a pedestal indeed, there sits no king.

"The prophet," a servant insists, introducing his master. There he is, bones in a worn tunic, no grander than the nomad bandits, a ragged bankrupt deity lounging on a silk divan—a man surrounded by riches, but draped in poverty. The contrast gives the man an ethereal and yet disturbing cast.

Beyond him, at the end of the hall, is an opening, an open door thinly cloaked by a gauzy blue cloth. The veil shudders, he notices. He can see that the veil is being touched, lifted even, ever so slightly by a pair and then a *few* pairs of thin delicate fingers. They are being discreet, the veil just barely rippling from their light fingers and heavy breaths. He squints his eyes to pierce what is barely there and swears he can make out the whites of eyes, many ghost stares. He listens closely and he thinks he can hear beyond the veil too—whispers, soft feminine vocal rustling like silk on satin, sibilant, husky, sweet. He recognizes it immediately: the spoils of conquest, undoubtedly, the harem. The women, the women and children, the women who are children . . .

The prophet asks if he can help him, in a voice that is too loud to be anything but a knowing interruption.

Darius answers that he doesn't think so, but then realizes that maybe he can. Suddenly his purpose there is clear—he is looking for something . . . someone . . . his child, *yes that's it* . . . it's been ages since he's seen his child . . . he is looking for his missing child . . . the prophet undoubtedly has *her*, he has taken his child. . . .

Your child? the prophet laughs. *And who is that?*

Darius, frustrated, trembling, now sure it is true, decides to get bold and yell it, but instead the word comes out like a gasp, as if through diseased lungs and corroded thorax, the word itself toxic: *Shireen* . . . and again *Shireen*, the two syllables sucking up any moisture left in his chest cavity, the name suddenly made coarse and gritty and painful, unlike its true sweet owner. But what can he do but try and try to say it again and again until it comes out, *Shireen, Shireen, where is Shireen, do you have my daughter?*

She's not your daughter, the prophet declares, and with a rapping of his fingers on the armrest, there she suddenly is: *his,* risen! Out of nowhere, the old dark ringlets, the familiar smiling face, the anomalous but trademark sundress, the inappropriately bare feet, Shireen, waving meekly, *Here I am!*

Darius opens his arms to her while she stands there paralyzed in her golden limbs and clean beam like a kid acquiescently trapped in freeze tag—and Darius, too, frozen, stands before her like a crucified madman with arms open wide, amazed to feel tears, the first drop of wet anything he's felt in years, wet with longing and desperation for his child, his Shireen: *My love! Don't worry, I am here— I'm going to save you!*

The prophet, with an overamused grin, snorts at that. He drops his shaking head into his hands with a couple of dry chuckles, feigning frustration. *Darius, Darius. You don't have a daughter . . . Darius, where is your SON?*

The very word "son" causes several of the guards to put their hands on their swords; at the same instant a sudden shushing and consequential hush from the harem. The atmosphere immediately becomes taut, with the prophet himself suddenly wearing a tense grimace. The palace feels like a balloon to Darius, pregnant to its maximum with tension.

Is this happening? Darius wonders to himself, almost thinking himself out of it. His mouth involuntarily opens and out pours, *Tell me, am I dead?* He wonders if this is that dark hot heaven of Islam, and if he is there because *he* is there. He looks for Shireen, looks to her for an answer, and when he looks before him, around him, even beyond the veil, it's empty. No trace of the women.

Are you *dead?* the prophet laughs. *Ask what you really want. Listen, this is coming to an end, don't waste it. Go on.*

His son, his son. It hurts to think. *But he's——he's alive,* Darius stammers. *I know that. He's spoken with my wife. He calls.*

The prophet nods again, in an overly thoughtful manner that Darius is sure is mocking. *Most of them are alive, you know, Darius. In fact, almost everyone there. We kept them alive.* He looks to his guardsmen and immediately one echoes, *We did, yes;* and the other goes, *Yes, prophet, that is how we kept them.*

Darius eyes the guards carefully. They are indeed young men, he notices, practically boys. In fact, they're more delicate than what one expects of guards, slender, lithe, with fine features, no facial hair, rosy skin. One could in fact mistake them for——

That's enough, get him out of my face! the no doubt mind-reading prophet suddenly snaps, putting one hand over his eyes like a visor, as if blocking out a particularly rude sun.

Immediately, the two guards rush to Darius's side, two hands gripping each of his lone arms.

Wait, Darius insists, *I'm not scared of this, you know?*

The prophet drops his hand and with narrowed eyes, hisses, *Oh, tell me, why is that?*

Darius thinks about it. He isn't scared——that was the truth, the foolish truth. But somewhere the thick fog of the dream state is thinning, and consciousness is seeping its gases into the chamber of the subconscious. He wasn't out of it, but he could sense it was coming, its universe was tiring of him, the atmosphere itself was fading in color and threat, somehow he knew he could get out, and that getting out would be nothing anyway, as it was something he did every morning. . . .

The prophet goes on, *Darius—his name makes me sick! I don't do kings, O Darius.*

Darius, your head didn't come to this, I came to it.

You left us, we found you.

You closed your eyes; so now open them.

But his eyes would not open and somewhere somehow he could feel a conspiracy, like it was timed, that if he stayed here too long he ran the risk of being led somewhere that even waking could not absolve, oh, he was running out of time, it could be only a matter of time until—

The alarm is going to go off, Darius. It'll freak you out.

And in a horrible explosion of accumulated panic—that elevator-dropping, stair-falling, cliff-jumping, semi-epileptic jolt that shakes the shit out of the unknowing dreamer—Darius startled himself to consciousness, yanked his eyes wide open, put his hand hard on the alarm clock "off" button, and got nothing but a moan in response.

"What the hell?" answered that automatically snappy whisper of Lala's irritable was-sleeping-now-woken self. She was still used to whispering her screams at night, as if Xerxes were sleeping in the other room.

"I—I the alarm," he muttered, rubbing his eyes, trying to piece things together while also trying to banish the bits that were coming to him.

"The alarm? Oh god, Darius, look at the goddamn clock."

He looked at it: 1:35 a.m.

"Yeah, according to my estimate, bastard, we had another five hours until the alarm," she snapped, "and we got less than two hours of sleep. You are becoming impossible to live with lately, even more impossible than before!" She angrily flipped her body to the opposite side and willed herself into a hard unsatisfying sleep.

Meanwhile, that night, that too-early a.m., Darius stared at the clock off and on all the way to sunrise. Two hours, she was wrong about that, he thought—he had actually climbed into bed sometime well before midnight, but remembered the clock making it past midnight last he saw it, and then his head still for another long while moving in circles, shuffling through the unfiled folders of the day's events, then the weeks, the months of such a troubling time, and yet the themes, the worries, the dilemmas, they were all the same, had been there for a while now, too long, all the unsolvables, unreachable but nameable, the thing in his life that was missing, the one that he'd admit was missing only at that hour when his figure would appear before him, like a mirror whose reflection had been missing for all too long. . . . In the end, it came only in mirage form—he would never make it as a character—only in essence, the corresponding reality less personal but always infinitely worse, his child mixed in with men he didn't know, anonymous wars, ambiguous history, eternal bloodshed, consistent violence and overall hopelessness, adding up to vacuums, uncharitable expanses, hot desolate deserts that were his own, sadly, all he and his kind had for landscape within their most secret nocturnal selves. . . .

It was at this time—specifically, late in the month of September 2001—that Darius Adam, trusting that he was in his life's last quarter, had matriculated to the logical finale after his youth's dreamless era and then his middle age's nightmare-ridden nights: the abstinence from nocturnal so-called rest that was the conscious mind's only way of combating the toxic subconscious. He had cultivated a phobia of sleep. What he didn't consider was how it could be seen as a miraculous act of reverse genetics, for three thousand miles away it was also proving to be the debilitating disease that defined his son's quarter-century initiation—his son, simply, calling it what it was: *fucking insomnia.*

*   *   *

Xerxes couldn't recall experiencing a full night's sleep in many, many, many months. Of course he knew he had to have slept somewhere here and there, some tidbits of snooze, just enough to keep the body and head going at a bare minimum, but he couldn't remember a "normal" night of it. Slowly, over the course of a few seasons he had felt himself fade more and more into a constantly living phantom, an uninterrupted consciousness that existed at a consistent, downgraded vibrancy—lit always, but always dimly lit. The lack of sleep, while it increased the quantity of his active life—if it could be called that, those wasted frustrated hours staring at clocks and praying to the thin air for even a few minutes worth of active-mind shutdown—sucked away at the *quality* of his life. He was always living, but day after day that living grew shittier and shittier. He never felt the cliché more poignantly—*every day we are dying*. That was it: without the inter-mission of sleep, all he had to face was that his heartbeats were running, but running out as well.

It wasn't until late September 2001 that he gave up even trying. He simply stopped sleeping for days at a time, not even getting into a horizontal position, not even offing lights, not even trying to kid it. He didn't *want* to sleep suddenly—who knew what could happen to the world if you looked away too long?

And as it goes, it was in this stage of his insomnia that his body and mind—closer to a sort of collapse than even Xerxes was aware of—snapped into emergency mode and began deliv-ering spontaneous bursts of sleep here and there, if just to save him.

Xerxes called it "passing out." "Blacking out." "Fainting." "Col-lapsing." "Uh, I think I was in a coma, officer, what time is it?"

They were especially strange because the moment the world would go blank to him, boom, he'd find himself in that other world—suddenly, dream life! His eyes would drop like a curtain on his real world and snap—*math class, third grade, Mrs. Lynch, but with students he doesn't recognize, he has to pee*—he'd find himself somewhere else, beyond questioning, beyond fighting out of—*Arizona, or Mars is it, red rock, Lala arguing, a birdlike dog or doglike bird appears, she screams*—beamed deep into it, in a way that almost implied he had always existed in that parallel universe—*the motion picture* Basic Instinct! *Malawi! An animated Eden Gardens! The White House movie room!*—but had just failed to tune in to it. . . .

—*and that's the way it goes, you know?* she was saying, when there he was again suddenly, before a grinning blonde in a tight small sequined pink vest, sheer flower petal pants, perfect ponytail, pretty pink grin. . . .

Barbara Eden?!

She rolls her eyes at him and in a lowered voice gently scolds, *Please! Jeannie.*

Right. Geez. Right. He looks around. They're in a palace of sorts, a palace marblelike, overdone, overprecious, somewhat like a palace constructed out of wedding cake. There's intricate white tiling on all walls, old Arabic style, all labyrinthine latticework. Somewhere he can hear the trickling of an indoor fountain. It's beautiful and ridiculous, like being in a museum's historical re-creation window.

As it goes, he doesn't question it.

Before he can process it all, she pushes him down to the floor. She bites at his collar—*oh, wow, a dress shirt* he notices on himself, he's actually wearing a dress shirt and a nice one—breathes hard on his neck, her hands wandering hungrily, her giggles everywhere astray—when suddenly there is a minor wrinkle in the dream, and he feels like it needs to move on, something is about to strike—*Shit,* he thinks, *just give me this episode, let's just go with this for a second,* this was greater than his boyhood dream, in all his fantasies, Jeannie, hell, he never even imagined fucking her—and so the dream maintains itself, tentative-feeling, however, but he doesn't mind, he helps her unbutton his shirt, even unzips his own pants, tries to get to her clothes, but like that magic that is her vocation, *phoosh:* her clothes are already gone, she's already her hairless, bare, blow-up-doll self—*Could we even do this? She's not a human after all, she's like a sprite or something, no?*—and she's pressing herself up against him and saying things he can't understand into his bare chest . . . when, of course, he thinks, the thing that has to end all dreams at the wrong point is going to come, *Oh shit, it's coming,* he can feel it—

Worse than waking up: a bad plot twist. They're being watched. They've been fucking behind a veil, a gauzy white veil that has now been lifted by several rough male hands. All he can see is their pupils, angry.

Get away from her, he hears one voice.

You have violated us, says another, *and you will be punished.*

Exit Jeannie.

Before he can fully register this truly grotesque rearranging of a perfectly good dreamscape, there he is with half a dozen guards around him, big men, dirty burly swarthy thugs who are taking him into another chamber. They have to walk down several spiral staircases into a basement of sorts, except when they get down there it's actually a cave. A dirt cave lit by torches with nothing inside but more guards. *What's happening?* his voice is echoing, his annoyance with this world of men and dirt and more men replacing the world of his dream girl and sex inside a wedding cake casa now eclipsed by sheer fear.

God is going to decide, Xerxes, is the only answer he gets from the chorus of men.

Finally he hears the footsteps down the stairs, and there are two more guards and suddenly there *He* is, the *He* they've all been waiting for.

He's wearing a turban and a tunic, all in gray or possibly a white that's just dirty. He has a beard. He is smiling.

The turbaned man, walking toward him, says, *In the dream you come to us, in reality we came to you . . . came to your country, you remember. . . .*

He doesn't have too much room to play with, Xerxes notices—the cave is small and the man is now getting closer than, say, two men in an office cubicle would ever get.

To your city, you will never forget. . . .

He is so close they could shake hands, Xerxes registers, noting that he can feel the man's very body heat. He's hot, like a heat lamp, like an August beach day, hell, like an unfiltered sun—Xerxes actually finds himself worrying he could get burned.

Just down your street, did we not . . .

Thankfully, he stops just short of his face. Xerxes, as much as he tries to memorize every line, every feature, every distinguishing facial characteristic, is destined to wake in a few moments, remembering nothing of this man's mug—the man will appear in turban and tunic and even beard, but completely and utterly faceless.

Were those your people? he asks. *Some would say I am your people.*

Of course, he would have his theories as to who the man was. He would understand why at that very moment another heat would be suddenly coming from within his own self, canceling out the man's threatening bodily air of apocalypse, why suddenly deep within him he'd feel a boil, the rage of several thousand men, enough for an army, men and women, all strangers of, *yes,* his city, his country—if it *was* his country—in one of his heads, twisted dream life or simple thoughtscape, he'd declare, *I am not a fool, I know who you are, where you come from, at the very least, and it's close to me, close to where I come from, yes, but aside from that we have nothing in common, and you are not going to destroy me, you have no chance, in this, I can turn you back in a second, poof, and then none of this, none of it, it's just a—oh fuck it!*

Just as he was vanishing away and Xerxes was rubbing his eyes furiously to get to reality and face the all-absolving day, he heard the faceless turbaned man's last words, residual dream afterthought, leaking paranormally into the virgin daylight of real waking life: *But, Xerxes, it happened.*

For weeks he would struggle to will himself back into that dream. Suddenly he didn't want the insomnia, but the insomnia had him. Not only could he not sleep, he just couldn't dream properly. Soon enough he'd collapse into his usual sporadic bursts of nonsense dreams, falling dreams, a sex dream here and there, none of them amounting to more than a few minutes at a time, when all he wanted was to be back at the moment of face-off in a cave far far away.

The one time he got close—*he is in a rural region, following a young girl, painfully young, no more than ten maybe, slightly resembling the young child version of a woman, a woman he had somewhere met, a pretty dark-curled thing, in a sundress, skipping barefoot on sand and dirt, telling him to hurry up, claiming she could show him the way, and indeed eventually taking him down, down, a dirt path, into, yes, precisely, a cave, with a heat he decides is familiar*—the phone rang, jerking him with migraine-inducing violence out of his dream cave.

Fuck me, he thought to himself. He grabbed the phone, without saying a word, furious that he wasn't one of those people who unplugged their phones at night—after all, he with his insomnia, these few moments here and there were precious—

"Xerxes, did I wake you?" of course it had to be his mother. He groaned. "Well, yes. Yes, you did."

"That's good! That means you were sleeping."

"True. Briefly. Yes." His ears were ringing, his hands were trembling. He tried to cancel out the strident Mom-talk with the strange yet soothing familiarity of the girl in his dream.

"If you had a job, you'd be up by now," Lala Adam thought it useful to point out.

"Nobody has a job over here right now, Mother. Please don't start on that." It always went back to that, the sorest of sore subjects. What she didn't seem to understand was that it bothered Xerxes, too. He had, after all, done his part: gone to an average liberal arts school, picked a degree that sounded innocuous and yet multipurpose and general enough to get him to more than one place should he ever decide where that was, got the BA in communications that they told him was good or good enough, graduated with a B/B– average that was supposed to be worth more than average or below average. But since he had graduated life had been a mess of temp jobs, long and short, only: administrative assistant, executive assistant, office manager, circulation assistant, production intern, creative services associate, transcription, consulting, data entry, reception, customer service. Jobs would end and he'd have to wait for a new call; he'd get hired for a month or two but before insurance could show its divine face, layoffs would ax him, or he'd simply be in a trance of boredom and mediocrity at work, it would show, he would get fired, always well ahead of the point where unemployment dollars could pad the blow in the aftermath.

His mother, who refused to understand the work world, would never fully buy it. "Well, obviously many people there do work, or at least several thousand did, as we saw with certain recent events, and if they didn't, well, they'd be as lucky as you—I don't want to speak about *that* actually."

"Neither do I." In every phone call since the event, she had found some unbelievably crass way to allude to *it*, always apologizing for it, always somehow managing to insult him further with her apology. She had no idea—he could excuse her, because she just had no idea.

"Xerxes, I just called to tell you about the hell I am going through and maybe then you could get over feeling bad about what's going on there."

He groaned and she began her long list of no-good-this and -thats: her blood pressure skyrocketing, their horrible mounting debt, the pains of menopause—

"Okay, okay. Thank you, Mother. You think it makes me happy to imagine your life is hell, too?"

It made her pause. "One more thing."

He considered hanging up. It was the *one more thing* that he always knew was the real reason she'd called.

"Your father."

Xerxes was speechless. She normally knew not to go there.

"You know, Xerxes, he's . . . well, he's really losing his mind this time."

Xerxes tried to distract himself with anything. "Mother, I have to go now, please. I have to start . . . my job hunting today, breakfast, stuff, you know."

"The other day he mentioned going to Iran. He does not sleep. He talks nonsense. He shakes, always sick. . . ."

"Please, I have to go."

"Xerxes, maybe if you could—"

"NO. I have to go. Please, leave me alone. Please do not force me to shout at you. I don't—" and as if in a stroke of magic, a flourish of miracle, the phone decided to drop itself, without anything more than strictly psychic help from him, managing to furthermore land itself square on its clicker, with a resolute *clang*. When he picked it up, ready to worthlessly apologize, all he got was the dumb drone of the dial tone that he supposedly wanted all along.

✻　✻　✻

Having a woman in his bed didn't help the sleep problems, he had to admit, but all in all, Xerxes was happy it had finally happened. They said sometimes it took a tragedy to bring people together, and so, suddenly, there she was, as if concocted from a deep delirium, her head on his pillow, a big brown mess of kinks and curls and thin skin and artificial flower smells and sometimes even reflex-like kisses. Or more. She was a healthy sleeper. He would humor her by lying down with her at night, but once her breathy half snores kicked in—if that barely-there motorlike purring of sleeping women could be described as snores—he would rise and tend to something. Usually it ended up being the worst things, like those endless hopeless piles of New York bills. *Can't they absolve this suffering city of that shit for a month or two?* he wondered. His bank account went from anorexic to cannibalized to overeaten of sci-fi proportions that September—oh, for the vibrant optimistic scenes of kittens and butterflies, balloons and palm trees, watercolors and Technicolor, on the face of those cash advance checks, as if its subscribers could believe it was a Monopoly ticket to invisible millions, as if they had forgotten it would remember them again once it had been double- and quadruple-dipped in the acidic invisible ink of interest. *Talk about apocalypses.* No, with a life like that, Xerxes was never bored—there was plenty of wreckage in his head to make busywork while the sleepers had their night.

When it would get too close to dawn he'd crawl back in, pretend he'd been there all along—sometimes she would know better, and he'd think, *Strange, this creature who doesn't even know me, but yet is on to the reality of my sleep habits*—and bury his face in her hair and its hair products and be thankful. He knew he wasn't alone in acquiring a bed buddy—he was just glad he wasn't the exception in that season of paramedic partnerships. It had spread through the city like a most desired virus: singles haunting bars to find not just flings but companions, the heyday's speed-dating sextravaganzas suddenly morphing into support-group-style coupling, fuck-buddies being fine but replaced by the finer and fewer who could play monogamy if not marriage, the desired dating being the dating that verged on holy matrimony, that said *constant,* that said *forever,* that said *life* not just *love.* The most desperate and vital and delusional emergency "love" was in the air. . . .

It took some time however. On the evening of September 11, it was safe to say this was the last thing on his mind when he first found her on his rooftop, when he had finally dared to face the unfiltered skyline.

She was sitting in the manner kids call Indian style, a tan tiny thing in a red calico dress that was stretched modestly over her knees. She was totally still, except for the effects of the evening breeze that made her curly dark hair move with an intimidating wildness. He had expected the rooftop, seven or so hours after the event, to be flooded with people in tears, holding hands and binoculars, crying, maybe even drinking to a bad miserable drunkenness. But this female—woman or girl, he couldn't tell—was all there was and so he cleared his throat with a theatric harshness in hopes that it would make her turn around.

It did.

Two outrageously large dark eyes met his. She was almost all eyes—later, for the life of him, he could not remember her lips (*were they lipsticked, were they thin?*), her nose (*big? upturned?*), the shape of her face (*egg? heart?*)—just her eyes and that unruly tiara of twigs that was her dramatically unkempt hair. Even looking right at her didn't help determine her age—*she could be nineteen, she could be thirty*, he thought. Most likely lost somewhere in between, like him, he hoped.

"Hi there," he said awkwardly—realizing they were the first words he had spoken to a live person that day, the second person at all, period, if he could count the phone call to his mother— adding immediately when faced with his awkwardness, "I'm sorry. I just came to . . . look."

She turned back to where her view had been directed before, the end of their world, the waterside, and—as if the water's head was steaming with demons—the great tower of dark smoke that bruised the late summer orange skyline like the most egregious metaphor's clotted lyric.

Finally, she turned around again briefly. "*Breathtaking*." she said simply and that was her only word. She turned again to the spectacle, this time with her head tilted downward, and didn't say another word as long as he stood there with her. Which wasn't long at all because after fifteen minutes or so the awkwardness *really* hit him, and he realized that was all their world was to be in the next long while—however long healing really took, who ever knew—everyone would be awkward, wanting to connect with one another for the sake of that shared milestone, longing to express and overexpress the deep truth within the surface melodrama of how none of them would ever be the same after that, needing to bring it up to anyone and everyone, all their blood brothers and sisters, the citizens of The City, the spectators of its fall . . . and possibly realizing, just as before, the sad disappointing truth that nothing had really changed though, had it—they were all different and all alone and would live and die, alone, even if all together, with one another, in a warningless blast, in a crumbling staircase, in a flame, in a fall—alone, awkward, much as they lived. It killed Xerxes just to think about it.

So, weeks later, in a brief unsatisfying spell of sleep, when he dreamed of the young girl in the sundress leading him down into an Afghan cave—*for the answer, for the retribution*—he knew it *was* her. A younger version of her but the same desert-sunbaked skin, the wispy insufficient sundress, the feral corkscrew mane, and the eyes. *My God*, he thought, *the eyes.*

For the first time since Barbara Eden he had dreamed of a living woman he did not know. Although unlike Barbara Eden, she was someone he *had* met before. And he would meet her again—

although when their next meeting took place, he would suddenly forget he had known it would—the rooftop episode a blur, more dream than the image deeply ingrained in his head of holding her child-self's hand as they wandered into some Hades of hers.

"Oh, hey," she said, with the total ease and confidence of a normal real human being just going on with her life naturally, when he ran into her at the Indian-owned bodega down the block.

"Oh wow. I know you . . . from . . . ," he exclaimed, without choosing his words, just dumbfounded, forgetting that in his basketless hands he was juggling a typical outing's worth of eccentric "groceries": toilet paper (the cheap thousand-sheet, single-ply kind), foot odor powder, and microwavable hot dogs.

"Yeah . . . you live in my building." In her basket were nicer items—he looked down to avoid her eyes, suddenly getting a flash of her in that toxic sundown, her and her single stunning "breathtaking"—she had jam (plum), a box of Frosted Cheerios, a carton of soy milk, a bar of soap (some nameless, brandless New Age kind the Indians sold), a Brita water filter, and laundry detergent.

He nodded slowly and put his stuff down on the counter at checkout. "Oh, you can go first," he apologized quickly. "I mean, I was just putting my stuff down, I had no basket, please, you first—"

"It makes no difference. Go head. I have a basket."

He nodded gratefully. As the old Indian man silently rang up his purchases, he turned to her and extended a hand, "Xerxes. Xerxes Adam."

To his surprise, it made her giggle. "What a name—sorry, no, I wasn't laughing at it," she clearly laughed on. *So what*, he thought. Oh, he was used to it. People, women, whatever, they'd sometimes laugh at his name. He wouldn't even bother, the way he used to in his late teens, ready to be defensive, to give them a lesson in Farsi, to go on and on about what it meant, the kings, the history, his heritage. Better left unsaid. He'd rarely even feel ashamed of himself when he'd just nod along with their "what a name" mockery.

He paid, got his receipt, and had nothing to do but linger. *A mistake to go first,* he realized, *now I'll just have to hang around like a creep until she's done. Or if I walk on and leave, I'd seem rude. But we are, after all, conversing—aren't we?* He was just relieved that his embarrassing purchases were covered with bags.

"Well, I'm Suzanne," she said, as they walked out.

"Nice to meet you, Suzanne," he mumbled, still looking down at her groceries, still looking more dignified than his though bundled in the same white plastic bags, just sitting in them better, more neatly, more comfortable, more adjusted. He knew part of his fixation had to do with wanting to avoid her eyes, which he remembered all too well, and worried about re-recognizing. For a second, he panicked to himself, *where to now,* when he realized this Suzanne was walking home—to his home—to their home—and that solved that.

"Well, it was nice meeting you, too," she said, turning down the hall, while he slowly walked to the stairs. Apparently she lived on the first floor.

"Oh, okay, yes, bye," he blurted.

"Xerxes, right?" she called, turning around before she made her way. He decided he needed to look at her—who knew, he might never run into her again, he certainly didn't have to, hell, he didn't even have to go to the Indian grocer's, it could be hers, he could give her that, whatever she wanted, they could see other people, why not, *oh what am I thinking, what am I not thinking*—and finally he did it: he looked right into her eyes. He felt as if he had been punched—their intensity was lethal, those two complicated bulbs, as bright as they were dark. Breathtaking indeed.

"Yes, perfect," he said, absently.

"Where is it from?" she called as she walked on down the hall, close to disappearing, just like that.

He wondered what she would think—in this era, in this time, who knew what a Suzanne might make of it—but he said the only truth that was his, his goddamn name after all, his goddamn appellation of his goddamn homeland: "Xerxes is Persian—Iran—Iranian."

She was out of his sight—oh, how he would have wanted to see those eyes then—but he heard her bags come to the floor and a jingling of keys, and her oddly calm though slightly delighted last few words, "How funny—I'm part Persian!"

He bit his lip so as to trap some undoubted mad yelp that he feared might jump out. He put his groceries down for a second. Was this Suzanne kidding? How could she just say that? Was it true? She looked the part, that was possible—she was, like all Persians, what an average New Yorker could dismiss as Jewish, Italian, Greek, Hispanic, pan-Mediterranean—but just like that? Didn't she see the importance of that connection, if it even be just a part of her that could offer connection?

"Really?" he called out . . . at the same moment her door slammed shut.

Everything is always too late, he thought. *But that girl, maybe she made it too late on purpose.* He went upstairs a bit spellbound, still thinking to himself about the importance of their connection, their part-connection. He let her name play on repeat through his mind: *Suzanne Suzanne Suzanne*. . . . The name had its part-Farsi aspect. There was the Farsi *Soo-san*, more commonly associated with *Susan*. But the presence of the "z" added an interesting dimension—a dimension he didn't at all want to assume fit this girl whom he didn't even know—a rather sinister dimension even: *soo-zan*, to stick to the phonetic, translated exactly to the Farsi word for *needle*. It was a name for needles. He didn't know what to make of it—*Let's just leave it at . . . it could go either way*, he told himself. Nonetheless it didn't really matter, he told himself, because he didn't really expect to see her again, or so he told himself.

But when she materialized again, it was in a way that was greater than anything he could have dreamed. One evening, behind a firm knock on his door, there she was announcing herself, "Hey, it's Suzanne!"

He paused at the door, angry at himself for looking so scrappy when he was alone, resorting to total shittiness in the expectation of absolute loneliness forever. His hair wasn't brushed, his socks didn't match, he was wearing a white T-shirt that might as well be an undershirt, and slacks that might as well be sweats. He looked low-budget (he was), a man who never had company (never)—hell, he looked like a kid just living away from his parents for the first time. She would have no choice but to love or leave the real him.

When he opened the door, he landed on the eyes, and to his horror, they were badly bloodshot.

"Hi, can I come in?" she said quickly, running a shaking hand over her face.

He nodded and let her walk in. She immediately went to the center of his living room as if the chairs didn't exist—as if to punish him for the lack of a sofa, he thought—and collapsed on the ground, with her head buried in her clutched knees. She began a long, thorough, wholehearted spell of sobbing.

He was terrified. He couldn't think of a single thing to say.

She carried on and finally, after a minute or two, looked up, red and puffy in the face, but still truly ethereal somehow, with those big universal-secret-holding eyes barely hidden under the fringe of rugged curls. "I'm so sorry," she said. "It's not like me to do this. And I don't know you." She paused. Then, as if opting against reserve, her pitch grew higher and she went on and on, "But I was just watching the news—and I don't know anyone else in this building—or very many people in the city really anymore— and earlier I heard some military planes and that freaked me out— and they had this account of this beautiful pregnant woman, seven months pregnant, whose husband was in the first tower, died in the staircase, they think, and shit, it just hit me, for the first time really—can you believe it—it's only been a a couple of weeks—it happened—here—my God—I guess that's all, that it just hit me— and the sound of the planes, these days you'd think they'd know better, instead they get so close—so I don't know, I got scared— that's normal, I would think, but then again I don't know what *is* normal these days. . . ."

He nodded over and over. He didn't know how far he could go— could he go over and put a hand around her shoulders, give her a friendly neighborly hug (*was there such a thing?*), tell her it would all be all right (*but was that even true?*), promise to be there forever (*oh, how*

could I?). . . . But he had to admit he understood her anxiety wholly—
what didn't make sense? The world had fallen apart and there they
were, right in the middle of it.

He brought her some tissues and she smiled, just barely. "Look,
I don't have anyone either," he said, proud of having said this,
knowing it was the right—not to mention, true—thing. "And I
get scared, too."

She smiled. A small sob came out and then a laugh, almost all
at once. "Xerxes," she said. "I remembered your name. I had to
look you up to know which apartment was yours. 'X. Adams' on
the mailbox. You'd be the only X, I guess. Although I didn't expect *Adams*."

"Adam," he muttered and then laughed dutifully along with her—
*Oh, his zany name, that kooky X, that shockingly unkooky Adams, correction: under-
kooky Adam!*—truly grateful that the clouds were clearing and she was
able to sit up and talk, and even watch a sitcom he'd never seen before. Ten minutes into it, he realized that he was hungry, that it was
past his dinner hour, and while he was ready to put a can of beans in
a pot for himself, he couldn't do that to her.

"I'm thinking of ordering food," he immediately decided out
loud, suddenly encouraged by the strange authority a needy crying
girl could lend an otherwise painfully insecure, indecisive guy.

"Oh, perfect," she smiled at him, then hesitated. "You mean
together, right?"

"Yes, together—I order food every night," he lied automatically,
digging through his cupboards for the Chinese place flyer, the Italian place flyer, something, anything. He added a partial lie to soften
the pathetic reality of his resourceless existence: "I mean, once in a

while." Then he added a truth, to soften the obviousness of the half lie: "And it would be nice to have dinner with you."

It *was* somewhat nice. Chinese. They ate together well, although growing more silent as the night went on. It was sinking in on them, he thought, the weirdness. He was less in control, he was running out of things to say. She was getting tired and, he worried, sullen all over again.

"What part of you is Persian then?" he finally blurted, once he ran out of food.

"Oh," she smiled. "My dad. My dad is three-quarters."

"Three-quarters?" He tried not to sound disappointed. That wasn't even a whole part of her. It was still something, but what is 75 percent of 50 percent of something?

"I'm three-eighths. His father was half Persian, half English and his mother was Persian."

"Wow," he tried to effuse. "And your mother is . . . ?"

"She's your typical white—Irish, French, Scandinavian, Eastern European, you know."

"So you're *almost* half Persian," he stated, as for a record, as if wanting her to withdraw or drop or give in percentagewise.

She nodded, with a proud grin. "You're full? Persian, I mean?"

He nodded back, without elaborating. It had to be obvious, he thought.

"What does your family think of . . . all this?" she asked, making a hand gesture that was both an indicator and a dismissal of the cosmos.

"Well," he took a deep breath. He thought this was going to be a long story, when he realized there actually wasn't much to tell. "I've only talked to my mother and it's the usual—worried but thinks it'll be okay. She's seen so much bad stuff in her day, so who knows?"

"Oh," she nodded. "My mother doesn't think so much about it, either." And then she had to ask it, the one thing she was not supposed to ask, *damn her:* "What does your dad think?"

It was as if the question alone had sucked the life out of him— suddenly he felt unconquerably exhausted. Suddenly, the novelty of a girl in his den of abysmal loneliness had worn off. Suddenly, he was looking forward to having her leave. He was not up for the real long story with this girl who popped into and out of the thin air of his worlds like a magic trick, an air kiss, a storm cloud. He had no reason to trust in her substance. "My dad and I don't talk," he finally murmured, getting up, hoping it would be uncomfortable enough for her to stop her probing.

And apparently it was. She nodded politely and yawned. He yawned back, as if in approval. He noticed her eyes were getting sleepy, too. It was barely 10 p.m. "Well, getting to that time, huh," he said clumsily. "Bedtime, huh."

She nodded, with a small dreamy smile. *A beautiful girl, though,* he thought, *Suzanne. A beautiful, exhausting girl.* He wondered if it was his lack of girls or simply his lack of humans in this girl-filled, human-over-congested city that helped him take her for granted so fast.

She rose wearily. "Xerrrrrxeeees," she stretched his name with a yawn in a way that made it sound foreign to him, so long, so arduous, so much more than two syllables, almost burdensome with its freak consonant. She wasn't moving, in no rush. She was simply gazing back beyond him to where his bedroom lay unannounced. "Would it be okay . . . ?"

He didn't want to be presumptuous so he addressed it at a minimum, with a slow lukewarm nod, and she nodded back. And that night—a night when he was truly too tired to register the shock value, the milestone, the novelty—he had a woman in his bed. A real live woman, sleeping, soundly even, immediately, without bringing it up, without any extra movement to imply a further want, a further need—for all he knew that implication didn't exist . . . and he lay there, as on any other night quite awake, but this time a bit less tortured, given the task of listening to her breathing the way most humans do when they experience the normal healthy erase-all antidote to a day's burdens, sleep.

Blame it on the setting, their era, those abnormal circumstances, September 2001, but soon they made a habit of it. This person, this new woman person, she became a regular. They shared several evenings a week. They had meals. She got to know him— him less of her, he felt, but a lot nonetheless. He got used to her in his bed and wondered how he had lived so long without it. And soon his insomnia began to eat at him a little less, because he came to know how bedtime could be used for other things, better things—you could chip at others' sleep time with something more productive, all the things that happened in a bed other than sleep . . . and afterward, to watch her fall deep, deep, deep into a thick slumber that he couldn't even break with a few soft kisses on the neck, atop her hair, a hand over her small satisfied body—no, his nights were better. Suddenly, he felt that everything, including the city and world, all because of her, had a stab at being okay again.

✳   ✳   ✳

If there was one thing that Lala knew about life, it was that you couldn't live like that, not the way her husband was suddenly "living." It wasn't even vaguely life, but suddenly it had become him, whatever it was that was eating him, making him the zero of zeroes, molding him into a big lump of the sum total of chronic sleep disturbances. That was the only way Lala could describe it: *There we are each night, normal hour, he's in bed, I'm in bed, "good night" we still even sometimes say, lights off, I'm out, I think he's out, and then there you go, I'm waking up two hours later from the entire bed shaking from his big stupid body suddenly jolted up. . . . I go back to sleep but you know, that's no way to sleep. I don't know what he does. I don't want to know what he does, to be truthful. . . .*

Usually, Darius wouldn't do much of anything. He would fight sleep, suddenly fall asleep, then wake up—head full of a foreign turmoil that came indeed from some ugly bored department in his own head—and he'd try to convince himself to lie down again— he'd lie down again, still be thinking about it, get close to nodding off, but then the worry that what he was still thinking about was about to coincide with him nodding off (therefore re-creating it again) would seize him and up he'd be yanked again. He could take only so much of Lala's curses—suddenly sleep to her meant something more profound than ever, as she had really *gotten a life* this time and it had unfortunately coincided with him losing his.

Lala Adam had, after all, triumphed over the season of her sudden friendlessness. Soon enough she was bowing out of drinking and watching movies with her two friends, she was skipping walks with Gigi to watch the news, she was cutting conversation short with Marvin to instead converse with her sick husband or her disturbed son. As sober autumn took over, more and more their giggles and nonsense talk and idle chatter just weren't enough for her when her thoughts were on her very alone son and his worrisome city. She did not want to escape, she wanted to be involved and help and heal, for once. The pulse of the world had let its weak self be heard and it needed every one of them. She had decided to put her spare time to good use, and as Darius took on less and less of a teaching load and the household income began to shrink, Lala Adam put the years of advanced English classes to the test. She began committing herself to work, really becoming a working-woman, taking anything that was there that paid but did not demand she really know things. So she looked to kids, the school system, and took whatever position let her remain credential-less. After helping in the cafeteria she was promoted to teacher's aide and soon she was assisting barely adult teachers assist barely five-year-old children. It was good for her, she thought, but it was physically taxing. And thus, sleep disturbances were not helpful. *Oh, I need every bit of right mind I can get!* she would remind him over and over.

He understood and he was sorry. Suddenly they were agreeing. *Yes, wife, something is wrong with me. I know. Yes, now more than ever, I know. I'm sorry.* Darius Adam was suddenly apologizing.

"When I was a child we had a dog," he suddenly mumbled to her one morning, after she'd begrudgingly shoved over his toast and tea, after a night when it had gotten particularly bad, when it was quite possible that neither of them had gotten any sleep at all. "This dog would howl all night. When my mother would tell him to stop, he'd bark. My mother would kick him, then he'd whine. She'd put him outside and he'd scream and throw himself at the door. The dog was a wreck. He never slept. Finally, after years of putting up with this dog, my mother one day took him outside to the shed, and all we heard was a single gunshot. He was gone. Nobody cried. We couldn't even bring ourselves to think we missed him."

He stared into the dark pool of his tea, waiting for her to say something, some mean-spirited quip even, like a snappy, *Are you suggesting something?* But he got nothing. She ignored him. The sleeplessness had begun to make him feel like a ghost—half or less of his former self at least—and now her treatment confirmed it.

It was effective. One day as she began to walk out the door without a "good-bye," he called to her, "Please!" It had been a while since he had pleaded with his wife. *Have I ever even?* He didn't recall ever caring enough.

She stepped inside and closed the door, for a second closing her eyes. When she opened them, he existed to her and she made sure he knew it. She said, "What the hell am I supposed to do?"

She said, "It's not your fault. You are sick, you are mad, I don't know and you don't know! I don't think you will go to a doctor! I don't think you will take pills! I don't think you will listen."

She put her fist in her other hand, as if in reminder to restrain herself. She said, "You know what I think. . . . I think you are depressed! I think you know you are killing yourself and you want that! For most people, I would say that is so selfish—forget a husband, but you're a father! But for you . . . well, you've made it easy for yourself, no? What do you have to feel selfish about? You pretend you don't even have a child. You're not being a father anyway! What does it matter if you were dead, right!" She flung her keys to the ground. She said, "I didn't come up with that. You did. Goddamn you, admit that was your thinking, not mine." Eventually she stopped waiting for him and left, slamming the door. That day—his worst yet—he didn't go to work. He didn't eat, he didn't do anything. He was in the same place she had left him when she came home, her face still red with anger and possibly some embarrassment.

She said, "Say something."

He thought the only thing he could report for the day was that he had tried to buy into what he was becoming, what she was seeing: a nothing. All day this thought had transported him to some abstract plane, where like the panic daydreams of his childhood, when he'd shoot down any idyllic scenes of old people hiking arm in arm with God through winding green mountain paths, he'd try to *really* envision death by first envisioning nothingness—the closest thing to it for him being a big white projection screen at a movie theater, blank and infinite and thingless not to mention thoughtless—and he had realized existing through a paralyzed brain like his was not so different from that nothingness. He had no thoughts.

He was so deep in the thick mucus of oblivion that he didn't notice the moment when her face crumpled a bit and her eyes grew moist—*Oh, the old Darius would have bought tickets to see this!* she thought— and so she sat down next to him and listened to him breathe for a while, trying to think of something to do, say, do, anything.

"Darius, if I suggest something will you listen to it without losing it, without blowing up?"

He didn't nod but he didn't protest either. She assumed it took too much energy to nod and she reminded herself of one of her favorite Americanisms: *silence means consent*.

"Okay, Darius, because it has occurred to me what it is—your mess of the head comes at the same time the world is in a mess of everything. . . . Wouldn't you say there is a link? And maybe a personal one? And that the link has a name? And that his name . . . Darius, his name, I am going to say it. . . ."

Still no reaction.

"Darius, would you really say it's an accident that you have become like this and just weeks ago, he, your son—yes, the son you stopped speaking to many months ago after a trip to New York, which, remember, came about because once upon a time you did not feel this way—in any case, can it be linked to how your son right now is living only blocks away from where one of the greatest tragedies of this USA took place, where they are still in a panic?"

Nothing.

"Darius, this is about . . . *Xerxes*." There. His silence was beginning to piss her off, making her bolder. "I am not going to be there for you, no more turning around when you beg 'please,' nothing from me, unless you do the thing you were to do months ago."

For a second, the cobwebs cleared—literally cobwebs, he saw, barely visible translucent strings of white, like that spit of spiders, clouding his eyes, as if his eyes were suddenly coated in the goo of his head, and soon his whole body, he wagered, entangled, surely it was trying to bind him up, so tight eventually he'd turn to goo-baked sculpture—but for the second the sickly web got punctured and he literally felt a blast of fresh air in front of him, he saw his house, his living room, his wife, her clothes, her hand, her question mark. Her hand that was on his.

He snapped out of it and managed to make out the one word in his head: "What?"

"You have to tell me what happened with Xerxes. In detail. Now." She suddenly saw his eyes go from blank to barely there to horror-struck.

"What are we doing? What happened?" he said.

"We made an agreement," she declared, and went to their bedroom to slip into some sweats, something comfy so she could stomach what she already knew was going to be epic, if it was going to happen at all. It was perfectly possible that she was about to spend an entire evening staring at her statue of a husband stubbornly, until he was able to burst out of his paralyzing, somehow protective, plaster.

When she finally came back to sit next to him, it was much later, he sensed, and she came with a glass of water and a bowl full of leftover rice for Darius, knowing well that he hadn't eaten all day without her and that this was the best a man who couldn't even muster the need for the toilet could stomach.

He managed a sigh, a nod. He looked at her and at the rice and water and was reminded of his old dog. Outside it was night, too, and he could see it, her guiding him by the hand, cooing him out, he for once without bark or whine, knowing something was coming, being taken inside, and *bang!*

"What, after all, do you have to lose, you jerk?" she said, brandishing instead of a shotgun to his canine head, a spoonful of rice to his slowly unhinging, dry, but still amazingly human mouth.

She had said a very true thing, he registered. He had nothing. He let the morsels of rice find their own way down his throat, let her flood them with a sloppy downpour of tap water that half-trickled down his chin as he kept that mouth slightly unhinged to remind himself, yes, sure, he'd go ahead, he could do it, he had nothing to lose, nothing at all, when he'd already lost the only thing a man, a father, had to lose.

*   *   *

Suzanne remembered everything—or rather, like all healthy sleepers, she remembered most things, enough for her to one day, late in the fall, seemingly out of the blue, turn to him and ask, "So why don't you and your father talk?"

Just the thought of that question—a question he often dreaded—inspired some horrible physical sensations in him. Immediately he felt his skin crawl as if being pricked by some supposedly-good-for-you but no-doubt-evil puncturing instrument, with a pressure and piercing that made him feel as if he was getting three-hole punched.

He opened the window and turned away from his computer, upon which he was once again job-searching—scrolling endlessly through fruitless Web sites, reading descriptions most of the day until it was time to go to Kinko's and fax his own descriptions back. It was awful. Suzanne had no idea—vocation and she did not compute. She was an artist, she said—she'd go to galleries, take a class here and there, read trendy art history books, and once in a while face a canvas fruit-lessly. She didn't work and she didn't need to—she had put it this way herself, "Look I don't want to say I'm exactly a trust fund kid. . . ." But she didn't pay rent. Didn't pay bills. Didn't pay airfare. Charged clothes and food and other items to "the account." It wasn't going anywhere. He was amazed more than he was spiteful.

Questions, on top of it all—they generated some spite and much anxiety. "Oh, Suze, it's such a . . . long and . . . long story."

"Well, not if you don't want to get into it," she said. "Never mind then."

He confirmed her kind *never mind* with a kiss but just days later, when they had decided to have a nice Friday night dinner out at Suzanne's favorite Italian eatery, she took his fairly stable mood and their many glasses of wine as a road in.

"Xerxes, you've dodged it before—and might I add, a little weirdly—but I do have to ask again—I'm scared I'll keep asking this if you never answer, let me warn you—but your father . . . are you never going to get into why you guys don't talk? I mean, just say it if that's the case and I guess I'll never ask it again—but, I mean, then it makes it sound so terrible, makes me think there's homicide or something involved, you know. . . ."

He groaned. He looked to the bottle for help and, frustrated at its emptiness, ordered another glass—for himself and for her. He knew it was hopeless and yet he didn't blame her. It was normal enough, the question, or so she thought. "But, Suzanne, right here, right now?"

She shrugged, as if to say *why not* and so, swiftly, suicidally, with a quick swig, he did it. Without too much backstory—which he knew was a risk, was no doubt bound to make the actual events, not to mention both father and son, all look like bad cardboard cutouts of some unrounded-out melodrama—he spilled the events of a little less than a year before. He tried to tell himself he was a different man then—*no better or worse, not fair to get into all that, just different.*

". . . ta da!" he concluded glumly. He was glad for the wine. He didn't know how it would have been possible—this rehashing that was barely five minutes of detached denouement—without some toxin to keep him burning inside.

She didn't say much, just nodded, opting to nibble at the last scraps of bread in the basket over her still half-eaten entrée.

"There you are," he went on, drinking away as if it was water, meanwhile ignoring his water glass altogether. "Happy, right?"

She went right on chewing dumbly, looking as neutral as a font, not saying a word, for once—and she was not a reserved girl, this Suzanne—until after dinner as they walked briskly home. To his own shock, it was he who had to bring it up.

"Well?!" he snapped, the alcohol fueling his fire all the more. "I mean, there you are, always begging for that story and there I go finally telling you everything and that's it! We stop conversing altogether? I mean, call me crazy but I think when someone goes through that, what I did, explaining their life's biggest problem, really, they'd deserve something, some kind of response! I mean, that's my everything!"

She stopped as he hoped she would and they sat down on somebody's stoop in the cold night. He had never blown up at her like that before, he who all along was just grateful, if not downright bedazzled, at her very existence in his world.

"Xerxes, do you really expect me to take that as your everything?" she slowly asked, pausing. As if sensing he would have no response to that, she went on, "That a visit with your dad last year, that had some rough parts, the boiling point being a walk with him at Christmastime in which he tells you about something fucked-up that he and some neighborhood boys used to do—which, look, I am taking very seriously by even saying 'fucked-up,' an expression I don't like to use, fucked-up indeed, and horrible, yes— but do you expect me to sit here and say, yes, okay, that makes sense, that is a very valid reason to totally disown your own father? It's a very valid reason to fight and maybe have it ricochet on to other fights, in which it becomes a symbol of larger things— I am assuming these are the dimensions it has taken or something—but to totally have the man shut out, when I'm willing to bet—based on nothing but my own parents, and yes, I know all unhappy families are different (how does that go?), but based on my own father, who's roughly the same age, I'll bet, where he's at emotionally at this time in his life, not to mention being a Middle Eastern man in a world like this, I'll bet he needs you, that he's not okay with this . . . and so why, oh, tell me why, Xerxes, would you really expect me to digest that perfectly?"

A million thoughts raced through his head—retorts, explanations, annotations, footnotes, translations, important paragraphs of backstory, a half dozen references, a few rewinds and a couple of fast-forwards, a logical outlining, a demonic explosion, an *I'm sorry*, a *you're right*, a *fuck you*, a *who the fuck are you in my life*—and he resorted to the most meaningless one to cap that destroyed night of their first true fight,

"Suzanne, your father isn't even fully Middle Eastern, if I re-member correctly, and so you want to talk about a Middle East-ern man in a world like this? Okay, sure, my father, but don't forget—sure, ME!!!"

He later thought about it some more and when it occurred to him that he wasn't regretting it the way he thought he would, he decided it was because it wasn't as meaningless as he had initially thought.

* * *

He thought it was possible that it was hypnosis: Lala's eyes drilling deep into his like that, waiting for his something that neither was sure was coming—but it was worth however long she had just sat there for if only Darius would give her that something, she insisted, all eyes—and so there he was pretending to think back, squinting his eyes for effect, mustering the energy to scratch a temple even as he imagined thinkers did, praying that his wife wouldn't lose patience with him, praying that instead she'd just tire of this and move on and leave him alone, and even if she didn't, he prayed that some-how, miraculously, her eyes looking at him like that would hypno-tize him and then he'd fall into some semiconscious state that he was sure had to count as a sleep of sorts.

"December 2000, Darius," she began whispering, whispering as if pleading, he interpreted, either that or he had hallucinated her whisper, or perhaps his ears were now giving way, too, that suddenly her speaking voice was registering as a whisper, *Oh God*. "December 2000, almost a year ago, you and Xerxes in New York. You and your son . . . an argument? C'mon, you."

It was like a riddle. That idea cracked him up for a second and he felt the laughter, like an only superficially soothing cough medicine, suddenly unnaturally lubricate his guts. It was good—temporary, but good. "Give me a hint," he said, hoping she would laugh back.

She scowled. "This is pathetic," she said, still speaking barely audibly. She thought back to that December 2000 week, discovering Gigi, perhaps Marvin, the long walks, the feeling of liberation, still expecting phone calls that didn't come until the day of Darius's arrival. "Not a single call that whole week but the day you were coming back, from the airport. I asked you how he was and you kept saying you'd tell me when you got here. Which you didn't. You know what else you said, Darius? You said he was doing badly. You made it sound like he hated us. That's a really cruel thing to say when you know you're never going to talk about it again, don't you think?"

She had a good memory. Once, he did, too. As if in homage to that old mind of his, a sentence, as good a duplicate as could be processed out into his extramental universe, leaked out of him: "I said, 'I don't want to talk about him ever again.'"

She nodded. "And yet here you are, going to do it. Darius, if you don't, I am taking you to a hospital—no, better yet, an insane asylum. You want that?"

He didn't. He wanted to remind her that they both knew he didn't belong *like that*—he was just . . . temporarily disabled. Still, that woman, his wife, you couldn't count on her—there was no telling what she could be capable of. The insane asylum could arrive like another bad chapter. "Okay, okay . . . it's coming . . . I can . . . I can feel it . . . slowly. . . ." he stalled.

She rolled her eyes, swallowed, sighed, and waited.

"Yes . . . yes . . . it's coming. . . ." he was genuinely trying to extract and assemble the old story: where would he start, where would it be right to start, what started it, what the hell really happened, why did it get like that, did he, did he, was he really not speaking to his son now for almost a year?! For a second it horrified him—the reality of it lay pulsing and raw in front of him, stripped of anything but the gory truth: he had abandoned his own son. It was awful. He thought he could feel something else in his system about to die out. Oh, an insane asylum, he wondered if it *could* help, perhaps just for a few days. Why did he ever go there, to him, in the first place?

"I went there," he began, wishing she could fully appreciate this, how difficult it was getting the words out, getting the words out at the same time he was examining the memory, difficult and even physically exhausting, "because I wanted to see for myself how he was. What he had become. Why he had left. *What we had done to him.* What being an adult made him. I didn't know him anymore. Every year that went by, I knew him less and less, it seemed. . . ."

He could detect a sudden light in her eyes, a hint of smile—she wanted to be encouraging but not overly so, as she did, after all, want him to go on. She realized she really had no idea what went on in his head, maybe ever. Who was this Darius Adam of hers?

"I'm his father, I have a right," he went on, and he closed his eyes, as they did in movies when they were about to be transported to another place and another time, and he was amazed to discover that it helped. "And his apartment, his life, everything was a mess.

He had no real job. He still doesn't, you say. He went to school, left us for, as I suspected, nothing but to be away. Food, even, you should have seen it—we ate . . . pebbles."

"Pebbles? Like rocks?"

"Well, no, but almost. A bad, crunchy, colored, dry thing—" the word for that breakfast food—the stuff you had with milk, the stuff kids liked, but sometimes adults also, especially the more boring type, the stuff in the cardboard box—escaped him. "Never mind. He had no food really. He hadn't even told us he was poor. Except somehow he had money for this apartment which cost more than ours. We never wondered how, did we. . . ." She had a hint of a shrug for that, he saw, looking at her through an open slit in his shut eyes. She never worried about the details. "Well, the entire week we didn't get along. Suddenly, here we were: just two men, two men." He stopped. That was deep.

"Go on," she said.

"Father and son, suddenly, *just two men,*" he repeated. "For the first time. Wanting to get to know each other. He didn't like me, either. I got on his nerves. I took . . . naps. He . . . went out."

"Okay, so you spent time alone," she said impatiently. "What was he doing out while you . . . slept, I guess?"

He thought about the instances. Outside it had been snowing. The paper, Xerxes would go to get the paper, and meanwhile he would sleep. Maybe dream even. Shireen, she had been there more than ever in his head, curling up at his side when her brother was gone, trying to console him, telling him she'd never leave. He couldn't tell her *that*—he looked at Lala's large, sane, logical eyes and never had they looked so sane and logical. The point was that he didn't know, he realized. He could barely admit to himself that he had no idea where Xerxes would go, knowing only that he would take a while and that he would barely miss him.

"Walks? That's what they do in that city, I guess. Anyway, he wanted to be away. . . ." and he could feel something come over him, maybe even hypnosis, as it wasn't sleep, but it was *something,* a spell, making the words come, words he hadn't even tried to choose, suddenly so slippery, so *out,* ". . . they take off . . . they fly away . . . WHAT?!" he suddenly heard himself shout, as if echoing a "WHAT" he thought she had said. She looked at him frowning, her mouth closed, closed for a while. He had said something. Something odd. *They take off, they fly away . . .* and in return he had gotten in his head, wings, wings flapping—he *felt* them as clearly as he saw them—a different time and place, white wings, flapping so hard against the canyons of his gray matter and their dull-throbbing neuron caves, a flapping that went from brushing to slapping, whipping almost, flapping back and forth wildly, madly—

"Go on, Darius."

—oh he could literally feel his brainstuffs being pushed around, loosened even, like balls bouncing askew all at once against a giant divine racket—back and forth they'd sweep him, chilling him with their breeze, blinding him with that white blur, white as all hotness, white as, yes, *fire,* flapping so hard that like stick against stick, feather against feather, they created fire—

"Oh, you're drooling." She wiped his mouth with her finger, trying to lower her eyes so he couldn't see it, again a tear. She couldn't believe what he had become—was this really it? Old age? Was it really over? She almost longed for that mad lively Darius, the old big boom of a bastard, the heavy step, the hot hand, the ready tongue. Her old man, where was he?

He was somewhere else: stargazing in a courtyard, lost in strange and parallel streets, Tehran, New York, young boys, grown men, kerosene and lighter, Christmas lights and Christmas lights, in his hand, in front of him, the smell of burning, burned nuts, in the distance hung and falling like fireworks, lit white and blue, hell, doves, peace—it was all, it was all coming together. . . .

Before he knew it, there it *really* came: avalanche-like, saved up from the decades, *oh, it has been a while,* that he knew as he felt the wetness from his unseeing eyes to his barely feeling face. He was weeping. "Oh, *Darius,*" he heard. He couldn't open his eyes long enough to see her matching tears—it was definitely a first, the couple crying together, as they hadn't even done that on their wedding day. "Darius, please." But he wasn't stopping, saying things in between heaves and sniffles that she couldn't understand, with his eyes closed, bawling the way infants do, holding on to her even, still trying to reason and remember, the helpless terrified wreck. It scared her to see it, she had to admit, and so she held him until, after a very long while, he grew quiet again.

"Okay, that's enough, Darius," she whispered, wanting to be gentle with him, wanting to give the poor guy a rest. Whatever it was, it was heavy. And besides, sleep deprivation made people emotional. "You're off the hook. Why don't you just lie there for a bit and try to rest? You want to try to have some more rice, some water, tea?"

He shook his head. But he wasn't done. He tried to say, *But you can't leave me like this, after all that, I had just begun, I am in it now,* but he couldn't. He opened his mouth and nothing. It was so frustrating that he couldn't feel embarrassed about crying like that, the embarrassment trigger in him, like the anger apparatus, certainly disabled as well.

She tried to pry his tugging hand off her. "Okay, okay, you're off the hook. Try to sleep, okay!" but he insisted. "For heaven's sake, what the hell, Darius? What are you trying to tell me?"

He let out what he hoped would be a rather normal yell, but instead he got a scream—*a woman's scream even,* he had to admit—just to tear his voice right out. And before she could even be horrified, he said, "I'm sorry, my voice was stuck, wait—"

"Darius, you're really worrying me, really really worrying me . . . *I* have to lie down now. . . ."

"I have to say something," he said, and so, wearily, she sat down and looked at him with the mixture of annoyance and care of old wives. And so before he could lose it again, he began, and suddenly his voice and thoughts were clearer than ever, realigning themselves like an old memorized prayer, everything falling into place—the boys, the night, the lighter, the kerosene, the birds, the stars—everything, it was out.

"Oh, Darius." Suddenly her voice was even smaller than a whisper. "Why did you tell me that?"

He had nothing more to say. Like a big man after his biggest meal, he was done. It was over, he decided.

"Is it true?" she asked.

No, nothing more. Oh, she can figure it out. I'm done, he decided.

"It's true. Fine, Darius. That's . . . awful. But what does this have to do with . . . what we were talking about?"

But he just had no more to say. Except "Xerxes," a final two-syllable mumble that came out of him, as she, to her joy, to her relief, saw him slowly descend to a state she hadn't seen for weeks—*sleep!*—and she turned off the lights. It was 7 p.m. *So what.* Her husband was sleeping! She ate dinner by herself, tickled by what music the sound of his usual obnoxious snoring suddenly had become for her. . . .

That night she delighted in going to bed by herself—*the entire queen just for the queen herself!*—as his snoring carried on in the next room. But instead of sleep came thoughts of drooling heaving Darius, juxtaposed split screen against young, bird-killing, nightmare-creating Darius. Suddenly she was having trouble sleeping. She kicked Darius out of her thoughts. And when it finally came over to knock her out, the slumber was deep and thick . . . as evidenced by how much it hurt to wake up at the sound of "Hey! Hey!"—suddenly the sound of her husband, a big dark dumb shadow in the dark of the bedroom. She didn't even have to look at the alarm clock—but she did: 3:15 a.m.—to know it was a bad hour.

"Hey!" he was saying, over and over, like a dumb overexcited child waking his parents on Christmas morning.

"I know, I know, you slept," she automatically snapped, trying to hide just how furious the hour made her. He had gotten eight full hours, she thought. Another, say, *month* of that and he just may be caught up, just may become a normal person. She couldn't wait. She buried her head in her pillow, wishing he'd vaporize.

"No, no," he said, and something about his voice—something about the old Darius, just in some small half-shadow way reappearing in that voice, giving a bit of the old growl to the recent shallow whine—made her want to listen. "Listen, I forgot to tell you the end."

"Of what, Darius? Really, look at the time. Please . . ."

"Yes, but before it escapes me," and like that overgrown child, and yet like the old Darius, too, he sat on the edge of the bed and even bounced for her attention and began.

He told her about the Christmas lights in the East Village, then the street with the doves, the blue and white lit doves of peace, and how it had made him snap.

"And you told him about the burning birds," she finished off for him. "Did that even really happen, Darius? I never heard of such a thing in Iran."

He didn't say anything to that, just carried on, like a man finally popping out of a coma, unable to get enough of the speech and thoughts and actions that characterized life, "and then he said he wasn't asking about that at all and I think I apologized—well, maybe not—but we walked back and it was very cold and we were very silent and I—I was leaving the next day, in exactly a day—I was hoping to sit him down, maybe that next day at least, tell him everything, my past, maybe yours, everything that was our history, the good and the bad, to let him know everything so there wouldn't be surprises—if you could call the birds story that—so that he could put things in context, take a story like that and know what to do with it, so he could know me. I wanted him to forgive us, to forgive *me*. That's all I wanted."

"Good, good, so what was the problem?" she muttered through the pillow. She was torn between genuine interest and debilitating exhaustion.

"Well, the next day, I couldn't face him. It was his reaction mostly, the hate I had seen in his eyes, the shock—he looked like he had been shot. Like I had shot him. He looked dead. I couldn't get that out of my head. So I spent the day out in the city, hating that city, doing things, whatever, to pass the time, meals, whatever, so sickened by that cold busy mean place that he had chosen to bury himself in. At some point I imagined he might die there and how awful that would be. How awful it was that I had taken my son from his homeland, his Iran, to this place where he might live out his days. I was in a state but by the time I got home, I felt ready to speak to him, but of course he was not there. He left a note saying he was out, had things to do. You know, all evening I waited for him and waited and waited. At one point I got worried—what if he *had* died? How would you know in a city like this? What if I had killed him? What if he was gone?"

"And then he came home. . . ."

"Well, and then he came home a few hours before my flight. I was amazed he even came then. He came then and then there was no time and it made me so mad to see that he had done that. More than likely, it was I who would die before we'd ever get a chance to be together again. Didn't he see that? And then, well, I was packing and suddenly he said he had to go downstairs, go out somewhere, and then he was just gone. I could have waited and missed my flight, but my theory was he wasn't going to be back until he knew I was gone. And I guess I was right. But I left thinking my son was lost—like a father whose son is really lost—and he made me leave like that. He made me leave him."

She slowly rose up and reluctantly turned on a light, which hurt them both. *So what,* she thought, *let it hurt.* It was all hurt anyway—there was no hope for peace that night after all that. She wearily asked—her right mind still caring, still wanting to know—"Darius, what do you think made him act like that?"

For a good five minutes—she was watching the obscenely bright green numbers of the alarm clock—he said nothing. Eventually she gave up, assuming his handicapped zombie self had to be back, switched off the light and lay down again. The minute she did that, of course, as life goes, as Darius goes, his voice—eerie in adopting the full weight of its old tenor completely now—burst loudly into that fresh, new, light-rid black of the night.

"It was the last of many crimes! It connected everything! It was the only story of my youth he had and suddenly it took on the burden of everything. Everything that was wrong with me, my history, my past. And I think for sons, they transfer that. It was a nightmare but a real nightmare. And that I told him, like that, out of what he thought was cruelty when really . . ." She could hear the last syllable break a bit, as if he was teetering on the brink of sobbing again, ". . . it was all about a different place, a different past, the land where he was supposed to be from, and all he ever knew of that place, all he ever knew were those nightmares, those real nightmares, that we real living humans could confirm for him over and over . . . and it was the first time I felt, I wanted to, to tell him that I was sorry for how hard we had made it, how much harder I kept making it . . ." and there the sobs came again with more defeat and yet more power than ever, "but maybe that's me—him, I really don't know, I don't know *what's* in his head! All I've ever wanted to know since he was a little kid—and unknowable even then—all I ever wanted to know was *him*, what *he* was thinking, what did *he* make of it all, and how did whatever it was make it okay to let it all go that day in New York, how, oh how?"

If his son had been there at that moment, he would have answered it in full—with every year that went by it became more and more answerable for Xerxes. He had collected the sentences, put together the pieces of anger and misery, examined all the most complicated emotions, and double-checked the evidence in his memory. At that moment he would have looked the man who shared his eyes *in* the eye, in his overflowing red eyes, and used that as an opportunity. Because part of the problem, Xerxes thought, was that they had never had the *opportunity* to communicate fully when he was a child. But as he got older, Xerxes found the narrative played naturally in his head—it would be the *real* face-off between him and his father, the opportunity to hold his father hostage and spill it all out like blood in his ears, the opportunity that he missed when his father challenged him in New York that day; it would be Xerxes with the power, his father with the anguish, Xerxes with the booming voice in the light, his father bawling in the dark, for once letting him get through it, through it all, or what he hoped was at least a start: *The sparking anecdote is only as big as the sum of its parts, Dad. Take the day you really beat me, that certain day out of a few of those days, but the day when I let the worlds mix and it meant the picture of us that you held so dear breaking in pieces, enraging you so much that you left me with two black eyes*

for school——I later dreamed all night of shooting stars and how they had blinded me from your blows, and then the day you told me about making stars out of the bloody burning feathers of living helpless beings, I thought of that, how you had made stars out of me, how you could do that, with a brandish of your fist force me into place, a place I didn't want to be, to a whole past that reverberated with another past, every layer deeper and more painful, from my past to your past to our people's past——when the hell could the symbolism stop? I was just a kid! You were the agent of ghosts, you'd reek of history and suffocate us with the bad parts. . . .
It was always in you, you taking your family out on a weekend drive, taking your family out on a weekend drive to a protest for your child to see a man burning out of nationalistic passion, a passion that I was supposed to understand, you wanted to tell me, a darkness that I was supposed to own, you were trying to instill in me. You didn't want me to belong to this country, but yet you wouldn't let me have the ease and clear conscience to belong to you, and so what happened? I ran away and, fine, the irony, even here the instability and turmoil got me: 2001! The worlds mix again, the horrible foreignness I fought to escape, crashing right into the phony Americanness I failed to pull off, the fear bringing me back full circle to my first fear, the nightmare born in a baby watching supposed enemy planes in the Tehran sky, fine, I got through it, but now I'm trying to break the circle, cut the connections, vaporize the voodoo. . . . I'm trying to find myself, an identity outside yours, outside nationality, outside ethnicity, outside family, outside history, foreign to them and to you and to everything, wholly my own lone person. The worst that can happen is I find out that the world I want to create cannot exist, that's all——that I just won't be able to make it like that—— that there are only graves for men who want that. But so what to you, you never wanted to save me from it, now accept that I won't be the one to save you, why would I when I don't want to save myself? . . .

What Xerxes couldn't imagine was that his vision of what Darius would be reduced to during his rant would actually look an awful lot like what Darius had become.

Darius was destroyed. The deep sobs running powerful currents through his body made him shake like a man at electrocution—he was losing it in ways she had never seen. She thought about turning on the light again, but couldn't deal with spotlighting his downfall like that, so she just blindly grabbed for his body, his quaking torso, and pulled him close to her. "You two will speak again, I will make sure of it, do you hear me," she whispered into his wet face over and over, until he partially bought it, enough at least to stop for a bit and let her feel effective, let her go back where she belonged, to being right, then to sleep, until she did, only after buying that he, too, was asleep, when really he was faking it all night, faking it with more conviction than ever, never giving up that ghost, hoping that if you faked a thing enough, especially a thing you had just done genuinely, a thing that had genuinely done you—and he *had* slept, hadn't he, just a while ago!—if you faked it long enough, eventually, there was a chance it could go back to just being.

Part Six

The Missing

In spite of it all, New York was given concrete consolations that came like firm orders: *Go About Your Normal Lives.* Be alert *but* also be *normal, be very very normal so as not to cause unnecessary suspicion because there would be tax dollars and new laws and more hatred if you pressed those buttons.* In a time when people were calling 911 on their junk mail, when an entire subway line could be frozen for hours because of a child's unattended backpack, when every plane looked too low and every man looked as if he knew something, normalcy was the new sanity even if it was hard to remember what *normal* had ever really meant.

For a smaller segment of the urban population, those who existed well outside the perimeter of society, the security of the homeland was not a factor. The apocalypse just a bridge or tunnel away had never hit home, the news was background white noise, and the voiced concerns of a nation had as much power as proverbs. Their lives would go mostly untouched. The only way it would get them, they imagined, was to kill them and that didn't matter either because dead men couldn't question what got them. They were the safest of all that season.

One of these men had become a regular at a Park Slope, Brooklyn, post office—a man of medium height and moderate build, who would have appeared just like any other man if he weren't wearing sunglasses paired with a baseball cap covered by the black hood of a dingy sweatshirt. The official start of winter was just a few weeks away and yet it was suddenly seventy-six degrees—everyone had pulled out spring and summer outfits except, apparently, this man. He had his reasons for his getup: he did not like to be exposed and he also did not like to wear the Kennedy Mental Health Center T-shirt out in the real world, so he put on one of the few cover-ups he had to face the supposedly "real" world. Still, people were staring and he thought it was because they knew where he had come from, as if they had X-ray vision and the T-shirt's message was loud and clear. As for the function of the sunglasses, they was a barrier between their eyes and his. Exposure again. Because these days when he would leave the facility, he needed all the protection synthetic materials could afford—and it was consoling to remember, these days, from the little he gathered, the country at large felt a little more naked than before.

It was just about the holiday season, so everyone knew to expect something bad, but just how bad, people had no idea: the line snaked itself into a tight unyielding J-shape inside the old postal building. He took a spot and counted eighteen people before him. *Fine.* What was not fine was that they were not going anywhere— he had to be back at KMH in a half hour. That was all the time they got before they were labeled missing and who knew what happened then—he didn't want to find out. But the minutes went by and by and even with five postal clerks operating, the line was just not moving. He wondered if he was imagining it—he counted again. Eighteen. *Okay, seventeen,* as one person walked out. Seventeen. The line seemed nearly locked. Something was wrong.

The other tip-off to the day's wrongness was the presence of police. In a post office with eighteen people in line, another dozen or so shuffling around and filling out slips and labeling boxes, and five clerks, was there really a need for four police officers? *Four police officers = four guns,* he thought. They were the big burly Brooklyn kind of policemen, the cops of 1970s movies. They also wore sunglasses—he assumed to avoid having the civilians follow their eyes.

The line continued to not move, but he had no choice—he needed stamps. There had to be another way, he thought. Suddenly, he had it: *stamp machines.* They still had stamp machines, didn't they? he thought. He stepped out of the line and headed to the back of the post office where the big black machines always stood. One was a soda machine; the other two were, indeed, stamp machines. Feeling relieved, he quickly took out his crumpled dollars. Before he could insert them, there was a tap on his shoulder.

It was a police officer. A huge black guy, shaking his head. He was also pointing to a handwritten sign posted above him, right on the stamp machine. "OUT OF ORDER," it read. *Oh,* he thought. *Oops.* He went over to the other machine, but it, too, had the sign: "OUT OF ORDER."

"The machines are dead," the police officer said. "You gotta get in line for them."

He nodded. He got back in line. There were now nineteen people ahead of him. Something was wrong indeed.

There were other tip-offs, too. For one thing, the clerks looked all wrong—sure, they were in the usual uniform but they were covered in other ways that were not normal, he noted. For one thing, two wore the masks surgeons used to cover their noses and mouths. And all five wore gloves, obvious white ones, made of something thicker than the hospital latex sort.

Then he began to notice that there were handwritten signs posted all over the place. "PLEASE HAVE YOUR ID READY," "ALL USPS MAIL REQUIRES VALID ID," "NO ID, NO DELIVERY, NO EXCEPTIONS." *ID?!* he thought. He couldn't believe it. Surely it was a mistake, surely it did not apply to him, this was just a post office, after all. . . .

He tried to remain calm and just observe, not judge. He was sweating profusely, but he did not put the hood down. He just stood there, hot and uncomfortable, wondering if things had just simply changed since he was last there. It had been at least a year, he thought. Maybe this was normal, maybe the future looked like this.

The man was feeling better until he got a tap on the shoulder.

"ID, sir?" It was another police officer, maybe the stockiest one, Italian, young, ready to be pissed.

"I'm sorry," he said, "but I don't understand. ID?"

"Everyone must have ID to mail out!" he said in a too-loud voice, as if to remind everyone else in line as well. The police officer lowered his voice a bit and addressed the man again, "Are you even sending anything out? Just buying stamps or something?"

He shook his head.

"What are you sending?" It seemed like a challenge, not just a question.

The man tried to cool himself down by telling himself he wasn't actually being challenged, he was just not used to this, and this was how normal people in the outside world spoke, he was in no danger, and everything would be okay. . . . He slowly removed a thin, slightly crumpled envelope from his back pocket and presented it to the police officer.

The police officer nodded at it, just barely reading the address. "Okay, so you need your ID, you understand?"

He nodded.

"Okay, so where's your ID?"

He was burning up, sure that the place was heated on top of the actual unprecedented heat of the day. He tapped his pockets absently, as if looking for his wallet, knowing well that he never carried a wallet.

"I don't know," he said to the police officer. "I didn't think we. . . ."

The police officer shook his head at him, as if exasperated. "No ID, no way!" he said again, in his louder lesson-for-the-masses voice. "I suggest you get out of line and come back when you have your ID."

He nodded and slowly stepped out of line. The police officer opened the door for him, as if to make sure he went out.

The next day, he tried again. Same hooded sweatshirt, same cap, same sunglasses. And same situation in the post office: same line, same clerks, same gloves and face masks, same cops, same signs. Even the stamp machines were still "OUT OF ORDER."

He was prepared. This time he had his facility ID in his hand, the envelope in the other. He felt better that day. Abnormalities always looked a bit more normal the second day around, he thought. It was back to cold, not yet seasonably cold, but *colder* and that was good. There were only twelve people ahead of him in line, and one extra clerk was working. The line barely moved but it moved and that was enough. A few still stared but that had to be expected. Soon it would be over.

When another police officer scanned the line, he flashed the contents of both hands at him. Envelope, ID. The police officer simply nodded.

When he made it up to a clerk, luckily one without a mask on her face, he presented the two objects silently.

"How are we today," the older woman stated absently, not looking up from whatever previous item of business she was wrapping up.

He shrugged silently.

She finally looked up at him and, although he suspected he could be imagining it, she squinted at him strangely. "*Hello*," she said emphatically, as if she was repeating it.

He cleared his throat. He had not been prepared to speak on that day. "Hello," he echoed back, and pushed the envelope and ID closer her way.

"Just this, regular mail?" she asked.

He nodded.

She looked at his ID first. She looked up at him, looked back at the ID, looked at him again, and back to the ID. She paused as if she were reading fine print on the ID. Perhaps she could not tell it was he, since he was covered with his hood and glasses and all, he wondered. Perhaps it was the fact that he was from a mental health facility that disturbed her. Perhaps his ID was somehow not valid. He was full of worries and doubts.

"Bow-back Nez-aim-y?" she stumbled, her finger pointing along what she read.

He didn't say anything.

"Am I pronouncing that right?" she asked.

He shook his head.

"How do you say it then?" she said, even smiling in a way he doubted was sincere.

He cleared his throat again. "Bobak," he said softly. "Nezami."

"Bobak Nezami," she echoed.

He nodded. "Bob," he muttered.

"Well, Mr. Nezami," she said, handing back the ID. "I just need you to fill out the return address. . . ."

He froze.

"The return address, please, we cannot have mail go out without a return address," she said, picking up on the fact that he was not about to move. "New rules."

He nodded. It had to be new. He couldn't believe it. He picked up her pen to fill it out, but then paused. He wasn't sure what to write, he hadn't given it much thought.

"Problem, sir?" the clerk asked, with a small smile still.

He shook his head. "I mean, yes," he corrected. "I mean, I hadn't thought about it. . . ."

She nodded as if she understood. "Well, Mr. Nitzoani," she said, slowly, thoroughly mucking up the name she had worked on in the process, "why don't you step aside and fill it out over by the form counter and when you're done you can come right up to the front to me and we'll take care of this, okay?"

He stood there frozen.

"Okay?" she smiled almost maniacally. She looked over his head to the rest of the line and called, "NEXT!"

He slowly made his way over to the form counter and thought about it. He was just not prepared. He decided to leave. Once outside, he realized he had forgotten to ask for a stamp—he could have just asked for a stamp before he left, surely that wouldn't have violated new rules? A stamp would have solved everything, he thought. After all, there were still mailboxes on the street, weren't there? He couldn't see one, suddenly. He was worried about just what it was that was so wrong these days.

He thought about going back and asking for a stamp but his time was almost up and he had been late the day before. He could not mess things up at the facility as well.

Upon returning to his room at the facility, he proceeded to hurl his fists into the wall behind his bed. No one heard, luckily, and he recovered well enough to carry the phone book from the lobby to his room. He closed his eyes and counted to thirteen as he carefully flipped through the white pages. When he stopped, he was on the page headed VACCARO–VARIETY. With eyes still closed, he slid his bruised fingers down a column and when he opened them up, he had it. Someone named "C Vane" with an address. He slowly copied the address onto his envelope, changing the name to his rightful one, "B. Nezami."

The next day when he returned—same getup, same lines, same signs, same law enforcement—he was *really* ready.

"Is everything okay, then?" he asked the postal clerk, a young man this time who had his face mask around his neck casually. His ID was checked, the sender address was there, it was weighed, he had paid, it was all done, he hoped.

The young clerk tossed his letter behind him into a giant bin and said, "You're all taken care of!"

He was happy; he had been waiting for those words for days. He bowed his head and smiled, and because he wasn't forced to speak anymore, he simply mouthed the words *Thank you.* He gave the post office one final glance, relieved that he would not have to return.

That night, he went home and sighed to himself, *There, my part of the deal is up, I have done what I can.*

He knew he owed something to the original sender as well, the man who called himself *M. Dill, A Friend of Your Sister's,* who had reminded him that he *had* a sister, who had explained her life to him in brief, who had sent her address, who had pleaded in his letter that he do it. He owed him a letter, too—it was part of the deal—to tell him he did it, to thank him and to tell him he was welcome both at the same time, but the idea of sending out another letter exhausted him. He didn't want to go there again. Plus, he had betrayed his sister in the end anyway—he had not attached his real address. He did not want M. Dill ratting him out, remedying the fake-address situation too quickly. By the time M. went around to bring the correct address to his sister, he would be gone from the place. There would be no Bobak Nezami of Kennedy Mental Health Center; he would be out of there and who knows where. It was a comforting thought. The possibilities were endless once they let you go. He dreamed of the island across the bridge just minutes away, he dreamed of the old continents he had once visited thousands of miles away, he dreamed of Tehran specifically and the smell of the year-round summer season in a city built over a desert, he dreamed of the quiet normalcy he was sure existed wherever it was you went when you were done doing what they insisted was living.

* * *

Gigi always loved December—one of her many reasons was because it was the season of good mail. Sure, there were the awkwardly bound packages of sugar cookies and fried cakes from the female relatives in the motherland, the recent photos from her children and husband tucked into simple gifts like scarves and coasters, the odd *Feliz Navidad* card from an almost forgotten friend from that other home . . . but the *real* deal for a promiscuously freelance housekeeper and nanny was the cash-stuffed cards of the season. This was the season when it all became worth it—when the Pasadena patrons remembered who exactly it was who was refraining from shuffling around their unguarded jewelry boxes, opting not to dip into their liquor cabinets, deciding against harming their million-dollar china, leaving their private school brats unmolested and unabused. "Housekeeper/nanny" was a lethal combination—everyone owed a woman like that. A woman who had your house and household in her hands, who was hired and rehired to keep her impoverished self out of the dirty dealings expected from housekeepers. Gigi took pride in being honorable because it was a trap—*when you're good, they owe you extra*—her being good only reminded them of how bad her type could be.

So when Gigi rushed to her mailbox compartment and did her

usual *nothing-can-hurt-me,* ignoring the many bills and austere all-capped collection agency letters, she inevitably found what she was looking for. There it was: an oversize red-enveloped Christmas card.

Oh yes, baby, who owes me?! She looked at the sticker in the upper left-hand corner for the sender and it said: Darius Adam, 7561 Arcadia Dr. #19, Pasadena, CA 91101. It only took her a second of *who-the-hell*-ing, when suddenly that awkward name rang a bell. *Oh no.* She ripped open the envelope. . . . *Oh yes, yes it was—the nerve* . . . Gigi was furious . . . *the bitch!*

On the face of the card was a generic green triangle of a tree and inside, *Happy Holidays* in the usual gold script. It was a cheap card, too—Gigi knew cheap cards well. But the kicker was what else the sender had filled the inside with: no, not money but that horrible overly-formal hodgepodge script that foreigners always had—*hell, it takes one to know one*—big dumb loops and overdone crosses and inappropriate caps and illegible intermediate lettering. And the weird English, well, that was *her* all right:

> Hello Gigi!
> Hope you are Happy and all things are Good!
> Sorry to not see you!
> But I'm thinking of <u>You</u>!
> Your old Friend, Lala.

She thought about ripping the card up but decided instead to call Marvin over for a dinner meeting and let the monstrosity be seen by at least one other person, one who was, incidentally, equally invested, she wagered.

"See, I told you," Gigi declared that evening, after he had taken a long disturbed look, over his one single untouched slice of frozen pizza. "Girlfriend ended up a bitch!"

Marvin nodded slowly, although he wasn't entirely sure what she meant. By the card's insult, at least—in real life, he got it. One could argue that in real life Lala Adam *was* a bitch, all right. The reason was simple: Lala had slipped out of their trio in recent months, but she seemed to add insult to injury by making it seem as if she had never been there in the first place.

He tried to remember when the hell she got like that and remembered that there was an exact date. How could he forget?— Just three months ago they were slated for their usual Tuesday dinner night together but on that Tuesday, September 11, 2001, they got a call from her saying it would be impossible.

Why? Family should be together! Gigi had said.

According to Gigi, she had snapped *Exactly* and that was why she had to be with her husband.

But since when did he become your family, sister?! Gigi had argued, adding another more emphatic, *SISTER!*

When Gigi had even gone as far as asking her to invite her stupid husband over, too, she had apparently said she could discuss it no further. Marvin and Gigi had spent that evening together with a rented movie that he couldn't remember. Gigi had insisted there was no point in watching the news, they wouldn't know anything for another long while anyway and why get miserable over something that didn't affect them, that was happening across the country—*what would be considered a whole other country or two if America was a normal country size!* she pointed out. It wasn't for them to worry about. Did he know anyone there? Marvin said he didn't. She didn't either. The people she knew lived in countries where far worse things happened. *Mexico!* she had cried. *Don't get me started. And, Marv, what about Africa?!* He didn't correct her; he let it go. Later, when they were saying their good-byes, Gigi had added, *It's just unlucky for her that her son lives there. Or so she says!* He hadn't thought about that. But he had let that one go, too. It wasn't in Marvin to hold anything against Lala anyway.

But then just a few weeks after that, he wasn't so sure. He had rolled into the Eden Gardens garage, waiting to pick up Gigi for their salsa class, and at that same moment, down through the garage, there she was: Lala with her usual outdated feathered and highlighted hair, her heavily made-up skin with its orange bronzes and bitter browns, her hard-heeled walk, her almost militarylike swinging arms, her clenching and unclenching hands with their always polished and always off-color nails, her squinting eyes and moving lips as if in dialogue and in dissent with some idiot apparition in her brain . . . but no longer in the jeans and plaid, no longer in the New American style they had seen her evolve to. She was in professional-looking clothes: a sweater set—pink knit cardigan over pink knit tank—a gray pleated skirt that came down to her ankles, and the comfort pumps of the workingwomen of commercials. Oddest of all were a backpack on her back and a pile of construction paper. Was she working? Arts? Crafts? College? Kids? What could that woman even do, he wondered?

He had honked, eager to tell her some news, that he'd had a lead on her what's-his-name brother—who, while his name had finally appeared right on the money eventually, was always doomed in his own head to the unutterable nonsense-nickname *Barback*

Noussaoui—that it had been easier than he had thought, that private investigations weren't even necessary if you had a computer and a search engine (*and were looking for a loony-tunes bro who had once made the news trying to off himself with hair spray and a lighter in the middle of a Kmart, for God's sake!* but he wasn't sure if he was going to tell her the full story there). He had honked again. *You want to know this, Lala-lady! Girl, this is big! I'm telling you . . . girl?*

By the fifth or sixth honk, he knew it wasn't necessary. She had to have seen him—at least had to have spotted the SUV, the SUV with the booming bass she had always *tsk*-ed at and the "MDILLZ" plate that had always made her laugh! But she just kept on walking, walking off and up the stairs, out of the garage and into her world, whatever the hell it was like in there. He was shocked. It had been a while, but really who was mad at who? What the hell gave her the right to suddenly be so cold, after all he had done for her, after all she didn't even know he had done for her. . . .

When Marvin thought about that—that aggressive disregard, that steely cold shoulder—he tuned back in to Gigi, and threw her a few strong nods as she continued to go on about the card. Suddenly Marvin felt the need to add, "Yeah, well maybe girlfriend had some bitch in her from the get-go."

"'Your old friend,' it says! Damn right, your *old* friend!" Gigi was hollering through bites of her third slice. "As if I couldn't tell you that. And does her towelhead ass even celebrate Christmas? What, is she trying to look normal or something? C'mon, Marv, you know, *they're* sketchy. . . ."

Marvin had to admit he understood that *they*. "Well, I mean, it's odd that we've never seen that husband of hers."

226

"I see all sorts of weird dark-haired guys in this building and I think it's him each time! But, hell, I don't know. *Their* type can disguise themselves—look Jew, look Hispanic, you know. That's how all those Jews get killed by the Palestinians—they disguise, I tell you, they look like whoever they want. But I'm telling you, *they're* sketchy and her man is sketchy. She'd tell me things, I mean, I *know* he was abusive. That's how *they* are with their wives—beat them and shit, put them in veils, they don't care, they'll get the virgins when they're dead!"

Marvin nodded. "She'd always have to sneak out, it's true."

"Yeah, her husband, her son! What the hell kind of woman has these hidden men that she has to run from?! And I tell you, her son being in New York, hmmm, makes you wonder. I mean, obviously he's okay or else she'd need us then—you can bet she'd be in here needing her old family if he wasn't. But he's okay, in New York. Wonder what he does? Piloting maybe?" She cackled wildly. "But you know what I mean . . . I'm saying, who are these people? Where's she from again, Iraq?! One of those countries, that's all I know!" She replaced her empty plate and his still full one with a box of supermarket-brand doughnuts for dessert. "I'll be honest, Marvy, I barely remember girlfriend—I mean, *Bitch*. Who cares anyway? I'm not caring about those places, those people, that's the lesson here—I'm just glad we're out in the west where we don't have to bother with caring about it. They don't want us. And you know what? We don't want them."

"I'd have to agree with you. . . ." he said, slowly, remembering something, a bit of evidence that could be the final nail in the coffin for ol' Lala, a now ancient insult that he had let flake off him like dandruff—oh, it had been nothing at the time but when he thought of it now, in the context of everything, oh, he could feel his ancestors shuddering. "I mean, do you know what bullshit she told me once. . . ." He was getting furious just thinking about it, how did he just take it, why did he just let her take him on that ride, was he even remembering right, could it really be . . . "that Santa in her country was black!"

"Bullshit!" Gigi hooted through lips and chin coated white with doughnut sugar, shaking her head, sending sugar gunpowder out her nose and mouth with every angry groan and moan, as if she were some incensed candyland dragon. "What bullshit she would send our way! What insults! Girlfriend Bitch was head-to-toe bullshit."

Marvin took half a doughnut, mesmerized by the memory of his acquiescence and her outright, unashamed, downright racist, yes, *bullshit*. "Big black Osama bin Santa!" he chuckled bitterly, in a voice and manner he found a bit unlike himself—but so what, he was angry. Anger could do that. After all he had done, he felt entitled. He was in the good and it felt good to be in the good. *Let her have her nutballs brother, they deserve each other.*

They both sat back satisfied, smiling silently at each other once it was all off their chests. They were even more content, however, once they changed the subject, both noticing they were starting to go into areas they knew nothing about—deep in their hearts they did admit this—and they feared sounding stupid even to themselves out loud—and besides, the conversation was doner than done to them, who the hell cared—and the whole matter, it was far away, East Coast and Middle East, and even though *she* was right there the whole time, just a few stucco walls away, she had in a way made herself farther away, to them at least. And that was just fucking fine with them.

*   *   *

It was a mistake that would bring Darius Adam back to his senses— or at least, back to his old self.

During his period of insufficient sleep and emotional breakdown, Darius had begun making more mistakes than usual. He'd write numbers on the chalkboard and they'd come out all wrong. He began letting class out early. He soon began canceling more and more classes. He considered taking a leave of absence, but he knew they couldn't live without his working. So he continued to operate some-how and the mistakes became more and more frequent. At home kettles burned, toilets overflowed, the car stalled and stalled and stalled, bills got misplaced, and messages got erased. The House of Adam was so seeped in chaos that Lala Adam didn't even think to get mad at him when he began accidentally opening the few pieces of mail she ever got.

He was about to absently toss all the day's mail into the trash, assuming it was all solicitations, when suddenly one envelope got his attention and snapped him out of his autopilot fog for a mo-ment. It was a strangely crumpled envelope, personal-looking, not businesslike, with their address in a human script that he could not recognize, a cryptic New York postmark and a Brooklyn sender address . . . he quickly added up that it could be about Xerxes, his only New York connection, and so with just that bare minimum of thought he tore into it, not bothering to note that it was addressed to "L. Adam," not "D. Adam."

It was worse than he thought. As he nauseously struggled to follow the dizzying loops and curves of the blue ink that ran against and over all the notebook lines, two things were clear: it was for his wife and it was from a man. A man who, even though he was writing in English, knew enough of the old her to call her *Laleh*—that word was piercingly clear. Darius did not hesitate to read it all the way through, or rather to read what he could of the impassioned scrawl: *I know, it has been years . . . I am sorry. . . . I wonder often about you. . . . Just thought in case you knew where I am now, that I am fine here. . . . It gets hard. . . . And I am better. . . . Maybe one day again. . . . I have been in Brooklyn, and many other places, in hospitals off and on.* And to end it, the most painfully legible words in the entire letter: *Yours, Bob.*

Hers! She had a fucking Brooklyn hospital Bob!

He sat there fuming, not sure how to proceed, so angry that he forgot to notice he had been jump-started back to his old self. Like a coloring book line drawing a kindergartner colors in crudely—adding so much vibrant color that the strokes jut out past the lines—the sick-barely-there Darius Adam began to quickly soak up so much of his old passion so quickly that the red hotness in his face could barely contain itself. He was almost glowing, over-injected with the heat of humanity suddenly—except in the bad way, the very very bad way.

After all, it was an emergency; there was a new struggle before him! He had never thought to suspect Lala of anything—now he wondered how could he have lived so naïvely. It had just never been an issue or a possibility. For all he knew, she had barely ever existed outside him. His woman who had lived only in Eden Gardens and their Tehran residence, what other life could she have possibly lived these years? She rarely went anywhere—some work, some babysitting, some palling with that old housekeeper . . . but who knew? He could certainly add "liar" to her list of crimes—and she did have a list. Lala was no angel—he may have never suspected *adulteress*—but he certainly never thought *angel*. Who knew what she did all day when he was gone? How she lived? How the hell could he expect a human to have lived all those years, just passing time alone like that anyway? Certainly he couldn't do it. What did she do with herself every day until he came home? Certainly boredom could breed mischief. Ah, the *jendeh*, he thought, *the prostitute,* certainly there was a chance he would do the same but . . . *BUT. Enough:* he could not allow himself to empathize. This was murder they were talking about. This was Darius Adam: done. His final undoing. A son who had cut himself off, a wife who was living the worst kind of lie—*Oh, how do men keep themselves alive with these fates? Or others alive?* He could suddenly feel the hot rage of movie villains, the blurred vision, the steely sweat, the headful of mayhem. He could not wait till she came home from work. Or wherever the hell she was.

As life goes, she happened to come home late that evening from the school, where they were having a winter recital.

Without noticing him, she kicked off her shoes, suggested they order pizza, bitched about some incident with the "damn Pledge of Allegiance" and what did the kids' barely mumbled "indivisible" really mean to anyone anyway?

When he was able to finally unclench his jaw to speak, when he could finally remobilize his muscles enough to present the torn letter lodged in his fist, when he managed to get the anger in him under control enough to do a thing like walk and stand, just stand, as close as he could up to her face—*her not-even-blinking, heavily make-upped, used, old terrible* jendeh *face,* he thought—he said one word: "WHO."

She was absently walking to the bathroom, when suddenly she was stopped by his hand on her wrist.

"IS."

She was forced to meet his eyes, eyes she had lately simply ignored as they had grown so dead. But this time she couldn't believe it. It was *him.* "Darius?" she whispered, squinting, trying to really make him out, like someone ascertaining the identity of a long-lost love. But it was all there, the redness in the face, the heavy breath, the fists, the awful energy—it was beautiful, she thought. "Why . . . hello!" she laughed. "Welcome back!" She wanted to cry with happiness—*What I would have given these last weeks to see this horrible old guy back! Oh, throw a fit, Darius, for me, please! Break something! Say something horrible, my dear!*

"BOB."

He waved the letter right up to her face and she tried to get a glimpse. "What, what are you up to?" she snapped, playfully. Too tired to solve riddles and too heartened by his newfound health to care, she waited for him to get to the point—it would come once his tantrum kicked in. It did, too, soon, and he took the letter, let it crumple just a bit—just to symbolically damage, but not fatally wound, the evidence—and then shoved it hard at her chest.

Shaking her head, she took one hand to her heart, and removed the paper that had actually managed to hurt, stabbing into her cleavage like that. Darius stomped to their bedroom, knowing if he didn't let it all go behind closed doors there was the danger that he'd let it all go on her, *Let it all go to hell, to hell, everything, wife, son, life, everything hell*—and he searched, looking in the room that held the bed they had shared for so long, for the perfect thing to break: bulbs, mirrors, framed photos, her perfumes, whatever could have the greatest hurt-power *for the rotten backstabbing slutting bitch,* when suddenly he froze at the sound in the living room . . . of Lala . . . laughing? But it was not her usual hard bitter laugh. He listened more carefully. No, it was a different sound, a sound he had rarely heard if ever, he thought. It was the opposite sound: Lala Adam was sobbing.

Good, he thought, *really good,* he tried to think further, but something was preventing him from enjoying it. It was a stranger, deeper type of crying, a type that didn't make him feel triumphant. It was—the only way he could describe it—the sound of a child, a little little girl, a little-girl Lala, suddenly broken in a horrible wounded lament.

He rushed to her to see if his instinct was right.

It had to be, as there she was suddenly on her knees—no, not in the manner of a woman with an affair exposed—hunched over the letter, which again was where he had shoved it, hard against her heart, now getting soaked by tears unlike any he had ever seen her shed, truly a bawling baby's, her sounds high and hoarse and wordless and unstoppable. He kept saying, "what-what," even trying his hardest to let the old anger melt enough to kneel at her side, to hold her, to forget he suspected—it just could not be, he suddenly now knew—to even kiss her, until she finally let the sobbing taper off to a raspy whisper.

"Bob," she almost mouthed, the sound was so small, "Bob is . . . Bobak."

A Farsi name, fine, he thought. But suddenly he got worried that it was still what he thought it was, only this time a Persian hospital-ridden Brooklyn lover. *Even worse.*

"And Bobak . . . is . . . ." her voice broke into sobs again, but this time she reined them in, still on her knees, grabbing for his hand in a gesture that was more for help than affection, "my one, only, brother."

And as if that wasn't enough for Darius to suddenly join her on his knees, too, about to lose it like her, too, finally lose it for that letter in the right way, she added through another round of tears, "That I had lost. . . ."

*　　*　　*

Three thousand miles across the country, on that big night of Christmas Eve, Suzanne found herself back at the old dazed complacency that made up the personality of her adolescent self. She was back in what her mother called Parlor Number One, one of several "parlors" in a house that wasn't quite her old house (it was, however, a replication of the house she grew up in) but close enough and in, of course, upstate New York as well. But this new one was not in their old Westchester of white-collar professionals—nobody really worked over here in Dutchess County, land of country homes and summer homes. Sure, the Westchester house still existed—handed down to some relative of Suzanne's that she didn't know—and there was the Upper East Side apartment which they rented out primarily to friends of Suzanne, but this, what her mother called the Dutchess Cottage—if by "cottage" one meant a nine-bedroom, four-bathroom estate, equipped with tennis court and pool, complete with garden and pond and a separate guest house over the garage—this was The One, as Suzanne's father called it, The One just being another name for what they were certain simply had to be true: it was everyone's dream.

Christmas Eve dinner was one of their few family traditions and so they all made the most of their time, while waiting for their final houseguest to arrive: the yet-to-be-met boyfriend, that Xerxes Adam. Suzanne's father Al (short for "Ali," which he'd conversely claim as a nickname for "Al," really, whenever, to his consternation, it revealed itself) and her mother Eleanor had been dressed for Christmas Eve all day, with nothing more to do than resign themselves to their favorite chairs. Anita their housekeeper brought endless rounds of holiday goodies: candied almonds, mulled wine, baked Brie, peppermint cakes, gingerbread crisps, eggnog, and even Eleanor's favorite, courtesy of the Starbucks Web site—*'cause if there's one thing I miss about the city it's all the Starbucks!*—eggnog lattes! It was truly a happy holiday for the couple with their one and only child in town, and she looking lovely as usual: Suzanne, just *exquisite, radiant, tremendous, darling,* in a dark green crushed-velvet dress, lightly patterned black tights, and patent leather heels. Her seemingly ungentrifiable hair was tamed and bound back into a single long braid, a style her mother adored as it somehow fell into a nice sync with Eleanor's own meticulously slicked, tightly bunned, amber coif. Eleanor, too, had opted for a little velvet trimming on a black satin suit, highlighted with pearl earrings and a pearl choker, further highlighted by her newly manicured red nails—a color she seldom visited, but, well, it was the holidays and a lady had to be festive. Al had agreed and put on a maroon tie—the closest he'd dare go to red—with his favorite three-piece gray Italian suit. Eleanor had persuaded him to give her hairdresser another shot— he was *getting so darn gray!*—and so that day he displayed a brand-new dark brown wavy head of immaculate, enviable, artificially toned hair. *It sets off that sandy skin so nicely,* Eleanor pointed out, Eleanor of the endless umbrellas and wide-brimmed hats, who always made it known she would rather die than be anything but her rightful porcelain. *Oh, how you all go together so well!* Anita would exclaim over and over, thus volunteering herself for taking endless rounds of photos on Al's brand new palm-sized top-of-the-line digital camera, special ordered from Tokyo, just in time for the holidays. Eleanor loved the movie function and so she had made endless strings of half-minute-long movies. "Look at this one we made for you!" she had immediately shoved at Suzanne, just moments after their driver presented her at the Cottage from the local train station. Suzanne took the camera and watched the tiny grainy version of her parents, all dressed up as they were now, both popping into the wobbling frame uncertainly. Eleanor was saying, "Oh, Suzi, we can't wait to see our little Manhattan belle for our favorite holiday—" and Al was saying "We're doing the maple duck again, your favorite—" and Eleanor was adding "We're upgrading you and—oh, Al, how do you say his name—" and Al was laughing, "Zer-ziss, yeah? It's an odd one, not a common Persian—" and Eleanor cutting in with "Yes, well, we're upgrading you and Zor— I'm gonna just call him Z! How's that! Well, you two are getting the *master*-master, you know which one, *master*-master Number One, and Anita put the sweetest—" and Al cutting in with, "it's gonna cut off, Ellie, wrap it up"—and Eleanor quickly shoving her face to take up the entire frame with a crackly, fuzzy, "We love, love, love you and Merry Christmas!" and Al ending it with a swift, sufficient "Yes!"

When she had shown up without "Z," though, it had taken them at least a half hour for his absence to register. Suzanne had to bring it up. "And I should tell you that *Xerxes*—that's how you say it, Mother—is late," she said. "He's coming. He's tied up in the city."

"Oh my! Working on Christmas Eve!" Eleanor gasped.

"Well, that's the city," Al mumbled.

"Well, no," Suzanne corrected slowly. "It's not his job. Not exactly. Not yet, I mean. It's a job interview."

Eleanor put a hand to her chest and widened her eyes in alarm. "You *are* joking, Suzi," she said. "On Christmas Eve!"

"Oh, well, I mean, if it's for a good high position," Al rambled on.

It occurred to Suzanne that she had no idea what it was for. These days Xerxes was going on so many interviews for just about every-thing, she couldn't keep track. Once in a while he'd even have jobs, though even their types changed often, it seemed. At times he would have freelance this and that, hold a job for an entire month even, design this, manage that, assist this, deliver that—she didn't really ever know what he did. The struggles of young working profession-als eluded her on the whole, but it did bother her that she didn't even know what areas Xerxes specialized in. She didn't think he actually specialized in anything, though. His major, after all, it was . . . Humanities? Liberal arts? Undecided? Could you even graduate Undecided?

"I'm sure it is," Suzanne muttered. "He's very studious. Always has something." She was unsatisfied with that phony defensiveness. "I mean, sometimes he doesn't have something, like now, but it's just that he's too good for, like, everything! He gets in there and they realize he's overqualified and can't pay him enough. Or he just walks out. He really should be, like, ruling the world or something. That type."

"Oh my, this Z, he sounds like *something* already!" Eleanor laughed nervously to herself, taking a big swig of her latte.

"Please don't call him that," Suzanne almost snapped and then, embarrassed by her tenseness, softened it with a, "His name begins with an X. Can you do 'X' at least?"

They spent that endless afternoon, then endless evening, being a family again, occasionally engaging Anita and, of course, Fyodor, Al's elderly borzoi; and Lola, Eleanor's Scottish terrier. Suzanne relaxed, even able to admit there were *some* good things about being home. Her spare, intentionally average East Village apartment made her forget where she came from—which was usually the plan, the preferred route of sanity, but once a year, once or twice or three times, when her parents invited her, it was nice to go back to that other style of living, *her* other style of living, that the Cottage, in fact, managed to re-create with almost alarming stone cold precision.

Finally, when dinnertime grew close, with Anita growing noticeably restless and still no Xerxes—*His train must be delayed, it's so busy this time of year,* Suzanne kept insisting, even pretending to dial his cell phone—Eleanor suggested that *a perfectly lovely way to pass the time* would be to hit the presents, a single present opened early for each, as ritual dictated. *Too bad for our tardy gentleman caller—he'll have to wait to open his!* Eleanor's sentiment made Suzanne nervous—of course they would have done that, gotten him a present. While she dreaded discovering what it could be, she decided it was best to quietly respect her family's all-inclusive class. Certainly there would be other battles to fight before the night was over. . . .

Suzanne had actually checked her bank balance on the way to the Cottage and assumed the well-measured fattening of The Account *was* her present but apparently not. She picked out the first box Fyodor sniffed in her pile.

"She can do that one if she does another one, too," Al said. "That one is kind of a . . . joke?" He looked to Eleanor for help.

"It's *really* not," Eleanor added, "but it, well, we like to think it *also* has a humor component."

Suzanne nodded, smiling, curious to know what could have inspired this unprecedented comic streak in her parents. The package, like all the presents, was in a perfect professionally wrapped box. She quickly made her way through the layers of gold and silver and lifted the lid to unveil a . . .

"Oh my God—what the hell?!!" Suzanne found herself almost screaming as she removed a very heavy, rather dirty-looking, black rubber-metal-wire-twisted . . . monstrosity. She had no idea. It looked like something out of a nightmare.

"Yes, well, it's a . . ." Eleanor laughed softly, a bit nervously, avoiding eye contact with the thing, pretending to be deeply engaged in petting Lola, while shooting a couple of glances to Al for help.

"It's," he paused, trying to smile, a bit embarrassed, until finally getting another glare from Eleanor to go ahead, "It's, you know, a gas mask. An Israeli Army gas mask. The real deal. They're hard to get . . . these days."

Suzanne confronted it, horrified, stunned. She lifted the thing close to her head but couldn't even bear a lighthearted trying it on. It was awful. It was not even funny. It was. . . . "Breathtaking," she muttered.

"Now, now, Suzi, it's like your father said, a joke!" Eleanor exclaimed, scrambling to liven the mood. "Kind of, at least! But you know, it's also for *just in case*—and that's like the silliest *just in case* ever, not even one in a hundred gazillion!—but let's just be silly and say that *just in case,* darling, it does work!"

Al cleared his throat and added, "What your mother's trying to say is that it's not something you're going to use, we know that. But good to have, no? You know, just pop it where the emergency kit is. . . . You live in Manhattan, dear, I know these things have been selling out like hotcakes, everyone has them. . . ."

Suzanne nodded. "Thanks," she said numbly, and was quickly shoved the other gift. She opened it on total autopilot, mind still reeling with *I can't believe they got me a fucking gas mask.* This one made sense: a large pink mohair bear with a pure silver Tiffany's choker tight around its fat neck like a collar. She thanked them with a smile and nod. Yet another Tiffany's necklace—*but their latest de-sign!* as Eleanor reminded her, as it had been all the other years— it was her third or fourth at least. She could add it to the *sell-on-eBay* pile.

Suzanne couldn't bring herself to complain—not about the necklace, at least. Her present for Al was yet another silk tie, after all—although this time a riskier grass green and from Saks, not Barneys—as it was every year. For Eleanor, too, it was yet another gift certificate to some trendy new downtown spa that she would never visit, but that Suzanne felt responsible for at least trying to expose her to. She found trying to be original or extravagant with the gifts embarrassing anyway—it was The Account that was dishing it out, after all, not her.

They all smiled and thanked and hugged and that was that. Eleanor revealed in a dramatic, hushed voice that Xerxes's gift was an extremely high-tech fancy alarm clock, also special-ordered from Tokyo. "I mean, we don't know him, so I thought the price of the thing could do the talking! Ha!" Eleanor laughed to herself.

Suzanne would have dry-heaved at that if she weren't nervously staring at her watch. It was late. Presents done, small talk over, Anita shuffling, stomachs rumbling, *shit.* Still no Xerxes.

Eleanor, true master of pretension, pretended it was no big deal. "Oh, let's just sit back, have some more mulled wine—Anita, can you get the fireplace going—and . . . talk! Tell us about him!"

"I hear he has something in common with seventy-five percent of your father," Al added, with a wink.

"Suzi darling, what does he look like?" Eleanor asked.

Suzanne thought about it. What did he look like? She remembered thinking that exact sentence a lot in their first few weeks of still undefined partnership—what was it that attracted her to him? Certainly she had dated more handsome men in her life—that one country boy in Tuscany, the several charming nearsighted and pea-coated New England college boys, the older chain-smoking Upper East Side architect with his many dogs and many hats, the Midwest musician with all the quaint tattoos, hell, even that one burly street poet from Brooklyn! Xerxes was not visually, say . . . *breathtaking*. He was not unattractive either—there was nothing wrong with him. But he wasn't . . . well, she could imagine her mother thinking he wasn't up to par with her visuals. And she didn't want the clichés to be true—*Oh, but he's so beautiful inside; oh, but you should see his heart; oh, but to my eyes he's the most*—but it had some true elements. She couldn't judge anymore. She loved him. She couldn't see him that way. He was hers. She'd started carrying pictures of them to show to girlfriends who'd always comment on them—*Oh, you're so cute together; oh, you guys look so happy; oh, he looks like he cares about you so much; oh, look at how content you seem with him*—but never on what she'd be getting at. What did they make of *him?* She didn't know and she couldn't tell, and when she thought back to her first encounter with him for evidence of what impression that initial exposure left, she was alarmed to register him as a nothing, remembering him as downright faceless, invisible, in fact, a voice, a presence, but certainly not a man, not obviously her man— and especially a nothing when juxtaposed next to that evening's historic black and bloody skyline.

"He's tall and dark," Suzanne said slowly. "And . . . handsome. Sure. He's, you know, Father, you know, from Iran. He has that look."

"Strong features, big eyes, curly hair," Al rattled off. "Lucky if he's not short and stocky, I'll tell you that. Thank goodness for my other twenty-five percent!"

"*Truuuly!*" Eleanor laughed along. "Okay, well, that's nice. He has that exotic thing, that's fun. Although these days . . . my, he hasn't had any . . . trouble?"

Suzanne could feel the conversation taking a bad turn. *Eleanor on Race:* it was always a doomed topic. She rolled her eyes. "We live in New York City, Mother!"

"Exactly!" she said. "Exactly my point. Of all cities, if any city had a right . . ."

"You know, she means people might take their anger and," her father paused, "act out, say, *discriminatorily.*"

Suzanne moaned. "Please, can you not talk like this when he comes?" she blurted out and then, a bit ashamed by the silence that she had caused, added, "I mean, I know what you mean. And no, as far as I know, he hasn't had any trouble."

"Where do his parents live?" Eleanor asked, reaching absently for a glass, a glass of anything, anything *alcoholic hopefully.* "And what do they do?"

"Los Angeles," Suzanne said, racing through the paperwork in her brain for their occupations. "The mother, she's . . . I don't think she works. And his father . . . I think teaches. Math and some science maybe, I think."

Al nodded approvingly. "Ah, they're probably one of those wealthy LA Iranians," he chuckled to himself, "who don't really need *job*-jobs. Jews?"

Eleanor eyed the Christmas tree in alarm. "Oh, no! Jew?"

Suzanne refrained from letting her annoyance take over and made do with a shake of her aching head.

More silence. Suzanne looked at Fyodor, Suzanne looked at Lola. The dogs ignored everyone. Al eyed Eleanor; Eleanor eyed him back.

"Well, okay. . . ." Eleanor murmured, gesturing to Anita to fill their glasses some more. "Then, so, one has to ask, what is he . . . is he. . . ."

"I mean, he has to be then, isn't he. . . ." Al wondered, scratching his newly thick-fringed forehead over and over in a ticlike reflex.

Oh, they were nervous. She knew what they meant. And Suzanne was happy she could say, "Well, historically sure, they must have been. But Xerxes has always told me his family and he himself . . . well, they're not Muslim at all."

Eleanor broke into a smile, eyed Al, Al eyed her back, *affirmative?* But Al still looked unsettled. His own family had been like that—*historically Muslim,* in fact, was a term she had heard him use—but it was his twenty-five percent that had propelled the move to America earlier in that last century and converted them to the New Land's unofficial religion. Al considered himself Christian—after all, you had to be something, which is why he couldn't take it and had to ask, "Well, what the heck is he then?"

Suzanne thought about that. She really didn't know. She didn't think he was anything. It was always what he was *not* that they talked about.

"He's not very religious," she said, quickly adding, "but believes in God." She couldn't even say if that was true, but it was very possible—and hopefully a means to cap the current conversation into complacency.

Eleanor smiled widely. "As long as Christmas doesn't bother him, whatever he is doesn't bother us!"

But later in the evening—as Anita's rounds of mulled wine continued and then were followed by Eleanor's request for spiked coffees, spiced rum Jamaican coffees, *Just for the hell of it,* Eleanor kept insisting, deep in the type of tipsy that demanded everyone be tipsier—Suzanne's mother started singing another tune. Suddenly it was the old Mother she remembered and remembered dreading, no doubt about to bring out the old Father she remembered and remembered resenting.

"So, what does he make of Iran today? Appalling, no?" Eleanor continued with her inquiry, her red lips now drunkenly curling into her old classic cruel smile.

"Your mother means their government," Al added.

"I mean, the country's just another nail in the Mid East coffin!" she cried, one hand in a fist even, suddenly. "Do you know your father doesn't know a single person in that dratted country anymore? Not a single! All the relatives, out! Paris, London, Stockholm, *out!* Thank goodness."

Suzanne looked at Al and he nodded along, preferring to observe Fyodor and Lola over either of them. The dogs looked half there, bored, sick, tired of life.

Suzanne could feel the evening's many exasperations heading to a boiling point inside her. Suddenly the many wasted hours and especially her mother, the ivory WASP sovereign, were getting to her, with her father as the almost exotic sidekick, and their warped morals and their pretty-sitting offenses—*and their fucking Israeli Army gas mask, just in case!* It was too much. She had to, for a second, be herself.

"You know, I would like to visit Tehran," she dared toss into the already troubled waters.

Eleanor took a highly indelicate gulp of the hot caffeinated booze that burned her throat, making her gasp out with an exaggerated grotesqueness, "Excuse me—I don't think so, Suzi, not so fast—oh, what, has your little boyfriend asked you to go to the motherland! Al, thank God, never ever—"

"There was never a chance, with the Revolution and all, and frankly I don't know the place," Al quickly, quietly, tensely interjected.

"No, in fact, Xerxes has never ever spoken of wanting to go," Suzanne snapped back, her own voice rising a bit, too, the force of the caffeine and alcohol equaling a perfect belligerence. "In fact, I think he has no interest. But I . . . you do remember, Mother, I *am* half Iranian!"

"Almost half," her parents corrected in perfect fucking unison.

It was true, but it upped the level of Suzanne's pissedness even more. "Okay, fine! But I think one day I would like to see the land where I am almost half from, damn it!!"

Eleanor slammed her glass, rudely snapping Fyodor and Lola back to consciousness. "Pipe down, Suzanne!" she barked. "This is Christmas Eve!"

"Your mother is just thinking it's not a smart idea to fantasize about the Middle East in times like this," Al added, a bit frantically, "when, let's just face it, there is no more dangerous region in the world."

Suzanne could feel her anger making her about to flip her lid. She was ready to lose it the way she used to when she was a teenager, when there were no people in the world more despicable than Al and Eleanor. "No more dangerous place! Hello!!! Try New York City!!!"

Eleanor cackled bitterly. "Oh, good example, good example, Suzi! And why is that? Why oh why is that? Because your darling little Middle East came to us!"

Suzanne wanted to rip that gleaming bun off her stupid head. She hadn't felt so violent in ages. "I want you to think about what you say, Mother, before you say it—September eleventh was not just about the Middle East—and certainly not Iran—and you can't just clump everything together like that, it's not right, it's downright ignorant, and frankly when I said I wanted to go to Iran—which I do and which I assure you one day I will—I didn't mean this month or soon, I meant one day! And I promise you I will and I promise you it will be fine and will resemble nothing like whatever your image of hijackers and fundamentalists and God knows whatever else is, goddamn it!"

"You can stop damning God right now, Suzanne," Eleanor hissed, pointing to the tree as if it were Jesus in the room. But she was outraged and now she was shaking, shoving her empty glass into Anita's stomach for more, Anita also shaking and shocked, used to nothing but Eleanor's immaculate WASP reserve. And she went on, "Because, Suzanne, you will never change me—your father never did! I know what I know and I know it wasn't me, it wasn't us, we didn't cause that hell, we didn't ask for trouble, your darling little Middle East, it came to us . . . !"

And just as it was all happening—Eleanor suddenly standing tall in her heels, shaking, practically jiggling in the equal but opposite way of, say, a Santa, face redder than holly and flushed deeper than a Rudolph nose, madly ranting, like the clockwork of bells, like the mechanized tidings of a battery-operated angel, over and over, "your darling little Middle East, it came to us!" only further cartoonized with Al trying to interject, looking to Suzanne yet at the same time managing to nod when Eleanor's eyes would meet his, and Fyodor and Lola suddenly tossing in every bark and whine known to canine in agreement/dissent, and Anita scrambling to the kitchen to prepare another highly complicated poisonous drink to obediently fuel her mistress's fire, and Suzanne just sitting there looking up at her mother as she did when she was a child, in disgust and fury and a little fear—and just as the words "your darling little Middle East, it came to us" were volleying from wall to wall with the spirited acoustics of an encored anti-carol, just as the Cottage's Christmas Eve had hit its all-time climax . . . the doorbell rang, and on the other side, indeed, it *had* come to them: a very tired, sweating, tall, dark, handsome-ish young man in an ill-fitting suit, holding potted grocery store chrysanthemums, automatically rattling off apologies.

*   *   *

And just like that the atmosphere in the Adam household turned upside down. Bob's letter ushered in the first season of happiness that they could remember since Tehran. Another dull California holiday season suddenly transformed into the first spring of Lala Adam's life—the next morning she called in sick, bought flowers, dusted and cleaned and scrubbed and polished, and instead of walking outside simply walked inside the length of the apartment, pacing barefoot on the carpet and laughing into the ceilinged heavens like a most blissful caged madwoman.

She referred to the episode only as *My Miracle.*

For days she even put off writing back. She let the letter sit there on her dresser and would wake up each morning excitedly to re-read it as if for the first time. But when she finally decided after a week that she couldn't delay it any more, the text came out quicker and easier—although more feverish and disorganized, she had to admit—than anything she had ever composed in English,

Dearest Bobak,

Hello it is your Sister Laleh—by the way, they call me Lala now, my Name is changed, but that's okay, call me anything you wish! But WOW, what an amazing Gift, what a most great Surprise, what a thrilling thrill! I thought, how can this happen, it is a <u>MIRACLE</u> really! WOW is all I can say!

I have a family here in California and my Son, who is 26, lives near you in New York somewhere and you should see him! But maybe I will see you soon too! I will come, tell me when! Why are you in a Hospital?

Most <u>important</u> is what is your Phone Number? Mine is (626) 791-2135. We must call and talk! A LOT! We lost so many years!

Do you speak Farsi still? You must but I write in English in case!

You have always been in my head—as they say in our language, *Khali Dellam Tang Shodeh:* My Guts Has Been Made Very Tight Because Of You Not Being Around!

<u>I LOVE YOU, MY AZIZ!</u>
Your sister LALEH or LALA
PS. How did you find me? WRITE ME SOON!

She thought she might know the answer to the last question but she wasn't sure. She remembered crying into Marvin's arms long ago and him assuring her the world was a small place and they would be reunited, but she could not recall how he thought he could help. Nonetheless she left a message on Gigi's cell phone asking for Marvin's phone number, since, to her amazement, Lala didn't even know his last name to look him up. Without getting into it too much, Lala's message to Gigi pleaded gently, *Please call me back, even though it has been so long you may not want to, but I may need you to, because perhaps I need to thank Marvin, I don't know.* She was not surprised when she did not get a call back—she decided perhaps it was for the best, as, after all, the mystery would be unveiled when her brother and she were reunited. In a way, she preferred imagining it was the work of the gods, rather than some thuggish New York agents of Marvin's. So she kissed the sealed envelope several times and gingerly placed it in the mailbox, as if without extreme love and care it would disintegrate and the whole dream would shatter.

Darius, meanwhile, was also better. He had his reasons: A) Of course, as her husband, he was simply happy for her and Her Miracle. B) It would no doubt mean a kinder, gentler Lala Adam, as he had always suspected that the tragedies of her childhood were what had made her so *hard.* C) Now she could focus on some other guy and leave him alone to obsess about his own messed-up life in peace.

And eventually D) came, just a couple of weeks after her letter was sent. Her Miracle became *His* Inspiration, as it suddenly set off a floating lightbulb over his head, so dazzling and pure that it could have been mistaken for a halo. Suddenly Darius, too, saw the potential for being *saved.*

It first came up on a particular night in their Season of Happiness, right after the first love they had made in a scarily long while. He was lying exhausted, entranced, amazed that her body could still feel familiar after so long. She was humming to herself like a schoolgirl, in a way he had never heard before, intensely alive. The world suddenly seemed safe, peaceful, loving. The darkness of night was suddenly nourishing and comforting, rather than torturous and demon-filled. Darius Adam was poised to be blessed, he decided. *What's the American saying again?* he thought, smiling to himself. *Something about how you get lucky when you get lucky?*

Her humming abruptly ended and in one sentence, she let the remnants of her luck pour all over him. "Oh, Darius! God, don't you think that's it?"

And as if he could feel something *hot* was in her, he didn't question it, he just egged it on: "Say it, woman, just say it. . . ."

"Well," Lala began, her voice sounding sweeter to him than ever, "You know, for many years nobody had any hope for my brother. When I say he was lost, I mean he *was* lost. People only had rumors, nobody could reach him, and soon I couldn't even reach the nobodies who couldn't reach him! He was gone to me. This is really My Miracle. But you know, all it took was my brother deciding to write to me and suddenly he was found. Things don't need to be lost always. There are ways to reach someone, and successfully. And if I can hear from the one person I was never supposed to hear from, certainly you could reach out, too? If I were more superstitious I could say this thing happened with something more in store for you, too! Not that it's a sign, but well . . . Darius, do you know what I'm saying?"

He knew immediately. "I could write Xerxes a letter," he uttered perfectly, as if hypnotized, like a magician's lovely assistant eager to submit herself for onstage dismembering.

She applauded and hugged him and kissed him and they fell asleep in each other's arms. That night, Darius slept well believing in it all, suddenly able to *believe*.

As it goes with Darius Adam, the sentiment did not quite last. The next morning, when he awoke, the whole thing had lost its shimmer—the bright halo had slipped down a bit, threatening to become a burning noose around his neck. *It wasn't My Miracle, it might not even be My Inspiration,* he thought. After all, what could a letter do that couldn't be solved with a phone call—Lala: *As if you would! Ha! You would never call him, you know that*—and she was right, but it was as if Lala was asking him to believe in something more abstract than the will of God . . . the inherent magic of letters perhaps, as if it were the medium her brother had chosen that had made the thing come together, as if those little pieces of envelope you shoved into those big blue boxes on the street would then go to some fairy farm to be placed into the beaks of mystical carrier pigeons, who would fly so high they would glaze the letters in the divine haze of the heavens, and by creating the invisible ribbon of connection across the globe at any distance, bequeath the lost with their long-sought communication. . . . *Oh, it's madness, even if beautiful madness!* Darius thought, again feeling pessimism coat his very afraid insides.

"Darius, there is no other choice," his wife insisted, bringing him a sheet of paper and a pen, as if the tools were half the battle. "Now you are going to do this."

The flip side was that when one considered to do *beautifully mad* things, one was already at the point where there was nothing to lose. So he nodded slowly, still slightly unconvinced, and took the pen. He noticed his hands were shaking badly. He could sense her watching him with a teary-eyed smile.

"You're going to just watch me like that?" Darius asked. "It will take a while, you know."

She wiped her eyes. "Just for a bit," she murmured, and a bit embarrassed, in a voice that was barely perceptible, added, "I want to imagine him—you know, see what it looks like when a lost man reaches out to his lost loved one."

It was too much, what she had said. He could not turn back, as much as he wanted to. And so he gathered the courage to, right in front of her, in wobbly script, write down the first two words:

Dear Son

He wrote several drafts that evening, all the way into the early hours of the morning. He even chose special stationery—that of a Zoroastrian temple he had once visited—hoping it would somehow, as much as he was ashamed to believe in it, "bless" the letter. In the end the draft he chose was the shortest, just a list really, summing up his life. He did not want to seem intrusive—he wanted to be *natural*. The problem was that he had forgotten how to be natural with his son—he worried they had never been natural to begin with.

Feel free not to respond, as I predict anyway, he decided to end it with, for Opposite Day's sake. Now that was natural. That was *him*. His son might even appreciate that—an old bit of the father he had to remember, as well as a gesture toward an out. Charm + utility!

Because as much as he longed for a letter back, he did not need Xerxes to be aware of that. The whole operation had to be blessed with normalcy—if it could come across as normal, while it actually felt abnormal to Darius, there would be some hope for success.

In the morning, with little sleep to keep him standing—still, the last few weeks of sleep disturbances had kept him used to operating in such poor physical condition—he took the letter to the post office.

"You really did it?" Lala asked later that evening, when he announced it to her. "You really, really did it, Darius?!"

"Yes," he said numbly. He did not know how to feel. Mostly, it made him nervous.

"Well, that is wonderful!" she cried. She looked at him piercingly and said firmly, "Darius, something will have to come of this, you understand me? Something will come, we must be patient!" Her words for a second seemed more desperate than assuring. It had already been several weeks since she had sent out her letter and, although she was nowhere near losing hope, the waiting was tough at times. "You have to want it so bad. Do you want something good to happen, Darius? Are you open to it?"

He thought about it and imagined the mystical great white carrier pigeon skimming clouds on the way to the other coast, finally presenting the letter to a boy whose face he could not see, the boy taking the letter in his hands, then the boy creating his own, handing that one over to the bird, the bird doing its thing again, and the magical ribbon of communication making it to its promised full circle. He nodded.

The letter made it. But Darius Adam never found out for sure, because the letter's ultimate home was atop a generous blanket of dust under the wire springs of a steel bed frame in one corner of the East Village apartment of Xerxes Adam.

And if the pigeon could have argued the delivery status in any way with Darius Adam, it would have insisted the ribbon had not yet snapped—it was just very tautly tugged now, as tensely as two points could pull a line before its breaking.

Part Seven
Homelands

They held the fort on New Year's 2002. That was their joke. *Oh, we're not going to do anything—nah, we think we'll skip it—we hate New Year's anyway—we're gonna play it safe—oh, we're just gonna hold the fort that night, just this year.* Xerxes shrugged it off halfheartedly. *As if the fort could be held,* was what he really thought. The fort couldn't even be counted on to properly exist, much less be held by anyone.

Still, people expected another worst and pretended they didn't, as 2001, to the *good riddance* of all, did away with itself.

8:30 p.m., Pacific Time: Lala and Darius's New Year's Eve celebration consisted of simply staying tuned. They had stopped making a big deal of it once Xerxes was grown—the young Xerxes after all was the force that would get them to tune in to Dick Clark one minute, that would, the next minute, order them to the balcony to watch the fire in the sky and listen to gunshots while he stayed inside holding his breath, reminding them to hurry back in when he sensed it had to be over, eager to trade in spectacle for normalcy. Their New Year's Eve observance was scheduled for exactly a half hour before the East Coast's New Year's, with the TV on as their link. On every channel the world unabashedly put its concerned eyes on Times Square—everybody was pretending that it was just New York's New Year that year. But the televised Times Square might as well have been a taped video of years before had it not been for the many American flags and the "We Will Never Forget" banners. The still indestructible stubborn hordes gathered in full for that pin to drop. It was as if they had to; if you didn't go on with things, they said, that other *they* had won. Lala loved this spirit, this fierce, blind, backward, overdone investment. It was as if they were burning their dinner on purpose—preferring coal to food. She had lived this way every day of her life—it was her secret to survival. You let your counterintuition take over and they don't win. Neither do you, but nobody's asking.

Midnight, Eastern time (according to Suzanne's watch, still 11:55 according to Xerxes's; but they didn't argue): Suzanne began counting down and Xerxes thought to himself, after correcting her gently once, then twice, finally *Who cares, let her have it*—after all, better she be early, in case. She could still have her countdown. Better, he thought, better that he be counting down negative numbers than having his countdown cheated of its hopefully still-as-hell zero.

9:05 p.m., Pacific Time: Lala and Darius went to bed before their own New Year's. The left coast's didn't matter. Darius reminded her, mumbling as they hit the lights and crawled under the covers, that their own Iranian New Year's was still over two months away anyway.

12:05 a.m., Eastern time: When the clock struck twelve, according to *his* watch, plus an extra second or two, Xerxes sighed. They had gone through two of their midnights—it was certain. They: okay. The fort: held. A New Year. 2002. A nice even number. Palindromic. Stable. Not the first year of a millennium, the second. The children's rhyme, how did it go? *First is the worst, second is the best.* Yes. They could move on.

January 2, 2002: California was fine. New York felt okay.

Nobody on the East Coast took the kind, lesser cold of that January for granted. They deserved it, New Yorkers said. Things were getting better and the weather, it was throwing them a bone. Suzanne swore she saw people smiling more, she felt that she was breathing better, easier exhales, as if her lungs were clearing themselves of whatever residual scarring they had undergone from the bad air of the last season. *The city is being born again,* Suzanne would declare, *it's as if winter for once means renewal not death!* He was glad, but how could anyone trust it?

Because there were days—perhaps just a few days after the terror threat level had been heightened, when the news had some new tidbit to dash like extra oil onto an already burning skillet—when Xerxes would get a wave of the old tension. One time in particular that January, Suzanne and Xerxes were taking a very packed rush hour subway uptown to meet Suzanne's friends for dinner. Xerxes, rarely having had the sort of employment that would require seeing what 5:30 p.m. on the New York subways looked like, was a bit horrified at the overcrowding. There was no chance of a seat so they crammed into each other in a corner, and he held her tight to him when noticing she was also crammed against three other men. He could hear waves of conversation, some louder than others, some whispers, many coughs. So many suits, he noticed. And police. One particularly fat cop, who was in the corner talking to a thin old cop, lifted his shirt for a second in a casual scratching gesture and, totally unembarrassed and unconcerned, revealed a whole network of wiring all across and up his fat white belly. Xerxes closed his eyes—*Maybe it would just be better to close your eyes,* he told himself. But Suzanne was going on and on about Valentine's Day, where they could spend it, an island, upstate, a different state, the other coast. *Doesn't sound doable, too extreme, dunno,* Xerxes was mumbling, while opening his eyes periodically and making some worrying eye contact with someone who happened to be staring right at him. *We could get off now, take a cab,* he thought to himself, but he imagined what hell it would be to make it through all those hordes to get to the door. Even when the door opened and the train stopped it seemed as if nobody was getting off or getting in. He did not think it was a horrible exaggeration to consider them all trapped. All it would take, after all, was a tragedy outside, a tragedy beyond the glass—hell, a tragedy inside, anywhere—for their situation to register as potentially fatal entrapment. He could feel himself growing hot, then cold, then hot, over and over. In a sort of distance, spiraling gingerly through his right ear, he could just barely make out Suzanne's almost motorized rambles. The crowd was squirming, arranging and rearranging like a snake taking the shape of its route, making way, making some natural way, apparently, for a blind man to get off. His guiding stick was helping but still, in a crowd like that, people were getting prodded and poked and trying their best not to hiss. With his free hand, the blind man grabbed for poles and when he got close to them, he actually grabbed Suzanne's shoulder by mistake. *Hey*, Xerxes accidentally snapped. Several people, including Suzanne, shot him dirty looks—*What's wrong with you, he was, you know*, Suzanne whispered, upset—but the blind man was off, and the train was rumbling on. It sounded louder than usual to Xerxes. *We could get off and try a different train, maybe they're not all so bad*, he thought to himself. But he couldn't imagine making it through. It was not until they were a stop away that the train actually froze, stalling between stops—something that Xerxes was well used to in the city, but this time, he panicked. *Great*, he snapped, *what do we do?!* Hot, cold, cold, hot. Suzanne looked at him perplexed, *No big deal, Xerxes. It's just a usual stall.* Xerxes waited for the conductor, even an automated one, but nothing. He never understood why the conductors didn't communicate better. Had they seen it all? Was that it? Nothing moved them? They had forgotten that the public might not think like them? Xerxes scanned the eyes of the passengers. The cops were chuckling loudly to themselves, all the others just reading their books, eying their papers, staring at their feet, a few still looking over at him. He couldn't take it. He was burning. It had been a long time. He was freezing. *What the hell, how long has this been*, he snapped under his breath. Suzanne kissed his cheek and told him to calm down, asked if he'd ever been to the Vineyard, maybe that was a good romantic possibility? Xerxes shook his head and stared at the door's glass. Pitch-black. He could vaguely hear another train zoom by on the other tracks, without a hitch. Where were they? Were they not telling them what was going on because they were worried about public reaction? Like not telling a kid bad news to prevent crying? Were they going to be surprised? Xerxes was irate; this lack of information, this black nothing, this entrapment—they were entitled to more. He wanted to stand up and scream, *What are we all doing here anyway?* But instead, he muttered, a light mutter that Suzanne either didn't hear or found it easy enough to ignore, *I don't get it, Su, why won't it open. . . .* He suddenly felt half his body turning into ice while the other was melting into ash, perfectly splitting off each other, as if sense and nonsense, heaven and hell, were trying to tear him apart in a second. He endured it. Giving up made his panic more manageable. *What do I have to live for anyway?*—he ran that question through his head all the while the train sat immobilized. Eventually it got moving again and once out and back up and in the New York air, Xerxes, like a spring, bounced back into form—that was what New York did to you, you were Gumby, you were superhuman, you could forgive and forget, because *if you could take it there, you could take it anywhere*—and like the rest of the residents of the island, he forgot moments like those enough to take it from day to day.

*   *   *

As the newness of January wore off they began getting restless. It was getting maddening, all the waiting for nothing. Getting the mail had become an exercise in extreme maturity, a daily drill in dealing with disappointment, a constant lesson in moving on and thinking positively. It was killing Darius more than Lala even. Every evening, he and his wife would review the day's stack of nonsense mail, coupon packets, and bills hoping for *one* of their dear New York male relatives to acknowledge them, but over and over, there was nothing.

I knew it, he would grumble. *I know my son! He hates me. Why would he bother to write me that in a letter?*

Stop giving up, she would say, glad that she could keep saying it, meaning he wasn't actually there yet. *Something might happen, who knows with these lost guys?* . . .

It was a given that she would hear from her lost guy first. But when she did, it was not what she thought it would be.

"Who the hell is Carla Vane?!" she shouted out loud when the letter from Brooklyn finally came, with a return address she knew was the one that had been on his envelope, as she had memorized it long before that point. It was all very perfect except one minor detail: the sender's name. It was not Bob Nezami, it was *Carla Vane.*

Inside the envelope was Lala's letter to Bobak and the envelope she had sent it in. There was a large Post-it note stuck on the letter, with tiny, neat, old-lady-ish cursive on it. It read:

> Hello, wrong addy, no BOBACK, VANES here
> for the past 18 years. Sorry it'd open, we don't get a lot
> of wrong addies here. Good luck —Carla Vane

Carla Vane's address was printed on a gold sticker in the upper left-hand portion of her envelope, so Lala proceeded to double-check Carla's address against the one that Bobak had written on his envelope. She couldn't believe it—the addresses were identical. Did her brother really write his own address incorrectly?! Was Carla Vane lying? Was she keeping her brother hostage?!

"Maybe he doesn't want you to find him," Darius suggested.

"Why did he write in the first place then?!" she snapped.

Darius thought about it. "He said he had been in hospitals," Darius said. "Maybe he's, you know, *not all there.*"

She knew he had a point, but still it hurt to think of him that way. She decided that, fake address or not, she would have to try other routes. Namely, the ones she didn't want to try, like tracking down Marvin for possible answers. She didn't know where he lived or where he worked or anything about him these days, so again it meant calling Gigi for his cell phone number. After all, she still wondered from time to time if he had had a hand in all of this—she thought he *had* to have, but wondered how he could be lying so low when his investigation had actually succeeded.

She prayed Gigi would pick up, even though she would see Lala's number and not want to.

However Gigi, feeling especially hateful, saw the number, and did. She picked up, without a word of greeting.

"Gigi, this is Lala," said Lala, her voice shaking a bit from nervousness. They hadn't spoken in many months.

"LALA??!! LAAA-LAAA??!!!" Gigi's shrill scream disintegrated into hellish cackles and before Lala could interrupt, she was given the only answer Gigi had for her: a dial tone, and thus a decisive dead end.

Damn it! It was frustrating but instead of killing Lala's resolve, it amazingly made her stronger. She wrote a thank-you letter to Carla Vane and moved forward. There was, of course, the 4-1-1-information route: he was, of course, not listed. And then there was the Internet: when she looked him up on the library computer she did indeed find him there—first, in the most shocking context: an article about a Bob Nezami who had tried to set himself on fire in a

Kmart; and second, with his name on some activist Web site that claimed he was *Bob Nezami, of Kennedy Mental Health Center, Brooklyn, NY, 11218.* She was overjoyed at how easy it *might* be and so she called.

"Please, I am trying to find my brother who wrote to me not too long ago," she blurted out to the KMH receptionist. "His name is Nezami, N-E-Z-A-M-I—"

She was put on hold for a long time. She did not care—she had waited her entire life for this, after all. But when the receptionist got back on, she reported with no feeling whatsoever in her voice, that there was no one with that name there.

"Oh, you're kidding!" Lala shrieked. The Internet information was several years old, but she refused to believe it could bear no fruit. "Well, he was at your hospital, right?"

"Confidential, ma'am," the receptionist said.

"I just want to know if he was *ever* there!"

"We cannot give that information, ma'am. Policy."

Once Lala really lost it and demanded additional explanation *of the stupid creepy slimy sick policy,* she was put on hold again. For an even longer time. Before Lala could commit to hanging up, a supervisor with a gentle soothing voice came on the line.

Lala told her the entire story all over again.

"Okay, Mrs. Adams, if you are asking me if I would deny if a Mr. Nezami was ever here in our facility," she said, almost sounding coy, "I can tell you *no,* I could not honestly deny it. How's that? Now that's all I can give you and that's already fudging a bit with policy, so . . ."

Lala sighed. "Thank you, that's great. Now when? Around when? The last year?"

"I would *not* be able to say he was *not* here in the last year, *no*," she offered. Lala could not tell if it was some kind of joke to her or really some legal loophole vocabulary she had to use. The double negatives were dizzying but Lala made do.

"Was he there, say, two weeks ago?" Lala said, cooperating with the game.

"I believe I *would* be able to deny it."

Eventually, Lala deduced that he had left a month or two ago. They could not tell her any more, nothing about who he was, the circumstances of his coming there, the circumstances of his leaving, where he was, nothing. Apparently they *couldn't* know where he was either—once patients were out, they were out.

Once again, Lala was at a dead end. She needed investigators, detectives, bloodhounds! There were few options, she knew that, and she was eventually left to conclude they could all be tapped with only one route of action. There was no other choice. If he wasn't going to come to her, she was just going to have to go to him. . . .

She had to go to New York. She had to try. And at the very least, her son was there. Just when the whole ordeal had felt too overwhelming for one woman to endure, she reminded herself it had come out of Her Miracle and she could save him and save *him*, too. She imagined herself swooping like some superhero over the skyline, swiftly coming in at them, and in one arm scooping up her brother and in the other arm her son, carrying them high above all the collapsing jets and the crumbling buildings and the horrific dead and the furious mobs. . . . *And in return, gentlemen,* she would shout through the wind, her hands morphing into talons, *you will like it! You will see you had been so silly to hide!* She would forgive them, but not without their first understanding that they had been wrong, that you simply did not leave Lala and Darius Adam hanging like this, clueless, in the dark of Eden.

✳   ✳   ✳

And planes were still being diverted, threats were still being aired, the crime rate—while they claimed it was lower than before—was still bad, there were killers on the news, burglaries in their building, rapists around the corner, a stock market that was crashing over it-self again and again, terror levels rising and falling but never falling to where they used to be, the news ignoring the new year, still strug-gling to work out 2001, 2001 over and over. . . . The only way to observe a change of any sort in New York was to notice that the posters all around the city of "the missing" were almost all gone. Xerxes couldn't imagine watching someone rip them off. Nobody, after all, a whole season later, was getting found. People were just learning to give up, which was very different from letting go.

"I just don't understand why," he'd say, "of all the places—and I don't ever have a real job or money or any real necessary reason—why of all places am I here? I'm not from here."

"Maybe you're here for me," Suzanne would offer, looking a bit hurt. "For us."

He'd kiss her on the head and rephrase, "Okay, fine, why the hell of all places are *we* here? We spend all our days glued to the news, gas mask by the door, waking up frantic at any noise in the middle of the night."

She would hug him and say she understood—even though he suspected she didn't, she of apocalyptic New York stock, whose coping mechanism was to never reveal that anything hurt her. But in her head she had a better reason, what was in most New Yorkers' hearts, what she couldn't really explain to him, so mystifying the allegiance was: she just could not abandon The City.

He would say, "I was dying to abandon fucking Los Angeles since I can remember." And then she'd retort that Los Angeles wasn't the greatest city, that was why, and then they would have one of their meaningless fights that was all about ideas and never about *them*. It bothered her that all this time the world had overshadowed them—they had barely had a chance to understand each other enough to fight about *themselves*.

One late night when he said it again—frustrated with the news now suddenly changing its mind and saying yes, their lungs actually *were* poisoned and the jet fuel *could* cause their children to be mutants, et cetera—wondering aloud, "Oh why, oh why, are we fucking here?" it suddenly occurred to her to say something that at first sounded like a joke, but then suddenly slipped itself into a seriousness, a seriousness so serious that she was doomed to keep it inside her, for just a little while, until she could really grasp what she even meant by it. . . .

She said, "Where would we go? What, Iran or something?"

He had glared at her, turned off the lights, and announced it was time to go to sleep, leaving them both awake and unready in the dark.

*   *   *

The truth was that Darius had been thinking about it, and seriously, on and off nonstop since the years following the Revolution, but he never knew just how real an option going to Iran could be. It could never be a vacation. To take that risk, not to mention the time off, the explanations, the throwing-all-practicality-to-the-wind—*it would almost have to be a move, wouldn't it?* The notion haunted Darius. But Iran felt like the precise remedy to fill all the many holes in his life.

And particularly as Lala began to fade from him more and more, her eyes now turning eastward, he felt less and less comforted by his faux home. He could see it already: he was about to lose her to New York, too. First his son vaporizing into the steaming pot-holes and dark bustling undergrounds . . . and now his wife, too, ready to run through the unknown labyrinths of that strange no-tion, *Brooklyn,* through every shady possibly dangerous brownstoned street to the buzzing white light of hospital corridors, searching for a man she never knew, this Bob, this brother that she had let go of in the moment when she went from daughter to orphan. She was looking for something she had never known, to add meaning to her life, to start anew with this lost element, while Darius was looking away from everyone he did know, to a place he once did, to start back where he began.

Nobody could ever prepare a man for the endless problems of family, he thought, sighing all the time, the way that old men he used to dread would, the way only his own old father never did.

Back when they were fresh from the Revolution, fresher at least, he used to think to himself, *Just wait, when Xerxes grows up I will go back to Iran, Laleh will come, Xerxes will return, too. Just let him finish school. By then, things will get better over there, another Revolution to cleanse the false Revolution of its bloodstains.* But nothing had changed—on the news the clips still featured those crowlike black-shrouded women, and men with their own faces hidden in beards, kids looking oily and thin and desperate, the streets blackening with the new neglect of only a few decades. . . . His homeland had become a cheap, grim, grainy, black-and-white horror movie.

Still, he asked: *What if we went back to our own country, woman?* It was a question he had asked her on and off, capriciously usually, out of nowhere, perhaps at the scent of a particular dish she had cooked, a glance at an old photo, a California landscape that seemed like something else—something *his.*

But that February, whenever he brought it up he would get a snap, *Are you kidding? We can barely live here in peace.* Or: *What own country? That country is not my country nor is it yours. We left all that just to go back to that, in a worse hell than we left it?* Or, even worse: *Right, and leave everything? Money? Debt? Our son? Or should I say, my son?* He had no answer. In a season of unrest, they always said men were supposed to crave stability, fear change, be more prudent than ever, more practical, more wise. Darius Adam wished it was the case for him, but it just wasn't. He needed upheaval more than ever.

He secretly began researching airfares, calming himself with the notion that he was doing it *just in case. Just good to know. After all,* he reminded Lala, *you never know when we'll have to escape this new country with all its own problems, just like we did our own.*

Lala would roll her eyes, knowing he was right to some extent, that he had some point, not a point that would take *her* back to Iran, but a point that was just as valid as any insanity in their era— she, however, was more intent than ever to stay on the continent. No, California was not enough—and as if her son's absence wasn't enough, here was another lost man in her life: her brother. Another man she could barely imagine from day to day, even though he, too, was her own blood. Another man in New York, this mysterious place where men seemed to go to get lost.

So she began researching airfares, but unlike him, quite openly. When he tried to reason, *Fine, you're doing it just in case,* she snapped back, *There is no "in case." If I have ever done anything worthwhile this will be it.*

And because all that was in his head was his own permanent move—the stability of the most unstable decision a Middle Eastern man in his era, in his situation, could make—Darius Adam took it as a decisive fissure in their partnership. They were over, was that it? Mother, with rights to child in child's city, on one end of the continent; Father alone, not even with weekend visitation, no money to send, no inclusion in any milestones, surpassing the continent altogether and fleeing to the other side of the globe. It made him miserable. He began looking at Eden Gardens with an air of strange nostalgia, like an old lost land, already viewing it as their past, their old temporary housing, a historic rest stop where they crashed long enough to make their most meaningful memories . . . and now, suddenly, because of the air of irrationality that had spread through the universe, they had no choice but to follow that wild crazy tide and be scattered, off away to distant unknowable futures, alone.

They had won, he thought to himself. All of them had become brain-damaged, all of them knowingly about to set forth on the worst decisions of their lives. Nothing was sacred, there was no place to go but down. They were about to erase everything.

This is not about Iran, Lala would insist. *This is still about Xerxes, I know it. . . .*

He did not argue; he let his already low spirits get further swallowed by any grain of truth in her declaration—Xerxes, sure, it might as well be. On the days when he helped Lala research for Bob, he realized that in some way he related exactly to his wife's long-lost brother: there was something to be said about fading men, always far away from the only things meaningful, making a stab at connection, throwing letters to the wind, letters that they had no way of navigating back to themselves in the first place.

* * *

He was going to be twenty-seven soon. It was, to put it mildly, disturbing.

Suzanne loved that his birthday was on Valentine's Day, the day of lovers, that everyone pretended to hate, because it meant she got to really lay on the spectacle. Plus, after its fall, the whole city declared that every holiday, every reason to celebrate, must be *extra stunning* this year. She and Xerxes deserved it, after what they had been through—they more than deserved it. It would have to be big—she envisioned a long line of spectacular gifts, all one by one growing hotter and hotter, as he got closer and closer, approaching the pinnacle, the one biggest bang of a present.

The whole Valentine's Day–birthday relationship embarrassed Xerxes. She knew this because once they had made it past just knowing each others' signs—hers Cancer, his Aquarius—and he actually revealed the day as "February fourteenth" rather than "Valentine's Day," she had laughed and given him a kiss, finding it so very *cute,* and he had suddenly snapped, *Please, it's bad enough that it is what it is.* He explained that he was a cesarean baby, born in Iran, where choos-

272

ing a date like February fourteenth meant nothing. He told her about being in elementary school and being tormented by all the teasing, all the *Cupid* and therefore *fairy* and therefore *fag* jokes, and not being able to pour some water over their flames until junior high, when his Sam just snapped, *Why the hell don't you just make it February thirteenth, you ass?* He told her it was because it was not true. She had rolled her eyes and snapped, *Shit, X, who the hell is going to tell on you? God?* He realized she had a point—although he was worried about documentation and *official* lies even at that age—and so as far as he could go with it, he went with February 13. It wasn't until college and the era of social security numbers and memberships and registrars' offices that he knew he would have to own up. Luckily, by then his world had grown up with him and nobody thought *fag* anymore when he muttered "Oh, two-fourteen." They just thought, at most, at worst, *cute.*

So Suzanne understood Xerxes enough to know just to celebrate the birthday part. He would not humor pink wrapping, Cupid cards, candy hearts. It would just have to be another birthday. In a way, it relieved her. They still felt like a new couple and she didn't want to do the wrong overly/insufficiently romantic thing—or expect him to do the right one and then be disappointed. It took everything off the hook. When friends asked what she and her mysterious invisible boyfriend—since they never ever saw him—were doing for Valentine's Day, she was able to say, *We're celebrating my boyfriend's birthday.* Every time they would gasp, *No really? Believe it,* she would say, proudly.

There was not a more inappropriate day for Xerxes Adam to have been born on. There was not a more inappropriate day for Darius and Lala Adam to have had their Xerxes Adam. *But the day means nothing to the Iranians*, they would throw back to the amused Americans.

Suzanne barely had to scheme. When it came to her, the right, obvious, and only gift—the one that she had admittedly dreamed of for him since early on in their relationship, when she'd press him more about his past, want his parents' stories, their parents' stories, tidbits of whatever memory, no matter how ugly or apocalyptic the refuse in his brain—she was astounded at how easy it all was. It wasn't cheap, but The Account's girth plus the fact that this boyfriend felt like an investment made it more than okay.

When she called her family's usual travel agent and said the name of the destination, Lo of TixTrix made a sound somewhere in between a choke and a laugh. "Are you kidding, Suze?"

"Not at all. We can go there, right? There's no, like, air ban or whatever?"

"Uh, no. Not that I know of, not today. But, Suze, I mean, they're worried about Americans in Italy right now. And you want . . ." It was the first request for that country that Lo had gotten in years, maybe a decade, maybe ever?

"Two tickets, please." Suzanne insisted. She wanted it done as quickly as possible.

"Oh brother."

"And don't tell Al," she suddenly remembered. "Please. My dad won't get it—I mean, I'll let him know, but I have to be the one to do it."

"Okay, yes, I don't think I'd have the heart to spill any beans on this one. Geez."

"Can we leave the dates open-ended?"

"Suzanne, are you sure? I mean, no, you can't. You have to pick a departure date, but I mean, I can switch it for you later. But . . ."

"Great, fine, what day of the month is March . . . say, twentieth? Never mind what day, we'll switch if we have to."

"How about I put a hold and you think about it overnight?"

"Are you ready for my card number?" There was no time for holds in a decision like this. When she hung up the phone she was amazed at how calm she felt. How right it felt—this crazy, crazy thing that she had done. A part of her wondered if Xerxes would be mad. He certainly wasn't impulsive. He couldn't even leave a city that he hated, that he had been jobless in for over a year now, much less leave the country. He had never done that. He had never even talked about vacations. But even if he didn't get it at first, he would later, she told herself. If that almost-half part of her was filled with such delight, such enthusiasm, spilling over to that just-over-half part of her that should have been nay-saying like Lo and any sensible American, then Xerxes would have to be into it, too. And that was what partners were for anyway, to bring out the best in each other—to show them a best existed. After all, he had no one—he acted parentless and she knew that she alone wasn't enough, *not even a damn halfie*, she couldn't bring it to him with her *person*, so she'd have to bring him to *it*. It was a big bang all right—it was the gift she always wished money could buy: a ticket to change your life.

When you have money, Al used to say, *nothing is too big. That's the problem with our class. Unlike their class, we can't find the thing big enough—bigger than us, bigger than we can afford—to want to buy.*

But she felt that she had done it. For days, weeks, it lay like a dirty secret in her heart, materializing only in that e-mail of the itinerary. She would have to build it up slowly, drop hints, maybe master a native recipe and cook it on his birthday, leave a trail of maps and tour guides, play indigenous songs, cover their bed in one big flag, learn to say happy birthday in Farsi—*tavalodet mubarak,* it was easy!—wear a belly dancer's outfit, hell, wear a veil!

It did wonders for her as well. She felt meaningful again in their partnership. When they held hands it suddenly took on a whole new meaning; when she said her "I love you" she had backing proof for it, bigger than emotion; when they had sex she had to fight not to let tears (*of happiness, fear, confusion, excitement, who knows, who cares,* she'd blink them all away) burst out—she couldn't give it away, couldn't let him know that she had just moved a mountain, had just given him something even God couldn't: his and partially hers, a homeland.

*   *   *

The words *Hamadan, Isfahan, Shiraz* danced on his lips—Darius, the Tehran city boy, more than ever missing his country's country— and he thought about that dry savory breeze, the one that made you think of how, in the old days, they used salt to preserve meats; how nourishing and self-preserving that ancient air felt . . . he could not resist it anymore. So he punched the letters with his usual hunt-and-peck: Tehran. They spelled it *Teheran,* he discovered, on GlobalAGoGo.com, but what did it matter? It meant nothing in English; it meant nothing to them.

A student of his who had been there—a tall thin blonde anthropology major named Wendy, who used to stay after class telling him tales of digs in his homeland, in desolate areas apparently so authentic that even he hadn't heard of them—had once told him it was cheaper to get there than people thought. When the number came up on the computer screen, he was still discouraged. He could do it, but he had to be sure—hell, he could, he *could* do it! It was a move—*a vacation, a trip, an overdue excursion*, he had been trying to convince himself, *nothing life-changing*—that he could actually make happen. If, that is, he was to really make it happen.

Day after day, he selected the "Hold Reservation" option. Sometimes the reservation was a month away, sometimes two, sometimes eight months away. One day he would do it, he told himself. Something would have to get him going. But in the meantime he could breathe easy, if for just a little while longer. After all, it wasn't selling out. Who the hell would want to go? There had to be only a handful—less, probably—of people on the continent, at the time, lost enough for a move like that to make any sense to.

*   *   *

He was nowhere to be found, she had accepted that. But quite recently, he had been there, alive and well, somewhere in that city, in Brooklyn, in fact, and he had written to her, probably intending to leave it at that, because he didn't know his sister, did he? *Bastard*. Lala Adam would get to her brother, there was no doubt about it. It would take the greatest city on earth to eat itself alive for her to feel stumped by him. *Brooklyn, get ready*.

There were, of course, a few minor obstacles.

"Ma'am, there is no Brooklyn Airport," the dead-sounding gum-snapping female voice on the other end stated.

"How far is New York?" Lala realized she hadn't done any additional research. She thought the greatest city would be great enough for them to know what she meant and simply work it out.

"Brooklyn is in New York, ma'am."

"Fine, New York Airport," she muttered.

"There are three that we serve, ma'am. LaGuardia, JFK, Newark."

"That's fine—I'll take the New York one."

"That's Newark, ma'am. The other two are in Queens, and Newark is in New Jersey."

"Brooklyn is in New York and New York is in New Jersey. What on earth is happening here, ticket lady?" If *this* was going to be so difficult she could only imagine her actual arrival. But once they got through the glitches and she heard the prices, she was relieved. It was something even she, an assistant's assistant, could afford on her barely above minimum wage salary. At worst she would have wasted a small bonus. It was nothing.

When she asked the ticket lady at 1-800-fAIRAIR why it was so cheap, she simply replied, "It's all promotions these days. The airlines want you to fly. Especially to New York. You know."

She did. Nobody was going there, she could imagine, but her. Nobody needed to as badly as she did. "You know, my son was there on nine-eleven—and my brother," she thought to add, so the woman would not be suspicious, so she would understand just a bit of her urgency, what she had invested.

"Oh no, ma'am. Were they in Lower Manhattan?"

It was the era when you could have full conversations about the world with customer service representatives.

After it was done, Lala sat trembling with unease. It would be her first plane flight alone. Her first important plane flight. Her first trip to that great city.

March 19: she had chosen the day their spring break began at the school. No reason to make things more difficult than they had to be. It was just before the beginning of spring, which meant Persian New Year. What a thrill, she imagined, to have her son and brother to celebrate a truly new year.

But Darius. Darius would have no choice but to understand. This was bigger than he was.

She tried to tell herself there were priorities: A) The Quest for Her Invisible Brother. B) Xerxes, and the Larger Significance of Saving Him. True, he was in his own way long-lost—most concretely to her husband, of course, as she'd manage to speak to him once in a while by phone. But it wasn't much. It was clear to her that he was trying to break himself off from not just Darius, but *them*. This notion pissed her off so much that she combated it with the extreme optimism required in believing in something much bigger than men and their quibbles; she decided to have *faith*, faith that he would be their son again, *because there was nothing he could do about it*. The universe would simply demand it. She recalled thinking on the twentieth anniversary of her parents' death, that if only she could have her brother back the blow that had come with their loss would once and for all entomb itself, that even the smallest lingering element of family would become her new full family, saving herself from the feeling that she had lost it all, lost every last drop of blood there was. She had decided rifts in families, no matter how permanent and decisive they seemed, had a way of healing by osmosis, by simple domino effect, by plugging in a different factor just slightly removed, by letting one situation rub off on another. Growth and shrinkage and distortions in the threads were a natural part of the fabric. Just as new stepfathers sometimes became *real* fathers to their unrelated offspring, just as grandmothers could raise children in lieu of mothers, just as adopted children could fill the holes in families—well, there were ways to add and subtract and multiply and divide which could create a new equation. Bobak and Xerxes were both required to keep the equation balanced, she decided. They were gone for a reason, they would be added back for a reason—after all, if Xerxes and Darius had always been a strong duo, providing a solid support system for her, maybe she wouldn't be running away to find this stranger, her brother; conversely, if her brother had been there all along, maybe she wouldn't have the phobia about lost men that would fuel her insistence that Darius and Xerxes reunite. So she decided that once she found her brother it would all have to happen, that the scales of the cosmos would demand the balance, that the circle would want to complete itself, that Darius and Xerxes would, like positive and negative ends of a magnet, dart to each other and lock in a never-again-violative embrace. Who knew by what real-life excuses it would *actually happen?*—once she unearthed her brother, Darius might be so moved that he would join her in New York himself and beg his son's forgiveness in person; Bobak might preach to Xerxes the merits of everything from letter writing to being-present-for-your-loved-ones and persuade him to approach Darius; both men might envy Lala and Bobak's blissful reunion and seek to create something beautiful themselves; the goodwill in the air might just gas them all, every one of them, until who knew?—the whole world might be forced into harmony instead of hellfire. All Lala knew was that it would happen because the world had naturally willed it and you could not get in the way of the world's natural will, the end.

And then there was C) The City. *Fine,* she could admit it. She tried to keep it there, in that C slot, tell herself none of this had anything to do with wanting so badly sometimes to escape that life in Eden—all the aimless weekend walking to pass the time, all the shit jobs, all the domestic hell, all the old fake complex-friends who didn't even notice her now, not to mention the husband who was always up to some new disintegration—no, none of it had to *entirely* do with wanting to see the world, now that the world was on everlasting finale, endangered in a way she hadn't remembered since the Revolution—and that had been just *her* world anyway, now it had become theirs—no, it had nothing to *really* do with the idea of losing her own self, in what she imagined it was like from movies, a place to get lost among those big almost bendable-looking silver buildings that went so high airplanes interrupted them, that loomed over those streets that were chained with an endless traffic of loud yellow cabs that stopped only for black-cocktail-dressed, diamonded and sunglassed and smoking Audrey Hepburns dashing to window-shop at Tiffany's, where inside the perfect marble halls there were the echoes of an old Old Blue Eyes crooning *these something-bond shoes are longing to stray right through the very heart of it,* all the way into the midnight as a lit red apple starburst its seed heart on a heavens-puncturing silver needle on top of another too-tall monument, to the cheering of millions, fireworks again and again and other times just plain fire maybe, the city running, feverish, the thrill, the kill—oh, Lala Adam prayed she would, if she should *make it anywhere*, she could *make it there.* . . .

* * *

Suzanne could see it now: the two of them holding hands through the bustling chaotic streets of Iran, she just another one of the women covered in a delicate black draping, her man leading the way, maybe with a camera around his neck, bartering with men at stands selling fruits she'd never seen, gems she'd never heard of, their hookah smoke perfuming the polluted air that somehow still allowed for palm trees to triumphantly sprout tall and proud like multibladed green knives into the skin-colored desert sky . . . the two of them running down cobblestoned streets where foreign automobiles dressed themselves halfheartedly as cabs, whisking locals one way or another, unused to visitors and vacationers, questioning them, wanting to know about *their* land, the two of them laughing it off, *You get the picture, it's what you think, it's exactly what you think,* or *We're the wrong people to ask, we left that heaven for this hell—who do you think you're asking, the people who don't want to be a member of the club that would have them as a member?* Or, best yet, *Oh, you don't want to know, better that you don't know, better that you just dream than know.* . . .

The dreams bowed out as the day arrived. Xerxes woke on his twenty-seventh birthday, covered in his girlfriend's kisses, to a sweetly whispered, relentlessly practiced "tavalod tavalod tavalodet mubarak!" She wasted no time handing him his gift.

"Oh, thanks, you didn't have to, of course," he muttered automatically, rubbing his eyes to attention, amazed at how very awake his usually morning-groggy, seldom-insomniac girlfriend looked. She was glowing, her face perfectly made up, hair done, as if she had been up for hours perfecting herself.

Even the present looked perfect, impeccably wrapped in metallic paper and secured with velvet ribbons. He struggled with the wrapping and he pretended to gasp.

There it was. Then he began laughing and she joined in, too, and for what felt like an eternity they held each other laughing.

"Dang, you're good!" he exclaimed, kissing her neck. It was something he hadn't thought of wanting in ages at least, and here it was. It was exactly right.

It, of course, being the *I Dream of Jeannie* DVD box set, with director and cast interviews and everything! He popped it into his computer immediately.

It was exactly what she had expected—better even—but his reaction calmed her nerves only slightly. She bit her lip and for the next hour or so let him peacefully watch as she pretended to watch along. There was still a cake and there was . . . the gift, the real one. She was getting nervous. The plan had been to get him in an ideal mood—humor, she would start with his good humor. The cake would be next. He would be feeling tickled and then fed and then . . . she could bring out the big bang. He wouldn't even see it coming. It would be a spectacle indeed. But the delay was giving her a stomachache. She wanted it over.

But Xerxes Adam, suddenly feeling comfortable as the birthday boy, decided to assert himself—it was his day, so he might as well act as though it was, enjoy it even, he thought—and so he declared the cake should wait until the evening.

"But what should we do now?" she asked nervously.

"Nothing," he insisted. More than anything he longed for a nice normal day of nothing. He had the perfect gift, the *IDOJ* box set that could take them through much of the day; the perfect girl-friend to perhaps have some promising birthday sex with; and *then* a cake. And then, if all the good luck could sustain itself, sleep.

Suzanne didn't know how to go with that plan. It wouldn't fit. She wanted time for them to talk about it—in case he didn't get it, the big gift—so she could persuade him to see it her way, see the beauty in it, that he could want it, too, and then they could daydream about it together. *And then, yes, cake, sex, sleep, fine.*

"There's something else," she said out of nowhere, when his contented silence grew too much for her, when seeing him all peaceful and lounging and fingering the Barbara Eden silhouette on the DVD case just got to be too much. "Another part to your present, I mean. In some ways, the real present."

His eyes grew wide. "Oh no! The Account! Has it gone buck wild for me?"

She tried to laugh. "It's the real present, I'll just say it. That, the *I Dream of Jeannie,* was just, you know, a joke."

He looked hurt for a second.

"I mean, a stocking stuffer," she quickly fixed, and reached into a little bag that was tucked deep into the wiring of his box spring, producing a little golden envelope.

"You wrote me a check," he grinned. "You gave me my own Account."

She was so relieved to see him in such a good mood, going along with it, being agreeable, that suddenly something about him felt irresistible to her, and with that gold envelope in her hands she came over and gave him a particularly passionate kiss—in her head, the kiss said, *Agree to come run away with me*—that of course got him riled up and led to a session of particularly satisfying *yes indeed, birthday sex!*—her manic nervousness translating to almost first-timer excitement and his birthday boy confidence giving off an I-deserve-it strut. They were stalling, she thought, as they just lay there as they always did, dazed in the aftermath. She faced the envelope, in her hand that whole time, now sweaty, too, from being pressed up against Xerxes's back. She bit a corner of it and wondered what to do next.

Xerxes let out a big snore that woke him up. Half asleep, he tried to cover it up with his usual, "Kidding."

"Right," she muttered. There was no better time. He had laughed, he had gotten aroused, he was coated in a cozy sleepiness—all pleasure points had been hit. There was no demon who could go from that to . . .

Suzanne doesn't like to think about the exact details of what proceeded because if she ever thought about it too hard 1) she would hate herself, 2) she would hate Xerxes, 3) she would be furious at the gift, 4) she would be furious for wanting to go through with it, and 5) she would discover she really was in love in that way that handicapped your ability to question, that made forgive and forget synonymous, that made impossible plans only seem all the more possible when anchored in the seemingly steady steel of ardor. . . .

In thinking about it further, she preferred to imagine she deserved it, in a way. She had, after all, killed one of his birthdays.

It had been bad, even worse. *But it had just been a slap on the cheek,* she told herself. *It had just been a "fuck you, how could you." It had just been a questioning of what sort of fucking position I thought I was in, prying so deeply into his life. Who did I think I was, anyway? I wasn't even one of them, fully.* He hadn't said the last part, but in her head she imagined he did and she imagined that was the part that had hurt the most.

"Look, consider the issue dropped," she had told him after it was all over. She knew there was no chance of that happening for her—or for him either. Even with half her face burning, fresh from her boyfriend's angry mistake, she still had that stubborn hope that he would come around. They just needed some time.

"You just don't get it," were the final words he said that night, before they went to sleep after a mostly silent day, Xerxes totally unable to look her in the face, so astronomically sorry did he feel. But he still couldn't muster the will to let her know he regretted it. He felt violated. If he had had any insecurities about this sudden woman of his—born out of the thin air of tragedy that September, so suddenly, so deeply wedged in his life, without rhyme or reason—here was the confirmation: she would go too far. And so, in return, so had he.

They lay there that night locked in the pitch-black confines of unacknowledgeable mistakes.

They said little else in the days to come. Suzanne watched the calendar inch through February, that sickly, slight month—soon it would be March. Sure, they could move the date around, but . . . what if they didn't have to? She began to comfort herself by indulging in the insulation of pure delusion, dreaming of pomegranate vendors and swimming in the Caspian Sea and faint reliefs on mountains of bearded and headdressed kings, soothed almost fully by blinding herself to the fact that the only relationship she had ever thought might have some permanence—for no particularly good reason, but a feeling—could be in danger. *But any day now, he will come around,* was how she got through those moments when reality would, crassly, momentarily, stab through.

When it occurred to her that it had been weeks since he had looked her in the eye, weeks since they had touched each other or done more than mumble, pass things at the dinner table, go to bed, et cetera, she consoled herself by thinking of the certainly many ways to fix it. She eventually came up with an idea. *You know, about the trip—and I promise I won't bring it up again, but I had an idea. I mean it was a present to you, so . . . you don't have to take me. You could still go and the second ticket can be anyone. Or you could go alone and ditch it. Or you could take . . . I don't know. Your mother. Your . . . father.* She bit her lip on that one. He was bound to take it badly. But she wished he could see she was turning to him with sacrifice. Admittedly, she didn't know how deeply she meant it, only how deeply she ought to—and she imagined secretly flying there anyway, avoiding him or spying on him, having her own trip while he had his, if it would come to that. *Or not,* she quickly thought to herself, reality again bursting another bubble. She could just let it all go. Part of her wished it had never happened, the birthday surprise, that idea that had given her stomachaches all along—part of her had known it would go like this. The big bang, indeed. She wished she could close her eyes and have it be September, closer to September at least, when they had become so close as the world fell apart. And here she had tried to sew the world up, to bring the world together with them in it, and here they were, falling apart.

But she did not expect his calm collected reply or his hand on her knee carefully, shaking a bit, placed there with the greatest of hesitation—as if to say, *Look, I care about you, but don't take this too much to heart*—and she definitely did not expect his eyes to meet hers. And she didn't expect him to come out with it, say something that she hoped was said in kindness rather than condescension—rather than his intent to pull himself out of the equation, rather than his wanting to say once and for all: *I lost him, I lost you, I've lost everything, I was born lost.*

After all, Xerxes Adam opened his mouth wanting to make one thing clear: that he knew he was disappearing. That to think he ever possessed *appearance* was probably a joke anyway.

He said, "*Suzanne,* I have an idea. Why don't you go? Why don't you go, *Suzanne,* and in fact take him? Take my father, *Suzanne.*"

She had sat there stunned at these first words, telling herself, no, it was out of kindness, he really wanted her to go and be happy, with his father, whom he actually loved. No, this was not the desert island to banish all the difficult ex–loved ones—he was saying it because he meant well. No, he was not repeating her name that way to be cruel, to hold some ugly mirror to her, to their difference, their ugly alienating individualities. *This was . . . his . . . apology,* she told herself.

Xerxes laughed, that violent bitter laugh she'd heard from weathered crazy homeless men, when he opened his mouth again to add, "You know, *Suzanne,* funny you would bring him up anyway. A little while ago he wrote to me. Did I tell you that? I didn't tell you that. He wrote me and I didn't write him back, didn't even consider writing him back. But in that letter, one of the few things

I remember, *Suzanne*, was him saying he was thinking about Iran. He said he wanted to go."

She didn't know what to do but nod. She didn't even know if he was lying. So his father had reached out and he had left it alone. She couldn't even feel surprised. There they were, one by one, all the old loved ones who had been so close to him, who for some reason he felt had wronged him, with their Irans, with their simple wish to for a second take him back, even if it meant just a brief walk, a brief recollection, a week's visit, through, sure, what might be a little bit of a hell—but so what, it was theirs, *his* hell, his father's hell, and in some way, partially hers, too, at least it could be hers . . . there they were, the cast of characters that Xerxes Adam was one by one banishing from his brain and now ingeniously clumping together.

They could have each other, Suzanne imagined he was thinking.

They deserve each other, Xerxes Adam was thinking.

"So go. Go. Meet him, *Suzanne*. You don't need me to educate you. Go, see for yourselves. See what's happened. See what they make of you, *Suzanne*. See what he makes of you. See all the hell. See what it was worth." He paused, and with a grin so despicable, so cynical, so hateful on his face that for a second she wanted to slap *him* with a final, Suzanne exit: *fuck off*—which of course she couldn't do—he added, "Go to the homeland."

Part Eight

Arrivals

It was over. Fitting, he thought, that their end would come as the Persian New Year was around the corner, his supposed home faintly trying to ring in renewal in this other land where the day was only a day that coincided with the commencement of spring. For many, the vernal clean sweep, amputating winter's last leg, ushered in notions of a fresh, positive season and possibly *era*—they were nothing but their prayers, with dread ingrown by then, used to hating even hope—but deep inside Xerxes Adam there remained hurricane and freezing rain and solid cold, a long way from the desired thaw. Over: *he* had made it over. For almost half a year he had had a girlfriend and it was good. And now—because of his own irreconcilable ignorance, stone-dumb stubbornness, general ineptitude for the simple setting right of seemingly remediable things, and whatever the sum total of this shortcoming of his many shortcomings was—she was lost. Xerxes had become his father. In a parallel universe he would have wanted to actually ask his father, *What was it that made you be like that to your own woman? And child? And what, what exactly would you have done in this situation? So I could do the opposite? What are you like, exactly, so I can work on not being you, please?*

There he was, in a state like a saying his father would screw up: *with the dropped ball scared stiff in his court.* He was cornered to a new impotence by the stifling silence of his only woman, his unhappy woman who was insisting on being *his*, still hovering under his wing, but fading fast. They weren't talking. In fact, he would sometimes spend eight hours at the public library hoping she'd assume it was some freelance job—he was armed with shameless lies, should she ask, which she never even did anymore. She spent more time in her own apartment downstairs and only came over for pretended responsibilities, things she needed, things that had to be checked up on, *things.* The few times she slept over, for whatever reason giving it a try, they would lie like two matches in a box, dead stiff, no chance of overlap. She would sleep the weekends away, slipping sleeping pills under her tongue if she woke up early enough to get anything done. He would spend much of his off days pacing through the apartment until he eventually thought of something, anything, to do outside. Sometimes he saw it was getting to her too—he'd go the bathroom and she'd suddenly be gone, off to take one of those long aimless sad walks that his mother used to take, he'd imagine. Meanwhile she'd leave him notes, include his laundry with hers, pay for his phone bill, his gas, his electric, all the usual. She'd still sign her name on little notes with a shaky *Love, Su* and sometimes her trademark "☺," but when it came to voice, eyes, a hand, she couldn't offer those. She knew he didn't want that anyway and was doing her best to steer clear on tiptoes. She was essentially—and this made him mad, too—waiting for him to get over it, whether that meant making up or breaking up.

What if I never get over it, Suzanne?

And yet there was the side of him that knew this was too much—especially when he couldn't figure out what his real problem was. He tried to separate the issues into lists in his head: lists of what simply irked him, what made it so impossible for him to turn to her and suddenly say, as he had rehearsed countless times over the last few weeks, *Baby, I'm so sorry and you're so sorry so let's move on with our sorry selves*, lists of what it was that made that so tough to chew, and further what it was that was making him erase entire humans from his ever-dwindling network. . . .

He boiled it down somewhat:

A) She had betrayed him.

B) She had betrayed him by going somewhere that it had always been clear she was not allowed to go.

C) She had betrayed him by essentially giving him a gift that was sending him back to his blood country, which she knew, had to know, had ruined his life, both by birth and by escape. She had mixed the worlds.

D) Not to mention that she had taken on this patroness role, making decisions for him, bringing in gifts with such gargantuan price tags and monumental significance that he was starting to get a dangerously shrunken head in her big hands.

E) Plus, she had not understood why it was inappropriate and almost unforgivable.

F) Therefore, she had made him slap her.

G) Which was further problematized by the fact that he had not slapped just any woman—bad enough—no, he had slapped a woman he . . . loved.

They had been saying their *I Love You*'s for quite some time, Xerxes realized. In fact, he remembered the first time it came up: a night when they had been asleep in a snug sweaty spoon, as peaceful as possible, her grinding her teeth a little less, him tossing and turning at a below-average rate, when suddenly a loud boom had woken them both up. *Oh my God, the gas mask!* she had automatically cried as she jerked herself into consciousness. He had gripped her arm, like a child with nothing to say but only able to gesture for protection. It had been a frightening sound, a sound they immediately assumed was the end of the world knocking, the one they had been living waiting for, it seemed. They got dressed quickly. She grabbed the mask and began to whimper, when suddenly it occurred to him to freeze the moment and say, *Wait*—should that instant be one of their last. He held her close to him, feeling her newborn-baby-bird tremors melt into his torso. She felt so small, so destructible. He had held her in a way that made him feel like a shell for her; he turned to the skies and said, *If you're going to come down, come now, on me, while I have her within me.* And she, she must have sensed this poignant gesture, for suddenly after another whimper she craned her neck to his ear and in that startlingly sexy sweet way of shaken female lovers said, for the first time, *Xerxes, I love you, you know?* He had nodded, choked up, and in that moment felt it was out of place to even question whether or not he should say it back—he just had to, and so he said it with all the depth the situation—more than he himself—could muster. *Yes, Suzanne, I know, I love you, too.* And then they had gone outside and seen that it was nothing—a huge garbage truck had rammed into an old brick wall of an abandoned alley—sure, it had made a mess, caused a scene, a minor catastrophe, but it wasn't *it*. Not yet. They went back inside, feeling slightly silly, and as they tried to go back to their sleep worlds, she sprang it on him again, as if it were the moral of the story still, no matter what, no matter peace or hell, it was there all along: *Still, I love you, Xerxes.* He had pretended to be asleep, feeling swallowed by sentiment's sheer size and shape—suddenly he, the mollusk in her shell—but soon enough he was finding himself saying it over and over like a trusty robot whose programming nobody need question.

She was always somehow trapping him into something—you could look at it that way, he realized. Her kindness, her love—it always had a forced aspect. He couldn't say no to her. She knew his nature was thinner than the tough he presented. He would always give in to her. She preyed on that. She was, in her own unseeming way, manipulative. And she had killed with kindness. She might as well have blindfolded him, popped him in a cab, put him on a plane, and taken the blindfold off only once they were in Tehran Airport— *or whatever the hell they call it,* Xerxes thought, annoyed.

He tried not to think about the actual problem that went beyond her line-crossing, that lurked behind his reaction—*the slap, my God, the slap.* She had given him the gift of Iran and nothing could possibly threaten him more—*and why, what was up with that, Xerxes?* he thought to himself. It was a question that he never tired of. What went on in his head that made his worlds, America and Iran, with their expansive oceanic and ideological gaps, so fucking threatening when considered—even worse, when *bridged*—in a sentence.

He tried to boil it down:

A) It was not only not his home—it was, in fact, his anti-home, if such a thing could be said to exist.

B) Iran was the only Islamic fundamentalist regime in the world. There were stories—his father's and mother's plus a trickle of anonymous gossip—of women getting mutilated for just having their hair exposed. No one was safe in a world like that. And who knew what his last name meant to the Iranian government, what sort of tabs the government had kept on his family and their fleeing. It was a dangerous place, not at all a vacation spot. *We're feeling near death on this turf, so let's go to Iran?* It was like deciding to honeymoon in Hades.

C) Didn't somebody—somebody wise, maybe Asian, somebody valid at the very least—once say *a man must go to his own world on his own time when he is ready* or something like that? No? Wasn't that just as good a proverb as any?

D) His father had suggested it in his letter; the root of it all could be traced to exactly that wrong person. Him, Suzanne, all these characters pointing east, plus a whole chorus of average New Yorkers warning that the city was uninhabitable—it suddenly felt like a conspiracy of the cosmos. They were making him go, these supposed do-gooders, telling him that it was his home, but essentially deporting him.

E) *She* had made it happen. Who was *she?* Who did she think she *was?* He couldn't go with his own family and so he was expected to go with this woman that he had known for about half a year? This *suddenly-she* of his? It didn't make sense.

F) It was just not his home, less than New York or Eden Gardens was. He did not miss it. It existed only in his barely born first vision of the bad pink light of anti-aircraft missiles, the news, their fights. Not only was it not his home, but it was the birthplace of his nightmares.

But ethnicity wanted to duel with nationality and often would win—it was hard to escape his birthplace even stateside. Sure, the Middle East had come to America, had chased Americans down and made its own private hells America's business, but suddenly it felt as if Iran especially was entering the scene. On the news one night, it began: the American government was planning to probe Iran's possibly full-bodied nuclear weapons plan. It was a beginning, Xerxes thought, The Americans were only beginning to bring *his* Middle East to their turf. It was the beginning of yet another end.

Suddenly a famous comedian decided to have an Iranian handyman on her show. He was going to be a regular cameo of pure slapstick comic relief, a lovable fat heavily-accented presence that would show Americans that Iranians were kind, cuddly, fun . . . fat handymen. Xerxes felt furious. He could imagine so did Darius. This man resembled none of them. But just his existence meant that suddenly Iranians were having to color themselves clownish and soft and obese, harmless neighbors, grateful shit jobbers, easy laugh track hacks. There were suddenly defenses and safeguards.

Iranian-American journalists began writing about the merits of Shiite Islam. As if to say, *We are them, but a little different. You are right, we are what you fear, but a little off. We're more okay.* There were suddenly overexplanations and misinformation.

The director of a dog-sitting company, one of Xerxes's potential employers, called Xerxes back, pronounced his name perfectly, and then asked, "Don't take my asking this the wrong way, but is that a Muslim name?" There were suddenly questions and entitlements.

Everyone seemed to be whispering, *Iran could be next.* Suddenly it was Iranians' season. Their kingdom was poised to come. Iran was everywhere.

It was all getting so deeply under his skin that he began to think he could give up. Give it all up. Say: *Yes, Suzanne.* Turn himself in. He imagined himself in the hands of prison guards being led to some infernal Tehran jail full of journalists and writers and artists and some Westerners and some plain old nothing guys like him, and himself declaring simply, *Iran, here I am; finally you got me.*

✳   ✳   ✳

Among the many notes that Suzanne wrote her supposed boyfriend —little Post-its that just put him in the know, like *Gone out for a walk, Love Su* ☺, or *Grocery shopping, need anything? Love Su* ☺, to let him know that, sure, she noticed things were off, that they were reduced to this, but there were ways, there was rescue, she was still there, at any minute she could be turned on again—among those were the few that she never ended up leaving, that she immediately crumpled and tossed out in the city's trash cans, lest he stumble on them in his apartment. They were ones that were flooded with vague, needless, selfless apologies—*Please, Xerxes, whatever I did, I didn't mean it the way you took it, you must know that,* or *Please, Xerxes, please, we worked so hard,* or, *Please, Xerxes, you were supposed to be meant to be, didn't you feel that*—that she knew would only annoy him all the worse. The only thing she could do was wait and hope he would come around. It would have to be his move.

But in the meantime, she could feel her spirits weakening so much that they were taking their toll on her physical self. She grew thinner and thinner, more tired, more restless, more sleepy, more sleep-disturbed. In the mirror she now saw the weary eyes and permanently creased forehead and tense jaw that all together perfectly created the frantic lost look of wasting women.

She rediscovered living in her old apartment. It was bearable but she was lost on how to fully exist as herself without him. She replayed their first meeting on the rooftop on that epochal evening over and over again. *You could not throw away a thing like that,* she told herself. *If you did, you might as well pretend, say, 9/11 never happened.*

She did not understand a world where people didn't come around, where people didn't grow sick of holding grudges, where the humanity inside humans wouldn't melt away their stubborn hold on old principles. It was inevitable that people had to go back to where they belonged, right? Return to those who had claims on a piece of their heart, right?

She could not live with the idea that *he* would be the exception to her rules.

She imagined speaking to and confiding in his mother on the phone—because she couldn't even let herself *imagine* his father, so taboo had that become—and Mrs. Adam saying, *Oh, don't mind him, they're the same, exactly the same, father and son—which is to say semi-hopeless. There is no point in waiting. Ultimately it will end if you don't find your own out first. Move on, go on. Get a life.* Suzanne imagined retorting back, *You don't understand and maybe you shouldn't. But suddenly without him, I'm nowhere.*

✻   ✻   ✻

It was going to be the 1381st Persian New Year and Lala thought that would provide the ideal miracle setting for their meeting: that just after arrival, just a bit after the cab ride to her hotel, just upon her first walk through that city's streets . . . there he would be. Bobak. Their New Year's present to each other. He would maybe be difficult for a moment, say, *Laleh, but don't you get it? I didn't ask to be found.* And she would hold him, and say in Farsi, *Oh, older brother of mine, that's just the hurt, the pain, that made it so hard—look, look what you've gained—look what your little sister has become—here comes the oldest new thing the world could have ever given us: us!* He would eventually come around, like all difficult men, and finally laugh, *Welcome to New York, little sister!* And there would be no talk of hospitals, no old family tragedy, nothing but the future and joy. Later that week they would find Xerxes—she'd show up at his door with her brother, hand in hand, and as her son opened the door she would announce, *Look, look what your mother has dug up: an uncle for you!* Lala imagined the two men shaking hands in shock. They would be nearly identical. It would explain how Lala would recognize him in the first place—her brother would be a Xerxes in the pure, a Xerxes without the Adam, a Xerxes who possessed a past that was entirely hers.

Oh, yes, there will be tears, she thought, but she couldn't wait for them. Darius, meanwhile, was appalled.

"It's already bad enough—I mean tough enough—and now you want to tell me it's a coincidence that you're going to be gone on Norouz?" Darius snapped. "Our first New Year apart in almost thirty years! This seems right to you?"

"It's not my choice—that's the start of the school's spring break," Lala insisted, "and I need a whole week. I am supposed to put off a single precious day of might I remind you very hard search work, so that we can get dressed up in front of the TV, eat some candy, count down by ourselves to Iranian radio? It's not like I am taking that day away. I'll call. Plus you'll be driving me to the airport that morning—we'll be together, since suddenly our damn togetherness is an issue to you."

"It has always been," Darius insisted, "and what's the point of that morning? The New Year will chime in the evening. We'll count down on the phone?"

"*If* my plane has even landed at that point, Darius," she said firmly. "The point is, we have to learn to live this way sometime, Darius. We won't be tied to each other forever, you know."

It silenced everything. Darius did not—although neither did Lala completely—know what she meant by that. Lala, who got a kick out of hazing her statements to a perfect nebula with manufactured *crypticism,* hoped that he might mellow out, interpret the reference to separation as a reference to their old age. In death, *they* would be done after all. But Darius, with his feet always resolutely on the ground, suspected it meant the divorce that he feared in his bones—that she would be off there rediscovering her old past suddenly, in the soil of a new slice of this new country, perhaps never to return or perhaps to pick up an even greater wanderlust that would take her farther, and he, he would be left to start a new life, or even a version of his old life, in that old land of his past. Their past. It was possible that they were over.

"I can't tell you not to go, woman," he grumbled. "So go, you get lost, too."

"Nobody's getting lost, Darius. It's the season for things to get found," she insisted. "It takes some work, you know. You have to put in some work."

Sure, if by work you meant magic, he thought. It took doing impossible irrational things that equaled hope, the frail pathetic human impulse that she was suddenly bound to. It took picking up a phone, dealing with his son's hanging up, maybe another unanswered letter, and then a flight of his own, and a walk he'd remember up and down East Village streets, to his door—a knock, a pause, an opening, and words that would kill for both of them, *Son, let me back in. I have come to make it better. Forgive*—ending with that hardest word of all. Maybe he would, maybe he wouldn't. But like his wife he would adopt that most desperate, urgent kind of trying, that shot in the dark, that myth of the somehow-sometimes-hit bull's-eye, whose very real life existence, although only once in a blue moon, made for the invention of the word *miracle*. He had to believe in miracles.

"Plus, I'll only be gone a week," she kept reminding him.

But that was enough, he thought, enough of a window for him to need to get out. They hadn't all melted away like this from him before—he was Darius Adam, once at the helm of that household of three in Eden Gardens. Everyone had needed him. Even other people's cats, even all those nobodies' birds. And now without his family's need, with just some piles of bills and a promise to sustain them somehow in their place, what was the point? He had felt the itch to go home months ago, if not years ago—even on the eve of horrific protests, the symbolic burning of otherwise happy men, the constant scraps of distant relatives' bad news, the somber images on the TV, all somehow amounting to more missing—and now, with her impending absence, the itch had a means to be scratched. They were leaving him in their own possibly temporary ways, within the great American landlock anyway, but little did they know he would have in store for them a leaving they could never imagine. Gone: he'd really be gone, a bona fide true goner. *Take that for loss,* he'd say. How the hell would any miracle dig him up? He would be beyond their finding, if they should even employ that—and he wasn't sure they would. On top of the feelings of giving up and truly missing his homeland, there was also a gesture of goodwill within it all: his getting lost/going back to where he belonged, maybe it was what was best for them *all* anyway, they might think.

He fantasized about arriving in the streets of Tehran on the big day itself, too . . . amid streamers and firecrackers and animal screams and delirious song—*oh, do they do the new year anymore?* They had to, even the ayatollahs had to know they had to. Darius could imagine—filled suddenly with an overwhelming dose of that soul-suffocating loneliness—getting there and pretending the celebrations of Persian New Year 1381 on his old city streets were simply his welcome-back party.

✳   ✳   ✳

And then one day he had enough. Call it the madness in the air of ever-bipolar March or just another world-sponsored breakdown, or perhaps a natural turning of the tide for a man who simply had nowhere to go but up—but one day, after wallowing for ages in the state of having lost it all, Xerxes Adam was suddenly snapped out of it. He was seized by a thrilling urgency that so welcomingly cut into that sick old air of their stagnation, so suddenly that all he could worry about was that all the newfound goodness equaled dying or something.

Fuck it. What the hell do I have to live for anywhere?

In reality, he was manic at most. Depression rust had frozen all yesterday's systems and here was mania's flame to morph the present into a possible future.

Counterintuition flooded him so deeply, so vigorously, that it was as if he had acquired a brand-new blood supply. It was more than an Opposite Day impulse. It was all that was left for a man who had hit rock bottom. Either you could let it all go and lie dead on that bottom rock or you could rise from your ashes and make life happen again, no matter how seemingly defeated the steps, no matter how insane and insulting and dreaded.

They say that only the manic realistically entertain the idea of suicide; the depressed are too depressed to deeply explore it, much less ever carry it out. He was suddenly unafraid of death. Let them kill him in Iran then—let fate do as it would—he would have died sooner or later in his old miserable post-birthday condition. He was at least now alive—if even too alive—for another round!

The air of acidic wellness had first hit him one morning when he woke feeling choked by something very dead-ended in himself, and just when it seemed serious, as if the demons were real and the options all too possible, *something* like a pump of death-defying goodwill shot through him and there he was . . . suddenly his arms wrapped around Suzanne's neck, maybe a bit too abruptly, for she actually screamed, a light disturbed scream, and then offered him her eyes, worried eyes that saw in his shake-up some sort of unstable newness, a profound new wave of upheaval so clear and so solid that suddenly relief and terror seemed siblings. It was the first time he had touched her since the fight.

"What's going on, Xerxes? Are you okay?"

He softened his clutch and dropped to his knees—collapsed really, but quickly modified the pose to make it look like a poetic chivalric stance—and held her face and began kissing it all over, over and over, as she kept saying, "Oh, Xerxes, oh sweetheart, but what, what do you mean?"

For a while, he kept saying, "Suzanne, I can't take it anymore, I just can't take, can't take it anymore," weeping a bit, the type of tearless dry weeping that he'd sometimes feel overcome by, those turbulent entrail-heaving fits of his child-self, when he was smaller than his own grief, when it wasn't just a matter of hiding it but a matter of controlling it lest it burst outside himself and swallow him up—*Oh, how could I explain it to her anyway?*—he himself could barely grasp what was happening, a breakdown, maybe that was what it was, maybe he had woken up refreshed like that because in his head were the new juices, the corrosive chemical formula of a breakdown. *But if it be, so be it*, he told himself, he had been beyond broken for weeks, let this breakdown, this insanity, this end-of-him be the new him, it was at least one last pulse to ride through—*Shit, maybe I am dying*—but who cared, who had time to analyze it all, when there she had been for weeks, all he had in the world, his old new girl, his only girl, hunched in a corner, counting down days to nothing, just silent and sick and fading—he had actually seen it the day before, really noticed it, how she had walked by just barely there like a hologram, and all he had seen was a skeleton of the old spirit, a faded image, a vintage newspaper clipping of a girl—oh, there was no time! No time for anything but revolutions. He loved her. He had maybe lost it. But there was no losing her, losing time, holding on to his impending self-destruction, imagining himself missing, lying at the bottom of a nowhere-land well, *no that doesn't have to be*—oh, he could almost pick up the phone and even call *him*, if he wasn't sure he'd just add new wrath to old wrath by shouting, *O fuck it all, father, let's fuck it!*—outside in those other worlds they were dying, after all, didn't they remember, dying of a capital-S Suffering he couldn't imagine, and so what was he doing, *Who the hell gave me that right to give up?* . . . No, he had no choice but to try it, no choice, nothing in the world but to live, live this sweet terrible Life!

"Can't take what anymore?" she was asking, "I mean, I know what, I think I know what, but please, Xerxes, tell me what you're thinking, can you?"

"I am thinking," he began and then paused a bit, "I am thinking, my Suzanne, I am thinking that we have to. It is time for a trip. We're going—and thank *you*—to Iran."

She smiled, embraced him, but didn't take a word of it seriously. She saw the mention of Iran as just a make-up gesture, just a way to present the old bone of contention and shatter it, so they could move on, go on with that love that she had been sure enough of to hold on to, even as she felt herself falling apart within that love's dark and dubious architecture. In her mind she had believed in the miracle of this moment and it had come. *Hope was a bitch, but when hope comes through, unfathomable the extent it can go,* she thought.

But as their union cemented itself more and more strongly, perhaps more strongly than ever, through the test of hours and then days, he only brought it up more and more—Xerxes made Iran the main factor behind his personal revolution.

"The point is, it's all perfect," he said. "What date do we leave?"

"March nineteenth," she said, hesitantly, sure that its being around the corner would put him off that track, sure that whatever charade he was playing would have to wear off and whatever lesson would reveal itself and just let them live on. She added, "So what's the rush? That's like in a week and a half, and my agent said if we decide we really want to, it can be changed. Let's put it off a bit, at least?"

The truth was that the whole idea made her sick. She had no desire to go anymore—the absence of desire was so real that she questioned if she had ever really wanted to go. What had she been thinking? Of course it was a bad move. She was ready to say Xerxes was right with his punishment—she had crossed a line. The best forgiveness she imagined he could grant her was just letting it all go and starting over.

But perhaps that was precisely part of her punishment: Xerxes was nowhere near letting it go. It was more than ever, more than it was ever allowed to be, the issue, and he did not even try to hide for a second that it was The Issue that had brought him running back, running madly, ecstatically, horrifically, back to her.

"March nineteenth? That's enough time! Ten days! That's all the time in the world, Suzanne! Let's do it."

She had decided not to talk about it, only nod at most. She hoped that as the day neared he would let go.

But then one evening as they were cooking together, his phone rang and with it came another world-mixing threat to their newfound harmony. Xerxes had decided to play head chef that night, reading off a pile of Internet recipes, announcing he would be showcasing a new special sauce for their eggplant rigatoni. He could suddenly cook—she couldn't believe it. He was elbow-deep in the slimy thin blood of tomatoes when the phone rang—"Can you get that?" he asked Suzanne, who was assigned to just chop vegetables. She put down her knife and carrot slivers and, with a quick kiss to his cheek, skipped to the phone.

As with other miracles of this time period, an old dream had come true: she was speaking to none other than Xerxes Adam's mother.

"Who is this?" Mrs. Adam had immediately snapped, her soft accent lessening the blow of the rude introduction, as if she was just confused and foreign and therefore required some extra understanding.

"Oh, hello, this is Suzanne. . . . I'm Xerxes's girlfriend. . . . I take it this is Mrs. Adam?" she had not realized in time that it might sound creepy to have come right out with her prediction like that. But she couldn't help it. It was an older foreign female voice with an accent of mixed-up Iranian though resolutely snappy mannerisms—who else? It fit exactly.

"Oh, oh, you are. . . ." Mrs. Adam didn't complete the sentence. She offered a few awkward chuckles. "Oh, hello then. Nice to speak to you."

"Oh, yes, same with me, I mean, so happy to finally speak to you," Suzanne stumbled.

"Yes," Lala repeated even more awkwardly. "You stay at his place, I see, yes?" She regretted saying it immediately—Xerxes would hate the way she asked that. She wished she could make her prying more inconspicuous.

"Oh, yes, sometimes," Suzanne said. "Well, I live in the building." There was more silence—she didn't know what the right answer was. "But yes, we stick together a lot!" And more silence. "Xerxes, he's in the kitchen, cooking, let me get him—"

"Oh, cooking? Him? Wow, what an influence you must have. Don't bother him. I just wanted to know if he got my message."

"Message? I'm not sure—"

"Yes, yes, I left it on the thing—" she stammered.

Suzanne paused. *Thing* equaled . . . *machine?*

"Oh? Well, let me get—Xerxes! Xerxes, phone!" Suzanne called over her shoulder.

"No, no, don't bother him," she insisted. "You must know anyway. . . . I am coming."

"Coming?"

At that moment Suzanne heard the housewifelike whistling-while-he-worked be put on hold. He walked in wiping his hands with paper towels.

But Lala was still going on: "Oh, yes, next week, Persian New Year, I get in to New York, he must have—"

"Oh, I didn't—oh, well, here he is—" Suzanne signed off as Xerxes immediately grabbed the phone out of her hand.

She plopped onto the couch like a rag doll. His mother was coming? Next week? Persian New Year? She had no idea. But suddenly she realized it was another layer of icing on the miracle cake—this would certainly push next week's trip to Iran out of his head, once and for all, no?

"Hello, Mother," he said, and while most of the phrases came out in a half-Farsi-half-English hybrid, some others, probably partly for her benefit, came out in crystal-clear English.

"Yes, yes, she is, yes, she's very nice, yes. . . ."

"Well, I'm sorry, Mother . . . really? Oh God . . . no, no . . . we'll just be missing each other. . . ."

"If you had told me earlier . . ."

"Well, Persian New Year, I figured it was coming, but I had forgotten the exact date. . . ."

"But it'll interest you to know that if it's Persian New Year then we're going to be doing something perfect!"

"I know, Mother, I'm sorry. . . ."

"Listen, stop right there—will you listen?"

Suzanne closed her eyes in dread. She could feel it coming.

"Because, Mother, the most amazing thing is happening and it simply can't be delayed—Suzanne and I—yes, we're cooking—anyway, the most amazing thing . . . Mother, next week—and now that I know our arrival will be on Persian New Year, that's an even better reason, certainly a sign—did you hear that, Su, March twentieth is Norouz?—anyway, on that very day, Su and I, we'll be in Tehran!" After either some silence or some too-brief response on the other end, he added more quietly, "I'm dead serious."

Suzanne went back to the kitchen to chop, trying to swallow back tears. She wished she could get back to that original foolish passion for the damn trip. She hoped she would, maybe when she could get used to trusting Xerxes's newfound enthusiasm—certainly it would be contagious, certainly she was still the girl who got the tickets in the first place—but the quickness, the date that she had so haphazardly picked—although apparently perfectly, clairvoyantly, picked, the damn Norouz!—rushing up on them, speeding way over any limit, head-on, ready for collision, it didn't feel right. . . .

"And the best part of all is," Xerxes yelled to her over the running sink, once done with his mother and back to his kitchen business, "can you believe it's Persian New Year? Now if that's not a sign, I don't know what is!"

Suzanne nodded, trying to smile. She started to set the table. "But your mother. Wasn't she coming to see you?"

Xerxes laughed, in a crude way that seemed wrong to her. "Oh, please! No. Not at all. She'd never do that. She has . . . other business. I can't even explain it—it all sounds like madness—but she thinks, she thinks she can find her brother."

"Her brother is lost?"

"Oh, it's a long story. But let's just say she's taking a vacation—from work, from my father, from her boring life. I've often wondered why she didn't do it sooner. But New York—who knew? It's too bad . . . but then again, who needs another one of my parents to visit New York and then God knows what. . . ." he laughed in that disturbed way again, while blindly pouring olive oil into the steaming pot with new wayward recklessness.

"Xerxes, are we really? I mean, really? Don't you think it's too soon, if we should even do it at all?"

He looked at her with bewildered eyes for a moment. Almost hurt, confused eyes. He shut them for a few seconds. When he opened them they were again wild, laughing, ecstatic, almost delirious. "No fucking way out, my dear!" he rushed up to her, swooping her up like a romantic-comedy bride, even spinning her in his arms for a second. They were both breathless, laughing. "Happy birthday to me . . . happy Persian New Year to me . . . to us, I mean, it's yours, too!" he laughed, kissing her head, burying himself in the wild wisps of the always untamable dark locks that had made her so otherworldly to him on first sight. "So many *happy* things," he continued, "so, Suzanne, let's just take it: right now we're a lucky people? Let's take it while it lasts." She nodded and kissed him back. They ate, washed dishes, napped, woke, had sex, and slept a full restful night as they had rarely managed before. And as the clock ticked on, as the days wasted away, Suzanne could feel herself regaining the old confidence, indeed letting him rub off on her, suddenly growing that thick skin of blindingly sunshined nihilism. *What else are there but risks these days anyway? What's so good about this new world anyway? So what if it all goes to hell?* she thought, without understanding that was his point exactly.

*   *   *

Because it was a hell of a history—twenty-nine Norouzes that they had spent together—Lala didn't have the heart to skip the usual preparations. In came the *Haft Seen,* the seven sibilant symbols of the Persian New Year—several spices, some goldfish, a red apple, a mirror, all arranged in a circle on a white-lace-draped coffee table, flanked by tulips. She even got the usual Persian cookies—chewy walnut clusters, delicate almond paste confections, chickpea wafers, honey and nougat candies, and dyed nuts. She loved the ritual. She set them down sadly, however, defeated by the notion that she wouldn't be around to put them away—or worse, that they would still be there when she returned, Darius undoubtedly letting the spices and apple and fish all sit and rot until she came back, a pathetic remnant of a holiday meant to be spent at home that she had instead spent in a city trying to turn miracles.

Should he be found, of course, it would be worth everything in the world. And should he be found, she would inflict the New Year niceties on her brother, too, hospital or not. Bob needed a nice long thorough Persian Norouz more than anyone else, she imagined.

For a few days she kept the news of Xerxes and his lady friend's trip to Iran a secret. She didn't know what to do with the knowledge—tell Darius and witness any number of chaotic reactions or withhold it from Darius and delay his wrath at her secrecy? Could she even afford secrecy—what if something happened to these naïve youngsters in Iran? A violation, border trouble, a run-in with

313

officials—say they ended up in one of those notorious Iranian pris-
ons that peppered everyone's Tehran-today gossip? Surely those
jails were full of unknowing Iranian tourists, people who were innocent, who had only made a false move or two or not even that,
people who had stumbled rather than slithered snakily through the
clergy's fascist state. . . . What would Darius do if she suddenly
told him their son was in prison in his homeland? O apocalypse
in the un-homeland, her head cracked on the *Haft Seen!* But on
the flip side, should he know about the trip in full? What would
Darius do with the knowledge anyway? Run to Iran, too? Ha!
On the other hand, maybe he would; he often spoke about it these
days, Lala reminded herself. Would he call Xerxes and encour-
age him even more? Tell him it's about time, give him some numbers, names of places to visit? Or decide it was too dangerous,
too full of the unknown, and call Xerxes and talk him out of it?
Or would he do nothing at all? Would he deal with it silently,
proud of his son for seeking out his homeland? Would he deal
with it silently, outraged at his son for going solo with some
nothing-woman rather than his own family? Would he deal with
it silently, upset at his son for again giving them the finger
by purposely seeking out what they had left behind, for con-
trarian effect—a homeland he and his American idealism and his
adolescent-level Farsi could barely hope to navigate—the homeland they had abandoned for him and his future alone?

She had no idea how Darius would feel about it because she herself had no idea how she felt. All she had wanted was for Xerxes—
and especially this new lady friend, who had gotten him all happy
on the phone, talking as he did, a bit lively, seeking roots, hell, cook-

ing!—to be with her in New York, to give her a tour, to be her anchor on this desperate mission, to ensure that even if she didn't find her brother it wouldn't be a wasted trip. She wanted the chance Darius had had, to see her son in his element, and to not fuck up that opportunity as he had done. Now, as it stood, it would be another long possibly forever while until her son became anything more than a voice on the phone. Not to mention that her own mission in New York looked bleaker than ever. To return empty-handed—when that was the realistic truth of it, to not even be able to say, *Well, at least I have my son*, to be able to say only, *Well, at least I have my son's city*—it was a devastating and highly probable possibility. She started to worry that her brother hunt was an excuse to find her son again, when really she had almost been convinced it was the incidental opposite.

She had even dared to imagine the four of them—Bobak, Darius, Xerxes, and herself—all together the following New Year. It was heartbreaking—it was also simply hard to imagine, but she had to. She was tired of watching Darius curse at what the daily mail did not hold, moaning about abandonment like a jilted child; she was tired of tiptoeing around her son's name as if it were an obscenity. She was tired of her shattered family. The broken circle and all the faith required to envision its completion were exhausting her.

Don't give up, don't be like those stupid cowards! she told herself over and over, pissed at all these men passively living their separate, tortured lives. She tried to remind herself that a reason for any hunt at all could be in simply finding a purpose—a purpose, the best out in any life—and through it a world, a mission, a goal, a dream, a life, and an afterlife outside Eden Gardens. She was being employed by the world, she reminded herself, the world—starting with her brother suddenly like a genie in a bottle appearing out of nowhere—was finally calling her and she had to respond. . . .

She swallowed her worries and faced her husband. But when Darius asked her if they should put some money in an envelope with a card for Xerxes—what they had done for every Persian New Year while he was away at college—and have her hand-deliver it to Xerxes upon her arrival, Lala couldn't take it anymore. She would have to let him know.

"Darius, I am not seeing our son," she said. As usual, in her attempt to have her words be bold and firm and *heard* it all came out too harshly. "I mean, he won't be in New York when I am there. I just found that out."

The idea of Xerxes not in New York, the New York where he had left him, immediately alarmed him. "What? He's not coming over . . . *here?*" He looked filled with fear and grief, but a thin, transient-looking fear and grief that could quite possibly unmask themselves as ecstasy and gratitude, she thought.

Lala shook her head gently and took his hand with a dramatic tenderness, like the stilted somewhat-off affection of high school stage actors in a love story. "Darius, he's not coming to *this* home, but he is going *home*. For a visit. *Home*. Do you know what I mean?" She tried to smile.

"Enough, woman, there is one home and that is—" he exploded, ignoring her nod—"and that is exactly where our son would never be!" He paused, seeing her smiling nods out of the corner of his eye as she tried not to face him, unsure what his reaction would be should he, could he, believe it. When he finally spoke all he had was a whisper. "It is not possible."

"I spoke to him and his lady friend and it's true. They are actually getting there on Norouz—celebrating it there, isn't that nice?—and they will come back after a week. Isn't that . . ." she didn't know what the right word could be, but it had to be nice, "really, really nice?"

Darius continued to avoid her eyes, staring at some other unknowable ghost in utter disbelief. The ghost of an ill-founded equation: *his son* + *Iran* = what the hell did that equal? What could he make of that? It was more than a surprise, more than a shock—it was an almost impossibility. Every one of the reactions Lala predicted ran through his head but all amounted to nothing, no single clear emotion. He was at a loss. His son once again had managed to kill him without even thinking of him.

He told Lala he had nothing to say about it and went to take a nap—he had a headache, he claimed, *unrelated by the way,* he added, *to our son.* But of course it wasn't. During the course of his pretend nap, Darius experienced everything from outrage to fury to pleasure to thrills. There was no knowing what portion of that spectrum was his true feeling. But one thought stood out and gave him a tiny bit of peace: he had mentioned to Xerxes months ago in that letter that he wanted to go to Iran. He had mentioned it before the idea had even taken on a particular urgency. It was just stated as a general fact, the exposure of a habitual feeling of his, written mostly to be taken as, *Son, one day it would be nice to consider a trip to Iran.* Hypothetical. That was all. Then who knows—power of his own suggestion maybe—Darius had suddenly realized that not only did he want to go to Iran, his whole world was kicking him out of his exile and sending him back. He had no other home but his original home. For weeks he had been desperate for Iran, and he had even imagined being there on the New Year. Now what calmed Darius a bit and gave him the preferred food for thought was, what if *this* was Xerxes's response to his letter? What if this was Xerxes saying, *Look, father, I am finally doing as you said?* What if it was a symbolic gesture, a white flag combined with a gift? He and his lady friend, what if this was their call for him to follow their lead, without explicitly asking? Xerxes, after all, had always lived in the realm of the implicit—rarely was he straightforward about anything as a child—and recently, with his absence from his father's life, he had become less than implicitly existing, he had become a specter of a son-past. But was this his way of reappearing, on his father's terms, in fact? Did Xerxes want his mother to leak this info to him and see what happened? Did he leave it to the last minute to test his father, see just how far he would go to get his son back? His son with a bonus, his son enveloped in the wrapping of his original package, his son in the only context that mattered, his Xerxes, a king in his own country? Was this his invitation to take back their kingdom?

In his head, as deep thinking with closed faux-sleeping eyes turned to genuine dreaming eyes, there she was, there she always was: a suddenly more adult Shireen, same wispy bright dress, same huge eyes and wild midnight hair. Shireen this time was in total peace, simply sleeping in a vessel in the sky. *Oh, Shireen,* he thinks, *Shireen, help me, Shireen. What do I do?* But Shireen, in her green-, white-, and red-striped sundress, sat limp against a pillow against a window. Her mouth was only slightly open and the only thing coming out was, barely, breath. Shireen was deep in someone else's dream maybe. *Oh, but Shireen, can't you wake for just a second and help your old dad out?* His own words bounced back to him, returned to sender, with a harsh echo so that he had to hear it again and again, *Help your old dad out, help your old dad out,* until he realized, for the first time really, that it was silly and bullshit, and this daydream, too, like all the others had no choice but to once and for all be shattered, once and for all crash and burn—because there was no daughter, no preferred sibling . . . if he wanted his child, he needed to get to the one he really had. He knew this and so he said again, hoping for just one last stir, *Shireen I just wanted to say good-bye, Shireen, and that I wish you well wherever you exist or don't, just a good-bye, Shireen?* but she couldn't hear him, not in that insulating coat of artificial silence, thirty thousand feet into the air, in the realm of constant sunsets and sunrises, cloud upon cloud, weather to new weather, of indistinguishable landmass and generic oceanic mileage, striped in invisible longitudes and latitudes, all altitude, all ungravity, pure heaven after heaven, over and out, over it all, over and oblivious to everything below, as if it was an accident, just dirt and grass and germ and concrete, featuring them, the ones with alleged souls, the ones that were doing and undoing it, over and over, day after day, and what was a day anyway but just another symposium of the star-crossed, and how could anyone blame her giving up like that, on humankind: what's not to hate . . . no, no, it was true, Shireen was already gone, Shireen was not about to stir for anything, anyone, certainly not him. He didn't take it personally, just kept his eyes closed enough to watch her and the big silver steel bird that held her burn through the layers of atmosphere, circling that pitiful dreamless grounded world, only bothering to wind down in sweeping swift spirals, makeshift circumferences, until it was clear that the vessel and its inhabitants were in a place where *home* was no longer a euphemism—the type of land that when you'd actually set foot on it, Darius smiled to himself, you'd want to shake yourself awake, wondering if this was really happening, wondering if you had maybe died and gone to the one heaven you could still imagine like yesterday.

XERXES: I didn't mean this the way you're thinking. Can we get that straight? I'm not inviting you. I'm better now, but not well. In regards to you.

DARIUS: In a way, from the beginning, this was how I saw it ending. This is the only way I imagined. You and I could never understand each other anywhere else.

XERXES: I'm not inviting you, Father. Now if you happened to be there when we were there, happened to run into us, me and my girl, if you were able to dig us out of a sea of our clones, our countrymen, then fine. I can't stop the inevitable if that's what has to be.

DARIUS: There is no other place for us. You won't know how much of that world you are until you get there. Then you'll see. You'll wonder how you can leave. You might not be able to.

XERXES: This is a trip. A vacation. I can guarantee you I would not be going if it were anything else. We are expecting to return. We are praying that won't be a problem. It can't be. It's curiosity, the politics of a relationship, my status in this new life in New York City, the ways of the world around me currently—those are the elements pushing me to go. It's not what you think. No longing for home. I don't know where the hell home is. I belong to fucking nowhere land.

DARIUS: I won't hold New York against you. So don't worry about coming back to me.

XERXES: I won't hold New York against you. So leave me alone.

DARIUS: Why can't I just call you right this minute and we'll talk?

XERXES: I'm trying to imagine you picking up the phone and calling me—me picking up, me hearing your voice—now what's
going to stop me from hanging up really? I still am not at peace
with you, my past, your past, where I come from, who I come
from . . . and this whole Iran trip, from the drama to the actual
vacation, none of it would be such a mess, such a conflict, if it
were not for you. All my life I have looked for a stability, a peace,
a wholeness that can't exist—because it's not only not in my
countrymen, it's not even in my country. My blood is fucked.
Yes, Father, I said fucked.

DARIUS: I don't think you'd hang up.

XERXES: You'll never know.

DARIUS: I'm dialing.

XERXES: Dial all you want . . . Father, we'll be together again in a
conversation, in a place, in a time, when it's right. Only then.
Good-bye.

"Hello?" Darius could barely recognize his own voice. It sounded
weak, shaky, elderly, particularly when bounced back against the
echoed "hello" that was all youth, vibrancy, confidence . . . and
femininity?

The bastard—it was not Xerxes—he had done it again!

"Who is this?" Darius said in his natural snap.

"Oh, this is Suzanne," she said nervously, the rude question seeming unmistakably like an Adam, even if it wasn't, as this was an older
man and it couldn't be, she told herself, it was not possible. . . .

"You are Xerxes's . . . ?" he mumbled, suspicion and unease and maybe even accusation, she sensed, deep in his throat.

She said she was. "Who is this?" she tried to ask just in case it was possible, trying hard to say it without sounding rude like . . . *them.*

"Oh, hello, this is Darius Adam," he said, with a hint of cordiality. "Is . . . is Xerxes home?"

She was relieved that he wasn't. She couldn't imagine being found lasting a second on the phone with that bugaboo of a man. "No, no sir," Suzanne said. "Honestly," she added, then feeling stupid for having added that because now it all sounded like a lie.

"Oh, I see," he grumbled, now sounding overtly suspicious. "Well. First, I need to speak to him. Can you let him know?"

She agreed.

"And then, secondly, maybe you can help." He had suddenly on the spot decided that there was no second to lose, *time becomes money,* he thought, *I must seize the second.* So he just simply asked it, "I hear you are going to Tehran?" and the way he pronounced that last word gave her goose bumps, it was so real, so severe, so in its original foreign-land form.

"Uh, yes," she muttered, amazed at how nervous she sounded, worried that again her truth sounded like a lie. He was an intimidating man—somehow she imagined more eccentricity, extra ludicrousness, a madman, a gong not an anvil—and he seemed to be controlling her every move just by speaking to her from thousands of miles away.

"Well, you see, so am I," he said, "and I can go anytime. I mean, I was planning to, that is. I wanted to just know when you were all getting there. Perhaps we can travel together."

Suzanne tried to sound delighted but couldn't believe herself—there she was, dangling off this stranger's marionette strings, suddenly dictating their itinerary, giving the dates, the times.

"Stopover in Frankfurt, you say," he repeated. "Okay . . . perhaps if nowhere else, I can first meet you there and we can all fly to Tehran together."

She said in a shaky voice that she would like that very much. She didn't know if she sounded as if she was lying, or if she really was lying.

"Good, good," he said. "Well, you have been a help. I need nothing else really. You, in fact, don't need to tell him I called."

She agreed.

The idea had occurred to him, he had flirted with finding a way, and then suddenly thanks to his history of ever-reliable absence, there *was* a way: he could drop a bomb on his son! "Don't, actually. Let's just say it can be a surprise."

She didn't say anything. Of course, she couldn't promise it, but he knew enough to not ask for a promise. He had just ordered, demanded—she could do with that what she dared. But she was amazed at how he just assumed she had no idea about their problems. She had no idea how a man could play it so cool. How a man could even be so lucky as to manage not to get the person he really couldn't speak to anyway.

"In fact, do *you* have a number?" he suddenly asked.

"A number?"

"Yes, your own phone number, can you give me that, please?" he chuckled. He was downright amused at the awkwardness he inspired, she thought.

She agreed.

"Okay then. Next week it is, huh! Well, I look forward to it and. . . ." he said, and then added an embarrassingly sincere, "and to meeting you!"

She tried to chuckle, to thank him, but a sound like a moan came out. "You, too," she croaked. She sensed he was about to hang up and she realized she had to say something, something to safeguard that fucked situation. Surely there was another disaster tucked into all the well-meaning deception. "Look, um, Mr. Adam, I can't guarantee anything is going to work out. I mean, even us making it there."

He chuckled, long and heartily, and totally misunderstood. "I have a feeling it's a different country. I don't think you'll be in any danger these days. No, I don't think we have any fear to worry about . . . but ourselves!" he laughed.

And before she knew it he was gone, and there she was with yet another potentially relationship-destroying—relationship-challenging? was that a good euphemism?—obstacle. Oh, Iran! Sure, they had nothing to fear when the thing was killing them already. How could Iran itself be the problem when clearly it was everything that came before Iran that they had to really worry about making it through?

✯   ✯   ✯

I can't take it anymore and hopefully you can just deal with it and it won't result again in me taking a blow—I'm sorry, I didn't want to bring it up again but how could I not—regardless, I have to approach you with it, be-cause we're not doing surprises anymore, that's what I learned—and I've had butterflies poking holes in my stomach for nearly a month now so I'd rather have it all explode now: Xerxes, your father is coming to Iran, too. So there.

She imagined she'd say it like that, all in one breath, like a car-toon God blowing clouds into storm. He'd have to take it. And then she'd take it. And there, another fight. This time one that she had nothing to do with. Oh, he'd be sorry. And maybe this once she wouldn't forgive him. She was getting sick of worrying about . . . everything.

She was imagining it as they sat eating microwave popcorn, ironi-cally enough, in front of the nightly news instead of the VCR, with the newscasters all riled up over some 9/11 black-box voice re-cording of the terrorists in one of the planes. As they got closer to airing it, she began feeling sicker and sicker. She couldn't take it. He, on the other hand, he was almost nodding off.

She got up, grabbed the remote, turned off the TV, and snapped, "Enough of this!" As she marched out, needing the vacuumlike solace of her own apartment to soothe her back into unfeeling, she heard a sleepy giggle from Xerxes.

"You sound like my father," he murmured, amused.

She walked back and just stood there, glaring at him.

He rubbed his eyes and smiled wider. "It's nothing. He just used to always shout *Enough!!*"

She nodded, biting her lip. She had to. She had to, had to. She let the anger and nausea in her bubble suicidally. *Oh, fuck him if he can't handle it. I'm sick of being sick.*

"Yeah, Xerxes, I can imagine," she began, with an almost malicious register to her voice. "I know exactly how he must say that. I can imagine it perfectly because . . . because I heard him." As if on cue, he squinted his eyes menacingly, just like a movie villain. "Yeah, get ready, because guess what? You know your whole brilliant Iran trip?" He was going to tell her it was *her* whole brilliant Iran trip in the first place—she seemed to constantly forget that, these days, with that always-anxious look on her face—but he didn't want to mess with her feelings. For once, Suzanne really looked as if she had had it. The light was out. "Well, here's yet another bonus to the whole thing—goddamn me and my goddamn birthday gift, the gift that keeps on giving—well, here you go: your father, your very own father, called the other day. Not long ago—don't freak out on that, I was gonna tell you immediately, it's just been a day or so—and he wanted to speak to you and lucky for everyone, I guess, you weren't here. Then he told me he heard we were going to Iran—from your mother, of course—and he said so was he." She paused, out of breath, trying to read his now wider eyes. "So he's gonna be there." He looked dazed and wordless. So she added another jab, just to shake him up, "Well, isn't that something?"

He nodded slowly. "Incredible," he rasped.

He lunged for the remote and turned the TV back on. Just in time for them to hear the voices of foreign men, jaggedly accented, over a radio speaker talking of bombs aboard, telling the passengers to stay calm and cooperate, and then a scream or two, and then just static. She wanted to run, run out and away from it and him and everything, but she couldn't bear to leave him. His eyes looked glazed.

As the TV played the sounds again and again, for no reason it seemed, but perhaps to display its own brand of terror, she curled up against him, feeling foolish at all her anger, and whispered, "So what do you think?"

He shrugged. "He knows what day?"

She nodded. He didn't ask if she had told him, but certainly assumed, she assumed herself. She felt as if she had just turned over her killer-lover to the cops.

Appropriately, he responded, "Well, he got me." He closed his eyes and laughed bitterly to himself and said it again, "Father, you got me."

"It's just a few days," she said. "We can ditch him. Or . . . you know, Xerxes, you keep forgetting, we *can* change the dates. Go a whole other time, when the world isn't that shit on TV, you know? Who knows if it's safe? Who knows if it's ever safe over there anyway? You know, we can just cancel it all, forever, you know. . . ."

He shook his head, shrugged, nodded, and finally let his lips rest on her neck, as he thought. He had become so gentle, she thought, almost kind-spirited. It scared her. Reminded her of all those profiles of the victims on TV, with their relatives talking about their night before, their last call, how they seemed so happy, so calm in their lives at that point. She always equated a new un-precedented calm as a calm before a storm. Especially with an Adam—she had heard about the father, but she knew firsthand from the son.

They went to bed early that night. She asked a few times, "But really are you okay?" All she'd get back was an "mmmhmm" at best and something that looked like a half-nod-half-headshake at worst.

And the next morning, she couldn't help beginning their day with, "So, Xerxes, what the hell are we going to do? Are we really doing this?"

For a second he looked tense and then there it came: that new laugh of his. That *God fuck us all* laugh. All he finally said—which helped her learn to drop it and go on with the plan, *this anti-plan, this anti-vacation of all vacations,* she thought bitterly—was a few final truly *enough* words,

"I never thought I'd ever have to see him again. But then again, I never thought I'd ever have to see Iran again, did I? So, fine . . . in an alternative or parallel or whatever universe, I'd say, woman, I suppose, *thank you.*"

Part Nine

Departures

The day before they were to take off, Xerxes Adam woke up feeling ill. *Are you all right?* Suzanne kept asking him and he'd nod away. *A cold,* he would say, *just a little spring thing.* She'd nod uncertainly until he would ask, *What about you? How are you?* She'd reply, *Just fine,* which physically she *did* feel, but in her head and heart she was in sync with his sickness. She was a wreck. Anything that came into her hands would be quaking along with the rest of her as if her nervousness was rubbing off on inanimate objects, giving them precarious lives of their own.

And so when she felt Xerxes also shaking in her arms, she cried, "Look at you! That's it—we're canceling, or postponing. You're not ready for this either!"

He held her face in his hands and looked deep into her eyes and said, "For the last time, Suzanne, don't be silly. It's you. It's just you. I'm ready. It's nothing."

But on that same day, when Al and Eleanor called for what felt like the hundredth time, still trying to persuade their daughter against the whole thing, Suzanne, in arguing *for* the trip's validity somewhat against her own will, found herself actually convincing herself that it could be okay. Blindly almost, like a debate team whiz, she shot everything they said down: *No no no. This is the most important thing I have done yet!* she kept trying to convince them/coach herself.

Meanwhile Xerxes coughed and sniffled as he packed with painful slowness in the background.

"Was that Z—was that a cough!?" Eleanor gasped.

"X, Mother, X," Suzanne, as usual, muttered under her breath.

"Is he all right?" Al said on the other line.

"Yes, yes, he has . . . a cold," Suzanne explained.

"Oh, stunning! A *cold* and you're putting him on a plane for what, twenty-four hours??!" Eleanor cried.

"Twelve," Suzanne said. "Seven hours to Frankfurt, five to Tehran." They were to leave New York at 4 p.m.; this would have them in Germany by 5:30 a.m., which was actually seven and a half hours. Then they'd have half a day to kill in the Frankfurt airport, till 2:55 p.m. They'd arrive in Tehran at 10:25 p.m., several hours after the Persian New Year had chimed in. Not only did the journey carry the appearance of twenty-four-plus hours, Suzanne was sure it would feel like a lot more. She did not admit this to her mother.

"Kids, they're kids, they know nothing!" Eleanor shrieked, so abrasively that Suzanne had to distance herself from the receiver.

"What Eleanor means is that we're trying to figure out why you wouldn't delay the trip perhaps until he's better," Al added. "Airplanes are just terrible for colds. And who knows, it could be more than that. People used to die of the flu—*influenza*—remember!"

"We're trying to get to Iran on the New Year," she snapped. "No delays."

"He could have some really horrible sickness!" Eleanor added. "You're not even looking into it! All you kids want to do is . . . party for New Year's! Well, I'll tell you what, missy, in that country I don't even think they do that—"

"You have a veil?" Al cut in.

"Mmm hmm," Suzanne said. "A *hejab*." It had been in her hands nonstop since she went over to the fabric store and got herself the most simple piece of black cotton they had. That was all you needed, they said. Sure, Iranian women were rumored to be more liberal these days, with more patterned ones in fancier fabrics, but Xerxes had warned her to risk nothing. They would have to lie low. *A halfie, who the hell knows what the Iranian government will make of you?* Xerxes would tell her, while adding secretly to himself, *and a halfie named Needle.*

Later that afternoon, Suzanne and Xerxes had their first fight since The Fight. *He* was back. In a way, she was relieved to see him fighting, no longer that strange ethereally beaming, *all-is-well* mantraed shade-saint of his old self. Resentment, wrath, and irrationality had been reintroduced to his system.

"It's just the cold—are you happy—just the cold that's making me an asshole!" he snapped, only somewhat apologetically. "And it's just the cold that's making you blow things out of proportion! And your parents—who, by the way, have NO idea what they're talking about—they just don't want us to go. The point is, I wish you'd stop fucking things up. Here I am trying to evolve, progress, do something good—"

"Fucking what up?" Suzanne snapped back. "We're less than twenty-four hours away from our . . . our *trip,* and you're a mess. Physically, psychologically—you know, I think it's your head that's making your body fall apart. You're a mess! Admit it, you're nervous, too!"

"*You're* making me nervous . . . about nothing!" Xerxes insisted, avoiding her eyes. "We're taking a goddamn vacation—a vacation that you planned, by the way—which I'm not opposed to, which in fact I was looking forward to—and you've been itching for some way out! I can't take it. . . ."

"No, no, it's fine, we're going," she said, with a defiant agreeability. "I just want to know what's wrong with you."

"Nothing! I have a *cold!*"

"Go to the doctor then," she insisted. "As is, I've never been so unprepared for anything in my life, Xerxes! So what would a last-minute doctor's checkup do to mess this mess up any further? Tomorrow, before the flight, make an appointment. Say it's an emergency. I swear, you have a fever. Just have it checked out. You don't want your sinuses combusting on a transatlantic flight, Xerxes!"

"Oh, please," he moaned, rolling his eyes, but he had to admit, he hadn't thought of that. No, he hadn't considered his sinuses. Now that he did, he could, in fact, feel his sinuses burning. His ears—he imagined the change in altitude and his ears popping, shattering, spewing blood! She had a point . . . but he had an argument. "Look, my sinuses will be fine. And there's no way in this city that a doctor will see me just like that!"

"*My* doctor will," she said. "He's . . ." She didn't want to bring her parents into it again, but weren't they already so awkwardly wedged in? They and the Account, the Account and its $3,066 in their combined airfare—The Account: wasn't it the real Iran-pusher in all this? "Look, Dr. Arnold knows me well. And this is an emergency. If you tell anyone, anyone at all, that we're going to Iran, they'll drop everything. Dr. Arnold certainly will."

Xerxes threw his hands helplessly in the air and began laughing, bitterly. "'Dr. Arnold, please help supply an out for our vacation! Oh, please tell me I have cancer so my girlfriend will be happy! Yes, Dr. Arnold, this was my birthday present from her, *but* she'd rather I have cancer. . . .'"

He went on and on. Before he knew it, Suzanne was in tears, half embracing him, half covering his mouth, shushing him like a baby, even though she was the one whimpering, pleading, "Stop it, stop it! I just want it all to be okay, to have whatever control we can over ourselves in all this. . . ."

Control: Xerxes grinned at her magic word. He continued, "After all, in Iran they don't have doctors! 'Please, Doc, diagnose me, because we're off to the Land Before Medicine!' That's what it is, isn't it—you're worried I'll fall dead in the old birthplace. In that old doctorless desert of a country! 'Oh, Dr. Arnold, please let me have my cancer in New York City only. . . .'"

When he finally took a moment to see that Suzanne was actually crying hard, he didn't have the heart to go on. He gave up and held her and promised that if it was possible, *fine*, for her sake, he'd go. He promised. *If* she promised one thing.

"Anything, Xerxes."

"That no matter what—even if I have to take medicine on the ride, there, afterward, whenever—that no matter what—okay, fine, if it's cancer for real, okay, that's an exception—but really Suzanne, no matter what the cold or flu or whatever, we're just gonna do it, do it and get it over with. . . ." Xerxes had that look: dead serious. And even though it didn't make any sense—the way he had made the doctor's visit totally inconsequential—she knew that it was too late. They had to. *Get it over with*—she blinked at those words, running like ticker tape across her mind. So that was how he thought of it all? She shook her head, knowing it would be worthless—no matter what, he'd come back saying he was fine anyway. Hell, he *was* fine, but let the doctor tell them that. It was just the last bit of *control* they had: ascertaining they were going into it wholly intact, knowing that should anything go wrong, it was not them—no, they were healthy and fine and in one piece before they got there.

*   *   *

There had been a plan and it had fallen through thanks to both of them. The plan: Darius would get himself to the airport by noon at the latest, after first driving her to LAX (they would wake up at 6 a.m. and get her there by 8 a.m.) and then going home, packing, returning to LAX for his own flight. The assumption was that Darius would be awake at 6 a.m. anyway, as he usually was.

Lala had opened her eyes at 6 a.m., without an alarm going off, even though she hadn't fallen asleep until 4 a.m. She had turned to him—his eyes were closed. She wasn't entirely shocked because at 4 a.m., right before she had fallen under, she had glanced over and there he had been, awake, glazed eyes transfixed on the ceiling. It made sense that two hours later, the eyes would give up and be gone. *So it's 6 a.m.—he knew, if he wants to be up, he'll get up himself, if not . . .* She did not wake him. She tiptoed to double-check her bags, all tidily packed and done.

He, on the other hand, had left all his packing to do that morning. *You're going on an international flight, spending a full week in our old third world country—don't you think what you take is pretty important? You haven't flown in years—since the Revolution, God, since Iran—you think you'll be so quick to get it all together?* In his head he had answered, *Oh, you'll be mailing much of my possessions to me anyway, woman. If this is it, if this is separation, if there is that chance that I am there to stay, then so be it! How does a man pack for that? I have to begin everything again—what's a few new shelves and shirts?*

But she knew that in spite of the lax preparations, Darius Adam had to be nervous. He had clearly been up worrying all night, because after she said *good night* to him at around midnight—and he said *good night* back, and they embraced a little more than lukewarmly for a minute, kissing each other's face with the soft defeated restraint of sick patients handling other sick patients—and pretended to sleep for the next four hours, she had periodically peeked through the corner of her eyes at his very awake face. His eyes were as open as a dead man's: unblinking, unexploring, owned by some compelling phantom point in the heavens. He was beyond pretending.

So that morning, as she tiptoed around him, she realized it was actually a relief not to deal with him and his end of the anxiety. She put on the nice dress she had chosen days before, applied a little makeup, and called a cab, without even a last look at him.

She focused on the image of her brother instead—gaining her brother, her blood, the person most like her in the world—and tried to have that shadow fall over the face of the sleeping Darius in her head. It got her and her bags out the door.

What she didn't know was that by the time the front door uttered its understated slam, Darius was already sitting up and watching her out the window. He had been awake and pretending to sleep. When she rose so sneakily, he thought, *Best this way. Best this way when you don't know what sort of parting a thing is.*

On the other hand, he hated that thought and its reek of finality. He told his head to tell his heart it would have to do everything in its power to not let their world turn upside down. At least not so fast, not like this. Certainly no good-bye meant no real parting.

He watched her through the blinds, struggling with her luggage, acting so surprised when the cabdriver helped her with her bags. He could see her overthanking him, but she'd probably forget to tip. He was glad she had left first—it made more sense, *her* leaving *him*. It was how he preferred it. His leaving would have to mean something else altogether—better the easy go first, better it look as if he had no choice, better he seem motivated by illusions of abandonment. He watched her face in the backseat turn to their window. She was smiling. She looked small and excited like a child, a girl far littler than when he had met her. She would have to be okay. The cab stalled for a second and he wondered if she could see him. Probably not. *Let her imagine me the way that's best for her.* Sleeping, peaceful, at rest, always there, always the ground beneath them —any other way would have to be her call.

They had been through everything, it felt, and he had always envisioned more.

He tried to promise himself that no matter what there would ultimately be nowhere to go but *back*—back here, back to her— but it was the word *promise* that got in the way.

※   ※   ※

Of all things to do the morning of his return to Iran, nothing could have been *wronger* to Xerxes than to be sitting patiently, at 8:30 a.m., in the frosty fluorescent-lit reception area of Dr. Reginald Arnold's midtown office.

"Have you seen Dr. Arnold before?!" the receptionist chirped the minute he stepped in.

"No," Xerxes shook his head, smiling phonily, sweating badly, making both nervousness and illness equally unknowable.

"Referral?!"

"No. Well, yes. Maybe." He told her who his girlfriend was and prayed that this was all that was necessary.

"Oh, *Suzanne* . . . Al's daughter!" the receptionist laughed. "Oh, wonderful! Wow, haven't seen them in a minute. How lucky you are!"

Xerxes nodded hesitantly. The receptionist had him fill out some forms and told him the wait wouldn't be long.

Forty-five minutes later, as he thumbed through the latest *National Geographic* in a cold sweat—Afghanistan, Iraq, Saudi Arabia, all featured, page after page, all of *his* somewhat-people and their dark faces and dead eyes and veils and wraps and tunics and inhospitable landscapes and dying animals and ruin after ruin—he finally got called in.

The nurse put him into a neat white room, took his temperature—"totally normal"—his blood pressure—"absolutely normal"—and left him, not without saying, "I hear you're a friend of Al's. Do say 'hi' to him! We miss him! It's been a while . . . how is he?"

"I assume very healthy," Xerxes said through clenched teeth, "if it's been such a while."

The nurse laughed hysterically, as if he had made the best joke ever, and left him there, where he waited another long—but slightly shorter—while until finally the door opened and a towering white old ghost of a man in a doctor's coat appeared before him.

"Reginald Arnold," he said as he extended his pale nearly translucent hand. "You are . . . er, Excor-sis Adams. Did I butcher that? Oh, friend of Al's, I see?"

"*Zerk-zees Adam*—boyfriend of his daughter's," he quickly corrected. He had never seen such a white, white man. He looked like an apparition. Like an old painting of a dead president, supernaturally, awfully, American. "Doctor, I'm actually in a bit of a hurry, you see. I'm going abroad this afternoon. . . ."

"Is that right?" He scribbled something into his notepad.

"Yes. Very far. *Asia*." Xerxes had thought about it beforehand and decided that Asia had just the neutrality that could slip past controversy. "I just want to make sure I'm okay." He told him the symptoms and the doctor nodded at everything. He checked his ears, throat, chest.

"Well, Mr. Adams, I'm not sure why you're here!" he said. Big smile, brown teeth.

Neither am I, Xerxes thought to himself, *neither am I.* "It's *Adam.* But, well, we just wanted to make one hundred percent sure, with this trip and all. I feel . . . fine. Or close. Or a little bad. But then, I always do—feel bad, I mean."

"Well, you shouldn't always feel bad. We'll schedule another appointment and see how you're doing nutrition-wise, run some blood tests—I see you haven't had a physical in years. But, as for today, right now. . . ." He smiled and shrugged and scribbled something on the notepad again.

"Nothing is off at *all?*"

Dr. Arnold looked up, still vaguely amused. "Tell me, what exactly do *you* feel is wrong with you? What feels off?"

It felt like a test. Xerxes tried to explain his symptoms, but every time he mentioned one, it sounded like an exaggeration or a justification for his presence there.

"Well. Have you been stressed lately?"

Xerxes thought about it. *Of course.* He hadn't been as aware of it—he had been so intent on living drama-free, going with the flow of life, of Suzanne, her plans, this dream, getting it over with—but clearly he had to have been. He told the doctor he was, although he always was.

"Hmm. Okay, well, trips can make one nervous, too. And Asia, you say! My! Japan?" he grinned widely, for no reason Xerxes could think of.

The spook had outsmarted him. Enter controversy. Xerxes slowly shook his head. "Well, actually, no. Less East. Middle, really. The . . . Middle . . . East."

"Oh, wow! Israel . . . ?" said the grin, resolute and, Xerxes thought, rude.

Xerxes shook his head, feeling near faint. He wished the doctor had taken his blood pressure at *this* point. "No, not quite." There was no way to gloss it over. He didn't want to get into it at all, but he wanted it over with. "Not at all, really." He paused and with closed eyes blurted it out: "Iran!"

When he opened his eyes, he saw that the doctor was all raised eyebrows, with a big grin to end all big grins. "Whoa! Okay! That's a first." He scribbled several things furiously on his pad again.

"I've never been," Xerxes lied, thinking birth after all wasn't such a lie. "My parents are from there."

The doctor nodded, still deep in the world of his pad and pen. He had suddenly grown quiet, busily writing more and more. Without looking up, he muttered, "Anything more I can help you with today, Mr. Adams?"

Xerxes thought about it. "Well, no. But according to you—everything, sinuses, et cetera—all okay?"

Dr. Arnold, still without eye contact, began to move himself and his all-engrossing pad over to the door. It was over. "Mr. Adams, everything seems perfectly fine to me. Have a fine trip. We'll check on you further, soon, I do hope!"

His "hope" had a bad ring to it.

"I hope so," Xerxes added, pissed that he'd repeated the h-word.

As the doctor began to walk out, Xerxes asked, just in case, just once more, "So nothing wrong with me at all, huh?"

The doctor popped his ghostly head through the barely opened door. "Nothing that I can see, Mr. Adams!" The doctor again put too much work into his grin, looking more than ever like some strange colonial specter, a weird ghost of a man whose ill-illuminated presence suddenly seemed to Xerxes to indicate something more, a significance that he was too sick to read, an omen that his disease-struck spirit was too battered to translate. . . .

"Well, good, thanks!" The door closed, and Xerxes shook his head roughly, as if to shake off all stupid thoughts, and got moving. On his way out he discreetly waved to the receptionist, who cried back, "Bye, and promise to send our regards to Al and the family, okay?!"

Once in the midtown sunshine he felt exhausted. He considered the nearby subway stop but instead, feeling drained and surely even sicker than before, he decided it was best to hail a cab. The suddenly-summer sun seemed to be draining him of any will. It felt as if a full day's emotional energy had been spent, and the day was just about to begin. *Asia*, after all, was still ahead of him.

The duration of the cab ride also felt too much to be true. When the cab pulled over at his block, Xerxes decided to tip better than he had ever tipped in his entire life, and like some kind of new, overly gentlemanly, but clearly God-fearing man, instead of his usual *Bye, thanks* he commanded the cab driver to take care of himself.

Just as he stepped out of the cab a homeless man, cradling an empty bottle, rammed drunkenly into him. *Watch it*, Xerxes snapped, appalled at drunkenness like that at 11 a.m. However, at his apartment door, inches away from his girlfriend and the world of final trip preparations, he paused. *Omens,* he thought. He had to learn to read whatever he could. He rewound himself back to the corner and thought, what would it hurt, there was some time, he was healthy, it would make him *feel* healthier at least, make him more bearable, with all the stress, the stress that after all could lead to illness should it not be attended to, why not? . . . He ducked into that same corner bar—the one he hadn't sat slumped in, hadn't so shamefully sought, hadn't ordered Scotch on the rocks after Scotch on the rocks, hadn't found himself hiding in just like that, no, not since his father had visited well over a year before.

*   *   *

Just before noon, Darius Adam was spotted sitting on a large piece of luggage outside of Eden Gardens, waiting for something, apparently.

Marvin, even though he had never seen him before and mostly forgotten he existed, immediately knew it was *him*. The man had that foreign look and it wasn't Mexican or Indian or anything like that. He looked Middle Eastern and a bit disturbed, the way he had always imagined Lala's husband looking.

Marvin had been on his way home from a sleepover at Gigi's— a late night of drinking that had ended up with him far too incapacitated to drive. He was heading over to his SUV parked on the Arcadia curb, when he identified the man and thought, *What the hell*— he couldn't help wanting to do it, now that it was finally upon him.

With Lala out of their lives, what was so wrong with him having a casual word with just another grown man in the universe?

"Hello there," Marvin called, adding a big smile and a wave. Darius Adam forced a tight smile and a nod, and that was that.

Marvin, hungover and therefore feeling a bit *fuck-it*, decided to really press the *what-the-hell*ishness in him that day. He went over and extended his hand. "Marvin Dill," he said. "I think I . . . know you, so to speak?"

Darius Adam took his hand reluctantly, adding a firm shake of his head. *Fine, hello*, it said, reluctantly, but *Enough*, it also said.

"I know your wife, I mean," Marvin clarified. "Not well or anything. We met. Through a woman named Gigi in the building. Your wife . . . Lala Adam?"

Darius Adam nodded slowly, looking more curious as well as more pissed.

"She's a nice lady," Marvin said awkwardly. "Haven't seen her around for a while."

Darius Adam continued to nod. He had to say something. "She's been here. Until today. Now she's . . . gone."

"Gone? What do you mean?" Marvin, of course, couldn't help equating *gone* with *dead*. For a second, his body stiffened in alarm.

"My wife went to New York," he said, still tight-lipped, as if only giving in to him in hopes of his giving up.

"Where your son lives, right?" Marvin was relieved she wasn't goner-gone, but had to throw that in for Gigi's sake. The whole New York thing had always seemed a bit bogus, so here was their chance.

"He's not there," Darius said, and just as Marvin was about to think *aha!* Darius clarified, "He lives there, but she's not seeing him."

Marvin nodded. Odd egg, that Lala, and obviously married to another odd egg, this Darius, who seemed fiercely antisocial in nature, and yet here he was, almost accommodating with info, spilling most beans. Sure, he was a bit gruff, but he had the gruffness of a man pissed about having nothing much to conceal. "So why is she there? She didn't move?"

Darius almost shrugged. "A visit, I guess. Her brother. She is going to see him, she thinks."

Marvin froze. *No*, he thought. *Hot damn, it couldn't be* . . . "Her brother? The one?"

Darius nodded, looking even more suspicious. "So you knew about that. Good friend, I guess? Yes, she thinks she found him."

Marvin nodded. "He found her? The one who was lost, since they were . . ."

Darius Adam nodded. "You know a lot. You met my wife a few times?"

"A few." Marvin paused. "He actually, really, finally did write to her, huh?"

Darius Adam nodded again, looking close to exasperated.

He couldn't begin to pursue this properly. He dropped it, his whole body nonetheless shaking a bit in shock. Slowly, he asked, "So are you going to New York, too, then?"

Darius laughed. "Oh no! Never again, I hope. I didn't like . . . well, I had a tough time there once. Anyway, I am going to . . . Iran."

Marvin wondered if Darius was fucking with him. He had never heard Lala mention either of them wanting to go.

"Going home, eh?" he tried to say it in a friendly way that he feared sounded creepy and mocking. He didn't want to alienate Darius—who seemed okay after all. He should have known that crazy Lala bad-mouthing him all the time meant that he was actually an okay guy at least.

Darius Adam didn't interpret it condescendingly. He gave a small shrug again, then smiled. "Back home . . . for good!"

"For good?" Marvin exclaimed.

Darius Adam's black eyes looked as if they were winking in the deep sunshine. "No, no. . . . I said, 'so good!'"

Marvin nodded. He had so many questions to ask, about Lala, about her brother, but he didn't know how he could ask them. He decided when Lala was back he would go and see her. He would sneak away from Gigi, never tell her even, and corner Lala for a chat. Maybe just a last chat—Lala couldn't hate him so much that she wouldn't dish the end of that saga, the happy ending that she had to know she at least mostly owed to him.

When Darius's car service arrived several silent minutes later, Marvin immediately went to help him stuff his luggage in the trunk.

"Thanks," Darius said, "but the cabdriver could have done that."

Marvin shrugged. "Just have a great trip. Maybe see you soon!"

"I don't know—maybe!" Darius said, with a rough laugh. As he got into the cab, he rolled down the window, and with a savagery that seemed intentionally comic or a comic tag that had an intentional savagery, with a definite wink, a wink or maybe a squint, but a smile, possibly a grimace, more than a smile—*Who ever knew with that crazy family?*—Darius yelled, "and stay away from my no-matter-what-still-wife please!"

There he was—the man Lala had described—and there he wasn't. Marvin waved impotently as the cab sped off. He sat there for a moment, on the Eden curb, contemplating what they all meant, that odd Odd-damn family, before he got into his SUV and went on with his life.

* * *

In spite of his hypothesis, the Scotches on rocks were not helping. He in fact felt sicker than ever. Butterflies in stomachs were one thing, but Xerxes Adam felt as if his entire gastrointestinal universe were infested by rats—they were gnawing and nibbling and regurgitating . . . it was too much. It was so much that when 1 p.m. rolled around—when he knew he was due just a few doors down, at his apartment, to gather bags, his girl, and that car service to JFK—he simply couldn't. The bartender eyed him sadly as he ordered his sixth drink.

"Please don't let me have another," Xerxes moaned miserably. "My wife . . . I have to meet my wife." He was calling her *his wife*. He couldn't believe it. The bartender was nodding, trying to juggle him against the animated booze-for-lunch crowd.

He finally made it to good judgment and closed his tab and was spending a long while just contemplating the bill when his cell phone rang.

The inevitable: "Uh, Xerxes. . . ." It was Suzanne, of course, sounding alarmed and annoyed, of course. "What's going on? I've been calling all morning. Is everything okay? The car service is coming any second . . . where are you?"

Xerxes tried to chuckle—he was going for a chuckle that would sound soothing and pleasant, a *no worries* kind of chuckle, but instead he feared it came out sleazy, irresponsible, drunken. He feared the chuckle's accuracy.

"Oh, Suzanne, Suzanne, Suzanne!" he stalled. He hot-wired his brain to emergency mode. "You see, I got out just recently—I'm sick indeed—nothing major, but bad enough—an infection—a mild one though—must get medicine. That's where I am now. Getting medicine. Pharmacy. Midtown. The Midtown Pharmacy. Waiting for the medicine. It's an obscure one—it might take a while longer—not too long—but you know. . . ."

Suzanne was silent for a moment. "Xerxes, are you *too* sick? What is it? You were at the doctor's for, like, four hours?"

"Well, yes," he chuckled again. "Got there—it took some time for him to see me—so last-minute, you know, the appointment— oh, the doctor says 'hi' to your dad—anyway, it took some time and then there were all the tests—blood tests, cancer tests, and whatnot —it took a while. Then I went to a couple of drug stores for this drug—hard to find—but they have it—once I take it, it will be fine."

Silence.

He added, "I'm coming. You know, I swear, I'm coming! I mean, we're going. Yes! All is well!"

Suzanne again paused. "Xerxes, you sound really strange. Look, we're going to miss our plane. And I'm worried about you. What can I do?"

"Oh, nothing," he said. "Nothing, nothing. No, you're right— shit—the plane. Su . . . you know, you should . . . you should take it!" His brain was fixing the unfixable. *Genius,* he thought.

"Take what?" she said, sounding suddenly as though she was approaching patience deficiency.

"The plane! I'll be . . . I'll take the next one." He couldn't be- lieve what he was suggesting. It was almost as if he was trying to get—*Oh, it was brilliant,* his head told him. It was the best idea he'd had in a while.

Suzanne sighed. He didn't sound right. Not even sick, just crazy. She didn't know what to make of it.

Meanwhile, the car service was buzzing her door. "The car's here, Xerxes. I'll cancel it. I'll cancel it now."

"No!" he shouted. "You listen to me—there is definitely a later flight—I will get it—probably with the long stopover in Frankfurt we can still take the Tehran flight together. It'll all work out . . . somehow. . . ." His own words shocked him. In the airbrushed universe of alcoholic buzz, he apparently had some solutions. That slight possibility of being right, having a way to make the mess work for once, was filling him with energy, the superhuman mania that could make emergency-struck men suddenly lift cars and bend steel. . . .

Before he knew it, she was in tears. *Nope, called that too soon, back to nothing working out.* Once again, he was making her cry. He wondered if he should just pay up and run over to her, then and there, pretend he had hopped into a speeding cab and made it. But he couldn't. He simply couldn't imagine seeing her, then getting into a plane and zooming off. Not in the state he was in. It could only make things worse. Plus, now he did feel sick. He finally felt *really* sick. The rats—he felt his stomach lining corroding— he was maybe even dying—yes, he had to be sure he wasn't dying first.

By some miracle, Suzanne finally agreed to take the cab—her exact words "Oh God, who the fuck cares at this point!"—and carried their conversation out onto the curb.

Phone to his ear, Xerxes ran to the bar door, where, through a little dirty diamond-shaped peephole of a window, he could see his girlfriend just a diagonal block away, struggling with two large bags.

"Oh, you didn't have to take mine!" he accidentally said.

"Your what?" she snapped. "I'm taking your bags, if that's what you mean. Wait, wha . . . ?"

"I know you!" he tried to laugh it off. "I knew you would!"

She was silent again. Once in the cab, she said, "I hate this. I want you to know I hate this."

"I understand," he said, trying to sound reasonable. He added a chuckle that was meant to be consoling.

"If you do, then why, oh why, are you so amused? Why are you laughing at this, Xerxes?"

He was silent. He had no more ideas.

"I'm calling my travel agent now to find out the next flight," she went on. "If what you suggest can actually work, okay. If it doesn't work, I'm coming back in this cab. But listen, if I go on that flight and land in Frankfurt and you never show up, Xerxes, I'm coming back. But not to you. It will be *so* over."

It was the first time she had ever made such a threat. In spite of its being quite fair, considering, it still pissed him off.

"Please, I'm sick, I don't need that," he snapped.

When they finally got off the phone, Xerxes suddenly felt washed in a disappointing wave of sobriety. *What did I just do?* he thought. He put down his money and thanked the bartender and got up. It was harder to walk than he imagined—aspirations toward sobriety were perhaps jumping the gun. Outside, the sunlight was piercing and terrible. But he couldn't wait to get to his apartment—his Suzanne-less, luggage-less apartment, his apartment before her and all the crazy plans.

But before he even got inside his door, there she was, calling again.

"There's a 9:30 p.m. flight, whole different airline, different deal, that my agent got you on," she said, still snapping and stony. "You'll only be five hours behind. You get in at 10:40 a.m. and then we can take the 2:55 p.m. to Tehran. It's the only way it will work. I'm actually amazed it *can* work."

"Great!" he said. It would give him enough time to really sober up, sober up and think, set his brain and stomach right again, get ready, and be off.

She gave him the flight details. "So be ready by six at the latest —I called you a car, too. Anyway, I guess I'll just be there waiting by myself in Frankfurt for hours . . . oh, your dad will get in, he said, around ten. So, we can have a little awkward time together before you get there, just me and your dad!" she sounded bitter yet restrained, as if she was holding back some serious fury.

His silence was heavy. It made her reevaluate her tone. "Yeah, um, he called again," she said sheepishly. "Wanted to confirm the times. . . ."

His dad. He had forgotten about that part. What a disaster. He didn't even address it, and consoled himself by thinking that without him how the hell would she find Darius anyway? It was better that she didn't. They could both just not find him until they absolutely had to. The idea of cutting down their dad-time—maybe never finding him at all, thanks to his delay—was a huge bonus, he thought.

"Okay, everything is fine!" he heard himself chuckle again to her. But she was already gone and all he had was static on his cell. He decided he had earned this time—a spare-time reward for cowardice and delinquency and deception—to enjoy his perfectly neat, perfectly comfortable, perfectly *his*, New York apartment for a last few hours—not last few, as in *last few*, as in *never again*, no, surely it wasn't so bad, *I'm not going to meet my death, it's a vacation, a vacation for me and my girl, and, er, my father, who we can dodge anyway, everything is fine, see, see, see*—to take in and then abandon, like everything else. Leaving, escaping, exiling, always running off and away—it was natural. It was in his blood, after all, he thought, chuckling still.

*   *   *

It was unusually bright outside, she thought, as her plane took off. Lala didn't remember it like this—well, not on *that* flight, twenty-something years ago, her one plane flight, from Iran to America— she didn't recall all that sunniness illuminating the thing's insides like that. It made her worry that all the light was actually from something burning. If she tried, she could smell it—something intense, chemical, plastic, worrisome. And the sounds, she hadn't remembered the sounds—the purring, the roaring, the screeches—just like a car, but worse. Like a cross between a big rig and a dragon—a monstrous thing whose mechanisms were altogether above their heads. She realized she had never had to pick if she was a plane-person or not, but now she knew she wasn't. The whole thing was making her ill.

Next to her sat a businessman—not a very fancy one, she decided, as there he was in her economy section, drinking Coke, with his tie untied. Every time she'd jump, startled by some unanticipated shake, rattle, or roll, she'd look to him, and either he'd ignore her or, once in a while, he'd look up and wink.

What the hell does that wink mean? she thought. But it seemed to sum it all up, the entire experience—signals, signs, omens—nobody in a plane communicated, nobody explained things, people just sat there suspended, knocked out, or else with all selfhood sucked out of them for passengerdom's sake, that belly of the beast just an accepted no-living zone. They could be their human selves, articulacy and reactions and all, once they were on the earth again. Here in the heavens they might as well be dead.

Don't say that don't say that don't say that! she scolded herself, shuddering. When the stewardess came around asking for drink orders, Lala paused, tried to plaster on a big charming smile, and asked, "Do you have anything that will . . . put me away?"

"Put you away?!" said the white smile of the stewardess, her blue eyes swelling dumbly like over-flooded globes.

"Put me, you know, away, off . . . out? Put me out, that's it, right?"

"Put you out!" the stewardess exclaimed, working the glossy putty of her face into an expression of exaggerated disapproval.

"Sleep," Lala said. "You know, like how everyone else is sleeping."

The stewardess laughed, again over-animatedly, so charmed indeed. "Oh, I think the sleeping ones may be taking something a bit *more* than a drink!" she laughed. "We don't have sleeping pills or anything, ma'am, none that we issue. Can I get you . . . tea? Wine?"

Lala shook her head, annoyed. Now that the stewardess had finally gotten it, Lala suddenly felt insulted. No, she didn't necessarily mean sleeping pills—she just wanted advice, a chat, a nice word about everything being normal and right. "Never mind, I want nothing," she mumbled.

When the stewardess came back, she brought water anyway. Lala took it without thanking her, chugged it down, and tried to shut her eyes.

It was even more annoying. Every time she tried to envision him—that grown Xerxes-looking brother of hers, say, in a tie, a tie and hat, smiling, maybe even a bit pleasantly plump, holding flowers for her, flowers and a hug—he would evaporate, evaporate and become. . . .

Darius. Big lanky Darius in a worn, cheap dress shirt and supermarket flip-flops, with his arms folded across his chest—a combined gesture of fiery agitation and icy condescension—Darius with his mouth open and going on and on, fists clenching and unclenching, arms throwing themselves in the air, hands running through his nearly extinct patches of shocked white hair—Darius pacing, Darius cursing, Darius demanding . . . it was all she got. Her husband; no brother. The plane; no New York. There was still no peace; she was still thousands of miles from the proposed peace.

Many hours into the flight, as the plane began its slow descent, she began to drift off—just as the cluster of skyscrapers began to appear out from under the clouds and passengers began to point and crane their necks for that perfect sunny midday panoramic view—and with shut eyes, she began to *see* again. But this time it wasn't him—nor *him*, not even her brother actually—it was just herself, herself in a black dress, juggling bagel-coffee-cigarette, hair done, sunglassed, all fancy and young and stupid, with her gloved hands pressed up against the glass of a big uptown jeweler that was of course *the one*, where she was pausing dreamily, sighing, leaning under the Tiffany's sign contentedly, as if it were her only home, perfect, hope-filled, and promising—until the tires hit the runway and she was jolted back hard to an appropriately breakneck, perfectly startling conclusion.

*   *   *

It had been well over two decades since Darius Adam had flown. In the plane it felt just like being home again: the grand rumble of the engines, the strange hiss of overhead air, the pilot's deal-sealing greeting, the pretty stewardesses, the free juice . . . it was great. He was so grateful for the ten hours in which he had nothing to do but not exist. Exit Darius. Fade out. Do nothing. Do not even *do* nothing. Just nothing. No thoughts even. Or say you wanted to think a thing or two—*poof*, it wouldn't count on land! He remembered having lusty stewardess fantasies on that ride to America and devising that theory then and there—it didn't matter in the heavens, only thoughts on earth did. Once on the ground, he would have to push those fantasies out. But in the plane, hell, Darius thought, there might even be an argument for pushing that foxy stewardess into a bathroom and getting away with it.

On this flight, it wasn't the stewardesses who were providing the forbidden thoughts. It wasn't even that strange black man and his wife, who were popping up in the paranoiac chambers of the anxiety department within his brain. It was just his son, his son, his one and only son, whom he could suddenly talk to and tell over and over—free in the space of his head, free in the space of the heavens, so far from the real dramas of the earth—*Son, I love you,* over and over . . .

*   *   *

Something went wrong.

But before that inevitable something took its wrong turn, Xerxes actually made it—against all odds, even though barely getting out of the fog of a hazy hangover by 6 p.m., Xerxes Adam made it to the airport. He arrived early even. He had sat in the terminal mostly calm—the remnants of the hangover taking the edge off of everything, sapping him of any complicated thoughts, of which there would have otherwise been many. He had reveled in the luxury of excess time by eating pretzels and drinking vitamin-infused water and watching as the clock neared the 9:30 takeoff. He was glad it would be night—he had no interest in *really* realizing he was leaving the continent. He didn't want to see all that water or the new foreign landmasses that would undoubtedly look different—they would have a different expanse from theirs, Mars-like, *more* unfamiliarly hued, *more* bodies of water he couldn't name, another mountain range to remind him of the consistently cumbersome nature of the earth's foundation. He would sleep, he decided. He would sit back, sleep, and in the morning deal with the reality of what he had actually done in agreeing to this nightmare.

But as life often went for Xerxes Adam, something had to go wrong. Only minutes after he had taken his seat—luckily next to an old couple, probably German, German-looking at least, who upon sitting looked instantly passed out—and the stewardesses had

355

tucked everyone in and the pilot had announced the flight time of seven hours and thirty minutes—just minutes after the plane had taken off into the dark clear New York night, they all saw that something was wrong.

Namely, in the form of a flash of gold and an apparently consequential rumble or two.

The problem was that with the very nebulous operating nature of planes, with their inner workings mostly a mystery to their generally ignorant patrons, who knew what to make of it? With their usual weird night-lights and such who could tell if it was an abnormality? Xerxes saw the flash; everyone else saw the flash, too. But certainly owing to the strange etiquette codes, behavioral requirements, and silently enforced social standards especially post-9/11, no one allowed himself to blink an eye. The ones with their eyes closed kept them closed. The ones engrossed in their magazines stayed engrossed. The ones zoning out into space stayed zoned. So Xerxes closed his eyes, pushed his seat back a bit, and tried to forget it, too.

He was trying to shove himself into the cusp of sleep when the pilot cut in with his garbled static-ridden message. It was clear something was wrong. It was not the usual monotone of pilots, though it was not hysteria either—it was just a deep gravity that meant business. The only words Xerxes really caught were "bird" and "engine." Which were enough. Soon, throughout the cabin everyone was whispering—*and why people whisper in planes, who knows,* Xerxes thought, *especially now!*—and the flight attendants, too were scurrying around like those battery-operated robot toys that bump into walls and redirect themselves over and over and over. The stewardesses were well-meaning, wanting to be there for them, be there and there and everywhere, but how could they or anyone in a situation like that . . . ?

A bird had blown out an engine, the story went. *How fucking perfect*, Xerxes Adam thought, *of all fucking ends, this ending. . . .*

His mind was struggling to slow down the chaos of thoughts coming sheet after sheet, slicing and dicing their way through his brain to his core, head to heart—the heart, the graveyard of all the truest, toughest thoughts. He thought hard and fast, as perhaps it was the last dance of the thinking device: *Now planes can fly on one engine, people say that, it's true—but there's a worst part here and it's not mechanics —bird, engine, fire, what does that remind you of—don't pretend like it's an enigma, asshole—birds like stars burning out in the night—oh, look what your fear has done, Xerxes—fuck, it's me, perfect ending—but you have the wrong Adam, wrong Adam, this is my father's fate, not mine—the bastard, where is he, here by now, there while I am about to be nowhere—oh, nowhere land, here I come, here I don't come—this is how it had to end, with this group of people, under the rules of my father's fate— and me, a Middle Eastern man dying in a plane crash, oh, what would they think— surely I am guilty, I mean, surely they would think I am the one, I am the guilty —Suzanne, Father, Mother, wherever you are, are you happy, are you happy—did I, I did, I did this to you, look, look, look what my fear has done. . . .*

His internal narrative was going nonstop—externally, he made sure to wear a calm collected smile that he hoped was sending out the message to the by-now-hysterical-and-no-longer-whispering passengers, that it was okay, it would all be okay, this happened all the time . . . *bird + engines = all good, we're gonna make it!*

And P.S., people: Yes, so technically I am Middle Eastern, but totally raised in LA, United States citizen, Allah hater, all-ish-American—and at this moment, people, I'd even go Republican! So don't worry about me—we are totally going to make it!

Except clearly they weren't. Not to Europe, at least. What they did hear the pilot say clearly enough was that they would have to turn back to JFK—not even twenty minutes into it and they would have to go back to where they started. Nobody was disagreeing with that move. The plane lurched and lunged as it deepened its descent—making only a few more bad sounds than planes usually make, Xerxes calmly consoled himself—and when they were just some yards from the apparently emergency runway area, Xerxes Adam realized the hardest part yet was seeing the ambulances and fire trucks waiting for them to hit the ground, hit it one way or another—and at the sight of them, just maybe a half minute away from touchdown, Xerxes Adam did the thing he had been putting off not just all flight, but all day: he began to wholeheartedly *cry.*

Part Ten

Landings

It was still pitch-dark midnight in Frankfurt at 5:30 a.m. when Suzanne's plane landed with such grace that she did not come to until her neighbor nudged her. Then she woke with a start and the young girl, with whom she had barely exchanged a word the whole flight, apologized and then muttered, "You missed the whole thing. It's over."

Suzanne awkwardly smiled and asked her how the flight was. "It's always bad, isn't it, though?" said the girl.

Suzanne shrugged. She had, admittedly, popped half a sleeping pill—she had taken it mostly to curb the stress of the day, with Xerxes abandoning her like that, with Xerxes sick or *something*, with her now all alone about to face his father, then him, and then the country where the trouble was only bound to begin. She felt sorry that she had slept because the flight was the part she was looking forward to the most—not being anywhere, not dealing with any- one. It was on the ground where the problems really lived.

The airport was big. It was white but not pristine the way she imagined the Germans would keep their airports—some parts were polished to minimalist immaculacy, other parts looked old and neglected. There were Mercedes Benzes on display in glass cases, maps of Germany, beer advertisements, fragrance vendors. She thought it was too bad she had no interest in the country or the almost ten hours of stopover time—half of which would be spent totally alone until her male companions surfaced—could be spent more wisely than, say, finding the first McDonald's—which she did—and sitting there with her head collapsed in her crossed arms—which she also did.

She was bored, agitated, a bit starving. She realized she should check her cell phone and see if there was any word from Xerxes. She hated to admit it but his whole plan for getting on another flight had annoyed her to the point of suspicion. How could he have been at the doctor's so long? And then the pharmacy? And what illness? Why did she feel he would try to get out of it somehow all along? Was that really what he was doing? Or was she a horrible person for doubting her poor ailing dear boyfriend? Was the world for once exactly what it said it was? She had considered calling Dr. Arnold's office and trying to figure out when Xerxes had checked out and what exactly he was diagnosed with, but she had no idea how to do that without sounding appalling to the office staff, who knew her and the family well. Plus, it was so insulting to Xerxes. Plus, it just made her look like a terrible scary girlfriend in a terrible scary relationship—and while theirs was many things, yes, terrible or scary she could not claim. . . .

So she had dropped it. Decided, *Whatever, Xerxes will come, and should he not, I'll just go back. Fuck the Account.* It could all go to waste, very possibly for the better.

She turned on her phone, eager also to try out her new international calling plan, and immediately she saw that there was a message from Xerxes. "Suzanne, hi, well, I know you're not going to believe this—" she closed her eyes tensely and thought, he was backing out, *the bastard,* he had sent her all the way there for nothing, she knew it, *oh, fuck him,* she felt very inclined to hang up, delete that message then and there, have a McMeal and get on the next flight back, back to a New York that she would find again without him, without that bastard . . . until she listened further and, to her own disbelief, *had* to believe it—"Well, so, we had an emergency landing. I know, crazy, after my delay today and all, and now this, you'd think some higher power or whatever doesn't want me to—ha, sorry, no, not thinking like that —anyway! Not a big deal, nothing really, engine blew out, they say it happens all the time, nothing really, but you know, unnerving, my first flight in a while, not so easy on the nerves, but anyway, Suzanne, no worries, not a problem, they're just putting us on the next flight, another one is taking off, surely without a hitch, what would be the odds, so it's 10:30 now and we're about to get on again, so I'll just be an hour off, an hour and a half actually, sorry about all the delays, the doctor, the everything, this morning, so sorry, it's all my fault, you're right to think badly of it, but I feel fine and about to take off again—" and her machine cut him off. Just like that.

She didn't know what to think except to believe it. Unlike earlier, with his chuckle and his easy plan B, this time he sounded more . . . dire. His voice was breaking up—more than just a bad connection, he sounded broken. He sounded bad. And she tried her hardest not to think anything of it, not to think, for instance, that their whole trip was totally cursed, a curse she had brought on, she and her dumb ideas, that their whole relationship was maybe even cursed —after all, 9/11 had brought them together—no, she banished those thoughts. Instead she made it through the McDonald's line, ordered a large coffee only, and went over to the airline information booth and found out that indeed there had been "plane trouble" and indeed another plane had taken off from JFK an hour and a half later.

She told herself he would be fine. He had had his bad luck and he would make it. But the passing hours of daylight were still saturated in a deep anxiety she couldn't deny and the bad coffee wasn't helping. She sat down at the food court, took another half pill, put her head down, closed her eyes, and let herself fall into an ugly forced sleep that held its own . . . until several hours later when her cell phone ringer snapped her out of it.

"Oh, hey!" she shouted into it automatically, convinced it would be Xerxes, without checking her wristwatch that attested to the sobering fact that it was still before his arrival time, only 10:25 a.m.

"A-ha," said the deep accented voice of none other than, of course, Xerxes's father. "You are here! I just landed. What a flight . . . over ten hours . . . and not so smooth either!"

Suzanne couldn't find the words, the appropriate greeting. She finally managed to say, "Yes, welcome, Mr. Adam. I am here. I am alone, however."

"What!" he shouted. "Xerxes, where is that guy? What do you mean?"

She did her best to downplay it—she used the phrase "plane trouble," checked her watch, and said he was just a couple of hours away at most. Somewhere inside her, although not *so* deep inside, she was grateful for all the delays that would hopefully add up to cutting short the trio's time together.

"Plane trouble!" Darius Adam laughed. "Oh, right! He backed out, did he?!"

Suzanne tried not to reveal how absolutely incensed that made her. "*No,* Mr. Adam, I swear, your son is on his way."

He noted the harsh register of her voice. "Okay. Okay, then. Well, so we shall meet first. Fine."

"Yes . . . fine." She was suddenly very annoyed and very, very . . . afraid. This erratic man, this notorious patriach of Xerxes's nightmares who her planning had somehow clumped them with— she was due to be alone with him for maybe two hours. Of all worst parts in the whole mess, it was to her the *worst* part.

"Where are you?" he asked.

"At . . . at a food court," she muttered, vaguely. She wondered if she could leave it at that and just leave their finding each other up to, say, a miracle. A miracle would certainly not get involved; there was no chance he'd find her. And Xerxes would love that: if they never did meet beforehand and were left to perhaps bump into each other in the aisles of the plane, where there would be no chance for anything more than a polite, perfunctory greeting. . . .

"The one near Lufthansa? The McDonald's and the German stuff?"

She couldn't believe it. She was forced to tell him it was indeed that one.

"I see it in the distance! I am at the pay phone just on the other side of the terminal! Don't tell me which one you are—let me guess! It'll be hard, so crowded and all—and, well, I don't know you—but I bet I'll find you!" He sounded so giddy, she couldn't help feeling disturbed.

He hung up before she could protest—before she could say she needed a minute, she had to go to the bathroom or check on his son's flight, or something, anything. She was trapped. He had her cornered. She had no doubt he would find her first, because she couldn't bear to look up. He could be anyone—but so could she. The airport was buzzing with people of all nationalities and origins—everyone looked different, everyone looked the same. His odds were bad. She even turned off her cell phone—at least for a second, she told herself, she could tell him it was an accident—should he call.

So she sat there staring into the messageless universe of her lap, trying to look inconspicuous, trying to ignore the fact that any minute the guillotine would drop. *No, it would be so impossible. How could he* . . . When too many minutes went by for her to believe he could really not find her, she eased up a bit and decided it was silly to leave her cell phone off. With a sigh, she brought it back to life . . . in the same second that she felt a hard—really too hard—poke on her shoulder. . . .

⁂   ⁂   ⁂

How he knew it had to be her, he wasn't sure—he had just known he could do it, and if he was wrong, who cared? He'd apologize to that wrong girl and try again—but when the hunched lone young lady by the German McDonald's slowly offered him his face, he knew. And it took his breath away.

His greeting came in the form of a gasp.

It wasn't just that it was *her*, that he had found her, his son's woman—as that was what her shy smile and immediate rising said—but it was just that it, she, she was . . . the impossible.

She was . . . *Shireen!*

"Suzanne," she announced and extended an arm, then quickly retracted it apologetically and replaced it with both outstretched arms, an invitation for an embrace—normally a gesture he would not have taken on, if only he had not been in such a shock, such a mind-tingling, spine-numbing, insane shock. Plus, now, how could he not, how could he not just throw himself into the arms of his long-long-lost, his always-destined-to-be-lost-but-somehow-here-found, his imaginary-girl-now-gone-real, *his* Shireen!

It was uncanny. Her hair that had the same surreal rugged beauty of twilight wilderness, her eyes that were like huge bottomless saucers of black tea, her outdoorsy brassy glow—God, she was wearing a dress even, a little dress, yes, a sundress of sorts, too! Here she was, just a little older than the girl of his dreams, his *his*, his *more-than-his*. . . .

How could he explain his tears? "It is very, very nice to meet you," he muttered, trying to blink them away, rubbing his face as if from sheer tiredness.

"Yes, it's a pleasure, truly," she said, smiling politely.

Perhaps she just expected him to be *off* in general, he considered, because if she was noticing something was off with him, she was refusing to let him know.

For a while, they just sat silently and then she asked if she could get him anything. "A coffee, too, perhaps?"

"No, please don't get up," he said quickly. "What I mean is, don't waste your money. I can—if you don't want yours when it gets cold, I can have that, but I don't even need it. I don't need a thing. I am . . . so . . . happy." He smiled, looking deep into her eyes, trying to see if she was seeing something, too.

She nodded. "Well, it's no problem, I was going to get something anyway—"

He was suddenly panicked at the idea of her rising, should she walk away and vanish back into the other world where she used to lurk. He got desperate—to persuade her to sit, he suddenly grabbed her cup and took a deep swig. He realized the gesture must have come across strangely and so he tried to laugh. "But you see, there, I'm done!"

She couldn't help laughing back. "Okay then." He was living up to everything. She looked away.

And so they sat silently some more. He just stared at her with a big foolish beam that he prayed she wouldn't think was creepy— *Shireen, forgive me, but how can I possibly explain it all to you*—but after a while, after she grew bored with feeling uncomfortable, too tired for tension anyway, she relaxed and smiled and even giggled once or twice.

"Xerxes should be here soon," she kept telling him.

He nodded slowly. *Yes, Xerxes. Xerxes would be here, fine. It would be fine. It would have to be. If this isn't a sign, what was? Oh, Shireen!* She had grown to live, really live, grown to be better than he could ever hope.

She eventually said she had to go to the restroom, again alarming him so much that he scrambled for a deterrent fast. "Oh no, don't leave! I mean, sorry, please, let's just move somewhere else, near your bathroom, where we can perhaps . . ." He thought hard, thought what he should have been avoiding thinking: what he could offer her, before his son would come and perhaps ruin everything . . . "find a proper food place so we can have lunch maybe?"

She paused and then said, with a sincerity he found heartbreaking, "I would like that." And she was surprised by how she meant it, then how quickly she rushed out of the bathroom to find him waiting outside, still with a sad dreamy smile that she couldn't fully understand—*Oh, the poor lonely old man, how could Xerxes have had the heart, so sweet, such a father he is*—and to show her gratitude at his suggestion, at his wanting to so badly create a nice moment for them at a time when they were so bizarrely duoed—just characters in Xerxes's story suddenly—she took his arm, smiled even wider, to show her absolute unexpected delight at his presence, a delight that even she couldn't begin to understand. The situation had felt bad in her and Xerxes's hands just moments ago, but in his, suddenly, she felt sure—something about him made her so *sure*—that it would have to be all right.

* * *

There would be no hope, were her first thoughts upon getting out of that cab, just pausing with her luggage in the middle of their town, their Midtown, to behold it all. *No, no chance,* Lala told herself, as all the reality in the world seemed suddenly concentrated in the ground beneath her feet—miracles, dreams, illusions, delusions, they would all have a rough time here. The whole cab ride there it had been evident: it was more, much more, than she could have asked for. In her head she had envisioned all that she thought it could be, but here, live, Lala could see that it was something much much more. There was barely enough room for her story, much less the story she wanted to create.

As she stood there on the sidewalk, eyes turned up to a heavenless sky, marveling at how those giant skyscrapers didn't even allow for any open air, people pushed and shouldered and rammed into her back and forth. One or two cursed. She didn't care—it actually made her want to laugh. The situation was so beyond her, it was only laughable.

She decided she was crazy to have thought there could be any real concrete hope.

In her hotel room—a miserable closet-sized room, pricey enough and yet somehow totally dirty-looking, which she had booked only because it was a skyscraper and they were able to give her a high room on the nineteenth floor, which apparently, now that she could see it all the city, wasn't that high at all—she couldn't do much. She couldn't sleep. She couldn't call Darius. Or embark on the brother search. All she could get herself to do was look out her window and take it all in again and again. The City. It was truly spectacular that there were humans behind it at all.

It was the America her schoolteachers used to hint at. Whereas California was modest-feeling yet unconquerably spread out, always green and a little yellow and even brown, with a Mediterranean climate she could too easily relate to—California, indeed chosen as the closest thing to their home—*this* was the real America, the America of their childhood dreams. She remembered a classmate once asking their teacher what the word *America* actually meant and their English teacher—an elderly Iranian lady—always claiming to have visited that continent, had declared without a moment's hesitation: *freedom*. Which, even as kids, they all assumed was incorrect, but still, she had never forgotten it. The fact that this old Iranian lady couldn't help equating the name with *freedom*—a word that she didn't think she ever even honestly considered until those days before and after they experienced their own terrifying slice of the Revolution—it carved a magical place for *America* in her heart.

And indeed it was magical, she thought, as she stared out into all the lack of space with her head at the eye level of all the other tall buildings, feeling herself halfway suspended into the heavens, towering over all the minor details, the human concerns, the little worries tucked temporarily in cabs, the same obnoxious eternally honking cabs of city comedies, guided by light after endless light, creating the loud neon buzz of the city, brighter than the sky, that barely open sky, that poked and prodded apparently island sky, still littered with more planes than she had ever seen before. She couldn't even fear their sight.

Of all feelings, she did not expect *peace* to be the one she would feel most wholly upon her arrival. But there it was. Everything else felt so distant—Darius, Xerxes, and, she hated to say it, her brother. Oh, she would try to find him of course—there was no stopping that—but she would not make it the end-all. She would instead take walks—real, invigorating, life-affirming walks, not those depressive time-killing walks at Arcadia Drive—she would go places at night, anywhere she wanted, she would talk to people, she would do all the things she never did in their new land, *or* in their homeland, in fact. She would for once embrace feeling alive. She would let go, she would for at least a week break from all the hurt, she would forget and for the first time find herself, her *freedom*. There would be insecurities, dark clouds, old goals, but like her brotherhunt, it was all hopeless, wasn't it? Never did she think, of all things, *hopelessness*—the freedom from hope's easily evaporating promises and suicidally rigid routings—could translate to the purest peace.

*   *   *

When their plane landed, a little after noon, several of the passengers—those who had been on the previous emergency-landed flight—clapped. They were applauding what was to be expected, Xerxes thought bitterly: a normal flight, a normal landing, as if normalcy wasn't deserved enough after you were about to find yourself trapped for many hours in an abnormal place like Germany. *Frankfurt*—for some reason, just the thought of it made him want to get out immediately. But not necessarily get *out* and get *into* Tehran. He was shaken up. He did not know if his fear had done it or if it had been the world, or, *or hell, just a fucking loose bird directed awry into an engine,* or—but he was, of course, worried that it was a sign.

What the hell are the odds of an emergency landing when you're already about to take the scariest plane ride of your life? Xerxes thought over and over. *Is that supposed to be some extra kicker to soften the final blow? Distract me? Tell me that no matter what I'm dreading, it won't be so bad, not in comparison with, say, your plane crashing and you dying, which you almost did?*

He knew he had to call Suzanne. And he was dreading it. Calling Suzanne, announcing his existence, would mean he was more than halfway there, on to Chapter 2, on to the new dread, on to the next big outcome-unknown thing. . . . He wished he had a second to think about the flight. Or, more importantly, to think about what he had thought about during his flight. He had, after all, thought about his father the entire time. At the moment of total loss, he had wished it had been his father and not him—because his father deserved it— not just any *it*, like simple generic death, but *that* particular end. He had tried to choose an end for his father, an end that had tried to choose him instead. It made him shudder.

Once when he was a young child, his father had told him about a documentary he had seen on PBS about monkeys. Xerxes knew his father was no fan of monkeys so he expected it to be a good or funny anecdote at least. It was not. It was about a mother and a child monkey *and in this experiment they had them in a bathtub-like thing,* Darius had explained. *Except it was like a hot plate. The scientists warmed the tub up, with the mother and her little child just standing there in it. Soon it got real hot, too hot. The two monkeys began to dance around a bit, jumping, scream- ing. They had no way of getting out, nothing to climb to, nothing to swing on and out. So you know what the clearly smarter mother did to get out of having her feet scorched? She rode on her child's shoulders. The child monkey suffered serious burns on its feet by the time the scientists turned off the heating device. But the mother was fine. The mother was fine and unbothered. The child, afterward and through its healing process, seemed fine, too. They went on together as if nothing had ever happened, putting that little experiment and what it had brought out in them be- hind them, would you believe. . . .*

Xerxes suddenly knew the real ending of that experiment, the ending he'd really believe in, which his father had not gotten into, which the scientists hadn't discovered yet. *One day, later in the parent monkey's old age,* Xerxes thought, *the child monkey, now an adult, would find another burning ground and have his chance to ride on his old mother's shoulders. Except his sheer weight and overdeveloped hard adult anguish might kill his elderly mother monkey whereas he, the child, had healed. Somewhat.* This was what growing up was: dealing with each other, finding the right deserved ways to deal with each other within the world's cruel and unusual experiments, he dreamed, he justified.

He turned the lights off on his thoughts—he had big important things to do, like call Suzanne, he reminded himself as he stood with his carry-on in the hallway of the arrival terminal. He turned on his cell phone and realized his phone didn't work. *Rats.* He hadn't considered that. Suzanne had international calling and he did not—his phone would be worthless the entire time. He looked around—phone book: check; gift store: check. He went into the store and bought a calling card and went back to the phone booth and eventually figured out how to dial.

Mostly he hoped she wouldn't answer and a little bit he hoped that she would.

But when she answered, Xerxes immediately noticed she sounded markedly different from when they last spoke, when she had been on her lone way to the airport and he had been across the street secretly, drunkenly, remorselessly, watching her. No, this time it was Suzanne who sounded drunk.

"Who's this?" she asked.

"Hi, Suzanne," Xerxes said. "It's me, Xerxes. It's a phone card. I'm here."

"Xerxes! Welcome to Deutschland!!!" she gushed, full of giggles.

"Hi. Well, I take it you got my message. It was so crazy, Su, this whole emergency landing—I really for a second thought it was all over—"

"Oh, we knew you'd be fine!!" she continued to giggle.

"No, really, Su, it was terrible. I mean, people were freaking out, even the flight attendants, and then there were paramedics on the ground and by the time we got on the next plane, well, I think we had all just lost our will to—"

"We're waiting for you, Xerxes! You should be telling all this to us in person! We have plenty of time, my dear!" Laughter, more laughter, all in her new weird giddiness.

He suddenly froze. Her words sank in. *We*. She had been saying "*we*."

"Uh, Suzanne, when you say 'we' . . . are you not alone?" He knew the answer, of course.

"Silly, as you know, as arranged, . . ." she began sounding more serious, then paused, and then again broke into a laughing fit, howling, "I'm with Dad!"

Xerxes felt every muscle in his body tense up. *We*. And now *Dad?!*

"Dad?!" he shouted. "Did you say—did I hear—did you just call him—"

More laughter. He could hear another voice, certainly his father, in the background laughing along. She continued, "Oh, sorry,

Xerxes, that must have sounded *sooooo* inappropriate!! But that's been our joke for hours . . . he keeps telling me to call him 'Dad'!"

Xerxes bit his lip to prevent the obvious obscenities from pouring out. He was beyond disgusted. He was sure he was getting a migraine.

"Why does he say that?" Xerxes muttered slowly, then snapping, "Why something so *stupid?*"

Suzanne paused in her cloud-puff delirium, not wanting to let the conversation escalate into anything that would jeopardize her ideal circumstances, the calm and peace and joy that she had suddenly been injected with since she had gotten to know Mr. Adam. She began to address the issue: getting Xerxes to them. She described the restaurant they were in. "It's a family-type place, big, bright, kids, moms, and. . . ."

Dads. Dad, he thought. He could not believe it. She was his, too, now. How could he have ever thought otherwise? How could he have believed her nervousness yesterday about being stuck with his father alone? Of course they would be like his. Oh, she was his, just like the plan, the whole fucking vacation, was *his* at root.

It had always been my dream that my child and I would one day return to Iran, Xerxes imagined his father had said dozens, if not hundreds, of times when he was a child, and now there they were, his son and his son's girlfriend, both his children, apparently—*as if he was God! Fuck!*—suddenly stuck in *his* dream, suddenly left there to act out as characters in his oldest, most impossible dream.

"Yes, I'll be there in a . . . a bit," Xerxes said. "I'm sure I'll have no trouble finding you, don't worry. I just need to use the restroom first and . . . and then I'll see you . . . you two."

"Lovely!!" she cooed again. She sounded breathless. What had she become? What had he done to her? He could not wait for the conversation to end so he cut in with a quick, curt "Bye" and hung up before he could hear another ecstatic breath.

He indeed had to go to the bathroom. Not to *go*, but he needed a place to sit, one that was not in plain view, that offered no visual distractions, that ensured he would not be spotted, where he could be left unbothered no matter how long he was there. Where he could consider his options.

He found one. He went in and shut the stall door behind him and sat in his pants on the toilet seat, perching his elbows on his knees and dropping his face into his hands. Every second or so, there was a chorus of chiming flushes, sometimes a ruder sound, sometimes a sigh, a cough, a snippet of conversation. Xerxes had so many troubles shouting through the chambers of his brain that the noise wasn't chipping into his attention much. He was worried, he was confused, he was angry, he was scared. It all had to do with *him. Darius,* now intensified by the presence of *Her.* How had he been so stupid to allow their meeting to just happen so slickly? Oh, he had believed in Suzanne's qualms, in Darius's misanthropic manners—he never in a million years thought there they would be, discovering some universe together, happy together, just waiting for the Xerxes-pin to pop their downright enchanted universe of bubbles. *Dad.* She had called *his* dad—a man he himself didn't even call Dad, a man he himself didn't *call*—*Dad.* This was the problem with Suzanne—like the trip to Iran, she was always able to go too far. And here she was innocently, accidentally even, doing it again. He felt his old anger about the whole situation build up again—suddenly he could see his hand, hot and hard, confident and crass, flat against her face, his own palm burning from that forbidden impact. Against that image he saw his own father running to her side, holding her injured, tear-streaked face, telling her it was all right, to ignore Xerxes—and she whispering, *Thanks, Dad.* They would maybe do just that—ignore him—in the airport, in the airplane, in the streets of Iran. This brought him to another problem: Darius would likely be by their side the entire time. There he would be, appearing like the world's greatest man—the father Xerxes saw as a young child, before his teen years tinted his vision more darkly and thus accurately—not letting himself unravel fully for her. Or maybe he would, like a snake, slowly shed so she could eventually see all the darkness—maybe he would show her everything. Under a sparkling night sky, he would direct her face up to the stars, pointing, and say, *Do you know, when I was a boy, such was my world: would you believe, we could make those in a hot second.* . . . Maybe he would tell her everything, in a different way from what Xerxes had recounted to her—maybe she would sigh, smile, find it magical, poignant. Maybe then, once in Iran, he would *really* show her everything: the blood, the incarceration, the hurt in the eyes of a culture, the baby hands on prison bars, the secret hushed hisses of women, the agonized prayer-cries of mortal men, everyone, not just the women, veiled in a deep unshakable blackness. . . . *Welcome to our world,* he might say, *welcome to Iran,* and maybe she would never want to leave. *This created your boyfriend,* Darius would tell her. *And I created this. For his generation. This is his. I come from some place before this. You wouldn't recognize. But we, we did this to us. We took our old Iran and turned it into this world. I made your boyfriend a world that he couldn't live in, but yet, look, he's here, he's living in it again.* . . . Maybe she would actually think, *It's not so bad.*

They don't understand. Maybe she would even say, *No, Xerxes doesn't understand. . . .*

The floor was getting hot and there he was, *Dad,* with his hands on Xerxes's shoulders, about to get on top of him. Xerxes could feel himself about to get burned.

He had to leave. It had been a while, he knew that. He got out of the stall and washed his hands for no reason. He was suddenly very alone—the bathroom appeared empty. He looked long and hard into the mirror. He was amazed to see that the cliché still stood—in spite of everyone always saying it would go away in the postteen years, go away with the acne and the SATs and the word "underage"—there they were: The Questions. The *who the hell am I?* The *what am I doing?* They were always there, always existed, they applied on all micro and all macro levels. He was as lost in the moment as he was lost in life.

He didn't want to leave the bathroom. Suddenly the limbo of Frankfurt appealed to him. In an alternate universe he was not just the missing boyfriend, he was simply *missing*—in two countries, two groups of countrymen were minus him, two countries far far away from each other, as different from each other as they were alike, both Xerxes-free. He was back to that feeling of not wanting to exist, wanting to let himself dissolve to something void of that ugly word *identity,* where the bloodless like him could disintegrate gracefully. Was it Germany? This big international hub in Germany? He thought, *Of all places!* Of all places that have quite a take or two in their histories on the issue of identity . . .

But as he walked out—the echo of the dirty white halls, the taps of heels on the ground, the German announcements cutting in back and forth, the blinking screens, and the other lost people—it felt right. Where else did he have to go?

The answer was in front of him: "WIRTSHAUS" said the neon sign, and "Pub" next to it. *Perfect*, he thought, there was a good sign, for once, a good omen. What he needed was a drink—things worked out much better when he was drinking, he decided.

He gave his face a few good wipes, tried to plaster on a smile even, and walked in. Before he could turn to the pretty young bartender and declare "Scotch on the rocks," he paused, distracted by something on the plasma TV screen. It was a show—in Germany unlike the United States, he gathered, sports were not the only pub-viewing fare—a show he knew too well. *Holy shit.* There she was, sign of signs, beautiful, beaming, and blonde, every inch of her—smile, words, aura, everything—bright as hell. *Jeannie.*

She was arguing with her mirror image, a twin, and quite heatedly, hands on hips, then hands in the air, ponytail shaking with fury, face in scowl, face in bitter mocking laughter. Her words were in German but there were subtitles in English. Before he could digest the twin premise, she was suddenly alone in the genie's bottle—the words underneath memo-ing her dilemma for him: "All I do is think and blink."

What were the odds? he thought.

The bartender came up to him and said something. He pried his eyes from the screen and just pointed upward.

She nodded, laughing.

"What were the odds?!" he exclaimed, not sure she would understand the English.

"Ha, yes, yes!" she laughed some more. He was still not sure if she had understood his English.

For a moment, he just stood there, his whole body cold and quaking. He had the chills.

Soon enough something told him to keep moving, *whatever you do, keep moving*—before he was too deep into the situation, before he let himself get all stuck in the bottle, the Scotches and rocks and Jeannies and thinking/blinking, he decided to shatter the sign. Omen or whatever, he was out of there. With a quick wave, he literally ran out, sure he could still hear the bartender-girl laughing over the strange German voice of his old Jeannie. . . .

✳   ✳   ✳

Eventually they ran out of small talk and he felt he had to tell her stories. Not just to keep her there—she wasn't going anywhere—but to keep her with him. To keep her charmed, allied with Dad. Any second his son could come and who knew what could happen to the dynamic? He would do his best, but how could he guarantee Xerxes would do *his* best? He had to earn her understanding.

Also, they were drinking and this encouraged stories. She had started ordering glass after glass of *wein*, and soon some untapped locks in his brain were coming undone.

So he told her the story he had never told him. It was the story he had asked for, the one he had mistakenly replaced with the other. He told her the story of that twelfth summer of Xerxes's, when Darius's one mission in life was to save the neighborhood blue jay population by putting bell collars on all the neighborhood cats.

"Gorbay, is that how you say it?" Suzanne was practicing.

"Gor*beh*," he corrected. "You need more *-EH*."

"Wow, you saved some little lives there!" she smiled.

"Can you believe that neighbor, she said the eff-word in front of him and everything?!" he laughed, adding more quietly, "Yes, I did save a few things in my life."

"Castro! What a name for a cat! I can't believe you remember!" Suzanne laughed back. "Another glass?"

"What do you call it—the underdog—I like to help underdogs," he went on. His face was getting red. He was not sure if drinking was a good thing with this girl. He hadn't drunk like this in ages. "No. No more drinks."

Instead, more stories. He recollected when they went to Disneyland for the first time and how Xerxes hated it—he was scared of all the real-life-sized suddenly alive Mickeys and Goofys and Donalds and Plutos, confused at their extra-animation corporeal existence—

"Oh my God, I had that same reaction!" Suzanne snorted in delight. "Same one, but Disneyworld Orlando! It freaks kids out!"

Her laughter was contagious. He went further, aping Xerxes for her: the scared-child Xerxes face, his melodramatic shudders, his hands over his eyes, his back turned against theirs, his hands folded across his chest, and he was laughing laughing laughing. . . .

Until suddenly—like an abrupt shatter to a frame of glass, *like that family picture of us all at Disneyland, the one Xerxes had knocked down, that had prompted me, made me, why oh why, strike my own goddamn child, worse than I had ever, and had I ever*—he was laughing so hard he was crying, and then just crying and crying and crying. . . .

"Oh, poor Dad," Suzanne muttered, hugging him without a second wasted. "You've had a bit too much to drink. My fault. And today's emotional, I know. . . ."

She was used to this, he could tell. *Ah, Xerxes.* Still, he could not pull himself together. Suddenly in Shireen's—*I mean, Suzanne's*—arms he could cry as he had rarely cried in his adult life.

He told her more stories, the worst ones this time—now that he had arrived, was already there, he had little to hide—and she didn't let on, not even once, that she knew more than one of the stories already and more than a few even that he hadn't gotten to.

✻ ✻ ✻

Xerxes was walking, pacing, to where he did not know. With every few yards of terminal he would cover, he'd arrive at another restroom. In he would dart, into a stall, and he would sit and think. He'd find himself ridiculous, no better than where he started, and he would go out again. And then into another restroom. Thoughts. Up and out.

He was going to run out of restrooms, terminal, time.

He went to the phone booth. He had to call Suzanne. He had to make himself a real out.

"Oh, geez, where are you already?!" she immediately cried, still in that new elated high pitch of hers. "Lost, I'm sure!"

Before he could offer anything, she was telling him where they were, speaking a mile a minute, somehow erasing all his thoughts with her explanations and directions and commands and expectations. He just listened.

"You got it?" she said. "We've been waiting, c'mon!"

"Suzanne, I'm sick," he said, suddenly more harshly than he even expected. "I'll get there, you know, when I get there. . . ."

"It's just that we want to get some food in you, too, before, . . ." and in came the horrible giggling again, "Oh, we're very excited, Xerxes. We can't wait."

Numbly, he echoed it back: he couldn't wait. He also told her his phone card was about to die, so he had to go.

He lied. About: his phone card—it was fine—and . . . ?

He hung up.

They were close. In the distance, he could see it: a bright indeed family-style tiki-looking café. Its logo featured a big yellow glowing bird in flight. He closed his eyes, then opened them slowly, blinked a few more times, then tried to look more closely. *Bird—no, not a bird. It actually could be a pterodactyl,* he told himself, deciding it was much more likely to be a prehistoric flying dinosaur of some kind—not quite a bird—than yet another omen, another ill-conceived sign. . . .

He walked to it, like a man stuck in the autopilot of a dream. Eventually he slowed down to a stop and snapped himself back to reality. *No.* He was too close. He examined the distance to the pterodactyl café and predicted he was the length of two men, two *dead* men, spread flat on the airport carpeting, head to foot, from it. That close. Just two lying men's length, that length of two inanimate men over and done with, into the belly of the glowing happy family-loving lit-up bird, where the representatives of the mixed worlds sat waiting for him in the best of spirits. . . .

All that rumination on dead men gave him an idea. It was a last resort, but at least it was an idea.

He looked to the signs to figure out how to get to the beginning, the ticket counter, the Lufthansa ticket counter all over again. If there was an out, that was the out of outs.

"Hello, madam," he said in his most charming voice, once he finally made it through the short but still excruciating line and was faced with a smiling old black Lufthansa ticket lady. Two good things: everyone spoke English and everyone smiled a lot in Frankfurt. He had those going for him.

"Hello, how may I help you?" she said, in good old American English even, with a sincerity that almost broke his heart. *Good omens.* He wanted to let her know just how badly he wanted her help, how very much she *could* help him, rescue him even, if she only knew. . . .

"Yes, well, you see, I am due to be on this flight," he said, taking out his ticket and pointing to the destination, no longer having it in him to say *Iran,* to deal with that on top of everything else.

She nodded, unfazed.

"Yes, well, you see, I can't get on it," he said. "There's been an emergency and I'm requesting to go back. Go back where I came from. Right back to JFK!"

She looked at his ticket. "You'd like to purchase another ticket?"

He shook his head. Oh no, he could not do that. His bank account looked closer to his age than the price of that ticket, or any ticket really. He had no means to pay for his out. This one had to be on Suzanne—and while he knew in a way he was jeopardizing the whole relationship, since after all she *had* threatened that on the phone, there was no other way. Suzanne had put him in this mess and she had to get him out. In his madness, he had decided the Suzanne-sacrifice would be the price to pay for his rescue, as well as the punishment for his cowardice. He would take being a coward, *a lying cheating coward, whatever,* over a man being forced headfirst into a dark vat of his greatest fears. . . .

It was not so easy. She could not charge it to the credit card if the credit card was not his. Also, the price would be much higher, since he was purchasing a ticket for that day *that day.*

He thought, *Of fucking course.* Suddenly, on the verge of the boiling point, when every last inch of him pointed toward breakdown, he decided to raise the stakes to the point where he had hoped he would not have to go.

"Of course, madam," he said, through eyes suddenly filled with tears. "You see, it was my girlfriend's credit card . . . she bought the tickets . . . and it's just that it's an emergency that I get back to New York . . . a very *bad* emergency. . . ."

She nodded, definitely aware of the tears, he thought. "I understand," she said, as if she really understood, as if she really grasped how important understanding was at that point.

He let the tears get the best of him, let his whole idea undo him. "You see, my father," he began, his voice cracking perfectly as if a sidekick in his hustle, "he . . . he. . . ."

"Oh my, sir!" she exclaimed, shocked by the abundant overflow of his tears, quickly reaching for a box of tissues and passing it over.

"Yes," Xerxes cried, amazed that there he was, really, really and truly, moved to beyond tears even, "my father has . . . *died!*"

"Oh, sir, I am so sorry, sir," the ticket lady murmured, gently. "Please know, in that case, there are options."

The tears were so real—tears of the day's many stresses mixed with tears of shame for going there mixed with tears of actual actor's catharsis in imagining the reality of the script—that his eyes refused to light up at her sudden resolution.

"Sir," the ticket lady continued, gently, "we have a policy where family members can fly at a discounted rate if they can present a copy of the death certificate or a letter from the attending physician defining the imminent death of the family member. Or if you do not have this, you can apply for a Bereavement Travel Refund after travel is complete. Does that help?"

He couldn't believe it. *No*, he thought. *It does not fucking help*. Tears of defeat were added to tears of stress, shame, and catharsis. There was no way out.

"But I don't have any funds for a refund! Hasn't that ever happened? Emergencies?! I mean, my father, my father—" he was losing it and he knew she could tell. She was looking around nervously, swallowing, trying to smile sympathetically, trying to hush him while he was raising his voice. "Don't you see, I have no CHOICE?!!"

She shook her head; she nodded. She smiled; she frowned. None of it was any use.

"MY FATHER!!!" he was shouting, crying uncontrollably. The whole line behind him was suddenly silent, then full of voices, everyone looking at him, everyone looking around. Other ticket ladies were suddenly joining the ticket lady, staring at the bawling skinny young man waving his ticket in her face, waving his fist, pounding it against the counter, wanting, needing, demanding things they could not do. . . .

"Sir," a man in a suit, a bit more official-seeming than the ticket lady, suddenly appeared, interrupting Xerxes's wails with a deeply accented voice of authority. "Sir. Please stop. You are causing a disturbance. We will have to . . ."

But it was no use. Xerxes Adam was holding on to the ticket counter as if it were the edge of a cliff he was dangling from; he felt that he was slipping and so to help himself he was kicking at it, trying to mount it, trying to get closer, to get right up to their faces, to let them see for themselves, he was falling, he had no choice, he needed help—and that there was something, some very real truth at the very least, to the very big deal he was making. . . .

You are having a nervous breakdown, his body told him. *It's okay. They can tell. You do what you have to do. You are having a nervous breakdown and the only bad part is that it's at an airport, in front of hundreds of people. That's all. But they've all been there—well, most, er, some. It's okay. One day it will be over. For now, you are just having a nervous breakdown, which is better than where you would have been had you not let yourself go through this.*

"Sir, sir," Suited Man kept insisting, getting Xerxes's attention only when he changed his song and went right ahead and got to what he assumed was the heart of the matter, "Sir, where, may I ask, are you *from?*"

It worked. Xerxes's hysteria came to a dead halt, as if the man had applied dry ice to his scalding wound, burning the lesion to complete frozen submission. He was about to say he had flown from JFK, he was a resident of New York City, he was raised in Los Angeles, he was a United States citizen, a Californian, a Manhattanite —when suddenly out of his mouth came a truth, a desperate suicidal truth perhaps more lethal than the hour's desperate suicidal lies: "I was born in Iran."

Suited Man nodded and looked away. The original ticket lady was still looking into Xerxes's eyes with her mix of sympathy/horror, while flanked by a group of other ticket ladies who seemed wrecks, too, unused to it all. They were pacing, panicked, turning to Suited Man, eyeing him for answers, eyeing the rest of the line as if fearing more of this Iranian madman's kind. . . .

Their shock shocked Xerxes. *But certainly this happens all the time,* Xerxes wanted to plead with them, *I mean, forgive me, so I got a little carried away, but certainly people have breakdowns in airports all the time? I mean, where better to have a nervous breakdown . . . ladies?*

But Suited Man's incisive question had calmed Xerxes or alarmed him into a survivalist calm, and there he was, wiping his face, straightening his shirt, patting his hair, trying harder than he had ever tried to just pull himself together. He wondered if it was having any effect. For a second he contemplated just walking off, but as if also clairvoyant, Suited Man raised a finger at him, a *one-moment-please-sir* finger gesture, and just like that, Xerxes Adam found himself immobile, absolutely petrified. Suited Man had powers.

Suited Man, of course, could only gesture because he was on the phone. On the phone right in front of Xerxes Adam the whole time, but talking in such a low voice that Xerxes could barely make anything out. He realized part of the problem was that he was speaking in German. Still, he listened and realized not all was lost in translation—the exclusivity of foreign lexica was fallible and some words broke through even the impenetrable German.

Specifically:

1) X-E-R-X-E-S A-D-A-M. His name spelled out not once, but twice. Then pronounced almost perfectly.

2) Iran.

3) Suspicious Activity.

Just as Xerxes Adam choked on those last words, as if they formed a mouthful of poisonous gas causing his throat to close in on him, Suited Man hung up and turned to Xerxes with a smile. It was the secret satisfied smile of a man who knew all too well his upper hand, only barely masked by the grandiose smile of a man who cared.

"Sir, if you'll step out of the line and come over with me," he said, "and *them*."

Before he knew it, behind him three large security guards had his shoulders. Luckily for Xerxes Adam, whatever that poisonous gas was that had gotten him had gotten him good and the wind was thoroughly knocked out of his lungs before he could process what a dire pickle he was in—before he could register Suited Man's *request for questioning*, Xerxes Adam, without any encouraging, without the slightest actorly sleight of hand, without any will whatsoever even, just gave in to his body and collapsed. Pure merciful blackout.

Some would point out that if it weren't for those guards and their ready arms, he could have cracked his head and . . . died even. Some would point out that if it weren't for Suited Man's security move, Xerxes could have gone off the deep end further and spent half a lifetime locked up. Some would point out that if it weren't for that timely collapse he wouldn't have arrived at the peace the mental shutdown afforded him, that allowed him to drift off into a happier alternative universe, where everything was okay again, all in that safe suspension between the blindingly chaste original light of heaven and the nuclear ultraviolet afterglow of earth, his father, his girlfriend, him, all together in a cloud-cuckoo-land all their own. . . .

✻   ✻   ✻

Darius Adam had become a new man recently, he realized then and there—*I am a man who cries.* Just months ago, it was into his wife's arms. Then on that day, it was in the arms of Suzanne, a girl who resembled the fake daughter who existed in the fake reality of his dreams. She could, of course, become something more, he thought, a daughter-in-law even. *Enough, Darius, enough, goddamn it, what are you becoming?!* The idea was a bit much for him, since how could he envision a bride when he couldn't even imagine the groom? Still, he could not deny that already she felt like family.

Especially at a time when family felt like less-than-family— Xerxes still missing, *somewhere there in the airport,* she promised, *just delayed,* she insisted, *he is very sick,* she reminded him—her easy family air was much appreciated.

Wine after wine, story after story, and the hours rolled by one against the other—sometimes, he thought, too slowly, sometimes too fast. Time seemed hit-and-run in Frankfurt, volatile, erratic, capricious—you had to check your watch against another clock and then maybe another just to reassure yourself you had the zones right. All he knew was that at some point time would get the best of them. They had a deadline.

Suzanne seemed to punctuate the increments of time by leaving messages on Xerxes's cell phone. *He can't answer it, he doesn't have the calling plan,* she'd explain, *but surely he's checking messages.* One by one, all still civil and sweet even, she left them, and turned back to Darius with ever-reassuring eyes. *It will be okay. Really. You'll see. Any minute.*

It took longer. They waited at the gate as their flight boarded and still no Xerxes Adam. They missed their flight, went back to the café, and waited some more. Nothing. They contemplated Plan B's and C's and D's for other flights to board, to buy more and more time, to give him a chance, wherever he was, whatever it was that was happening—and still not a sign of Xerxes Adam. Since Suzanne swore one thing was for certain—he had made it to Frankfurt—they had nowhere to go but stay. They checked in at a nearby airport hotel and made do.

In New York, Lala Adam was beside herself on the phone to Darius. "Should I come? Should I go home? Do you want to come home? What the hell? Look . . . what did you do to him, really, Darius?!" she would shriek. He had made the mistake of calling her early on and having little to say about what was happening. She would hang up on him only to call back again hours later.

For days, the father and the son's girlfriend were suspended in a dreamlike haze of shared mixed feelings—terror, anger, remorse, guilt, anxiety, anticipation, every emotion that's bigger than its carriers. They tried every airport hotel, the police, info lines, the news, hospitals—*nothing nothing nothing nothing nothing.* Then one morning—after a long night of belatedly "celebrating" their Persian New Year, in tears at a Turkish Frankfurt pub, a dark place to drown out their hopelessness in the alcohol that had discovered both of them suddenly—news came in the form of a phone call from where they least expected it.

Lala Adam: "Darius, I found him."

* * *

It was of course not *him*. Her brother was not found—that was not going to be the purpose of the trip, she realized soon enough. It would take another decade, until she finally did the unthinkable and made it back to that native land that she thought she was done with. . . .

She had gone to Tehran still without many links to her old family—and the few she had she had hesitated to use. But soon enough they had found her—a cousin who recognized the family eyes stumbled on her pacing their old neighborhood and brought her into his home. She had reluctantly let herself be smothered in hugs and realized it was not so bad. From this cousin she was led to another cousin and soon dinner parties full of cousins. All that family shocked her, eventually in a good way—it washed over her like a wave that at first chills but then soothes—she thought, *I have my people and it's not so bad!* That alone was a gift, but the gift of her life was still waiting at a certain dinner party. Finally, he came, the last guest, a man with little hair and kind eyes and a slouch, with a young child in his arms. Whispers caught up with them and when the man approached Lala the whole dining room went silent.

My sister, my God, he said.

It took an hour of convincing for her to believe it—this man, her closest of kin, entirely different from what she had expected, a whole man with barely any scars of old fragmentation, a father even, a brother suddenly. It took another three days, the only days left for her in Tehran, of nonstop contact and conversation, tears and laughter, for her to be able to accept it and let it go.

One could imagine that the simple lesson for Lala Adam would be how you could find a thing—how a thing could find you— when you first learned to let it go. But a decade earlier, on her first trip away from her family, when she had eventually thought she *was* letting go of everything, another lost thing had found her and taught her that some things wouldn't let you lose them.

And as much as the earth lore would dictate *People never change*, apparently some would. As if it were an adolescent hormone, the cynicism in Lala Adam's system seemed to run dry as her days went by. So much so that when finally in midlife she could look back on two of her losses found, she thought, sometimes you had to wonder about hope, and whether it did truly have a mind of its own.

* * *

Hungover, for days sleepless, lying in a twin bed in a fancier hotel than he could ever afford, across from a hungover sleepless girl-being in a twin bed who had afforded it all for them, Darius Adam shook himself awake to the reality on the phone.

"Darius, did you hear me?" Lala was shouting. "I said I found him!"

Darius tried to muster some enthusiasm for her cause. "Bob? Really?"

Lala groaned. "Who are you worried about here? No, stupid! *Our son.* I have him. He's here. In New York. We're together."

He asked her to say it again; surely, he hadn't heard it correctly.

"Darius, I have him. You heard me."

She had him? She had him. Holy big wow.

Before he knew it, Darius was roaring into the phone, just roaring like an overfed lion. When he could finally form words, he told her to hold on and shouted the news in some barely coherent form to Suzanne who, half dressed, jumped to his side.

"No!" she cried. "No! No! YES!"

Darius finally asked the question of questions: "What happened to him?!"

"Oh, a lot—don't worry about that now," she said. She didn't want to put Darius through it. She could barely believe it herself, how her trip to New York had taken on such purpose in such a swift turn. It had all happened very fast—specifically, on the tail end of one of her longest days, which she'd devoted to going from park to square to bigger park to barely square throughout the boroughs. She had returned to the hotel glumly, feeling a bit depressed after yet another vacation day alone. Bored, she had decided to call home and check the messages for no good reason. There was one, to her surprise, but it took several listens to understand who it was, much less make out what it said. The most important words came through, *I need help,* he had said over and over, wanting the hand of the only one of them not involved, the one who was the cleanest of conspiracy for his newly rattled self, fresh from the eye of paranoia. As much as anticipation would have prepped her for its being her brother, she knew, a mother knew, even in spite of the seeming impossibility—because of all people it shouldn't have been, it was her son, not in Tehran, not with his girlfriend, but at a hotel outside JFK, where he had been questioned overnight and then had just stayed, unable to decide where home was exactly. How the hell do these things happen, she thought? Of all reasons to be in New York, she couldn't believe it: to rescue her most lost man, her poor son. When she got there, she found a version of her son she hadn't seen—shaking, exhausted, wasted, *grateful*. She took him back to his own apartment and spent the next day cleaning it manically as bit by bit he told her about Frankfurt, his questioning, and his apparent future date for further questioning. Her eyes would grow misty every time they would meet his; it had been years since she had been in a room with her son.

Twenty-four hours into their reunion, it occurred to her that she would have to share him with the others and call his father and girlfriend. But it was not her story to tell, she knew. So she told him, *Xerxes, this is it. Now I want you to help yourself. I want you to make it better. I know you can. Come to peace, Xerxes, you know what I'm talking about.* He knew for the first time, and he didn't fight it. And they went over that final move, over and over, until he could do it and breathe at the same time.

"Woman, what? What should we do now?!" Darius was shouting.

"Well, to begin with, you guys can take your German vacation and transfer it over to New York," Lala ordered. "But before that, Darius, because this is not even for me to explain, I am pleased to tell you your own son has asked to speak to you."

Darius gasped, he hoped inaudibly. His heart was not going to endure this day, he thought, there was no way.

He asked her to repeat it. And again.

"Stop it, Darius, you heard me, you're hearing everything I say, old man, wake up! Your son is going to speak to you now. Hold on. . . ."

There was a pause. Darius, with his eyes getting watery again, mouthed to Suzanne the word *Xerxes,* and she—eyes horribly slick, too—made a silent clapping gesture with her hands. He nodded, tried to smile, but in truth he was also afraid.

Scary thing, having died and died and died and now gone to heaven, he rationalized. And so here it was. The kingdom indeed.

On the other end, in another world altogether, Xerxes Adam—a different Xerxes Adam, even Xerxes had to admit, even if he feared a smaller, frailer, post-fall new man—found it in himself to sit back in his mother's arms and listen to her whispers, *Here, you can do it, you said you can, now go, my dear, let's move forward, let's come to peace, remember. . . .*

He took the phone as if it were the man himself. Immediately the obstacle: an old sentence rushing at him—*They had both decided they would do their best to make that moment, the one about the heaviness of carry-ons, the last time the two men would speak ever again*—and just like that, in the highly flammable chambers of his old mind, Xerxes lit the sentence like the wick of a dynamite stick and let the words combust into shattered particles of forever-rejected memory refuse. . . . There was nowhere to go but *on.* He paused for just a few seconds and took a deep breath that felt like his first, and so he chose his oldest word, the best one, his first word. Originally produced at a time when his infant tongue was taught to take in only Farsi, this one English word he had digested tenaciously, echoing what had come from them strangely enough, as if with his parents' name-dropping of it they knew where their near futures would take them—what fate, what land, what new tongue would replace the native tongue— so much so that the baby Xerxes, without any prompting, uttered its simple syllable, its lonely three letters, loud and clear one day in front of them. And here a quarter of a century later—once again after many months of crying wordlessly for intangible things, grasping fruitlessly for communication and its ajar if not simply open doors—he said that first word he knew he always had in him somewhere, the one word that never left him alone: "Dad?"

Acknowledgments

Thank you to my tireless powerhouse of an agent, Rosalie Siegel; and my ever-wise ever-patient editor, Amy Hundley. My gratitude to Grove/Atlantic for their unflinching dedication—Elisabeth Schmitz for bothering to flip through that anonymous manuscript on her desk the year before and Morgan Entrekin for hearing her out and ultimately taking the risk. Also, a million thanks to my mentors Alice McDermott, Stephen Dixon, Melvin Jules Bukiet Danzy Senna, and Victoria Redel. Without Johns Hopkins University and Sarah Lawrence College, I would never have possessed the courage or the tools to face this.

Thanks as well to Jonathan Ames and Donald Antrim for their constant pats on the back, sage-like wisdom, and occasional wisecracks.

Thanks to Candice Tang for humoring this dream for twenty years.

Thanks to Brian Frank for breathing life back into me and teaching me to live through this.

ACKNOWLEDGMENTS

Thanks to my incredible readers Daniel Maurer, Matthew Remmey White, Alan Lawrence, Jason Mojica, and—most essential—my brother Arta Khakpour (who is not Xerxes Adam, no matter what they say).

Thanks to my parents Asha and Manijeh Khakpour for putting up with this . . . and everything.